More Than a Crush

JESSA KANE

Table of Contents

My Best Friend,
My Stalker

CHAPTER ONE

Peyton

P ANIC SPEARS THE walls of my throat.

I run through the trailer where I live with my stepbrother, my toe catching on a piece of raised carpet and sending me sprawling. Hearing Tony's footsteps behind me, I scramble to my feet, knocking empty beer cans in every direction. Tears make my vision blurry, but I've lived in this trailer all my life, long past the point I wanted to, so I know it like the back of my hand.

"Get back here, Peyton, or I swear to God."

Leaping over the partition that stands between the dining table and the front door of the trailer, I jerk the knob and throw myself out into the night. The summertime humidity hits me like a brick wall, clogging my windpipe. But I have to run. I have to get away from Tony. What he tried to do...

Drunk or not, it was wrong.

I had no warning. Never could have expected it.

Skin crawling, a pitiful sound breaks from my lips and I force my legs to go faster. I sprint through the dark trailer park on bare feet, not daring to knock on a neighbor's door for assistance. None of them can stand me. Ever since I started working as a kindergarten teacher at a private school on the nice side of town, their nickname for me has been Miss High and Mighty.

"Peyton!" Tony screams in my wake. "No one is going to believe you!"

All I can do is run faster, my nightshirt floating around my thighs.

When my stepmother passed away earlier this year, joining my father in the great beyond, I was just getting ready to finally, finally move out. To be on my own in a clean, empty apartment miles away from this place. But I stayed after the funeral, even lost the security deposit on my new apartment, because my stepbrother was so grief stricken, I didn't want to leave him alone. Sure, he's mean as a snake, but we're family. And there was no one left to cook his meals, make sure the bills are paid. Without my financial contribution, he could have ended up homeless. So I stayed.

Remembering the way he clapped a hand over my mouth tonight and tried to pull down my panties, acid churns in my gut. I'd been fast asleep so it took me a moment to realize what was happening. Who was trying to…to…

To what?

Thank God I never found out. My instincts kicked in immediately and I swung the book in my lap, bashing Tony in the nose. Ran like the wind. And I'm still running now, the road coming into view up ahead. What am I going to do when I get there? Ideally, I'd flag down help from a driver, but everyone in town knows Tony. He's a well-loved local DJ. Odds are, whoever pulled over would doubt me and take his side. What if they refuse to help me escape in time and Tony reaches me?

With no choice but to continue running along the road, my heart flies up into my mouth when I hear the purr of an engine approaching from behind. I throw a frantic glance back over my shoulder to see if I recognize the vehicle. In a small town like this, normally I would. But I've definitely never seen the vintage, black Mustang before. It rolls past me and I lock eyes with the driver…

And time seems to stand still.

In the space of a single heartbeat, I sense that everything is going to be all right. There's no reason I should feel that way. The man with a hand draped over the wheel is a stranger. I place him in his late twenties, but his eyes speak of a profound maturity. They're deep set, full of knowledge. They betray a heavy soul.

His hair is dark, eyebrows drawn. A groove on his forehead grows more intense the longer we stare at each other through the passenger side window. In the sleeve of his white T-shirt, his bicep jumps, a line moving in his jaw. There's an attractiveness to him that is nothing short of sharp, dangerous.

So why do I feel like my savior just arrived?

The brakes of his Mustang grind to a dead halt

and I stop running, my breath continuing to fly in and out of my lungs. Throwing the car into park, he gets out, comes around the front bumper, looking around. Searching the area with those soulful eyes. Lord, he's tall. At least six foot three. "Someone after you, honey?"

"Yes," I breathe, shame heating my face. "M-my stepbrother, Tony."

Malice darkens his expression and oddly, that reaction comforts me. It makes me feel as if I have an ally for once in my twenty-two years. He sweeps me with a glance, his attention ticking to something over my shoulder a split second before I hear the footsteps approaching. "There's the vermin now," murmurs the stranger. "Why don't you get in the car and I'll handle this?"

I start to do as the man asks, desperate to escape Tony, but I stop short, my hand frozen on the metal door handle of the Mustang. Why am I so quick to trust this person I've never met? I don't even know his name. "I, um...how do I know it's safe to get into your car?"

Without taking his eyes off my stepbrother, the stranger pulls a knife out of his back pocket, flips it open and gives it to me, handle fist. "How about that, honey?"

I'm not a fighter. Never have been. I don't own any weapons. But the second that pearl-handled knife touches my palm, I'm given back the control I've been lacking since I was rudely awakened tonight. And this man gave it to me so easily. Let me have the power I needed to even the ground. Gratitude wells up in my throat. "Thank you." I open the car door and start to climb inside, but hesitate. "What is your name?"

"Granger Hoskins." If I'd named him myself, I couldn't have come up with a more fitting moniker. It suits this sharply handsome man with the gravel voice and clenched fists. "And yours?"

Before I can answer, my brother shouts the answer. "Peyton Pruitt," he snarls, alcohol slurring his words. "Get back here, you bitch."

With a whimper, I lock myself into the car and close my eyes, rocking back and forth in the seat. My eyelids fly up when I hear the first bone-crunching thud. I turn around in the seat and watch the scene play out like something from a dream. I've never seen anyone fight like Granger. There is cold precision in every movement. He's predatory. His expression is almost dispassionate as he plows a fist into Tony's jaw, picks him up off the ground by the scruff of his neck…and slams him face first into the road, leaving him unmoving. Seemingly as an afterthought, he kicks Tony's unconscious figure down the embankment, watching him crash through the foliage without blinking an eye.

And I should be scared of him, right? Why aren't I?

The sound of my breathing is loud inside the silent car as Granger turns his head and locks eyes with me through the rear windshield. Fog wafts behind him on the road, his slow gait carrying him back toward the car. Why don't I have the urge to run? It's almost like his gaze pins me in place, the promise of his protective energy making me want to stay, despite what my head is telling me.

That's there's more to him than meets the eye.

A lot more.

Finally, he reaches the driver's side and opens the door. My grip closes tightly around the handle of the knife and he watches it happen, his eyes ticking between my face and the weapon. "Look. You're smart to be scared of me. But I'd stab myself before I hurt you." He gets into the car, slams the door and starts the ignition, pausing for a long moment. "Your stepbrother," he asks stiffly, his dark eyes lifting to the rearview mirror. "What did he do to you?"

The engine vibrates beneath my bare legs. "Shouldn't you have asked me that question before you beat him up?"

A half smile curves his masculine mouth. "He deserved that and more just for scaring you." His attention swings to me and it's laser focused in its intensity. "I just need to know if I should have to kill him, too."

Haltingly, I shake my head, marveling over the fact that I'm still not scared. What is wrong with me? There's just something about the way he holds himself, as if he's poised to take a bullet in my honor. After a lifetime of being threatened and treated like a burden, it's like wading into a hot spring. "No, you don't have to do that. He...he tried to..." Suddenly, I'm blinking furiously trying to stop the flow of tears, my earlier panic coming back in a thick wave. "He tried. T-to touch me. But I woke up and ran. It was the f-first time he'd done anything like that."

It was the first time for me, too. Not that it went far enough to be considered sexual. Not for me. But I'm worried. I'm worried because I used to look forward to the future, when I would enjoy physical intimacy with a man.

Now?

Now the idea terrifies me. Puts me on the verge of hyperventilating.

Granger's eyes have grown brilliantly bright, like twin diamonds. "That won't be happening again," he rasps, jerkily putting the car into drive. "Put on your seatbelt, Peyton. You're coming home with me."

"But I don't even know you."

A muscle slides up and down in his throat, the first hint of vulnerability I've seen from him. "Would you like to?"

Something compels me to tell the truth, the absolute truth, to this man. "Yes," I whisper, clicking my belt into place. "I would."

Is it my imagination or does he let out a held breath before gunning the engine? Watching the trailer park disappear in the rearview mirror, I get the distinct feeling that I'll never see this place again. Because...he won't allow it.

Am I crazy to be comforted by that?

Am I crazy to feel like I've finally found...a friend?

CHAPTER TWO

Granger

IF I COULD? I'd eat her whole.

She'd never come up for air.

I couldn't believe what I was seeing when I took that curve in the road and she came into view. Peyton is something straight out of a fairytale. All doll-eyed and innocent, sweet as hell with her big brown curls. I've been on the verge of coming in my jeans since that very first glimpse and now, as I gesture for her to precede me into my apartment, I'm still right there on the edge.

I'm overcome by every detail. Her scent, the slope of her throat, her thighs. The pale blue nightshirt she wears without a bra. The pink nail polish on her toes and the indentation in the center of her bottom lip.

Jesus. My pulse is going a thousand miles an hour.

I'm almost dizzy just having her brush past me in the doorway.

Acting normal is next to impossible. Acting like I haven't found the goddess I plan to worship for the rest of my life. If she didn't look shell-shocked and pale right now from what that bastard did to her, I'd already be down on my knees, whispering prayers to her ankles and licking up the insides of her thighs, begging for a chance to worship.

Nothing affects me like this. Hell, nothing affects me at all.

In my prior profession as mob muscle, I was known for having ice in my veins. A stint in prison made that blood run even icier. Right up until her. Now I've got lava flowing through me, rushing all different directions.

Forcing myself to regain control, I watch Peyton walk through the apartment, wearing nothing but a nightshirt, feet bare. Protectiveness expands inside me, shoving at the walls of my chest, nearly busting me wide open. Mine. This fairy is mine to protect. No one is ever going to harm a hair on her beautiful head.

Not ever again.

She turns, rubbing the outsides of her arms. Is she cold?

Without taking my eyes off her, I adjust the thermostat on the wall.

"You live alone?"

Polite conversation isn't something I'm used to, but I do my best to make the opposite appear true, needing her to be comfortable with me. To trust me. "Yes, it's just me." I study her, memorizing her coloring. "I assume you're done with that place. The trailer park."

She lifts her chin, nods.

Good girl. Wouldn't have let her return anyway.

With a deep breath, I nod at the second bedroom,

which I've been using as a gym. "That's the guest room. You're welcome to it."

"Oh," she says on a breathy laugh. "I couldn't impose like that."

I suppress the urge to storm toward the girl, pick her up and lock her inside the room until I can figure out how to exist now that I've met her. She's not leaving. I cannot let her leave. Am I capable of maneuvering her into staying without making her a prisoner? Yes. Yes, I have to be. Otherwise she'll think I'm no better than her soon-to-be-deceased stepbrother. There's one important difference between him and I, at least. I'd never lay a fucking finger on her if she didn't want me to. The idea of her running away from me—or anyone—in fear makes me want to punch a hole in the wall.

"You're not imposing," I say, struggling to sound normal. "I was actually looking for a roommate."

Lie. I'd never voluntarily live with someone, except this fairy named Peyton. After sharing a prison cell for years, I vowed to live alone forever. But everything changed when I saw her in the road.

Peyton swallows and I watch the play of muscle on her throat the way a cat observes a canary. "That's really kind of you, Granger." I have to swallow a groan. That's the first time she's said my name out loud. Fuck. My cock is so hard, it's giving me a toothache. "But…after what happened tonight, I think, um…I think I'd be a little nervous living with a-a man. I hope you're not offended. I know nothing about you that would suggest you're anything like Tony. You actually saved me tonight. I'm so grateful for your help. But...but..."

I notice the blood is beginning to leave her face.

Alarm blares through me and I push off the wall, crossing toward her quickly. "Peyton?"

"I'm sorry," she says, squeezing her eyes shut. "Now that the adrenaline has worn off, I'm feeling a little shaky."

I catch her as soon as her knees begin to buckle, bringing her up against my chest roughly to keep her from falling.

Two things occur to me at once.

One, if I could go back in time, I would snap Tony's neck for scaring her like this. Of course her nerves are shot now that some time has passed. That bastard was twice her size. Obviously his intentions for trying to force himself on her in the middle of the night weren't honorable. She's probably in the process of realizing exactly what could have happened if she wasn't so brave.

Two, from this moment forward, I'll never be able to survive without her in my arms. Jesus, she's so goddamn sweet. She fits me like we were carved for one another, her head tucking right beneath my chin, her breasts and pelvis settling into me like a missing puzzle piece. It feels so good, I'm seeing double.

"This is humiliating," she grumbles. "I teach kindergartners for a living. I'm supposed to be a little tougher than this."

A kindergarten teacher in the arms of a felon. Former mob muscle.

Somewhere out there, fate is laughing hysterically.

"You are tough, honey. That was you tonight who ran away. That was you who survived the fear." A little bit of the tension leaves her and she sighs, snuggling into me somewhat, turning my heart upside down. "You know..." My voice is deep and hoarse, so I struggle to clear it. "You know, we've established that if anyone messes with you, I'm going to kick their ass. Staying here with me might make you feel safe, instead of scared." I inhale the vanilla fragrance of her hair. "But if that's not enough, I could install a lock on the inside of your bedroom door. You'd have the only key."

Her breath warms my neck for long moments. "Granger, are you doing all of this because you want to sleep with me?" She looks up at me and I permanently drown in her wide hazel eyes. "I don't think I'll want a man's hands on me for a while after...tonight. I get nervous just thinking about it." Pink spots appear on her cheeks and she can no longer look at me straight. "I don't have any experience to begin with, so..."

Christ. A virgin.

I don't know why I'm surprised. Maybe because I come from a world where innocence is taken away at an early age. Not just for females, but for everyone. There's no such thing as being naïve. God, I should have known she'd still have her cherry, though. It's in her shyness. It's in her guileless expression.

It's in the way she presses into my erect cock like she has no idea what it is or why it's bulging up against my zipper, just dying for a shot between her legs.

"No experience, huh?" I choke out, ordering myself to keep my hands off her ass. "I don't have a lot, either. What I have done is not worth remembering."

I'll never remember anyone but her.

I'll never want anyone but this girl. Every second I stand holding her gets her deeper into my blood. My bones. I just need her to stay.

I'm not sure how I'll handle it if she doesn't, but it wouldn't be the last time I see her. The idea of never seeing her again is laughable. I'd be trailing her the second she touched the sidewalk outside my building.

Trailing her.

Following her.

My dick gets stiffer at the prospect of protecting her even when she doesn't know I'm there. Watching her every move.

"Do you think we could be friends?" she asks, peering up at me.

Being friendly is the last thing I think about when I look at her. I want to rope her wrists to my headboard and fuck her into next week. And when I'm done, I want to rock her like a baby, run her a bath, buy her presents. Take pictures of the love marks I leave behind on her skin. Dress her up and pose her for me. God, I don't know if that makes sense and I don't care. But none of this is going to happen any time soon. She's too spooked over what happened…and if I want her to trust me, I'll have to put my lust in check and play the long game.

Whatever gets me near her. Whatever gets me access.

"Friends? Nah." I tilt her chin up and smile. "We're going to be best friends."

CHAPTER THREE

Peyton

WITH THE LAST of my students scurrying off toward their parents at pick-up time, I return to the school building with a smile on my face. There is nothing more satisfying than teaching children, watching their little faces brighten during the surprise twist in a story. Or when they take the morals about kindness they learn throughout the day and employ them with each other. Sharing, giving, caring.

I open the door and move down the waxed hallway of the private school, passing framed portraits of the last five school board presidents. Artwork isn't posted in the halls of the prestigious institution, but I more than make up for that rule in my classroom, which is an explosion of color and happiness.

Before I can reach my door, however, where I plan to collect my things and take the bus back to the apartment I now share with Granger, a fellow teacher steps into my path.

"Hey there, Peyton," he says warmly, sticking his hands into the pockets of his khaki pants. "Thank God it's Friday, right?"

A frisson of alarm passes through me, my pulse

beginning to pound. I try not to let the fear show on my face. How long after Tony's actions am I going to feel this apprehension every time a man comes close to me?

After a week of living with Granger, I'm beginning to relax around him (the lock he installed on my door doesn't hurt). After he went to the trailer park and collected my things, I officially moved in and we commenced a comfortable routine. Granger cooks breakfast and drives me to the school, before heading to his job at the garage repairing cars. When I arrive home, I prepare dinner, since he doesn't get back until later. We watch television together, do the dishes side by side, laugh at each other's workplace stories. It's so…easy.

And he doesn't try to touch me. Ever. Not so much as a graze.

Sometimes I feel electricity on the back of my neck when we're both in the apartment. When I turn around, though, he's busy working on an engine part or chopping vegetables in the kitchen. I have to confess, when he asked me to move into the guest room, I worried it would end up being a bad idea. Granger is mysterious—we've never spoken about his past and I haven't brought it up, wanting to keep our relationship light and friendly. I grow more curious about him by the day, however, this man who has become my friend. My comfort.

The one who makes me feel safe.

I don't feel safe right now with my fellow teacher

standing so close to me. My brain tells me he is just being normal and I'm the one who is messed up, so I paste a smile onto my face. What did he say again?

Oh, right. Thank God it's Friday.

"Yes," I say, slowly edging back toward my classroom door. "I love the kids, but it's nice to relax and regroup."

"Absolutely," he agrees affably, shifting in his loafers. "Speaking of relaxing, I was wondering if you wanted to get dinner over the weekend." A flush darkens his cheekbones. "You've only been working here a short time and we haven't really had the chance to get to know each other."

My legs are stiff. Frozen.

I'm being silly, aren't I? Nothing actually happened with my stepbrother the night I ran away. It's more what could have happened that keeps me awake at night. That and having my safe space compromised. Being caught off guard when I thought I was secure. "Um…" I don't know what to say, so I stall. "I'm sorry, I'm so bad with names. Can you remind me…"

"Wow, I really jumped the gun asking you out, didn't I?" He laughs, shakes his head. "I'm Paul. I teach algebra to the older students."

"Right. Paul." I vaguely remember being introduced to him on the first day of school, but being a new teacher, I met everyone at the same time, so a lot of the faces blended together. "Thank you for asking. I'm just not really…dating at the moment."

Why can't I get Granger's face out of my mind?

I can almost feel him frowning. Which is ridiculous. We've decided to be friends and that's exactly what we are.

"Oh," Paul says, still smiling. "That's fine. I totally understand." He hesitates. "I hope you don't mind if I try again in a few months. Just in case you decide to start seeing people. I don't want to miss my opportunity."

It's on the tip of my tongue to tell him I'd rather he didn't ask again, but I don't want to get a reputation among the staff for being impolite, so I nod. "Sure."

An hour later, I'm putting away some groceries in the kitchen when Granger gets home from work. His hooded gaze locks in on me as soon as his boots cross the threshold and my muscles tense involuntarily. But not the way they did when Paul approached me in the school hallway. It's more of a zapping jolt of awareness. And really, I'd have to be dead not to be aware of my new best friend.

He's a presence.

When he enters the room, the temperature seems to rise.

He kicks off his boots, toeing them neatly into place beside my black ballet flats, staring at the line of shoes for a few seconds, before slowly advancing toward the kitchen. I've noticed Granger has this habit of plowing fingers through his hair and holding on to it at the crown of his head, leaving his arm raised. Bent and flexed. Why is that slick bulge of muscle so distracting? In combination with his intense focus on me, I'm caught between feeling treasured…and like a bunny rabbit caught in a trap with the hunter approaching.

"How was your day at the garage?" I ask, picking up a knife and slicing a red pepper down the middle.

"Fine." Finally he drops that hand away from his hair, gesturing to his clothes. "Messy."

"I can relate." With him standing so close, I really have to concentrate on cutting the pepper, moving my fingers out of the way of the blade. "Although the messes I clean up are finger paint accidents instead of grease."

His mouth ticks up at the corner. "Do kids still put glue on their hands and peel it off?"

"Yes," I whine. "They especially love to pretend their skin is melting off to terrify me. I don't get the fascination."

He props a hip against the counter. "No, I bet you were a teacher's pet, bringing in a shiny apple on the first day of school and raising your hand for every question."

I lift my chin and give him a prim look. "There's nothing wrong with that."

"No, honey," he drawls. "There isn't."

I don't quite disguise the odd shiver that wriggles up my spine when he calls me by the endearment. "Am I to assume you were the kid who spent lessons carving his initials into the top of the desk?"

His slow rasp of laughter warms me. "Guilty as

charged." He pauses, watching me thoughtfully. "Maybe I should have paid better attention. I wouldn't have ended up with the wrong crowd."

My interest can't help but be piqued. No matter how much I tell myself I want to keep our relationship casual, I can't deny my eagerness to know more about Granger. "Did you? End up with the wrong crowd?"

Tilting his head down, he tucks his tongue into the corner of his lips. "Honestly?" I can barely breathe when his eyes zero in on me like this. "I was the wrong crowd, Peyton."

"Oh." The knife is forgotten in my hand. "Where did that...get you?"

"In bad places. Working for worse people." His jaw flexes and he takes a step closer to me, coming up short when I draw in a gasp. "Sorry."

"No, it's okay." I duck my head. "It's crazy to still be on edge like this a whole week later."

He jabs the counter with his index finger. "No, it isn't. Don't doubt your instincts. Here I am telling you I worked for bad people. That's a pretty good reason to back away."

My hand moves on its own, dropping the knife to reach out and curl in his T-shirt. "I'm not backing away. It's just...you usually don't come so close and I wasn't expecting it." I look him in the eye. "I'm not scared of you, Granger. No matter what you tell me about your past."

"Yeah?" It seems to cost him an effort to inhale and exhale steadily, his eyes fixated on the place where

I clutch his shirt. "What if I told you I'm a convict? That the night I met you, I was coming back from the final meeting with my parole officer?"

I wait for the surprise to hit, but it never comes. Perhaps I already sensed Granger's past included doing time. There's a rawness to him, a restlessness that reminds me of an animal pacing a cage. Or a cell. "I'd say…it sounds like you did your time." I wet my suddenly dry lips. "There are bad people out there with no prison records at all. Like Tony. Now I know there are good people with records. You wouldn't have helped me otherwise. You wouldn't have brought me in, made me safe."

Ever so slightly, he leans into my touch, pressing his hard stomach to my fist. Up and down it heaves. "Maybe I'm only good with you."

What happens in that moment to my body is something I've never experienced before. There's a wet trickle down the center of my womanhood and the whole of my flesh begins to pulse like a heart. Thick, heavy, slow.

No idea what it means—and needing to process it—I drop my hand from his shirt and force my attention back to the task of cutting peppers.

With a breath that doesn't sound entirely natural, Granger pushes off the counter, walks around behind me and opens the fridge. The drag of glass tells me he's having a bottle of beer, like he usually does after work. "So…" His voice is low. "The kids gave you a run for your money today, huh?"

"As always," I manage, going still. "Actually, today was weird…"

I trail off, realizing I'm about to confide in him about Paul asking me out. Somehow, though, relaying that information to Granger is totally inappropriate, even though we're friends. Something stops me.

But he picks up on my hesitation, coming up beside me to study my face, tipping the bottle of beer to his lips. "Why was it weird?"

I've never been a good liar. I flit around to nine different potential fibs, before giving up. It's useless. He'll know I'm full of baloney. "One of the other teachers asked me to have dinner with him—"

The bottle of beer shatters in his hand.

I yelp, dropping the knife and staggering back from the counter.

"Granger. What—" I sputter. "Oh my God, you're bleeding."

"I'm fine," he says dully, his eyes kind of unfocused. "Don't come over here. You'll step on the glass."

His odd tone of voice throws me off for a few beats, but I shake myself and get moving, crossing to the front door and slipping my shoes back on before returning to Granger who is still standing eerily still. I pick up one of the kitchen towels and crunch toward him in the shards of beer bottle, making sure there is no glass in his cut before wrapping the towel around his hand. "Granger." Why does the sight of him in pain make me want to sob? "You need stitches."

"No." Visibly, he pulls himself back together. "No, I've needed stitches dozens of times in my life. This is just a scratch." His eyes bore into me and I start to shake. Not out of fear. Out of…being drawn so deeply into a moment with another person that it feels like the world is no longer turning. "What did you say to this co-worker when he asked you to dinner?"

In all of the commotion, I forgot what we'd been talking about prior to the bottle shattering. Surely he isn't upset over Paul asking me out? "I said no, of course. I'm not ready for that." Anxiously, I watch the kitchen towel turn red. "Anyway, I'm not…"

"Attracted to him?"

"No. I'm not."

All over my body, even in my most private places, my skin feels warm just from having this conversation. Growing up, I didn't fit in very well with the other girls in the trailer park. The girls who lived on the nice side of town called me names at school, like trashy. The girls from my side of town thought I was snooty. Having fallen somewhere in the middle of those two groups, I never had another female around to confide in. Talking about attraction for the first time, especially with someone as magnetic and good-looking as Granger, makes me feel even more vulnerable than usual.

Still, he never makes me feel awkward or judged or like I'm overreacting. Maybe fate made me wait this long for a friend because I was going to receive the best one of all. "What…" I lick my lips. "What does it feel like, when you're attracted to someone?"

All he does is stare at me. Hard. For a moment, I don't think he's going to answer. "For a girl? It depends how attracted you are." His voice is like gravel. "Sometimes you can be objective about a person. You might think they have a pleasant face or a fit body. But you don't get, uh…" He stops for a long breath, his gaze traveling down the front of my T-shirt and pajama shorts, resting on the seam. "That wet clench between your legs that can't be ignored. When that happens, it's a different kind of attraction."

Before I can stop them, my thighs shoot together and I cross my ankles, squeezing. Not…not because I'm experiencing the very thing Granger is describing. Right? No. No, it's just because this whole conversation is indecent.

That doesn't stop me from wanting to learn more.

"A different kind of attraction," I repeat slowly.

"Mmm."

"If you can't ignore it, what…what do you do?"

Granger takes a step closer and my tummy turns ticklish on the inside, the sensation reaching up to my breasts and making them fuller, more sensitive. "If you can't ignore the attraction—and it's the same for him—then you fuck, honey. If the man knows what he's doing, you'll get a nice reward for being so wet and sexy."

I can no longer control my breathing. I can't believe he's talking to me like this. His voice is wrapping me in some kind of spell, a bead of sweat rolling down my spine. "And th-the reward is…"

"An orgasm, Peyton. For both of us." A long pause drags out and I notice perspiration has formed on his upper lip. "I meant, for you and this man you're attracted to, of course."

Swallowing hard, I nod vigorously, wondering if I'm coming down with the flu. I'm having hot flashes and my muscles are tense, jumpy. What is wrong with me? "Anyway," I say, forcing a laugh. "I don't even feel the objective kind of attraction for Paul, so it's a non-issue."

"Hmm." Am I imagining things or does Granger seem extremely wound up? Like coiled metal primed to spring. "Will you save me a plate? I'm going downstairs to work out."

"Oh." I frown as he pivots on a heel and stalks to the door. "Didn't you work out this morning?"

"Yeah."

The door closes on that single growled word and I'm left wondering what the heck just happened. I'm not sure, but something tells me it was significant.

CHAPTER FOUR

Granger

I'M HIDDEN IN the trees across the street from Royal Oak Academy where Peyton works and I can taste blood in my mouth. After a weekend of hitting the punching bag, doing pull-ups and jumping rope until the sweat poured down my body, I should be too worn out to feel this much wrath. But I'm starting to realize there are no rules when it comes to my obsession with Peyton. It's a living, breathing part of me and it demands to be obeyed.

Paul.

It only took me a few minutes of searching online to find the math teacher's picture on the school website. Now I watch him through the window of his classroom, my fingertips ripping off a strip of bark and crushing it in my grip. Did he think he could just waltz up to my fairy and ask her on a date? Did this two-pump chump divorcee think he was worthy of her presence? Did he?

I'm here to set him straight.

And it's obviously not enough to live with Peyton. To spend my nights sitting in the corner of her room, guarding her as she sleeps. Counting her breaths and straightening her blankets when she kicks them off. It seems I have to be with her during the day, too. I have to be there to make sure other men keep the hell away from what is mine. No one will have her but me. No one will come close.

I push off the tree and pace back and forth behind the tree, attempting to get myself under control. In the past, my profession has required me to intimidate people, to scare them, but I was always in control of the anger. I'm not in control anymore. Hunger and possessiveness for Peyton have taken over.

She's close.

She's close to letting me in.

Friday night in the kitchen, I swore she was about to acknowledge the wild chemistry that boils between us. I swore she was going to admit her feelings for me go beyond friendship, but she wasn't ready yet. That's okay. I can wait. There is never going to be another female for me. My fairy will take all the time she needs—but in the meantime, I have to keep the weasels away.

Faintly, I hear the bell ring across the street and that's my cue.

I pull the baseball cap down low over my eyes, tuck my hair into the sides and jog across the street, skirting along the edge of the brick, ivy-covered building. Security is tight at the school, as I discovered on their website, so I came prepared. There is a blog section on the site and I scoured the pictures until I found what I needed, a picture of the janitor. After a quick trip to a shop that sells work gear, I'm wearing a boxy-gray uniform shirt tucked into black pants, identical to the ones worn by the janitor.

Now, I locate the broom I left propped against the side of the building earlier and circle around to the back door. Only about five minutes passes when a teacher exits and lights a cigarette, propping the door open with a shoe. When she sees me, I smile and breeze in through the entrance, mumbling something about forgetting my keys. And like most people, she doesn't pay the janitor the slightest bit of attention.

Based on the online schedule, it's lunchtime at the school, so the children are in the cafeteria. I stalk down the empty halls, broom in hand, turning left at the end of the corridor and entering the classroom where Paul teaches. He's taking a sacked lunch from his backpack when I enter and I don't give him a chance to register surprise. One second he's jerking back from his desk, the next I have him pressed to the wall with the broom lodged against his windpipe.

"Hello, Paul," I growl through my teeth, enjoying the way his eyes widen with terror. It's familiar to me. I've been making men piss themselves ever since I realized I'm stronger than most of them. Less given to fear. I can keep a calm head in any situation—except for this one. Except when someone wants Peyton. My Peyton. "Listen very carefully and I might not ram this broom handle down your throat. Are you listening, Paul?"

Eyes bulging, he nods, the smell of his urine turning my stomach.

This coward actually thought he was good enough for her?

I press the broom handle tighter, eliciting a pathetic whimper from this grown man. "Don't look at Peyton Pruitt. Don't speak to her. If I even catch you looking like you might be thinking about her, I'll come find you in the middle of the night, Paul. I'll burn your house down while you're still inside. Am I making myself clear? Forget she exists or I'll make sure you don't anymore."

He nods as well as he can under the circumstances.

"You tell anyone about this, I won't be happy, Paul." I let him see the madness inside of me. Madness for her. "Do you want me to be unhappy?"

"No," he gasps.

"No," I agree, shaking my head. "You don't."

I let another few seconds pass, watching his skin turn chalky, before I step back and let him sink to the floor, covering his piss spot in shame. With my lip curled in disgust, I open the window closest to the road and climb out, not bothering to hurry toward where I've parked my Mustang half a mile away. There's no one coming after me.

And I hang on to the broom and the uniform.

If I'm going to watch Peyton during the day, they'll come in handy.

I JAB THE punching bag with my left fist, plowing my right into the leather quickly after, shaking the equipment's chains where I've secured it to the rafters. A storage bay in the basement of the building is where I moved my workout area when she moved in and it's where I've been forced to spend a lot of time. A single light bulb hangs from the ceiling. Sweat travels down my bare chest, soaking into my gray sweatpants. My knuckles are beginning to bleed, but I keep punching, my lips peeled back in a growl.

I should be upstairs with Peyton, but my need for her is growing more excruciating by the second. Every time she flips her hair or smiles at me, my cock stiffens, throbs. I'm at the very edge, always seconds from pushing her down on the couch and climbing on top of her, ripping her out of whatever clothes she's wearing and finally, finally burying myself between her thighs.

The night we met, I made myself a vow. The next time I come, it will be with her. For her. So I haven't jerked off once. God, no. She owns my sperm now. It's hers. Every single fucking drop. There is nothing that can derail me from that promise, but it's getting more and more painful, leading to me coming downstairs and working out until I'm ready to collapse.

When I hear a creak on the stairs, my head comes up, salty moisture dripping into my eyes. I swipe it away and steady the bag, my heart shooting up into my throat when I see Peyton's delicate toes come into view, followed by her smooth, slender calves, knees, the lacy hem of her pajama shorts. My dick aches with anticipation, wanting her, needing to be around her, while my mind rebels, knowing it's a bad idea. Knowing I'm so close to snapping when she needs more time.

"Hey," she says lightly, hesitantly, walking into my den, complete with a bench press, pull up bar, weights and punching bag. "Are you coming back upstairs?" she asks, twirling a curl around her finger. "I was going to make popcorn."

There is nothing I want more in the world than to sit beside her on the couch and watch a movie. Every time we do it, she sits a little closer, her wariness of being around me ebbing. It's a double-edged sword, though, inviting me to take too much. To take it all. "I think I'll hit the bag a while longer," I rasp, my gaze tracing the low neckline of her tank top. "Go ahead without me."

"Oh. Okay." Her disappointment is obvious and it burns me alive. "Is it…me? I hope I'm not making you feel uncomfortable in your own home."

"It's our home, Peyton." My throat feels raw, my cock is pounding and I want her so bad, I'm shaking. That's probably why I let the next part slip out. "You make me uncomfortable, honey. Just not in the way you're thinking."

Her eyes widen. "How?"

Against my better judgment, I step out from behind the punching bag and let her see my erection.

Without my shirt on, there's nothing to hide the hard ridge that stretches the material. My hand goes to it without a direct command from my brain, stroking the length once and gripping. "Uncomfortable like this," I grunt.

"Oh." Her complexion deepens with color, her fingers twisting in the hem of her shorts. "I, um...I know men have to relieve themselves from time to time. Do you feel weird about...doing that to yourself when I'm home? I could take a walk—"

"No." The idea of her going on a walk by herself at night makes my stomach churn. If she ever attempted it, I'd be following her in the shadows. "No, you don't have to go anywhere. Ever. If I just hit the bag a while longer..."

What?

My erection will go away?

There's no chance of that as long as she walks the earth.

What if this moment is an opportunity, though? Hopefully my lust-fogged brain isn't causing me to make a mistake when I say, "You could watch me."

Her perfect lips part on a gasp. "What do you mean?"

No turning back now. And I don't want to. It feels too right talking to her about sex. Any form of intimacy with her is like breathing fresh air. "I mean, you're nervous around men. This could be a way of facing your fears without being touched. If you watch me pleasure myself, maybe you'll get more comfortable with the idea of touching." I saw the heel of my palm up and down my length, causing it to swell drastically against the front of my sweatpants. "You're scared because you were vulnerable that night, Peyton. So watch me at my most vulnerable. See how helpless I get at the end...when I'll die if I don't come."

By the time I finish talking, her little nipples are pebbled against the front of her tank top and she's squeezing her thighs together, the way she did the other night in the kitchen. Yeah, she's horny. She just doesn't know what to do about it yet.

Good thing I do.

I just need an opening. I need her trust.

Is this the way to get it?

"Come here, honey." Her progress across the storage cage is slow and I meet her halfway, stopping just shy of touching her, my hand still busy on the bulge in my sweats. "You've never seen a man's cock before."

A statement, not a question. Nothing has ever been more obvious.

"No," she whispers, looking down between us. "Do you really turn...helpless at the end?"

"Yes," I say raggedly, turning our bodies without touching and walking her backward until she's pressed to the wall of the cage. I prop my left forearm above her head, getting as close as possible without touching. My balls are heavy and throbbing in anticipation of finally getting relief and I'm powerless to do anything but shove down the waistband of my sweatpants and fist my dick. Holding the hard length of it up and showing it to her. "You can tell it hurts just by looking at it, can't you, honey?"

Her nod is jerky, her breath starting to come faster. "Y-yes."

I let my head fall back and start to jack myself. "Ohhhh fuck." My jaw is slack, eyesight blurring. "It's been so long. It's sensitive."

"It's b-bigger than I thought," she stammers.

Peyton commenting on my size causes semen to bead on the head of my arousal and she gasps, bringing more and more milk to the surface. The pressure in my balls only intensifies, though. "Yeah. It's big, honey, but it would fit inside your pussy like a fucking dream."

"Granger," she rasps, her fingers reaching back to curl into the cage links, those gorgeous tits of hers heaving up and down. "You shouldn't say things like that." Her eyelashes flutter. "Sh-should you?"

I start to twist my strokes, my thumb swiping over the sensitized head and it's so hot with her watching me, I let out a long groan. "I can beat off in front of you, but the line is drawn at talking about your pussy?"

"I...I don't know."

"Do you want to talk about it?" I lean in and let my mouth hover right above her ear, as close to touching as I can get. "Bet it's so creamy and tight, baby. Bet you're too shy to even touch it in the shower, aren't you?"

Laboring to breathe, her head falls back against the

cage. "Yes."

"Goddamn. That's okay, Peyton. I'll do it for you." I devour the sight of her tits from above. The perky swells in her neckline, the valley between the beautiful pair, the outline of her erect nipples. I make a hoarse noise and my hand moves faster. "Ah, Jesus. Your tits are going to make me come."

She seems to marvel over that fact. "Really?"

"Fuck yes." My orgasm is a runaway train at this point, eating up the tracks of my thoughts. Loosening my tongue. Making me forget to go slow, not scare her. "Pull your top down for me. Show me those hot, little virgin tits."

"Granger—"

"Do it for me, baby. Please." I drop my left forearm from the wall—and with the most intense climax of my life bearing down on me, I wrench down the straps of her tank top, clawing the garment down to her waist, barking a curse when the sweetest pair of breasts ever created come into view, all supple and puckered for me. Quivering with her attempts to fill her lungs. "Ah, shit. I'm there. I'm done." My body moves on its own, flattening her to the cage wall, rattling it, my hand moving feverishly between our laps, jacking my cock. "There's only you. Only you making me come. I'm your servant right now, Peyton. Can't you feel that, baby? Huh, baby? Imagine me getting this fucking helpless when I'm about to blow in that sweet little cunt. I'd rail that goddamn thing just trying to fuck the pain away and you'd have the power to help me. Only you."

I'm out of control. Of my actions, my words.

Some part of me knows it, but I can't make myself stop.

The lust, the closeness of her has me spinning out.

Before I'm aware of my own actions, I'm yanking down the shorts of her pajamas and coming all over her pussy and thighs. My bellow echoes off the walls of the basement, almost drowning out her whimpers. But I hear them and they egg me on, my loins twisting, producing more, more, more spend to paint her in.

"Mine," I grit out, burying my teeth in her shoulder, locking her against the cage and pressing my spurting dick up into the folds of her sex, stopping just short of entering her, but needing to get my come as close as possible to her womb. "All fucking mine and don't ever question it."

I lick over to her neck, move higher and grind my open mouth against her ear so she can hear my moans of her name. So she can hear me coming apart for her. Finally the last blistering drop leaves me and I go boneless, staggering into her—and reality roars back, turning the sweat on my skin to ice.

My actions over the course of the last few minutes replay themselves.

My roughness, the crude language, the way I manhandled her.

Disrobed her. Jesus, her pajama shorts are around her knees, tank top bunched at her waist. She's covered in come. And she's trembling.

My God, what have I done?

"Peyton," I say, sounding strangled.

I give her one inch of space and that's all she needs to wiggle out from beneath me and pull up her shorts, crossing her arms over her bare breasts and running for the staircase.

"Peyton!" She doesn't stop and I'm too immobilized by shame and horror to chase after her in time. A moment later, I hear our apartment door slam. With my heart pounding in my ears, I sprint after her, entering the two-bedroom and throwing myself to a kneeling position in front of her door. "Honey, I'm sorry. I got carried away. I'm a fucking animal. Please open up and let me in." I twist strands of hair in my hands, all-out madness threatening to take hold. What if she's crying in there? Crying because of me. "I can't stand this. I can't stand you being upset."

"I'm fine, Granger," she calls through the door, sounding more dazed than anything. "I just need some space for a while. Okay?"

Space.

That's the one thing I can't give her.

Maybe I don't have to, though. I'll just give her the illusion of it.

God, I messed up. I was supposed to make her comfortable with the male body and instead I took it too far. Probably horrified her. Having her want to stay away from me is no less than I deserve. But that's not all I deserve.

With a suitable punishment in mind, I grab my car

keys and burn rubber to where I'm going. If I don't have enough willpower to be what she needs, I'll simply have to take away my will.

CHAPTER FIVE

Peyton

IT'S AFTER HOURS at the school and I've stayed late to work on report cards.

This is something I could have easily done at home, but home is a distracting place to be lately. It's Wednesday night, two days since the…incident in the basement. Since my body hung on the verge of something exciting, every muscle tightening as if an explosion was about to happen. All because of Granger and his voice in my ear, his sweaty, chiseled torso.

That long, thick appendage being so roughly handled between us.

A breathless sound escapes me, loud in the dark, quiet classroom. Setting down my pen, I place both palms flat on my knees and drag them higher, slowly, bringing my skirt to the tops of my thighs. My breasts grow full and achy almost on cue, a telltale pulse starting deep in my core.

Women can give themselves orgasms, same as men. I know that much. But I've always been too timid to touch myself there, afraid I'd like it too much. Afraid that once I started, I'd be required to do it all the time. There are entire stores dedicated to pleasuring oneself and all of the choices always seemed overwhelming. Like a time-consuming hobby.

Obviously I'd just never been inspired enough to need it.

To have no choice but to touch myself there.

I've resisted for two days, but alone in the classroom, the moon having risen in the sky, I part my thighs and trail my fingers up and down on the sensitive skin, getting closer to the edge of my panties with every journey of fingertips. Electricity races all over my skin, my breaths sounding hollow in my ears. And I can't help but close my eyes and think of Granger.

His flexing six-pack of muscles, his white knuckled grip rifling up and down that hard, angry part of him, lip caught between his teeth.

God help me, heat inundates me when I remember the way he pulled down my tank top. Without permission. Exposing my breasts. My palms grow damp when I recall him yanking down my shorts, sinking his teeth into my shoulder. The sounds he made, like a wolf mating during a full moon.

With that grunting rasp ricocheting in my head, I finally slide my fingers down the front of my panties, my middle finger stealing into my slick folds—and I jerk, a shocked moan sailing from my mouth, my back arching involuntarily.

Oh my God, what is that spot?

I can't seem to stop rubbing it, twisting a corresponding bolt inside of me every time my middle finger passes over the tingling nub.

His name comes to my lips unbidden. "Granger," I gasp, feeling his male seed bathing my feminine flesh, running down my thighs. Watching his mouth fall open, his eyes going blind as he attacks me, pushing me up against the chain links—

My phone rings loudly on the desk and I screech, quickly pulling my fingers out of my panties, looking around the room guiltily. There is no one here, of course, it's just my phone making the commotion. But when I look at the screen and see my roommate's name scrolling by, I might as well still be touching myself. That's the effect thoughts of him have on me now. Just knowing he sleeps one door away has kept me awake and restless for two nights, the pulse between my legs refusing to calm. The way he behaved should have sent me running in the opposite direction, especially after what happened with my stepbrother, but instead…

I've had to stop myself from running to him.

I might have given in, too. I might have knocked on his bedroom door and asked for his help in extinguishing the new fire inside of me. But he's been acting so strange for the last two days. He moves around the apartment looking as if he's in physical pain. Every time I walk past him, he hisses a breath.

Being near me seems to put him in acute agony. And yet he never takes his eyes off me. It's like he's waiting for me to run so he can give chase.

I never took myself for a reckless girl, but I can't

help it.

There's something inside of me that thrills to the idea of being caught.

My phone continues to vibrate on the desk and I pick it up, pressing talk, taking a deep, bracing breath and holding it to my ear. "Hi, Granger."

"Peyton." His exhale crackles down the line. "What are you doing?"

His voice jolts my pulse into racing. "I'm working on report cards."

A long silence. "Is that all?"

The hair stands up on my arms and I turn my head, searching the pitch-black windows for a face. Some sign that he's watching me. That he caught me touching myself. But that's crazy, right? My roommate is not standing on the other side of the glass. I'm being paranoid. "What do you mean?"

"I mean, you should be home by now. Is there something you're doing at the school that you can't do at the apartment?"

I'm not sure why I whisper, "Yes." Perhaps because he showed me his vulnerability in the basement on Monday night. Showed me how badly he needed release. And here, alone in my classroom with no one nearby to judge, I confide in the only person who has ever made me feel safe. Wanted. "I'm doing something I've never done before," I say shakily, dropping my free hand back between my thighs and tease the front of my panties with two fingers.

"Are you touching yourself, Peyton?"

"Uh-huh."

He releases a guttural sound. "Why?"

I swallow hard, rubbing now. Rubbing my sensitive spot through the white cotton of my underwear, creating a wet spot. "I can't help it. Ever since the other night, I've felt different...down there."

Do I hear footsteps in the background? "Different how?"

"H-hot." I bite my bottom lip hard. "Damp."

He's breathing in short, rasping pants. "If I was there right now, baby, would you let me pump my dick inside of it?"

Those words blast me like an inferno, my fingers moving involuntary to slip inside my panties, finding my soaked flesh and stroking it eagerly. Granger between my legs, his hips thrusting vigorously. The imagery makes me restless, the upper half of my body falling back in the chair and arching, thighs spread. "Yes," I say finally.

And then he's there.

Framed in the doorway of my classroom.

He lowers the phone pressed to his ear, shoves it into the pocket of his jacket and advances toward me—and God help me, I'm too turned on and achy to question how he arrived so fast. All I can do is be consumed by those eyes. They're black and tinged with madness, but it's madness I feel, too, in this moment. Like I would do anything for this ache to be lessened and my body knows, instinctively, Granger can help me do that. He's the only one who can.

Halfway to me, he strips off his jacket, drops it on the floor.

Grabs his T-shirt behind the neck and tosses it aside, leaving him bare-chested in jeans and boots, his hair in disarray. My femininity clenches at his blatant sexuality, his magnetism, the corded stomach muscles that flex with every one of his panting breaths. Granger doesn't stop until he reaches me, plucking me up by the waist, depositing me on the desk—

And then he surges between my splayed thighs and kisses me.

I've always felt like prey in the spotlight of his attention and that sensation is amplified now. I'm being devoured whole. His mouth is wild, wet, moving over mine the way a man eats a meal when he's been deprived of food. He's on the verge of starvation and I'm the only thing that can save him. My lips become pliant along with my body, need screaming through my nerve endings, wanting him, burning for every stroke of his tongue inside my mouth, every moan we release together.

As we frantically try and get our fill, his hands don't remain still for a second. They scrub up my thighs, pushing up my skirt, and when it won't go any farther, he wraps a forearm around my waist, lifts me and leaves the garment bunched around my waist. This is unprofessional and scandalous, sitting on my desk with my wet panties showing, but my lust doesn't care. It's demanding I let this happen. Let him have me, show me what it means to be helpless and desperate.

We're mid-kiss when Granger breaks away, groaning brokenly. In pain.

"What's wrong?" I manage around my laboring breaths.

With his forehead pressed to mine, he hesitates a second. Then he reaches down and unzips his jeans, shoving them down. It takes me a moment to believe what I'm seeing. His erect manhood is there, but it's wrapped in a silver cage, swollen and miserable. Locked in a device that's preventing it from growing to the huge shaft he masturbated to an orgasm on Monday night.

"Granger," I gasp, tracing the smooth metal slats with my fingertip, causing him to jerk and curse. "What is this?"

"Cock cage," he says through his teeth. "My punishment for pushing you too far the other night. I scared you. I made you run from me."

"It looks painful," I say, emotion in my voice. He did this for me? As penance?

His nod is jerky. "Every time you make me hard, it reminds me I behaved like a bastard and not to do it again." His face falls into the crook of my neck, his fingertips clawing at my hips. "Ah, baby. I'm hard all the time. Your skin, the way you smell, the sound of you showering, even your shoes sitting beside mine near the door. It's torture. It's torture and I deserve it."

"No." I'm suddenly frantic to stop the pain. End his suffering. "Take it off."

"That was the other vow I made myself. Only you can take it off. I put the key on your ring." His stuttered breath bathes my ear. "You own this cock. Torture me or free me, Peyton. You decide."

I have the sense that I'm on the precipice of a major decision.

If I unlock him, there's no going back. My body knows it. Once we take this relationship to the next level, we'll never be just friends again. Maybe we never were just friends to begin with and I was just in denial. But my instincts ring loud and clear, telling me that I'm swimming into a deep end that has no bottom.

So be it.

Offering my mouth for another kiss, a comforting one this time, I search the desk for my keys, finding and lifting them. They rattle in my hand. I feel for the unfamiliar key I never noticed, locating it after a few seconds. Small and jagged.

Pulling back, I study the cage around Granger's hard sex and find the lock, inserting the little golden key and twisting. When the contraption falls away, landing on the floor of my classroom with a clank, he catches his rapidly swelling shaft in his hand and shouts a curse, his eyes turning a darker shade of black, masturbating himself roughly, his attention blazing a path toward the place between my thighs.

Teeth bared, he releases himself, takes hold of my panties at the waistband and rips them clean off my body. Gripping my buttocks, he yanks me to the edge of the desk with a growl. "I wonder if you realize what you just unlocked." He stamps his mouth down over mine and I feel it, that thick head prodding my entrance, our flesh oh so slippery. "It's never going back in the cage, honey. I'm not just talking about my cock. Do you understand what I'm saying?"

"Yes," I whisper, my subconscious answering on my behalf. Some part of me knows I've just made an irreversible decision to be his. I'm not sure everything that entails yet, but I know I can't survive the night without him giving me pleasure. Showing me what it means, feels like. "I understand, Granger."

"Good girl," he rasps, pressing his erection there, pressing, shifting it, grunting in frustration. "Ahhh Christ. Tight virgin kitty we've got here, baby. I've got some work to do before I can teach you to fuck, don't I?" His kiss doesn't allow me to answer. It absorbs my thoughts, distracts me as Granger props one of my ankles on his shoulder and presses his steel sex against my core again, spearing me with the engorged tip, punching his hips with a groan, delivering more. More. Sweat appearing on his forehead, his teeth clenched, eyes obsidian. "So wet. So innocent."

"Is it going to hurt?" I hiccup, my fingers curling into the edge of the desk.

"As soaked as you are, honey?" He shakes his head, his hips starting to roll forward and back in a sensual undulation, his jeans slipping farther down his legs. "Not for long. I'll make it good, Peyton, just have to get it all in first. Have to."

The deeper he gets inside of me, the more pressure

begins to mount, but I trust him not to hurt me unnecessarily. It's my first time with a man, in any capacity, so I have nothing to compare to this stretching sensation. The fullness of his flesh inside of mine, wedging deeper and deeper, until he releases a satisfied growl, our hips flush, his mouth panting on top of mine.

"You're taking all of me now." He rocks gently, hissing a breath. "Goddamn, I knew this pussy would be sweet and tight, but it's like being in a fucking vise."

I breathe through the tinges of pain. "Is that bad?"

"Jesus, no, baby. It's so damn good." His lower body ebbs back and grinds forward, his mouth falling open on a broken moan. "It's so, so good. It's heaven and I don't deserve it."

Those words distract me from the pain and I find myself relaxing, even opening my legs wider to him. "Yes, you do." I reach up and unbutton my shirt, pulling it open and watching his expression slacken with lust, riveted by my breasts. "You deserve this. I wouldn't have waited for you otherwise."

"Peyton," he rasps, leaning in to kiss my mouth long and thoroughly.

Lovingly.

"I want to watch you get helpless while you're inside of me," I whisper against his lips, flexing the intimate muscles that cradle his manhood. "Want to watch your need turn...critical."

"It's always critical," he grunts, taking two handfuls of my backside and squeaking me closer on the desk, his hips beginning to pump faster. Faster. "Christ. Stop squeezing my dick so hard. You're going to make me come."

But it's too late.

I'm addicted to giving him pleasure.

Amazing how it happened in the blink of an eye. I went from a clueless virgin to understanding my power, my ability to make his body come undone. And it turns me on, suddenly holding the key to making this man's willpower snap. I arch my back and show off the bounce of my breasts in the opening of my shirt, I throw my other ankle up onto his shoulder—and that is what breaks him.

"FUCK!" he roars, pitching forward and bending me in half, his hips slapping down against mine roughly, possessively, his sex hard and swollen, ramming in and out of my entrance, a touch more violently every time. "Do you know what it did to me? Watching the sweet little kindergarten teacher rub her clit, that tight ass wiggling around in the chair? No idea how to come. Just knowing it feels good. I almost broke the fucking cock cage, baby." He rakes his teeth up the side of my neck. "Horny little fairy needed a big bad dick, didn't she?"

My eyes are rolled back in my head, a heady sensation beginning to wrap around me, beckoned by his gloriously crude language, the friction being created by our straining bodies. And oh God, even the ferocious sounds of this man mating me turns the dial on my pleasure to a fever pitch until I'm moaning right along with him, lifting my hips eagerly for his forceful drives.

"Granger," I whine.

He pushes his thumb into my mouth and I suck it automatically, wanting any part of him inside of me, desperate for his taste. "Yeah, that's the first and last name you'll ever fucking moan, do you understand me?" He bears down with his hips, smacking into me with punctuated pumps. "This is your first and last cock, Peyton. I'm your first and last man. Say it."

"First and last," I whimper, my thighs beginning to tremble. "First and last!"

I'm not expecting the rush of bliss to blindside me, but it does, it careens into my loins, squeezing, and I scream. Somewhere in the back of my mind, I register that I'm having an orgasm, but surely this feeling can't be whittled down to a single word. It tears me apart, my womanhood clenching to the point of pain, pleasure, pain and all I can do is ride it out, accept Granger's animalistic humping, vaguely hearing the bump of the desk inching along the floor.

And then Granger jerks to a halt, shuddering, his muscles in a tight clench, head thrown back as he calls my name, letting that hot liquid pulse into me. It's unlike anything I could have imagined, opening my legs to allow a man's seed to enter my body, knowing I'm responsible for making him hard, for creating the need for him to thrust and rut and sweat. I'm not just addicted. I'm the addiction, too. And I was right, there is no way to go back to a time before I knew what this man felt like inside of me. I'm almost fearful of how much I love it.

It's not merely my libido that has reshaped itself.

There's something in my chest. A righteous yearning when I look at him.

His eyes meet mine and something passes between us.

Wonder. Desire. A promise.

Obsession.

If I'm looking at him with a fraction of the intensity he's looking at me, it's a wonder the whole school doesn't go up in flames. It's that intensity in Granger's eyes that reminds me of how he looked when he arrived. Hot. Determined. Starved.

But there is something that doesn't make sense. With my pulse going back to normal, my thoughts settling, a bigger picture knits together.

My nerves begin to dance. Trying not to show it on my face, I take my ankles off his shoulders and scoot forward, hopping off the desk. Granger is standing so close that my breasts graze his bare chest and we both break off a sound, my womanhood constricting. If he pushed me back onto the desk and entered me again, I would wrap my legs around him and ride the ride again. My body, my insane attraction to him would give me no choice. But he seems too focused on my face to act, as if he's intent on reading my thoughts.

"What's wrong, Peyton?"

"Nothing," I murmur, fixing my clothes, watching

Granger slowly do the same. "How did you get here so fast?"

I ask the question carefully, but his hands pause in the act of buttoning his jeans. And that's when my pulse kicks into high gear again. I can hear the oxygen moving in and out of my lungs, my fingertips tingling with alarm. Fight or flight.

He got here so fast because he was already at the school.

Following me. Watching me.

His eyes turn predatory, as if he knows the conclusion I've drawn.

My legs are burning with the need to run, but…oh God. I don't know what I'm running from, do I?

Granger.

Or the fact that him watching me unaware makes me feel…treasured.

Coveted.

Hot.

So yes, when I turn and sprint for the door, there's a possibility that I'm running away from what this man has awoken inside of me. Something dark that likes to be possessed. Likes to be on the receiving end of an infatuation.

I wheel around the corner into the school hallway and skid to a halt. There, on the floor in a heap, is a janitor uniform. And scenes from the last two days come back in a blinding rush. The janitor moving past my classroom door at odd times. The janitor watching me pull out of the parking lot from the shadow of the building, his baseball cap pulled down low over his eyes.

Granger has been dressing as the janitor.

Granger has been stalking me.

A scream builds in my throat, but I never get the chance to let it loose because I'm being thrown over Granger's shoulder. He storms down the hallway, easily subduing my attempts to get loose, his mighty forearm clamping down on my legs to keep them from kicking.

"Let me go," I breathe, twisting to try and free myself. "Let me go now!"

His laughter is deep and devoid of humor. Villainous. "Too late for that, Peyton," he says; his voice is crafted of iron. "You said first and last. First and last," he shouts, then takes a minute to rein in his volume, but not his madness. That has clearly been set loose. "You'll keep that promise, even if I have to make you."

CHAPTER SIX

Granger

I PACE BACK and forth in front of the bed.

My stomach is in fucking knots. A lot like the ones I used to tie Peyton to my headboard. This is bad. This wasn't supposed to happen. I told myself as soon as we were in a real relationship, I would stop following her, watching her at work, during the night, following her everywhere she goes. But she found out about my extra-curricular activities before I could make myself stop and now I could lose her.

There's a logical part of me that knows I never would have stopped, though. Twenty years into our marriage, I'd be stalking her. Until the end of my life, I'd be watching from the edges of her awareness, making sure no other man tries to claim what's mine. Making sure she's safe and happy. What else am I supposed to do when Peyton walking the earth is the equivalent of having my heart walking around outside my body?

I stop pacing long enough to take stock of her pale face, her chattering teeth. She's scared. Might as well rip out my insides. Peyton experiencing fear is the last thing I want. It's worse torture than the cock cage.

"Granger, you can't keep me tied up forever," she says, pulling on the restraints. "Please. I'm scared."

"Scared?" I rip my fingers through my hair, frustration clawing at my throat. "Don't you know I'd put a bullet between my own eyes before I hurt you?"

Processing that, she wets her lips. "I won't call the police."

"Peyton, the police are the last thing I'm concerned about." My voice is threadbare, raw. "I just can't have you running away from me. I'll go insane."

She goes limp on the bed and I can't help it, her surrender turns my dick hard. I've never seen anything more luscious in my life than Peyton tied to my bed with her blouse unbuttoned to her navel, the skirt rucked up from struggling. Maybe I am sick. Maybe I'm a psychopath. Her fear horrifies me, but this...this offering she represents has a very different effect on my body.

A voice in the back of my head urges me to kiss her, fuck her until she gives in and understands this relationship is inevitable. Until she wants me back again. But my refusal to do that is what separates me from her stepbrother. I need her to need me back. I need her to look at me like she did when I showed up at the school. As if I was her savior. As if she couldn't live without me.

"How long have you been following me?" She watches me carefully. "Did it start b-before that night on the road?"

"No." I shake my head. "No, we met by chance. I

turned the corner and there you were. A beautiful fairy. Mine to love, mine to keep safe."

Her lips part on the word *love*. And I want to say more. Want to tell her exactly how deep my feelings run. Love? Love is only the tip of the iceberg. But I bite down hard on my tongue and tell myself not to dig myself a deeper hole.

"You've been dressing like the janitor so you can watch me," she whispers, squeezing her eyes closed, tipping her head back on the pillow. "These last couple of days, I felt something odd. A tingle at the back of my neck."

There's something about the way she says the words in that throaty tone of voice…it's how she called my name while I was planted inside of her. Curiously, I study her body language and find her thighs pressed together tightly, her stomach dipping and creating a hollow, as if her pussy is flexed and it's uncomfortable for her. It's too much to hope that she's turned on by my stalking, though. It's purely wishful thinking.

"After that math teacher asked you out, I couldn't take any chances," I say, turning away from her and sitting down on the edge of the bed. "I physically couldn't do it. Let you dance off every morning looking so fucking sweet and pretty, knowing there would be men around who'd covet you. Allowing that would be like hammering a nail into my skull, Peyton."

"Well you didn't need to worry. The next time I

saw Paul, he ran from the room as if I had the plague..." The bed springs creak behind me. "Did you have something to do with that?"

"Yes." I look at her hard over my shoulder, unable to disguise my possessiveness. "And I don't regret it."

"You're crazy," she whispers, but her eyes turn slightly glassy, her legs shifting, rubbing together beneath the raised hem of her skirt.

Stop reading into everything she does. She thinks you're crazy.

You are crazy.

I take several bracing breaths, searching my mind for a way to make her understand me, my actions. "Where I come from, the way I grew up, Peyton..." It's unnatural to talk about my past. I haven't done it before. Confided in anyone. "I spent most of my days starving, trying to find scraps just to stay alive. My parents were never home. They tried to make ends meet in the beginning, but feeding three kids on minimum wage is hard. It's a daily grind. And when they lost those jobs and leaned heavily on alcohol, that's where all the money went. In my house, in my neighborhood, if you wanted something, you had to fight for it. Power, food, money, sometimes my life. Same in prison. Everything is life or death. And then you...you appeared." I dig my fingers into my knees, wishing I was touching her instead. "You're the first person I've ever needed. I had to fight to keep you the only way I know how. Playing dirty. Playing for keeps. Playing not to lose you."

Peyton is quiet so long, I'm starting to wonder if she heard me. Then, "I know something about that kind of life, Granger. You know where I grew up." Her voice turns hesitant. "But I wouldn't stalk someone I wanted. Following them and—"

My groan cuts her off. It comes from deep down inside of me. "Ah honey, the thought of you stalking me…" I angle my body so she can see my erection. So she can watch me scrub my palm over it roughly. "If I came home and found you going through my things, if I caught you spying on me across the street from my garage, it would make me fucking burn, baby."

Her breath comes faster. "You would like it?"

"Like it? No, I'd be in heaven. I crave it." I pull down my zipper because I'm getting too hard to remain trapped in my jeans. My cock pushes out through the opening, protruding against the front of my briefs and I shudder at the semi-relief. "If you even showed a hint of jealousy, like I did over that math prick, I'd spend a week eating your pussy until the feeling went away. I'd find whoever made you jealous and I'd fuck you right in front of them. You would know I'm yours. But you…doing things to ensure it…I can't help how hot it makes me."

"It makes you feel…secure," she whispers throatily. "Important."

As if she understands.

Does she?

I look back at Peyton over my shoulder and notice the dazed expression on her face, her heels digging into the mattress, hips shifting. Is it possible that she's turned on instead of scared? "Peyton, talk to me," I demand raggedly, turning and climbing onto the bed beside her, running a finger in circles around the hard peak of her nipple. "Your body is telling me you need a fuck."

Her back arches into my touch, her teeth sinking into her bottom lip. "I don't understand it," she says, so quietly I almost can't make out her words. "Is there something wrong with me that I still…"

I search her face eagerly. "Still what?"

"Still want you." Her exhale is shaky. "M-maybe even want you more…knowing what you've been doing?"

The sky above me is opening up and light is pouring through. Am I dreaming or did she really just confess to wanting me, despite my actions? That her desire for me has been amplified because of them? Hope ripping through my chest, I scrutinize her expression and find her peeking up at me through her lashes, cheeks flushed. In need of reassurance. In need of me, against all odds. "No, honey. There's nothing wrong with you." I straddle her hips, bracing my hands on either side of her head and leaning down to kiss her, moaning jaggedly when she actually kisses me back. "There isn't a single bad thing about you…" I kiss my way down her throat, licking a path between her tits. "My sweet little obsession is perfect. Perfect in every way."

I slide my fingers into the waistband of her skirt

and pull it down to reveal her drenched panties. She tries to cross her legs and hide the telltale wetness from me, but I don't allow it, pushing her knees wide on the bed. "Granger..." She squirms, starting to pant. "I d-don't know if I want to let myself be okay with this. I don't know what that means about me. I'm scared of who I'll become if we..."

"Let this obsession run wild?"

A beat passes, followed by her nod. "Yes."

I drop my mouth to her stomach, dragging my tongue over her belly button and dipping it inside firmly, wiggling it until she whimpers. And all the while, I'm tugging the panties down her legs, baring that exquisitely tight pussy to me completely. "Let me do a little convincing, baby," I mutter thickly, settling my mouth over the top of her slit and inhaling deeply, then slicking my tongue through her damp folds. "Good girl, tasting like my come."

The restraints groan as she jerks, whining my name when I go to town, spreading the lips of her pussy with two fingers and bathing her with my tongue. Her taste combined with mine is so goddamn sweet and right, I get dizzy, my hips struggling for friction against the edge of the bed. I sip on her clit, loving it roughly, then gently, trailing my fingers down her inner thigh so I can slide my middle and ring fingers inside of her. Fuck. As hard as I pounded her earlier, she's still virginal in her tightness. So much that I struggle to get both fingers inside, moaning in victory when she gets wetter at my touch, easing my way in.

I think of her stalking me, stealing my things, rolling around in my bed naked when I'm not home and secretly watching me while I shower. The imagery has me fucking the bed and grunting like a boar, trying to get my cock some relief, even as I focus on hers. Even as I work my fingers in and out of her slippery, little sex, feeling her clit swell on my tongue with every stoke and jiggle until she's crying out, yanking on the restraints and wrapping her thighs around my head.

After what happened tonight, I thought I would have to beg for this. I thought it would take me months or even years to earn the privilege of pleasuring her again. But she's not only allowing it, she's so fucking hot for my tongue, she grinds her cunt down on it, her breathy whimpers filling the room. Filling my head. And with a shaking twist of her hips, she orgasms, coating my mouth, my chin, with the bliss I've wrung from her beloved body.

"Granger," she gasps. "Please."

We're connected. She's a part of me and I'm a part of her, so I don't have to question what she wants. Needs. I climb up her body, cock in hand, and deliver it between her spread thighs, rutting her violently without hesitation. And she screams for it, her small tits bouncing wildly with the force of my pumps.

"This is your stalker fucking you, baby," I growl in her ear. "You're going to cream for the man who obsesses over you and this pussy every second of the day. Do you know how many times I had to lock myself in the janitor's closet and bash my fucking fists against the wall because I needed to be inside you so bad?" The headboard slaps the wall in quick succession, in perfect timing with our smacking flesh. "I'm going to eat you alive, you tight little fairy."

Her eyes widen and I think I've gone too far. Until she says, "Do it."

I can almost hear the creaking hinges on the cage inside of me, the beast charging free of its prison. Keeping my cock buried deep, deep enough to make her whine loudly and dig her heels into my ass, I reach up and free her wrists from the restraints. But I don't give her a chance to use her hands. No, I slide my shaft out of her sleek body and drag her off the bed, pinning her facedown to the floor.

Retrieving the rope from the bed, I bind her wrists quickly at the small of her back, blood and obsession and lust pounding in my head. Once her hands are secured, I knee Peyton's thighs apart roughly and drive into her from behind, my roaring curse ringing out in the bedroom.

I clap my hand over her mouth to muffle her screams and fuck her, gnashing my teeth against her ear, some sick, animal part of me taking over, having been given the freedom from her acceptance. To run amok. To take without reservation.

"This is what would have happened if I didn't put my cock in that cage," I say hoarsely, licking the lobe of her ear. "Feel how badly I need you, honey? Feel what happens every time you blink or breathe or swallow? You ever run away from me again like you did at the school and I will chase you down. Do you understand me? In less than a minute, I'll have you like this, face down, tied up and wiggling around on my dick trying to get an orgasm. Mine forever. Mine. Forever."

She wails into my palm, her sex clenching around mine, her knees trying to dig into the floor so she can meet my thrusts. But I keep her flat beneath me and sneak a hand under her hips instead, positioning two fingers where she can grind her clit down on them. Her resulting scream makes me laugh darkly in her ear, my hips thrusting all the faster, feeling the ripples travel through her core, turning her into a hot, milking paradise for my cock. So wet and warm and tiny, I can't stop my own climax from approaching with the speed of a bullet being fired from a gun.

When Peyton stiffens beneath me and begins to shake, crying out into my hand, I give myself permission to let go and my balls pulse, sending hot seed up my shaft in waves. I drop my hand from Peyton's mouth and slap it down on the floor, along with my other one, my hips ramming forward quickquickquick, desperately, spurred on by my obsession with the girl beneath me. Claiming her, possessing her, making her mine. Now.

"I love you," I gasp into her neck, pleasure and affection untying the knots inside of me one by one. "I love you, Peyton."

I'm not disappointed when she doesn't say it back

to me. No, I've been given a gift. More than I ever could have expected—and I won't be greedy. She isn't leaving me. She still wants me, even though my dark obsession has been revealed. Over time, I will do everything in my power to make her return my feelings. Even if she can only develop a fraction of them, it'll be leaps and bounds beyond what I ever expected to receive in my lifetime.

Picking her up off the floor, I gently untie her wrists and bundle her under the covers, my heart rapping against my ribcage. And when I climb into the bed beside her and she tucks her head under my chin, I'm the happiest man alive.

That doesn't mean I'm letting my guard down.

Not when I can still hear her words ringing in my head.

I d-don't know if I want to let myself be okay with this. I don't know what that means about me. I'm scared of who I'll become…

I band an arm around her, my body poised to chase her if she tries to escape.

CHAPTER SEVEN

Peyton

M Y PHONE BUZZES on the nightstand, waking me up from the deepest, most boneless sleep of my life. I'm not even sure how or when my phone was placed there, but Granger must have grabbed it on the way out of my classroom, since the last place I remember seeing it was on my desk.

I try to reach for the phone, but the muscular male arm around my midsection refuses to budge, and helplessly, I sink back into the warmth of him. It's so simple to let the contentedness take hold, safety and security making me almost drowsy.

But I fight against it, forcing my eyes to stay open.

I'm in bed with a man who stalked me. Based on how he's holding me now, the possessive way he spoke to me, I don't see him stopping.

And it excites me.

Makes me feel needed and important for the first time in my life.

More than anything, I want to ignore the warning voice in the back of my head telling me this is dangerous and let Granger consume me. He gives my body unimaginable pleasure. He loves me. Wants to care for me and protect me.

With the deepest recesses of my soul…I want to let him.

I want to give myself over to this obsession I feel building inside of me. It's not one-sided. I've been fascinated with him to an unhealthy degree since the beginning—I just didn't realize it. Didn't know what the hot quaking of my body meant. Or the constant, rupturing sensation in my chest. But I know now that our deep, abiding fascination is a two-way street. Now what am I going to do about it?

Let myself get carried away?

Or break free before I end up in a dark, co-dependent, sex-fueled relationship with a man who spied on me, followed me, all but admitted he'd been fantasizing about pinning me to the floor, covering my mouth and taking me without mercy?

Realizing I've grown wet between my thighs, I struggle for focus.

What is the right thing to do for me? Stay or go?

As if Granger senses my thoughts, he stirs behind me, that arm tightening ever so slightly. Almost like he doesn't want me to notice.

And I like it.

I like him holding me as if he's ready to fight to the death to keep me.

I shouldn't, though. I shouldn't be breathless and achy over his treatment.

"Who would be calling you this early in the morning?" Granger asks in my ear, his voice deceptively calm.

"I don't know," I say honestly. "Can I look?"

When his sex thickens against my backside, I sense he liked me asking for permission. Oh God, I liked it, too. I loved it. So much that I can almost feel my pupils dilating, my nerve endings zapping. "Yes," he says, finally, but he keeps a firm hold on the back of my neck as I lean toward the side table to retrieve the phone.

"It's the school," I murmur, frowning at the screen. "I hope nothing is wrong. They left me a voicemail."

"Listen to it." His open mouth glides along the breadth of my shoulders, making my eyelids flutter. "On speakerphone."

I nod jerkily, tapping the screen and settling the phone back onto the table. I'm stunned when I hear the principal's voice sounding grave on the recording. "Yes, hello. This is Principal Laughlin from the Royal Oak Academy. Miss Pruitt, if you're listening to this, we know you've been taken. The security cameras captured footage of your abduction last night. We have sent the police to your apartment to determine if you're there." He clears his throat. "If this is Miss Pruitt's captor, please return her home safely. We have your imagine on camera and the police will be much more lenient if you cooperate."

The voicemail ends.

Neither one of us breaths, but the tension coils in the man behind me.

JESSA KANE

"The school has this address?" he asks mildly.

"Yes," I whisper. "I updated their records when I moved."

"So they're coming. Here."

Without saying the words out loud, I know we're thinking the same thing. The police are under the impression that Granger abducted me—and to be fair, they aren't wrong. He caught me when I ran, put me over his shoulder, took me home and tied me up. But I have a choice to make. I can allow the police to believe Granger is my abductor and free myself from these addictive shackles.

Or I can change their minds.

Slowly, Granger's hand curves around my throat. "Do you think prison bars would keep me from you, Peyton?"

God help me, my sex clenches, my heart firing on all cylinders in my chest.

I close my eyes and search for the right answer to this situation.

Let this hunger take root and grow gnarled and twisted or rip it out before there's no turning back?

But is there turning back now?

His skin against mine is warm, his heartbeat strong against my spine. Even his hand on my throat is thrilling and grounding at the same time. Granger came into my life like a dark, avenging angel and even then, on that road, the connection was already forming between us. It strengthens by the minute, leaving little hope of severing it.

This isn't the life I pictured for myself, though.

I've always craved normalcy. A respectable life that would separate me from my past struggles. This relationship with Granger…it's wild and turbulent.

What should I do?

There's a loud knock on the front door of our apartment—and I'm no closer to deciding the best course of action. My heart climbs up into my mouth and I turn to face the man behind me, his brow drawn in worry. Panic. Not from the police. Oh no. This is not a man who fears anyone. The panic stems from the decision I'll make.

We stare into one another's eyes for long moments until another, louder knock echoes through the apartment.

"You have to let me answer," I whisper. "This isn't going to go away until they've spoken to me."

"No," he rasps, his throat working with a swallow.

"Yes." I smooth out the furrow of his brow with my thumb. "If we're going to be together, you'll have to trust me."

"You ran from me less than twelve hours ago."

"I know." If I'm going to get to that door, if I'm going to have a chance to decide my own destiny at all, I need to find a way out of this bed. So I lean in and kiss him long and full on the mouth, my chest tightening at the way he kisses me back. Like he's never going to see me again. "Things are different than they were twelve hours ago, aren't they?" I murmur against his lips.

He takes two hasty breaths. "I don't know."

"They are," I say, kissing him again, stroking the hair back from his forehead. "Trust me, Granger, okay?"

His nod is stiff, but he gives it. And I don't wait. I climb out of bed and find my skirt, zipping it on while the knocking grows louder, more insistent. Granger sits up and watches me from the messy sheets, his eyelids hooded, mouth in a tight line.

That's the moment I realize I love him.

I love him for letting me make the choice. For giving me his trust, even though it's hard for him. I love him for his jealousy, his possessiveness, his protective nature and the way he's made himself vulnerable to me, despite how hard that must be for someone like him.

Dressed now, I take one last look at him and leave the room on trembling legs, calling, "I'll be right there," at the rattling door, afraid if I don't say something, the police are going to break it down.

The walk to the front door is the longest of my life, the distance seeming to double with every step I take. And that's exactly why I know I'll never be happy without the man in the bedroom behind me. Because each step in the opposite direction of him makes me miserable. All I want is to be back in bed with him. I want his obsessive hands all over me. I want his darkness spread all over me so I can revel in it—and I want to give him my own in return.

I could open the door and tell the police that he

did, in fact, kidnap me and hold me against my will. It just wouldn't be the truth. Even being restrained in his bed gave me a deeper sense of rightness than I've ever felt in my life. I can't live without it. Or him. The very thought of him being taken out of here in handcuffs makes me so anxious, I can barely breathe as I settle my hand on the lock, sliding it across and opening the door.

The faces of five officers stare back at me. They don't look relieved to see me alive and well. No they take one glance at my disheveled state, the red marks on my wrists, and their attention sweeps the apartment behind me, trying to find Granger.

The threat.

"Can I help you?" I say, my throat scratchy from screaming.

"Are you all right, ma'am?" One of them draws his gun slowly. "Is there anyone else in the apartment?"

Moment of truth. "Yes," I answer. Then louder, "Yes. My boyfriend."

That gives them pause. "Your boyfriend." They exchange looks. "You were abducted last night at your place of work by a man known as Granger Hoskins. A felon, ma'am. Is he in the apartment with you?"

"Granger is my boyfriend." I wet my lips, a sense of purpose settling over me, making my voice sound more confident. "And he didn't abduct me. We were…roleplaying. We didn't mean to alarm anyone."

"Roleplaying," one of the officers echoes doubtful-ly.

The newly twisted part of me chooses that moment to rear its head. I'm surprised by the pride that comes along with it. I want to own what I have with Granger—and I have to, if we're going to be happy.

"Yes, roleplaying." My voice dips to husky and I lovingly rub my wrist marks against my cheek, sensuality uncurling inside of me like smoke. "I went willingly. Very…willingly."

I sense movement behind me and turn to find Granger outlined in his bedroom doorway, one forearm propped high on the door. "Hello, officers," he drawls. His voice is casual, but his eyes are rife with intensity, boring into me, making me feel feverish. "Let me put on a shirt."

Granger turns in the doorway and I gasp.

His back is covered in scratch marks. Fresh ones.

In slow motion, I look down at my nails and find them tipped with red.

Heat climbs my thighs at the visible proof of my pleasure. At it being broadcast rather inappropriately. Intentionally. To let the other men know how satisfied I am in his bed. It's bad. It's good. It's us.

An officer coughs behind me. "I, uh…don't think a shirt will be necessary, Mr. Hoskins. We'll let the school know Miss Pruitt is safe and sound."

Granger nods once, his expression hardening, no longer friendly or casual. Instinctively I know he doesn't like men near me. At all. He prowls toward me and I turn into his arms, tipping my head back to sigh over his gorgeous face. The jealousy displayed there.

"If you'll excuse us," he says to the officers, reaching over my shoulder to close the door—and immediately backing me against it, our mouths fusing together wetly, desperately.

My skirt is ripped up to my hips by impatient male hands and I wrap my thighs right where they belong. Around his waist. He grinds our foreheads together while reaching down and unzipping his jeans, a moan breaking past my lips at the feel of his shaft prodding the entrance to my sex.

"Let them hear you," Granger rasps in my ear, filling me in one savage drive. "Just in case they have any more doubts that you love riding this dick—and this dick only. You love it. Tell them."

"I love it," I whine through my teeth, Granger pounding me roughly against the door, rattling the hinges. "And I love you, Granger. I love you."

He pauses, lifting his head to stare with a look of wonder on his face. "You…chose me. I can't believe it."

"Feel me," I whisper, wrapping my legs as tightly as they'll go, clenching my intimate muscles where they cradle him. "Believe it."

"I love you," he groans, burying his face in my neck. "My fairy."

"My dark prince," I whimper back, the door beginning to shake again with each one of his frantic drives. And for the rest of our lives, he certainly lives up to the name.

EPILOGUE

Peyton

Five Years Later

I'M NOT THE same girl I was five years ago.

After some profuse apologizing for having inappropriate relations on school property, they let me keep my job, so I'm still a kindergarten teacher who is given to blushing. But I'm a lot braver. Which is why I'm walking through the trailer park on a Friday afternoon in the summertime, memories reaching out to me from all corners. I've decided to come back and face my final remaining fear—my stepbrother.

If Granger knew I was here, he wouldn't like it, which is putting it mildly. He's a fearless man, though. The kind of terror I experienced in this park all those years ago is something only a woman fully understands. And I'm here to purge it. Over the last five incredible years together, a lot of Granger's courage has worn off on me.

Among other things, such as his passion.

His lack of boundaries when it comes to how he loves me.

How he takes me.

Our hunger for one another is an insatiable thing

that only continues to twine and twist and grow more complex. We married on a mountaintop in fall with only the preacher as a witness, but we don't have children, because we simply can't share each other. My job gives me all the affection and fulfillment I need from children—and the rest of my time is spent being stalked by my husband.

Stalking him in return.

He isn't following me today because, ever since he bought the garage where he works, weekdays demand his attention. I've left my cell phone at home so he won't track me here, like he normally would. We go nowhere without each other's knowledge and I love that. Crave and treasure it—the sense of being on an undefeated team. Love being confident in the fact that he is watching me constantly, thinking and yearning and counting the seconds until we're back in the apartment, dragging each other under with the spell of obsession.

I'm here today for myself. Because I want to look my one and only demon in the eye and let him know I'm not scared of him anymore. I want Tony to look at me and witness the confidence that love has given me and know he didn't win.

I reach the trailer, which looks almost exactly the same, except for a few potted plants out front. But when I knock on the door, someone I don't recognize answers. A woman in a shift dress with a baby on her hip.

"Yeah?"

"I'm sorry, I…used to live here. Is Tony at home?"

"Tony?" She seems to be searching her memory bank. "Is he that fella who disappeared back in the day?"

"Disappeared?" A tingle climbs the back of my neck. "No, I don't think so…"

"Yeah, he's the one. Lived here before me. He up and vanished one day and this trailer sat here until the bank repossessed it." She bounces the baby. "That's why I got it for so cheap."

"Right," I say, dazed. "And when…when did you say he disappeared?"

She looks up at the sky, thinking. "Must have been five years, since I was pregnant with my first."

I swallow the knot in my throat. "Thank you."

The woman closes the door and I stand stock still, processing several things at once. One, Tony is gone. Two, he vanished soon after I met Granger. Three, there is no way that is a coincidence.

On unsteady legs, I turn and walk back out of the park, people peeking out at me from their windows. Do they know?

I reach my car and slide into the driver's seat, locking the doors and staring straight ahead, not wanting to acknowledge the hot shivers creeping up my legs, meeting at my sex and turning it damp. It's not right for me to feel this way, having just realized the lengths my husband will go to avenge me, keep me safe. But over the last five years, haven't I learned to live in the gray area where right and wrong are just suggestions?

My husband is a savage when it comes to me—and I love the darkest parts of him. They call to something inside of me I didn't know existed until he barreled into my life and now? I can't turn it off.

My pulse accelerating, I reach up beneath my skirt, lifting my hips to remove my panties. Setting them beside me on the passenger seat, I put the car in drive, one destination in mind. The same one I always have. Him.

Granger

I'M RESTLESS TODAY.

Intuition pricks holes in my gut.

I check my phone for the tenth time in as many minutes, studying the blinking dot that tells me my wife is at home. But there's something off. She was acting too casual this morning over coffee. I took the mug out of her hands, slammed it down and fucked her on the kitchen table—and she was one hundred percent with me then—biting and scratching and grinding into my thrusts. Still, a few minutes after we came, she started giving me those too-quick answers again when I asked about her plans for the day.

Summertime is hard for me. She's a teacher, meaning she doesn't work for three months, and all I can think about while I'm at the garage is how I'd fucking die to be home with her. Holding each other in the bathtub, making meals in the kitchen and spending hours wringing myself out in her tight pussy.

Out of the sheer sexual frustration that never leaves me, I slam my fist down onto my desk, upsetting a cup of pens. I swear to God, every day I sink a little more into this Peyton-induced mania. If we didn't have bills to pay or basic errands to run, I don't think I'd stop touching her for a single second. Not while she showers, not while she sleeps. Her skin, her voice, her existence are my addiction. I'm a junkie and my goal every single day is to overdose or I'm not alive.

I stalk to the glass window overlooking the garage, gratified to see it full of cars, more in the lot awaiting repairs. Over the last five years, with Peyton's encouragement, I've expanded into the property next door and doubled our clientele. I never could have done it without her. Never would have believed myself capable of being a businessman without my wife.

That—and a million other reasons—is why I'm surprising her with a house tonight. A secluded cabin-style home beside a river. Lots of space.

Most importantly, privacy.

I can already see her wading naked into the river in the summertime, smiling back at me over her shoulder, her tight little ass bruised from my fingertips.

Fuck this.

I'm going home to her. My cock is already stiff thinking about walking in and taking her wherever she stands. I need her. I can't think straight without her.

I yank open my desk drawer to retrieve my car

keys, my hand pausing in mid-air when I find a pair of panties sitting there instead. My balls draw up tight and I have to grab the desk to maintain my balance under the onslaught of lust. Of course, I recognize my wife's panties on sight. I'm the one who buys them for her. I'm the one who picks which pair she'll wear every morning.

These are black and white and red, a heart pattern. I bought them a size too small. When I brought them home, I made Peyton put them on—only them. Nothing else. And then I told her to lie facedown on the bed and hump a stuffed animal I won her at the county fair until she climaxed. I came in my pants after a mere minute, then again when she hit her peak.

Yes, they're a particular favorite.

I'm already rubbing them against the bulging fly of my jeans. Not only because I know they've touched her sex. But because she put these here.

My wife is here.

Stalking me.

A hoarse sound climbs my throat and I push off the desk, stuffing her panties in my pocket on the way out of my office. I hear nothing, see nothing, except the path in front of me. The one that will lead me to her. My breath sounds loud in my ears, my tongue thick in my mouth. I check my car first to see if she's there, but I don't find her. I sweep the property, growing more and more aroused the longer it takes me to track her down. Finally, I enter the lot full of cars waiting for repair—

And I catch a flash of brown curls.

They disappear behind an Acura and I stride in that direction, taking her panties out of my pocket and pressing them to my nose. Quick footsteps tell me she's running from me. I close my eyes and listen, trying to judge the direction she's taking, and when I figure out her course, I jog back three car lengths and take a fast right, catching her around the middle when she careens around the next curve.

"Got you now," I grunt, dragging her to the hood of the nearest car and throwing her facedown over the hood. My wife, my Peyton, whimpers as if she's scared, as if she doesn't know I would die for her in a heartbeat. And she struggles as I yank up her skirt, finding her delicious ass bare, as I suspected I would. "Did you think you could sneak around and not get caught?"

I crack my palm against her backside, producing a broken moan from her perfect, beloved mouth. Then my fingers find her. Two into her incredibly narrow channel. Hard. Pumping in and out. "I...I thought..."

"You thought you could leave the sweet scent of this pussy in my office and I wouldn't track it down?" I push my fingers deep, as deep as they'll go, leaning down to speak in her ear. "I'd kill for this hot little thing."

Her breath catches, eyelids fluttering. "You have killed for it."

My heart stutters in my chest.

She knows.

For a long time, I worried she would find out I ended the life of the man who dared touch what's mine. Who dared scare her. We are twisted in a lot of ways, my wife and I, but murder is another level of dark entirely, so I hoped she'd never find out I left her sleeping the middle of the night five years ago and woke Tony up with my hands wrapped around his neck. But she did find out.

And she's still here.

She's not just here, she's...tilting her hips up, begging me without words for the rough treatment of my shaft. When I growl into her neck and buck into Peyton's heat, we're embarking on a whole new level of depraved. Of trust and connection. And I welcome it, crave the additional closeness of her with every fiber of my being.

"I love you," she whispers, turning her head so we can devour each other's mouths over her shoulder, the vehicle rocking back and forth between us.

"I love you, too," I heave, and then I chant those three words over and over again until they blur together...

THE END

My Husband, My Stalker

PROLOGUE

Evan

I'M CLEANING MY Glock after tonight's hit when I see her face on the news.

A full minute passes before I remember to breathe.

Without registering my own movements, I find myself on my knees.

Inches from the screen of the motel room television.

Who…is she?

Her face is exquisite, but God, she's tired. Her strength is fragile, though very much alive in her big, golden eyes. Beneath her beautiful face are the words "Kidnapping Victim Speaks at Sentencing" and my blood is already beginning to boil as I turn up the volume.

"Miss Dubois, what was it like to come face to face today with the man who kidnapped you?"

The question jars the young woman, but she hides it well, tucking a loose strand of chocolate-brown hair back into her ponytail. "It wasn't…pleasant. But hopefully, someday, seeing him put away will be part of my closure."

Her voice sends my blood rushing south, my cock

stiffening painfully behind the zipper of my jeans. Soft, husky, resilient, pure, honest. I've never been so drawn to a sound in my life. But here I am, pressing my forehead to the screen, my breath fogging up the glass. My hands grope for the sides of the set, all but pulling it off the cheap dresser in a need to be as close to her as possible. Who is this girl? Who tried to hurt her?

I will end their life. I'm a professional, after all. It's what I do.

And I will do it for her. One glance and already I would do anything for her.

Miss Dubois tries to pass through the throng of reporters, but they pipe up in a grating chorus, daring to block her path. "Miss Dubois! Jolie!"

Jolie.

That's her name.

Jolie Dubois.

I don't bother writing it down, because it's already engraved on my brain.

There are claws in my chest, rearranging organs and making me new. Making me into whatever she needs me to be. I will worship her. I will find this sweet girl and protect her from any harm. She is mine to guard, to keep, to marry. To fuck.

I've never had much interest in females. They are merely objects that need to be avoided so I can kill the men I am contracted to execute. They are occasional, faceless tools of comfort. This one is my angel. She was sent for me. My singing blood is telling me so.

On the screen, she draws her bottom lip through her teeth and I come very close to ejaculating in my pants. The pressure behind my fly becomes too intense and I have to unzip, have to stroke myself, standing on shaky legs and showing it to her. Letting her see the last cock she'll ever have between her legs.

"Jolie," I choke, dragging the head of my erection over her face.

"What will you do now?" a reporter shouts at my girl. Mine. "How will you move on after such a terrible trauma?"

That question draws Jolie up short, her golden eyes crowding with worry. Thoughtfulness. And God, I am a miscreant. To be able to rifle a hand up and down my dick while she deals with such intrusive questions. While she speaks about this terrible thing that happened to her. But I will atone as soon as the sun rises tomorrow. I will make it up to her. Perhaps the anticipation of giving her real closure, making her happy, is part of the reason I'm so hot. So sick with the need to come.

Finally, she answers the question. "What I hope for is…a quiet, normal life. Blessedly normal. And if I'm lucky, some laughter." She ducks her head and pushes through the crowd. "Thank you. Excuse me."

Quiet. Normal.

Can a hit man give her these things?

No.

No, but someone else can.

I will simply have to become someone else.

The news station moves on to another story and I turn, stumbling to the bed and falling face down, fucking my fist like an animal, imagining her big, beautiful eyes flashing up at me. Imagining her sopping wet pussy clenching around my shaft, that sweet voice calling my name.

She's woken something inside me. An instinct to mate. To claim. And I snarl into the scratchy comforter now, my hips jerking forward and back violently, vowing to find her.

Vowing to stalk her, until I know exactly what will please her.

Vowing to make her my wife.

When I come, it's a boom of thunder that changes me irrevocably. Into her man. Into her perfect husband. My spend soaks the bedclothes and bubbles over the tight grip of my fist, wringing me out, making me roar, until I'm slumped over, visions of Jolie rotating in my head.

I'm coming for you, angel eyes.

I'll be there soon.

CHAPTER ONE

Jolie

One month later

I'M GOING TO go to the block party.
No more hiding in this house.

The neighbors were kind enough to invite me via a note in my mailbox, even though I've locked myself away from the world since the trial. A full month of people leaving brownies on my doorstep and checking the locks every hour. But now…

I glance down at the newspaper, the headline still there. I didn't dream it.

"Kidnapper Murdered in Prison."

Not just murdered, though. Carved up and hung from his ankles in the recreation yard.

My fear that Joseph Hynes is going to jump out of the shadows has been irrational since they put him behind bars. But now, my fear is even more unfounded. My therapist has been urging me to take small steps to reinsert myself back into society. A block party is a bigger step than I was hoping for. The supermarket might be a better option. But the headline in the newspaper seems like a sign. That it's time.

After several calming breaths, I pick up my phone

and hit the controls to brighten up the entire house. Lights flip on and banish the shadows, illuminating the back hallway leading to my bedroom and I pad in that direction now. My heart pounds wildly in my chest, even though logic tells me no one is hiding around the corner. No one is going to jump out and grab me, drag me to the basement, tie me up.

I shower and do my hair, makeup, for the first time in a month.

My favorite cream-colored slipdress hangs from my frame, due to the weight I've lost from being too anxiety-ridden to eat. So I add a belt and a cardigan, buttoning the sweater all the way to my neck to make myself feel more secure.

There's no telling how long I stand with my hand on the front doorknob, breathing, counting to one hundred and back, attempting to garner the courage to walk outside, but I finally do it, armed with the knowledge—in black and white—that Joseph Hynes is no longer a threat. He is gone. He can't hurt me. It's broad daylight and I can hear the neighbors outside, can hear the music playing. This is safe.

I open the door...

And I see him immediately.

A man I don't recognize, but must be one of the neighbors.

There is a group of men congregating around a barbeque and he stands slightly apart from them, a bottle of beer held at his side between two knuckles.

He's handsome. In a sharp way. Like he has to

concentrate on holding himself still. Dark-haired. Tall, wide-shouldered, muscular, his broad chest contained inside of a simple, blue button-down. Strong. His eyes are focused as they fix on me, widening slightly.

I'm caught off guard when my mouth goes dry.

When my pulse skitters with…interest?

I'm twenty-two. In the past, I dated, but it never got serious. I was always too focused on interior design school, learning everything I could about beautifying homes, to worry about the drama the opposite sex always seems to bring. Traveling, going dancing, reading, swimming in the ocean. Those were the things I used to enjoy. Boys were kind of an afterthought. Not that this man could even remotely be referred to as a boy.

He's a man. A man whose thick thighs test the seams of his jeans.

A normal man, though? A quiet one?

Why am I wondering about him? I'm not open to a relationship. I've barely made it to the end of my front path yet. I have a lot of recovering to do before I can even think about dating. My God, that's probably years in the future.

Besides, I'm sure he isn't clamoring to ask out the traumatized virgin hermit next door.

I give him a polite smile and lower my eyes, going in search of Nancy, the one who left me the note. I saw her deliver it through my peephole. She's a petite blonde in her forties who favors brightly colored leggings and always wears a visor.

When two minutes has passed and I haven't spotted her, my palms begin to sweat.

Is it my imagination or is everyone whispering about me?

They must know who I am. I was all over the news for months.

I was probably invited as the entertainment. For everyone to gawk at.

Another minute passes and I'm just standing there like an idiot. I have to get back inside. That's where it's safe. Where I don't have to worry about anyone but myself, my own space, and the locks on the doors.

I turn, walking in a fast clip down the sidewalk toward my house, but before I can veer down my front path, the handsome man I noticed before breaks from the barbequing group of men. He doesn't block my path like I expect him to do. Instead, he takes a hesitant step in my direction, hands in his pockets, a lopsided smile making him even more attractive.

"Leaving already?" he asks, in a husky baritone that makes me shiver hotly.

I haven't spoken to anyone in person in a month. Before that, it was mostly lawyers, cops and doctors. So my voice sounds unnatural to my ears when I respond. "Yes. I can't find the lady who invited me. I don't see her." For some reason, maybe because his eyes are so patient, I blurt, "There are a lot of strangers here."

He considers the packed block, nodding, as if that was a completely normal thing to say. "I see your point." He lifts his beer. "That's what the alcohol is for."

A laugh sneaks out of me. "Actually...I don't drink anymore."

A beat passes and I assume I've disappointed him. Then he turns the bottle so I can see the label. "Non-alcoholic," he says, kind of sheepishly. "I didn't want you to think I was..."

"Flawed?"

His eyes are the most intense shade of blue and it deepens now. "Isn't everyone, though?"

It's the strangest thing. Those three words feel like they're being whispered to me across a pillow. We're standing in a sea of people and yet...this encounter is so intimate. Like no one else exists. The other voices are just buzzes of sound. His eyes are a lifeboat in a huge, turbulent ocean and I can't seem to look away. "Yes. Some more than others."

Did he move closer or am I hallucinating?

"I don't want to be forward or anything, but..." He looks over his shoulder. "I happen to know where I can get you a tasteless non-alcoholic beer, too."

My heart starts to pound. So loud he must hear it. I'm not ready for this kind of thing. At all. Sure, he's kind. But having a drink with a man? A man I'm attracted to? Where can it lead when I'm not even capable of walking into a room unless the lights are blazing and I've pep talked myself for ten minutes? "I don't know," I whisper. "Um...no, I can't."

"Of course not," he says, visibly exasperated with

himself. "I haven't even told you my name. That's supposed to come before asking the beautiful girl for a drink, right?" I'm still reeling from him calling me beautiful when he holds out his hand. "I'm Christopher. New to the neighborhood. I live next door to you."

"You do?"

He hums in the affirmative.

New to the neighborhood. Does that mean he doesn't know who I am?

If he doesn't now, he will eventually. People talk. But I can't help but think it would be nice to sit and have a conversation with someone who doesn't know I was kidnapped and terrorized in the basement of an old house.

Shaking off my nerves, I slip my hand into his without thinking, shocking myself. "It's nice to meet you. I'm Jolie."

There's a flicker of something in his eyes and an answering crackle breaks across my palm. Electricity. It turns my nerve endings into buzzing little sources of sensation. "Jolie," he says gruffly, his attention dipping to my mouth. "It's nice to meet you, too."

"Do you live...alone?" I ask.

"No." I try to take my hand back out of his grip, but he holds on. "I have a temperamental Husky named Winston."

"Oh." Wow. I think I almost got jealous there, assuming he had a wife or girlfriend. How embarrassing. I've only known this man for a matter of minutes.

What business do I have being jealous? It makes me feel silly. For making assumptions. For being so freaked out over having one measly drink in broad daylight with a neighbor. You have to start living again, Jolie. "I guess one drink sounds nice."

He smiles, lines fanning out from the corners of his eyes. "Thank you."

CHAPTER TWO

Jolie

CHRISTOPHER LEADS ME to an empty picnic table on the outskirts of the crowd, leaving briefly to get me the same non-alcoholic beer he's drinking. When he sits down across from me, it feels a lot like a date and a flutter of panic takes wing in my throat, but his affable smile puts me at ease. "You're in luck, Jolie," he drawls, tapping the neck of his bottle to mine.

"Why is that?"

"Because in my short time living on this block I've picked up a lot of neighborhood gossip. And I'm about to fill you in."

"Oh my gosh." I press my palms to my cheeks, surprising by the pressing need to giggle. "I shouldn't be so excited. Gossiping is mean."

"Only if we get caught," he says, winking at me.

I gasp with mock outrage. "You're bad. You must do something evil for a living." I narrow my eyes. "Lawyer?"

He leans forward on his elbows, grinning broadly. "Nope."

"A magician?"

A laugh barks out of him. "Magicians are evil?"

"It's common knowledge. They operate in the dark arts. Sawing women in half all willy-nilly." I shrug, take a sip of my beer. "And just being generally cringey."

"I can't argue with that. You get one more guess."

"Hmmm." This is flirting. I'm actually flirting. And I can't believe it. Except there is something about Christopher that makes it so easy. Makes me feel completely safe. At ease. There's attraction, yes. But there's no pressure. No anxiety. It also helps that he's seated me in the exact right spot where I can see my front door. Did he do that on purpose? "Russian spy?"

He laughs into a sip of his drink. "Sorry to disappoint you. I'm just a normal, boring, run-of-the-mill insurance salesman."

"Normal isn't a bad thing," I say honestly. "In fact, I think normal is the best thing."

"Do you?"

I nod slowly.

We simply look at each other, the day passing in flurry of color around us, but our bodies remaining perfectly unmoving. "So…" I whisper. "About this gossip."

"Right," he growls, though it quickly turns to a cough. He must have had something stuck in his throat. "Let's start with the man operating the barbeque. He's obsessed with his lawn. I once caught him in the middle of the night on his belly, trimming it with scissors."

My mouth falls open. "No, you didn't."

"I did. And it's all because the man who lives across the street is his high school football rival. You didn't realize we were living in a sitcom, did you?"

"I had no idea. Competing lawn care fanatics. Now that's a show I would watch."

"Me too." He glances back over his shoulder and I take a moment to appreciate his physique. For a man who sells insurance, he is obscenely fit. Like cut triceps and flexing shoulders and hands that look like they do a lot more than tap at a keyboard. He must do CrossFit after working hours. Otherwise he's very naturally gifted.

This is healthy, right?

Noticing men and their attributes?

I'm already excited to talk to my therapist about it.

"Okay, next up is the older woman holding court by the snack table. You see her? Fire engine red hair. Hard to miss."

This time, I can't stop my giggle. "I see her."

My laugh seems to distract him, but he swallows and keeps going. "She dyes her poodle's hair pink and posts pictures of it in costumes on the town's online bulletin board."

"Oh, please say she dressed it like an old timey sheriff."

"A sheriff, a mermaid, a milkman, a flapper..."

I almost choke on a sip of my drink. "No insurance salesman? What a terrible oversight."

"Right?" He shakes his head sadly. "We get no

love."

"Are you..." Don't ask. Even if there's an odd sense of connection here, you could be imagining it after such an upheaval and departure from regular society. And it's too fast. Too soon. "Are you...looking for love?"

A light of awareness comes on in his blue eyes. Until his finger traces the small of my wrist, I don't realize his hand is close enough to touch me. "I'm looking at you, Jolie."

It's suddenly hard to breathe.

That rough fingertip of his travels into my palm, moving in a circle and there's an answering wetness between my legs. From such a simple touch.

My nipples ache in my bra.

I've never been this drawn to someone. Not in my entire life. Never knew it was possible. But I find myself allowing Christopher to weave our fingers together, holding my hand across the table. Like we're a couple. Like we didn't just meet minutes earlier.

And I'm shocked at how right it feels.

Maybe the newspaper headline was a sign.

At the reminder of my trauma, the sounds of a hysterical male voice filter into my thoughts, along with the sounds of me begging, sobbing, wood splintering.

I suck in a breath and take my hand back, standing abruptly and knocking a hip into the table. Christopher shoots to his feet as well, shoving long fingers through his hair. "I'm sorry. I'm...please. That was too much."

"No, it's me. It's..." I look around, my cheeks turning numb when I realize the sun has almost completely gone down. How long was I sitting at this table, looking into this man's eyes? Did I leave the house later than I thought? It's possible. I spent a long time trying to psyche myself up to go outdoors. And now. And now...I'll be walking into my house after dark.

My worst fear.

"Jolie," Christopher says in a calm, resonant voice. "What is it?"

I turn in a circle, alarmed to find that most of the neighbors are heading back inside, the music has stopped and the barbeque is no longer smoking. "I just, um..." I wipe my perspiring palms down my dress. "I don't like coming home after dark."

"Why?"

"You really don't know?"

His brows pull together. Slowly, he shakes his head.

I lower my voice. "I was taken from my home. Kidnapped. After work one night. He'd been hiding in my bedroom for days. The...the man was an older co-worker of mine. He'd formed some kind of...infatuation with me and imagined this whole relationship between us. There was nothing, um...sexual. It was almost like he was courting me." I stop for a breath. "I played along until he let his guard down. Until I could call the police. It...it was in the news."

I wish I didn't have to talk about this out loud. Not to this normal, good-looking man who has every right to avoid a girl with baggage like mine. Not when he made it possible for me to feel light for a while. To be the kind of girl who flirts and has drinks with cute, easy-going insurance salesmen.

Christopher has been very still while I related the story. Now, he says, simply, "I'm sorry."

He doesn't glance away uncomfortably or try and relate my experience to another horrifying story. He just says the right thing and leaves it at that. Right where I need it for now.

"Thank you," I murmur, stepping away from the table. "And thanks for the drink. But I think I'll head home now."

Putting his hands in his pockets, he nods gravely. "Good night."

But when I reach my front door, I can't seem to get a foot over the threshold.

The lights are blazing inside. I've turned them on with my phone. There's no reason not to walk through the door, but I can't. I can't—

"I could go in with you." Christopher's voice carries from the sidewalk behind me. "I could check the rooms and make sure it's safe. Then I'll leave."

I nod without turning around and he appears to my right, tall and strong and reassuring. My immediate neighbor. A man everyone saw me with. Surely letting him inside briefly is safe.

I want him to come inside, too, I realize.

There is something about him that puts me at ease. It's the manner in which he speaks to me, as if he's well aware of the invisible boundaries.

Without another word, Christopher steps inside and I follow him. We move room to room. He checks even the ridiculous places, like inside my kitchen cabinets. Behind the vacuum. Everywhere. He goes down to the basement and does a thorough sweep, his manner efficient. Powerful, even. So able and masculine, I once again become aware of my damp underwear and the coil in my loins. My sensitive skin.

Logically, I know I can take care of myself.

But I...like this man being protective. I like his care. His attentiveness to detail.

The way he doesn't judge.

"There's no one here," he says, looking me in the eye, letting his assurance sink in. "Everything is locked. You're safe."

"Thank you," I whisper.

"Any time. I mean that. Any time."

He hesitates, his chest expanding, then starts to leave. Makes it all the way to the door.

"Wait."

His back muscles tense, his hand pausing on the doorknob. "Yes?"

This is crazy. I can't really be considering asking this near-stranger to stay the night. We just met. I'm not mentally healthy enough to do casual or serious. But I'm already walking toward him as if in a trance, already sliding my palms up the range of muscles on his back, absorbing his shudder. How can this feel so inevitable? Almost…foretold? "Stay."

He braces a palm on the door, and once again, I marvel at the size and capability of his hands. The way one of his knuckles is crooked and scarred. But I'm distracted from my thoughts when he says, "Stay and have coffee? Or stay and take you to bed, Jolie?"

"I don't know," I say to his back. "I just know it makes me feel safer to have you here."

"There's irony for you," he mutters.

I frown. "What do you mean?"

His fingers curl into a fist on the door. "Nothing."

Long moments pass and all I can hear is the sound of his breathing, my racing pulse.

"I've never spent the night with a man before. Am I doing this all wrong?"

"God, no, honey." He drops his hand from the door and turns, expression sincere and strained all at once. "You are fucking perfect."

The look in his blue eyes knocks me back a step. He's…aroused. Very much so. The crotch of his jeans protrudes at an angle, his jaw slackening while he looks me over, head to toe, a low sound coming from his throat. He's so huge. The muscles of his forearms are in tight ropes, his pupils expanding to encompass the blue. Starved. For me.

When my back meets the wall, I realize I've been putting distance between us.

"I'm already scaring you," Christopher says raggedly.

Is he?

I'm wet. Growing so damp, so rapidly, my thighs are trembling. My skin is crying out to experience those large hands. Have them rake my flesh. I'm drawn to him like nothing else. And yes, the attraction is so immense it startles me, but I think I'll collapse if he leaves.

Christopher shakes his head, reaches for the doorknob again, signaling his exit. "This is moving too fast. It's my fault. I—"

Quickly, I unbutton my cardigan, from my neck to my waist, shedding it.

The belt is undone next, dropped heavily with a metal sound to the tile below.

When there's nothing left but my dress, I curl my fingers in the hem and wait only a moment before stripping it over my head. And then I'm standing in front of this magnetic man, my neighbor, in a matching bra and panties set. White with a red rose pattern. All of the lights are on. There's nothing and nowhere to hide. It's also the reason I see every emotion cross his face. Awe, hunger, surrender, lust. Lust like a battering ram.

He takes one step and flattens me against the wall of my entryway, his mouth coming down on mine with a groan. His fingers slide into my hair and cradle my nape, our hips meeting, thighs pressing. He kisses me with lips only, pulling at my top one, bottom one, slanting his mouth on top of mine until I mewl, arch my back, and he finally slips his tongue inside, stroking it against mine, his breath catching. I've felt nothing but fear for so long that I race toward my own need, flinging myself into it like a cliff diver into a blue lagoon. It feels so good to be alive, to have this man's touch, and I'm suddenly greedy, desperate for more.

I scale his sturdy body, slinging my legs around his hips, the kiss taking hold. Going deeper. With more urgency. He slides a hand down the back of my panties and kneads my butt, pressing my upper half to the wall, his lips racing down to my neck, my throat.

"I can't believe this is happening," he rasps in between kisses, those eyes intense, exploring. "I've needed you. I've needed you."

"I've needed you, too." My fingers work to unbutton his shirt. "Take me to bed."

No sooner are those four words out of my mouth than I'm ripped off the wall, carried down the back hallway at a fast clip. He false starts toward the guest room, but I point to the right door and he changes directions, entering my bedroom. All the lights are on. Every single one. And I'm grateful for that when I finally get Christopher's shirt open and it parts to reveal tattooed muscle. Weathered brawn. Slab upon slab of inked steel.

"You must sell a lot of insurance," I breathe.

The corner of his mouth ticks up. "I had a wild youth." He lays me down on the bed, shrugging off the shirt and tossing it away, flicking open the button of his jeans. Those blue eyes blaze over me, drinking in every inch. "I'm still a little wild, Jolie." He hooks his fingers in my panties and shucks them down my legs, a shudder wracking him. "But all of the wild inside me is for you now," he says thickly, tracing the seam of my womanhood with his thumb. "Do you understand?"

I'm having a hard time concentrating on anything when he's touching me with such possession, but I capture his meaning. He's going to make love to me with abandon—exactly what I want. What I need. I don't want to think of my past or my trauma. I want to see and think about and feel only Christopher.

His thumb parts my folds and grazes my clit. "Do you understand, Jolie?"

"I understand," I gasp.

"Good girl."

Something about those two words set off fireworks in a secret, unknown part of me, sharpening my lust like the tip of a pencil. Good girl. They're still echoing in my head when Christopher drops to his stomach and kisses my sex. Reverently. Breathing in and out against it, his hands coasting up and down my bare thighs.

"Knew you'd have a sweet, juicy, little pussy," he rumbles, nudging me with his nose, groaning brokenly. "Savor this," he says, his words muffled against my flesh. Is he talking to my womanhood? "Savor your last seconds of freedom. Because I'm never going to give you a moment's peace again."

As if my body already knows what he's capable of, my fingers twist in the sheets, preparing—and he starts to eat me. With long, crude licks. Thank God I invested in a good home waxing kit, because it would be a travesty to miss a single stroke.

Oh lord, I've never done this. Never even come close. But instinctively I know there isn't a man alive who could perform this task half as well. He's obscene and cherishing. Nasty and worshipful. Those blue eyes bore into mine, lust clouding them, the wet of his tongue flashing in the light, dragging up through my sex and teasing my hotbed of nerves.

"Oh Jesus, Jesus, Jesus," I whimper, tearing at the bedclothes.

I can't breathe. The release that's rolling in is a beautiful monster and it turns me into a creature I barely recognize. One who pulls a man's hair and bucks against his mouth. One who rips off her own bra so she can clamp greedy fingers around her aching nipples. The monster snaps its teeth, digging into my lust and I go off, my body trembling wildly, pleasure spearing me deep, deep in the center of my body, making me rear up off the mattress.

"Christopher!"

My scream is still echoing in my bedroom when he lifts his head, moves up my body in a slow, purposeful crawl, his eyes black, chest heaving. "I could live off the perfect taste of you," he says hoarsely, unzipping his jeans. "But we need to take advantage while you're wet."

I don't understand. "What—"

He takes out his shaft and I suck in a breath, my

legs closing instinctively.

Or I try to close them, but he blocks my progress with his hips, stroking that enormous appendage in a clenched fist. "No. Please don't be scared of it." He plants his free hand beside my head, leaning down to kiss me thoroughly, until I'm breathless, head spinning. "Once you're used to this cock, it's going to give you nothing but pleasure. You're going to shake every time I walk into this fucking bedroom just knowing I'm about to put it in that tight-ass cunt."

His words are rude. Disrespectful. They should outrage me.

Why am I nodding?

Why do I feel like this man has cast a spell over me?

I can't tear my eyes away from the intensity of his stare, can't do anything but open my thighs and welcome his domination. His nostrils flare with triumph at my compliance, his mouth capturing mine in a slow, wet kiss, his huge shaft pressing into me, not taking no for an answer from the resistance of my body. I cry out into his mouth, but he only advances further, deeper, growling into our kiss. "Tight baby girl," he grits out, punching his hips forward slowly. "Aren't you a snug little virgin? So fucking sweet around my dick. Shhhh. I promise it's not going to hurt forever."

I'm sobbing, but it's more from emotion than pain.

I can feel myself being possessed by this man.

I don't have an inch to breathe or worry or even think. There is just Christopher blocking out the world around me, filling the cracks in my soul and demanding more. More.

There are ripples of hurt in the vicinity of my womb, but they dull the more he kisses me, our lips growing hungrier, his hips beginning to flex, to push forward and back.

"Does it feel better now, Jolie?"

"Yes."

Visibly relieved, his left hand drags down the center of my body, between my breasts and stomach, circling around to take hold of my bottom. Clutching it roughly as he rocks deep. So deep that both of us moan, my heels burying in the flesh of his ass. "You feel it, don't you? That we're one now. It was meant to be like this."

I can't deny it.

It's the coming together of two beings. A collision.

"Yes," I gasp, my nails raking their way down his back involuntarily. "We're one."

His eyes flash, revealing the wildness he spoke of before.

And my own untapped wildness answers.

Something inside me is in charge now. Is it my heart? My soul? My lust? I don't know, but we're suddenly grappling with each other, Christopher's mouth burying in my neck, sucking bruises onto me, my hands gripping his thick buttocks and yanking him deeper, the bed slamming against the wall with the force of his thrusts. I'm being fucked. Filthy and raw. And he was right. That's all I can think. He was right about that massive part between his legs giving me pleasure, because I quickly become its servant, whining and straining to take more.

He gives it.

He shoves my legs open and ruts into me with smacking pumps of his hips.

"Mine." He looks me in the eye. "Mine."

"Yours."

His mouth sears me with a kiss. "I will be everything you need. This is where it begins, angel eyes. Listen to me. It begins here. If you ever feel lost, come right back here to the beginning and find me. I'll always be right here."

My orgasm is cresting and carrying his words away, but they make me glow on the inside all the same. His trunk of flesh saws wetly over my clit, again, again, the muscles in his broad shoulders flexing, tattoos rippling in the light. He winces in pain, his features screwing up tight. A man trying to hold on to his control—and that visible proof that I undo him causes the eruption of lust in my belly. It cascades down and snares my loins in a breathtaking seizure.

"Good girl." He pants above me. "Come for your Daddy."

I scream.

That word makes me scream.

Pleasure like I've never known wracks me. I bow up off the bed, but he pins me back down, bucking his flesh into my constricting heat, bellowing my name into my neck. "Jolie." He grips the slamming headboard, powerful arm flexing. "Giving you my come. Ahhhh, honey. Got so much for you."

True to his word, I'm filled to my limit with piping-hot spend, the excess rolling in beads down my buttocks and thighs, Christopher groaning loudly above me, his deep voice joined by the sound of slapping flesh. When he finally falls on top of me, his huge body depleted, not a single second passes before his arms wrap around me and I'm pulled into the warm cocoon of his embrace, his mouth moving in my hair, whispering my name in awe.

It's the first night in a long time I don't sleep with the lights on.

There's no need.

I'm safe.

CHAPTER THREE

Evan

One Month Later

I UNDERESTIMATED HOW much of a struggle this would be.

Pretending the way I feel about Jolie is normal.

I'm getting ready for "work," standing at the kitchen counter in a tie I once used to strangle a man to death, sipping coffee and trying like hell to remain still. To look like a regular husband. This is my morning process while she's in the shower and getting dressed, humming so prettily to herself. I stand here and struggle against the blinding urge to storm into our bedroom, pin her down and fuck her again. Again. Again. Even though I already had her twice this morning. Once on her hands and knees in bed. Once on the edge of the bathroom sink.

My cock is strangled in my slacks, begging to be let out.

But I have to control my lust for her. I have to keep it at bay as much as possible, so she can believe me to be her normal husband. That's what she asked for. That's what she needs.

And it's working for her, this normalcy.

In addition to her own strength, our routine, the support of having someone at home who loves her...it's part of what's healing her.

So I will stay the course.

The day after we spent our first night together, I slowly started moving in. Leaving boots in her mudroom, my toothbrush in the cabinet. A shirt in her laundry.

I fucked her blind every night. Addicted us both.

God, we are so very addicted.

The privilege of calling her my wife only deepens the constant ache. I was able to wait all of two weeks before asking Jolie to be my wife, presenting her with a diamond surrounded in yellow topaz stones that remind me of her eyes. My sanity hinged on her saying yes and she did. She did, tearfully, throwing herself into my arms, and I could barely believe my luck.

It happened.

I found my angel and made her mine.

No, I have to keep her. Safe. Happy. Untouched by anyone but me.

Forever.

My hands grip the edge of the counter when I hear the distinct slither of her panties being dragged up her thighs, hiding away the pussy I crave sixty minutes out of every hour. If I concentrate hard enough, I swear I can hear her heartbeat from the other room. My pulse beats in the same tempo, same speed.

Jolie sails into the kitchen, her face bright and flushed and gorgeous.

She's wearing yoga pants and a snug T-shirt that molds to her gorgeous tits.

I almost break off the edge of the counter.

"Good morning." She bites her lip and ducks her head. "Again."

"Good morning." I order myself to back up and refrain from kissing her. It's painful, but neither one of us will ever make it out the door. "I made your cheese toast," I say, triple-checking my handiwork, then handing her the plate.

My wife gives a little intake of breath. "Thank you."

If she knew what I was, if she knew I was lying, would she love me?

Would she try to leave?

These fears echo inside me constantly. They probably will forever.

They might drive me madder than I already am.

Jolie leans back against the counter and takes a bite of her favorite breakfast. Multigrain toast with a slice of cheddar on top. "Mmmm." She swallows, smiling at me while I watch her throat, mesmerized. "It always tastes better when you make it."

"You didn't realize you'd married a culinary master, did you?" I say, straight-faced. "Toast. Cereal. Putting ice cream in bowls. There's nothing I can't do."

Her giggle sends my heart into a fit of skipped beats. "I like cooking, so you're safe. Besides, you kill the spiders. That's what really counts."

I kill a lot more than that, honey.

For instance, the man who kidnapped you.

It's good to have contacts on the inside.

I wasn't always a killer. I grew up relatively normal in the suburbs, although I didn't have a lot of friends. Relating to people never came naturally. My interest in books about the military history and war led me to join the army out of high school and there...there is where I was taught how to kill. How to compartmentalize and execute without emotion. When my tours overseas were over and I was at loose ends, I fell back on what I knew. Easy as that.

Now she is all I want to know. All I want to study.

I continue to do jobs, but my mind is always here now. On her.

"Are you ready for today?" I ask Jolie.

She swallows with a little more effort, her good mood dimming. "I don't know. Maybe I could put it off until tomorrow?"

The quiver of nerves in her voice causes an anguished twist in my chest. What I wouldn't give to take away her painful memories. Crush them like bugs. I can't do that, though. So I can only do everything in my power to show Jolie how strong she is. It would be easy to protect her myself for the rest of her life—and that is my instinct. Wrap her up in my arms, hide her away, keep her in the shadows where she's comfortable. But she's capable of more. She needs more from herself to be happy. Making her happy is my job, but over the course of our first month together, I've learned we have to share the job, whether it's hard for me or not. "There are only women in the self-defense class. It's taught by a woman, too. It's a well-lit studio."

Jolie nods. Says nothing.

"You can do it, angel eyes. I know you can." I reach over and brush a hand down her ponytail. "I'll be with you in spirit. And I'm one phone call away."

Well. I'll be parked down the block.

But she doesn't need to know that.

"I guess if it goes terribly, my therapy session afterward will help smooth things out." She comes off the counter and turns, looking at the clock on the stove. Her eyes widen. "Chris! You're going to be late for work."

I wince. "Shit." I tug on the knot of my tie. "It's a good thing I outsell everyone or they'd never put up with me."

"You're worth the wait." She sets down the remainder of her toast and holds out her arms for a hug. "See you tonight."

I panic.

If I put my arms around Jolie, I'm going to back her against the counter. Rip those thin, ass-hugging pants down her legs. Pound my cock into her until she's screaming...and she'll never make it to self defense class. Or her therapy session afterward. But the fact that I'm an insurance salesman will become even more unrealistic if I don't adhere to the schedule.

I can't leave her hanging, though.

She's already beginning to look at me oddly for hesitating.

I bite down on my tongue as hard as I can and pull her close, settling my cheek on top of her head. Immediately, the beast inside me howls, my cock protesting being trapped inside my pants. Her lilac scent drifts upward and I drop my nose to the crook of her neck, inhaling roughly, my hands tunneling into her hair, fucking up her ponytail. I can't hold the obsession at bay when we're touching. My control withers.

My hips pin her to the counter. I dip my knees and grind up against her pussy, forcing a whimper out of her, her nipples turning to little torpedoes inside her shirt.

Stop. I need to stop.

I'm her husband, the one who does what's best for her—and the best thing is to keep up the pretense of being a normal man. Not an obsessed stalker. Not a hit man. Just plain old Christopher. The best thing for her is to learn how to defend herself. Not because there will ever be a need, but because it'll give her back the confidence she lost.

Her weekly therapy session is also a must.

It's how I find out what's happening inside of her head and compensate.

You have to back away.

I press my bared teeth to her ear. "No matter what happens today, remember your husband is going to fuck you so filthy tonight, your legs will be shaking for a week."

Jolie moans, her fingers grappling with my belt, but I step away before she can get it loose, risking a kiss to her perfect mouth to ease the sting of leaving.

"I love you," I say, looking her hard in the eye.

"I love you, too," she whispers.

With the willpower of forty men, I turn and walk out the door.

Then I drive my car to the end of the block and wait for her to leave, so I can follow her.

WHEN I FOUND the self-defense classes for Jolie, I didn't suggest them to her until the studio had been thoroughly vetted. I went at night and checked the locks. Looked through the private files of every employee, searched them online to make sure they weren't hiding deranged boyfriends or shady pasts.

It's squeaky clean. As close to being worthy of her as anything can be.

I also installed a camera and microphone in the corner of the room, so I could monitor every single second. This is what I do. I stalk my perfect angel of a wife.

There is no insurance to sell. My money is made at night, by the gun, while she's fast asleep, exhausted from making love.

When Jolie first became mine, she didn't leave the house very often. Only for therapy. Slowly, she started going to the store, clothes shopping, to the beach for walks. And so I began doing those things, too. She just couldn't see me.

If I tried to explain this burning need to watch Jolie every second of the day, it would come out sounding unhinged. Maybe that's what it is. I'm not the kind of man who could just go off to work and leave his wife's safety to chance. I know more than anyone how dangerous this world can be—I am one of the dangers. She was kidnapped once. It won't happen again.

Other men do not approach her without consequence.

It has happened once or twice and I have handled the situation.

And it is bound to happen again because she is not only fucking beautiful, there is a light inside of her that glows so bright, people can't help wanting to get near the warmth.

It's why I refuse to miss a single second of her day. I hold my breath every time she smiles, I groan when she discreetly fixes her bra, I hang on every word that comes out of her mouth during therapy. My dick is hard all day long as I miss her, need her, think of her.

Now, I sit in my car down the street from her self-defense classes, watching on my phone as she is called to the front of the room. Her hands are wrapped in the end of her sweatshirt sleeves, her posture unsure. But she comes forward and gets into the defensive stance as instructed. For most of the class, she has been standing back and watching, but now she performs the moves they were taught—striking the instructor—and she kills it.

"Fuck yeah, Jolie," I shout in my car, startling a woman passing with a stroller.

My eyes zip back to the screen in time to witness her shy smile, the way she hugs herself afterwards and I want to hold her so bad in that moment, my throat burns.

When she calls my phone ten minutes later, she has no idea I'm watching her exit the building in my rearview mirror. It's a challenge to keep my voice even. "Hey, angel eyes. How'd it go?"

"Amazing," she breathes. "All the other women were so nice and non-judgy. And I just...I-I kicked the instructor and it felt really good. Like I was...I don't know. Taking control. I want to go back. I'm so glad you bullied me into it."

"Bullied you?" I laugh.

"Fine." She smiles into the word. "You finessed me."

"Much better." I hold the phone so tight, I'm risking snapping it in half. "I'm proud of you."

"I'm...proud of me, too." She blows out a breath and climbs into her car, so I can't see her anymore and I subdue a note of panic. After all, I know where she's going next. "I love you so much, Christopher."

A swallow gets caught in my throat. "I love you more."

Trust me.

We hang up a moment later and I follow her to the next destination. Therapy.

Truthfully, I felt conflicted about taping the microphone beneath her therapist's desk two months ago, but it was too tempting to have full access to Jolie's hopes, fears, musings. Since I started listening, they've mainly talked about her kidnapping. I've been discussed, too, and there have been no complaints. Although her therapist, Elmira, did question Jolie's rush to get married.

I didn't like that.

Thankfully, the issue wasn't pressed and they went back to dealing with what happened to Jolie at the hands of Joseph Hynes.

I'm sitting in a coffee shop across the street from her therapist's office, listening through an earbud as Elmira greets Jolie. The husky warmth of my wife's voice makes me immediately stiff under the table and I check my cell for the time. Four more hours until we're home and I can be inside of her. The only time I can let this obsession run wild is when we're fucking and it's like letting suppressed air out of a valve. Four more hours. Four more.

"I was wondering if we could talk about something different today," Jolie says—and I wish I'd installed a camera, too, because I know she's tucking hair into her ponytail. I love it when she does that. It reminds me of the day we met.

"Of course," Elmira says smoothly. "This is your time."

Jolie exhales. "It's about Christopher."

My hand tightens around my coffee mug, my pulse starting to sprint. She can't be unhappy with me so soon, can she? What have I done wrong?

I'll fix it.

I'll listen to every single word and I'll repair myself to suit her better.

"Okay," the therapist prompts. "What about him?"

Jolie laughs quietly. "It's kind of embarrassing."

"There's no judgment here. Only truth."

My wife is silent another moment. "The first night Christopher and I were...intimate...he called himself Daddy. He hasn't done it since that night. And, um, I liked it. A lot. I don't know how to tell him I liked it and that I want more."

More.

More.

That word bashes around in my skull. I haven't been giving her enough?

Unacceptable.

"What do you mean by 'more'?" Elmira asks, not a hint of censure in her tone.

I lean forward in my chair.

"I mean...my husband is the first man I slept with, so sex is kind of new to me. Still, I'm not naïve. I know our sex life is..." She releases a shaky sound. "Incredible. But ever since he said that word— Daddy—I've had fantasies about pushing that boundary."

"Role playing?"

"Yes. Is there something wrong with me?"

"No."

"Even if I daydream about taking it…far?"

"Define 'far'."

It's a moment before Jolie answers. "I don't have daddy issues or anything. I have a perfectly normal relationship with mine, even if we're not super close. It's warm. So there's no underlying problems. Christopher is the only one…inspiring this." Her pitch deepens. "He has this way of building me up, encouraging me outside the bedroom. But in the bedroom, he's dominant. Extremely so. I hand over my will and he takes it." She pauses. "You see, he's all these things at once. Everything. Filling every need. And it just puts me on my proverbial knees. I want him to have that ultimate power role…because I trust him."

My fucking breath is sawing in and out of my lungs.

Between my legs, my cock is a stiff pole, pressing against the table.

I'm drawing attention to myself from nearby tables and that's not good. I'm supposed to be blending in. Being normal. But I never expected to hear my wife confess to wanting me to act as her Daddy. To have the ultimate power role. Jesus, those words are like a drug to me. To a man who craves control when it comes to his wife. I'm one stroke from coming in my pants.

"I want him to be…parental. In bed. That's what I mean by taking it far." A pause ensues. "I just want to make sure this doesn't connect to my trauma in any way."

Elmira hums. "In my opinion, it doesn't. Joseph Hynes wasn't a father figure. The two of you didn't have sexual contact, nor did he force himself on you. I don't see a connection."

"Okay," Jolie breathes, sounding relieved. "Now I just have to nudge him, I guess."

I laugh without humor and drain the rest of my coffee.

Nudge me?

Oh, angel eyes. There won't be a need.

CHAPTER FOUR

Jolie

MY FAVORITE TIME of the day is when Christopher walks through the door. He's always rumpled from sitting at his desk, tugging at the knot in his tie, briefcase in the opposite hand. But the fatigue always flees from his blue eyes when he sees me. More often than not, he boosts me onto the entryway table and whatever I had cooking burns while he takes out his stress on my body, bucking into me savagely, my hair wrapped in his fist.

Tonight when he walks through the front door, there's something different about him. I can't quite put my finger on it. He's watchful and calm. Intense as always. But there's a new thoughtfulness to his expression that somehow sets my pulse thrumming.

He kisses me on the back of the neck where I stand at the stove.

In the reflection of the microwave, I watch him slowly remove his jacket and tie, his eyes tracking down over my butt and thighs. I'm always wet when he's this close to me, but I swear I can feel my sex pulsing now, his measured breathing filling me with anticipation. It's probably due to the conversation I had with Elmira today. One I've been meaning to broach for a couple of weeks. Wonder how long it'll take to actually act on my decision to tell Christopher about it?

I stir the simmering tomato sauce, my eyes closing when I hear my husband remove his belt. Looking down and to the right, I can see the long strip of leather dangling from his fist.

"How was therapy today?"

This is your opening. Take it.

"Good." I smile at him over my shoulder, but it fades when I find him looking positively wolfish, his hair even more finger tousled than usual. "We're making progress."

"That's great."

"Yes." God, I feel so breathless. Probably because he's usually inside me by now. The anticipation is turning me hotter, another degree for every second that passes. "Combined with kicking and punching another human being, I'm like a new woman."

Christopher huffs a sound. "A woman?" His open mouth comes within an inch of my neck. "And yet you're dressed like a teenager."

"I am?"

I look down at my outfit. A pink tank top tied up between my breasts, no bra, itty bitty jean shorts that don't even cover my backside. And it dawns on me what I've done. I've dressed younger. Probably as a way of forcing myself to tell Christopher about the fantasies I've been having. The fact that he's noticed and that his voice is like gravel makes my nipples peak painfully.

"Yes, you are." Slowly, he hooks the leather belt between my legs, one end fisted at my belly button, the other at the small of my back—and he pulls upward, bringing me onto my toes with a whimper. "It's almost like walking in and finding a little girl instead of my wife."

A sob scratches from my throat and I drop the spoon I was using to stir the sauce. "Christopher..."

This is not the first time my husband has seemed to read my mind. When we're in bed, he knows what I want before I do. He knows when I want to change the channel of the television or drop a subject. He knows when I'm nervous or happy or annoyed. So I'm not surprised that he walked in here, took a look at my outfit, and knew there was something afoot. I'm grateful for his intuition now. It's going to be so much easier to talk about what's on my mind, because he's pushing me there. Giving me no choice.

"Which is it?" He tugs the belt harder, pushing the seam of my shorts against my clit, and I heave a sob. "Are you my wife or my little girl?"

I squeeze my eyes shut. "I could be both. A-at different times."

"Interesting." He gathers more of the leather in his fists and I have to grip the stove for balance, my thighs starting to tremble violently from the arousing pressure between my legs. The belt isn't even moving and I'm sure to climax. It's inevitable. God oh God oh God.

"Let's say you're my little girl right now. What does that make me?"

My heart is going to beat out of my chest. "I…I don't know."

He clucks his tongue. "You don't?"

"No." The belt is yanked. Hard. I scream. "Daddy! You're my Daddy!"

"Good girl. Now you get a reward." He starts to saw the belt between my legs, up and back, dragging the denim seam over my clit, creating friction everywhere. Everywhere. Even on my back entrance, which shouldn't feel so perfectly good, but it does. So good, I can barely maintain my position on my tiptoes. "One more question." His mouth is right up against my ear. "If I'm your Daddy and you're my little girl, where does that leave your mother? Is she in the picture?" The belt. The belt. It moves faster, making me moan. "Do I have a very short window of time to exercise my rights?"

"Yes," I gasp, groping blindly to turn off the stove burner.

He knows. He knows every naughty thought in my head without me having to say a word.

Accepts even the parts of me that are a little wrong. A little twisted.

"I see," Christopher says, dropping the belt.

I whine over the loss of friction, the promise of an imminent orgasm, but the sound gets caught in my throat when I'm spun around, picked up by the waist and tossed onto the edge of the kitchen table. And oh my God, his eyes are pitch black, sweat dotting his upper lip, which is curled up in a snarl. His shaft is thick, filling out one leg of his pants. And his fingers, they undo his shirt buttons quickly, jerking the garment open and treating me to mouthwatering muscles, tattoos layered above flushed skin.

"How long do we have?" he pants, stripping off his shirt completely, dropping it.

"Fifteen minutes," I whisper.

He growls, as if frustrated by having so little time, and goes to work unfastening my shorts, lifting me up against his chest to get them down my hips, then jerking them further, past my ankles and away. "We'll leave on the shirt and panties, so you can get dressed fast."

"Okay."

I'm hypnotized by the sight of his thick fingers lowering the zipper of his pants, the bulky ridge that comes into view, hidden only by thin white cotton. It's the first time. He's my Daddy and we've been tempted too far. "I can't take it anymore. Having you so close and not being able to touch," he rasps, pulling me to the edge of the table, fastening his mouth over mine in a forbidden kiss. "You're the only thing that makes me hard."

Our mouths devour, tasting hungrily, his hands lifting my tank top to my neck so he can fondle my bare breasts, groaning brokenly as he does it.

"So supple," he says, dipping his head to suck a nipple into his mouth. "So sweet."

My fingers twist in his hair, holding his skilled mouth to my breasts, but I drop one now, sliding it into the V of his pants, exploring his erection, gasping excitedly over his size. "You're so big, Daddy."

He groans at my praise, tugs the silk strip of my thong underwear to the right. "Oh Christ. We shouldn't be doing this."

"I won't ever tell."

I open my legs wider, bite my lip, and he loses the battle between right and wrong.

In one rough move, he stuffs me full, capturing my shocked mewl with his mouth. "Fuck," he grits, pumping into me crudely, his hands going to my buttocks and clutching, yanking me into his thrusts, causing the table to bump wildly on the floor. "Not going to be able to get off any other way now, am I? Now that I know what this tight cunt feels like."

"No." I pout. "Only with me."

Roaring a curse, he pulls me off the table and pins me against the fridge, driving into me with powerful, greedy hips, his breath frenzied in my ear. "I put a roof over your head. Food in your little belly. Now show some gratitude and get those knees up around my hips, girl."

My knees fly up and hug his muscular body.

"Good girl." He licks his lips. "Look at those little titties bounce."

I gasp at the violent constriction of my loins.

I'm not sure I knew how deep this fantasy ran. Or how potent it would be. How much it would arouse me, score me with lust. But it does. My nails are buried in his shoulders and I'm holding on for dear life, my mouth in a permanent O, receiving rough thrusts of his huge sex and feeling my own pleasure dam begin to give way, even though I want more of the game. More of the depravity and pull between good and evil. More Christopher.

"You have to come, Daddy," I whisper in his ear. "Or we're going to get caught."

He makes a hoarse sound and rails into me harder, his erection thickening inside of me, signaling the end. "God help me, I didn't use a rubber and I'm not pulling out."

"You'll take care of me." I kiss his neck, his shoulder. "You always do."

"That's right." He latches onto my mouth. "Every day of your life."

It's that tender promise of care that sends me sailing. I'm being pleasured without mercy or gentleness, but I'm also being comforted, treasured, loved, as well. This man is the best of both worlds and he rocks into me just right when the climax hits, holding himself deep inside me and growling as I shake, making sure I'm well over the finish line before he hits me with a series of savage pumps, looking me straight in the eye, and finally his seed geysers up inside of me, reaching every corner of my womanhood and dripping down my thighs, onto the floor, soaking into my thong.

"Go ahead and get pregnant, then." He grinds out into my neck. "No one will blame me. The pussy was just too ripe."

A second orgasm crests, catching me off guard, and I scream his name, my flesh squeezing, squeezing so intensely that I can barely stand it. And he watches me, my husband. He watches this second peak hit me with blatant satisfaction in his eyes, almost like he's triumphant and fascinated, the corner of his mouth edged up into a smile.

"That's a good girl," he murmurs, still rocking his hips. "Let it all out."

I've never been more spent in my life. I collapse forward over his shoulder, desperately trying to fill my lungs, and while his breathing is shallow as well, his shoulders covered in a sheen of perspiration, Christopher is sturdy as ever, carrying me to the bedroom and laying me down on the cool sheets.

Right before I drift into unconsciousness, he kisses my forehead.

"You have no secrets from me, angel eyes."

CHAPTER FIVE

Evan

M Y TARGET IS late.

Right after Jolie fell asleep tonight, I received a text from my boss ordering the hit. A Greek businessman named Constantine who fucked over the wrong partner at his flashy firm. I don't ask questions or philosophize about whether or not someone deserves to die. I don't have any code, except for refusing to kill women and children.

I lean back against the concrete piling and exhale, anxious to be back home with my wife. With her head tucked under my chin, an arm wrapped around her waist. After the new way we made love tonight, I'm hungrier than ever for her pussy. If I was home right now, I'd be teasing her clit with my middle finger, arousing her while she's sleeping. She'd be rolling over on top of me, half asleep and humping me, confused and disoriented to wake up wet and throbbing, whining until I took care of business.

Keeping an eye on the parking garage where my target is having a clandestine meeting with his business partner's wife, I can't help but replay what happened in the kitchen when I got home from "work." I walked in with the intention of slowly unraveling her secrets, but I went a little too fast. I have to be more careful with how I respond to the information I get from her therapy sessions or she'll get suspicious.

I look down at my automatic, long-range rifle and worry twists sharply in my chest.

She would leave me if she knew.

She would leave me.

Anxiety rears up and threatens to make me dizzy, but I breathe through my nose and find my balance. I'm starting to wonder if lying to Jolie like this was the worst move possible. She's smart. She will eventually realize I'm leaving in the middle of the night, question where I'm going. She will eventually ask to meet co-workers and attend Christmas parties. And Jesus, she deserves better than a man who lies about his identity, his job. Spies on her. Follows her.

Listens to the private thoughts she speaks aloud.

What if I'm no better than the man who kidnapped her?

What if...she should be scared of me?

I am obsessed beyond measure. My every waking thought is about her. But if she were to find out the truth, would she understand the love is real? This connection between us cannot just be the delusions of a sick mind. She feels it, too. Before I even opened my mouth to let out a lie, we looked at each other and experienced the undercurrents. Much of my identity might be fake, but the fact that I would die for her is not.

I'm distracted when my target walks out of the building, his jacket over one arm, tie askew. He paces to his parked car, sending only a satisfied smile at the woman who emerges from the parking garage behind him. I don't give him a chance to reach for his door handle, firing a single bullet through his temple and watching him crumple to the ground.

A female scream hangs in the air, but I pay it no attention, escaping into the shadows at the edge of the roof and melting down the back fire escape. Dropping soundlessly into the alley. I get into my car and calmly exit the alley, turning down the side street.

What...

What is the odd prick in my throat?

I don't know why, but I'm thinking about the woman screaming.

The affectionate way the dead man looked at her before I killed him.

I take a hand off the steering wheel to rub at the spot. For some reason, I'm not feeling as detached as I usually do after a hit. Am I beginning to develop a conscience?

Troubled by that thought, I press my foot more firmly on the gas, positive I will feel better once I'm back in bed with Jolie. She cures me, makes me whole. I'm all but sweating by the time our house comes into view, throwing the car into park and spilling out into the garage. I don't like coming home to her after a hit. I never have, but it feels worse now, because this love...it's making me more and more human.

I make it to the bedroom and finally, finally, feel like I can take a deep breath. There she is. My wife. Nude. Covered in love marks from my mouth. Curled onto her side, hugging a pillow. Safe. Breathing. My evil deed didn't kill the only positive thing in my life. She's still here.

Letting out a shuddering exhale, I fall into a chair beside the bed, tilting my head to look at the lithe, sensual length of her. I should be stripping off my clothes and getting back into bed before she realizes I've been out, but I can't seem to move. Can't do anything but be arrested by the beauty of my Jolie. Daddy, she calls me. Daddy. Daddy.

Before I even know what I'm about, I'm yanking down my zipper and fucking my hand, lips peeled back in a wince, my balls so high and tight, I'm probably going to go off in seconds. I stand and walk toward the bed, looking down at the slightly parted crack of her ass and I swallow a groan, semen beading at the tip of my cock.

I'm almost busting when she stirs, humming a little in her throat and rolling over onto her back, yawning. I can't let her see me like this, dressed in all black street clothes, touching myself while she sleeps. I can't. So just like earlier on the roof, I step back into the shadows and watch her without breathing, hoping she'll just drift back to sleep.

But she doesn't.

She looks over at my side of the bed and I'm not there, her entire body stiffening with fear. "Christopher?" Her sob almost rends me in two. "It's dark. Where are you?"

I can't stand her fear for another moment. As fast as possible, I strip down to my boxers and attempt to even my breathing. Go from feral to normal. Normal, like she wants. Needs.

"Sorry, angel eyes," I say, stepping into the moonlight where she can see me. Her body collapses back onto the pillows, hand to her heart. "I went to get a drink of water."

The lie burns in my gut. I hate myself for being untruthful with this loyal, honest, courageous woman. It gets worse every time.

She's given you a conscience.

"S-sorry," she stammers. "I shouldn't be freaking out. It's silly. You should be able to walk to the kitchen at night without me having a panic attack."

"No," I say firmly, crossing to the bed. "Hey. There is nothing silly about you. Or what you went through. I should have been beside you. I'm sorry."

She really has no idea how much.

I get into bed and pull her up against my chest, groaning inwardly at the pure decadence of her body molding to mine, her leg draping over my hip. "Do you want to talk about it?"

The day we met, Jolie told me she'd been kidnapped by a co-worker. I know the full story from the news and her therapy sessions, but I've never pushed her to elaborate for me. Probably because it felt extra deceitful, asking her for painful details I already have.

Why would I want to put her through that?

Now, however, Jolie nods into my neck. "Yeah…I think I want to talk about it a little bit. Maybe the self-defense class gave me even more bravery than I realized."

I tug her tighter against me, stroke her back. "Say whatever you want to say. I'm here."

Her warm breath fans my throat. "Sometimes I feel guilty. About everything that happened to me."

Above her head, my frown is ferocious. "Why would you feel guilty?"

"For not fighting harder. I was too scared, but I should have sucked it up. I should have fought and…I should have recognized earlier there was something wrong with him."

A swallow sticks in my throat.

Heat swamps me.

There was something wrong with the man who kidnapped her.

There is something wrong with me, too. I'm…a stalker. I stalk this woman.

My wife.

Someday, she could be saying these exact words about me.

"There had to be warning signs I didn't recognize, right?"

"I don't know," I choke out, my right eye twitching. "Sometimes monsters hide in plain sight."

"Yeah…" she hedges, tracing a finger along my collarbone. "I guess so."

"I do know you can't blame yourself for not fighting," I say, sincerely. "You survived. That was your job—and you succeeded."

Sighing with gratitude, she snuggles into me. "I'm tired of talking about myself. It seems like that's all we ever do. When we're not…you know." Her laugh is breathy, uneven. "I want to hear more about your childhood. College. Your parents. Your friends."

"I told you," I respond lightly, kissing her temple. "My parents passed away, my friends are scattered around. Seattle, Texas. Hell, I can barely keep track. Someday I'll take you to where I grew up in Utah. We'll make a whole trip of it."

Lies.

More lies.

"You've never even shown me pictures," she says, quietly. "Why is that?"

I force myself to stay relaxed. To stay afloat among the alarm and guilt.

Jesus, only tonight I worried about this eventuality—and here it is. She's starting to press, starting to expect more from this man she married impulsively.

I distract her the only way I know how. The only way I know will succeed.

I take my wife's hand and place it on my stiff cock. "I'd rather talk about why you haven't done anything about this yet, little girl." Next, I take frame her jaw with my hand, applying a small amount of pressure, tilting her face up to mine. "Daddy is getting impatient."

Her breath hitches.

There is something in her eyes, a new curiosity that tells me she sees through my attempt to distract her. I'm worried she's going to voice her concern and lean in to kiss her before that happens, but her hand strokes my dick and I end up groaning against her lips instead.

"Like this?" she asks innocently.

"Yes," I hiss, my shaft sensitive as hell from my own rough treatment.

Another squeezing rake of that hand. "What do you want me to do about it?"

"I want you to suck it," I pant, putting pressure on her jaw until her mouth pops open on a gasp. "Just enough to wet it. So I can get it up your tight ass."

Jolie blinks at me in surprised excitement.

I recognize my motivation. Claiming her like this for the first time. Taking full ownership to balance out the fear of losing her. The fear that is suddenly seeming more and more real.

Desperate to regain that ground, I surge forward, pushing my wife onto her back, getting on top of her and walking on my knees along the outside of her body, until I can notch my cock into her gasping, little mouth. Sinking in a couple of pulsing inches. I almost never ask for this. I definitely don't expect this perfect angel to suck me off, but I want her mouth around my dick right now so bad, I'm going to snap. I want to witness her attraction and be reassured she's still with me. "Big and salty, isn't it, little girl? It's got no place in a virgin asshole, but that's exactly where it's going, so suck it sloppy. Make it slippery for your own good."

The filth coming out of my mouth makes her moan, her fingernails dragging down my thighs so she can double fist my cock, pulling on the fat girth of it, trying to get as much of it between her lips as possible, stretching bravely to make it happen. Watching her struggle to take me into her mouth is enough to make me come, but I bite down on my tongue and stave off the rising tide.

I rest my hands on the back of my head and flex, watching her eyes go molten. She's made no secret about loving my road-worn body and I give her a show now, rolling my hips toward her mouth, letting her enjoy my muscles chasing each other across my abdomen. I spend a lot of time killing hours in the gym when she's safe at home and I'm supposed to be at work. It pays off now when she whimpers and lets in another inch of my shaft, her hands stroking feverishly, her tongue bathing me, lips suctioning, teeth grazing. If I let her go much longer, I'm going to finish too soon—and I need that final, untapped privilege of her body tonight.

I pull my cock from her mouth and lean down to kiss her swollen, gasping lips. "What did I tell you the first night I fucked you?" I catch her throat in a tight grip, looking her hard in the eye, love and obsession and power coursing through me. "Once you're used to this cock, it's going to give you nothing but pleasure. That's what I said, isn't it? That you'd shake every time I walk into the bedroom just knowing I'm about to put it in your tight-ass cunt?"

"Yes," she breathes, her eyes at half mast. "I do. I shake. Please…"

"What about when I'm going to put it in your ass? Huh?" I release Jolie's throat, flipping her over onto her stomach, separating her cheeks roughly and giving myself a look at her untouched entrance. "Maybe you'll just find something to bite down on."

Her fingers curl into the pillow. "I want this," she says huskily. "I want to feel you there."

A groan rumbles in my chest. "Is it any wonder Daddy can't stay away?" I spit on her puckered hole and push forward with my hips, wedging my cock between her cheeks and riding, riding, thrusting against the promised land I'm about to claim as mine. "I'm probably going to get three or four inches in and bust, baby, you're so fucking sweet."

My addiction lies in getting this girl off, however, so I reach for the bedside table, taking out two things. A butterfly massager she's had since I met her but hasn't used since. And a small bottle of lubricant—which she also hasn't needed. I turn on the massager and slide it under her hip, moving inward until I can press it tightly to the juncture of her thighs.

Jolie's whole body shudders, her hips dropping to grind into the vibrator. "Oh!"

"Fuck it for Daddy," I rasp against her ear. "Fuck it while I defile you."

Jolie sobs, her thighs jerking a little wider, giving

me more access to where I need to go. I take it with a growl, using my knees to push hers open even more. If she could see my face right now, she'd be scared to death. I'm fully her stalker in this moment. I'm the wolf in sheep's clothing. I'm the man who steals hair from her hairbrush and licks the rim of her coffee mug before it goes in the dishwasher. I'm an obsessed felon who assaults men that try and speak to her. I am fucking insane. And I'm working two fingers in and out of her fuck-tight ass. A dream come true. A fantasy come to life. She has no idea the battle I fight not to hold her down, get inside of her, and roar myself hoarse about everything that makes her irresistible. Addicting.

Mine.

I spit again onto her entrance, then replace my fingers with the thick head of my dick, inching inside with a low, jagged sound of a man overcome. A man on the verge of imploding. Or going insane. Or both.

"Let's see how deep I can get it," I growl into her neck, working my flesh through the damp, stretching resistance. "Let's see what a good little girl you are."

The mounds of her ass are so soft against my belly, her back is such a sweet curve, bisected by the feminine ridge of her spine. Her cheek is pressed to the pillow, so I can see her open mouth, the shallow breath coming in and out. The black fan of her eyelashes. She's a revelation. A goddess walking the earth. And so tight. So motherfucking tight around my dick that I'm making hoarse panting sounds, a bead of sweat rolling down my temple. "Daddy," she whispers when I sink in another inch. "I'm all yours."

I choke out her name and a shudder wracks me. "Fuck, fuck, fuck."

My orgasm seems to spear up from a deep, untapped part of me and I'm already overflowing her little asshole, barking curses as white streams roll down the slopes of her buttocks, filling the parted valley in between, sloshing up onto my belly, because at some point I started thrusting and she started encouraging me with yes, yes, yes, and I wrap around a hand around the slapping headboard and fuck into her clenching hole, releasing everything inside of me. Every drop she inspired.

"Mine, goddammit. Mine forever."

"Yours."

I fall on her, shaking violently, and without the use of my usual shield, I gather her up like she might disappear and wrap my body around her, as if we're under attack. I rub my open mouth across her forehead, up into her hair, holding her so tight she's gasping for air. I'm supposed to display more control than this, but the dread inside me won't allow for caution.

"Don't you ever leave me," I rasp into her ear. "Don't you dare."

"I won't." Our kisses are quick, frantic, everywhere. "I won't."

Momentarily, I'm reassured.

But in the back of my head, there is a voice saying we'll see.

We'll see about that.

CHAPTER SIX

Jolie

I STAND IN the shower watching water slide down the white tile, unsure of how long it has been since I moved. There is something bothering me, worming its way under my skin, but my brain wants to ignore it. My heart, too.

With Christopher, lovemaking is always intense. An emotional, full contact sport. But last night, there was something different. A desperation that still clings to my skin, as if he left it behind by accident. As satisfying as it was, it…jarred something inside of me. A wakefulness.

Feeling as if I'm waking up from a trance, I soap my body and rinse, going through the motions, even though there is something hot prodding me in the gut.

For some reason, my mind drifts to two days ago. When he came home and seemed to read my mind, playing his role as if he'd been anticipating it. Like he knew what was going to happen the moment he walked through the door. Knew what I needed.

I think of how he avoids any conversation about his past. Heck, his present.

I don't even know where his job is located.

My heart is beginning to beat faster. I replay the last month in my head. It has been blissfully happy. I've made progress personally, separate from Christopher, and he's been there rooting for me, pushing me. At home, we've been locked in a constant state of lust, but our conversations are always about me. Or they're funny and lighthearted.

Or they're vague.

Like wisps of something deeper we never delve into.

Communicating without really getting into finer details.

This man I married is protective, funny, thoughtful, supportive, sweet.

He's also primal, intense, mysterious and dominant.

There is a part of the picture of Christopher I'm not seeing, though, isn't there?

Standing here in the shower, that seems so obvious, while before, I was distracted by a fog of desire and love and excitement. Part of me wants to step back into the fog and forget the pieces that are suddenly stark and coming together, but I can't.

With a hard swallow, I climb out of the shower and go about my routine. I get dressed in a loose shift dress that brushes me mid-thigh and I blow dry my hair, applying a little makeup. When I walk into the kitchen, Christopher is standing at the counter dressed for work, a coffee mug to his lips. He turns to smile at me, just like he does every single morning, but this time I'm looking for something else—and I see it. Right after he spots me, just before he smiles, there's a flash of something wild. Obsessive.

It sends a cascade of nerves down my spine, but...it also turns me on. Makes me short of breath, my thighs clenching together. If he backed me into the bedroom right now, I would go. He would make me moan and claw at his body and I could go about my day as if there isn't anything wrong, but...I think there might be. And I can't ignore that.

I've missed warning signs before and it got me kidnapped.

Terrorized for days.

I'm stronger and smarter now, though, aren't I?

"Hey, angel eyes." He says this so casually, as if he didn't hold me like the world was ending in the wee hours of the morning. "Made your toast."

Christopher turns and leans a hip on the counter, running his tongue along the seam of his lips, checking me out without shame. And God, the man is so gorgeous, he turns my mouth dry. His hair is slightly damp from his shower, full and dark, styled with fingers. Tattoos peek out at the edges of his white dress shirt. His smile is adoring and wolfish and male.

This man does not sell insurance.

That fact hits me in the face like a stack of overdue bills.

"Are there women in your office?"

I'm not sure why I ask this. Maybe because it's a roundabout way into a conversation about his work life, which I'm sure...yes, I'm suddenly sure he's lying about.

Oh God, my husband is lying to me. Why?

A chill crawls up my arms, making the hair stand on end.

Christopher rears back a little at the question, laughs. "Sure. Why are you asking?"

"You're very attractive. Don't they...show interest?"

His blue eyes sparkle with humor. "You can't actually be jealous, Jolie." When I say nothing, his humor winks out, replaces with visible panic. His coffee cup rattles when he sets it back down on the counter. "Did I do something to make you doubt me? Tell me what I did. I'll never do it again."

I shake my head, wanting to reassure him, despite my growing suspicions. "No, you didn't do anything."

He's already coming toward me, capturing me against his chest. My lord, I can hear his heart slamming against my ear at a thousand beats a minute. This is not a typical reaction. It's not. All I can do is stare wide-eyed at nothing while he rocks me, kisses my hair. "I'm in love with my wife. I live and breathe and ache and fuck for you. Only you. I see nothing else. Nobody else. Please don't say things like that, Jolie. You might as well put a knife in my chest."

"Okay." I wrap my arms around him. "I'm sorry."

Why am I apologizing?

I don't know. Except there is an intuition, a positivity that he is not lying about loving me. About living for me. Aching on my behalf. Those parts are true. My heart is backing me up on that, sighing with contentment at his words. Loving his embrace as much as ever.

It's obvious that my concerns aren't going to be assuaged via conversation.

Not when my feelings for him overwhelm me into stopping. Don't rock the boat. You're happy, satisfied and safe. Why look for holes?

Because I was fooled once. Pride won't let it happen again.

And there's also the question of why? Why does he have to lie?

What is he hiding?

"Are we okay?" He pulls back, scanning my face with concern. "I don't want to leave for work with something between us."

I force a laugh. "It was silly. I walked in and you looked so handsome, I thought, the women at your office must wish me dead."

He says nothing, simply studying me with a crease between his brows.

Trying to make things light, I poke him in the ribs. "If I worked in an office with a bunch of people you'd never met, you'd wonder. You'd feel that natural jealousy, too, wouldn't you?"

"You have no idea, Jolie," he says, calmly—and I see it again. That same fleeting flash of wildness flicker in the depth of his eyes.

I keep my smile, though my pulse turns skittish.

I keep it until he slides a hand up the rear of my dress, over the right cheek of my backside and into my panties. "I could stay home." He kneads me firmly, turning my breath to hot puffs of air. "Spend the next eight hours fucking the doubt away." He breathes hard against my mouth. "I could start by licking that sweet, little cunt."

Yes.

My body, heart and libido say yes.

But my brain rebels. I can't. I can't surrender to this insane attraction any longer.

Not without the truth.

"No, I um…" I back away but reach up to fix his tie to soften the rejection. "I was actually thinking of pulling out my sketch book and working on some designs. You know, update my portfolio so I can think about interviewing again someday soon? I'm getting there." I wiggle my fingers at him. "I'm getting itchy to work. That's good, right?"

Slowly, he nods.

I go up on my toes and kiss him. "I'll be right here waiting when you get home."

"Okay."

He seems hesitant to leave, but finally, he walks out the door.

And then I follow him.

CHAPTER SEVEN

Evan

I'M NOT SURPRISED when she follows me.

When she walked into the kitchen this morning, I knew I'd been made. Maybe not completely, but my behavior over the last couple of days pulled back the curtain too far.

Watching the little blue dot of her car move on the map on the screen of my phone, trailing so close to mine, takes bite after bite out of my sanity…and now I'm even beginning to unnerve myself. Because there is a part of me that wants to yank that curtain back all the way. A part of me that wants to show her everything. Show her how much she has been worshipped for the last two months, ever since that night I saw her on the news.

I want to offer my sick devotion up to her on a platter.

I want to show her Evan and have her love me anyway.

That's not going to happen.

You're delusional if you believe she could love you.

Not Christopher.

I bare my teeth, swipe at the perspiration forming

on my forehead. Look in the rearview mirror and see her four cars behind. What choice do I have but to show her the real me? To step into the light? I'm supposed to be going to an office job right now. I could go to the building I'd designated as my fictional office. I could duck inside and possibly stave off her suspicions a little longer, but I can't keep the two worlds from colliding forever.

Maybe I should have tried to work a real job. If I'd done so, who knows how long this ruse might have lasted? But I know deep down, I never would have been able to maintain it. This need to follow my wife, to watch her every move, owns me. Working behind a desk and indulging this obsession with Jolie could never have happened simultaneously.

I'm had.

I'm caught.

I saw the knowledge in her eyes that something is wrong and I can't lie to her anymore. This conscience she inflicted on me won't allow for it. The guilt gnaws at me now every time we're together. I have to come clean and hope like hell she doesn't hate me.

What if she does?

With that question lingering in my mind, I drive another two miles and turn in to a familiar parking lot. One of the places I come when I'm supposed to be selling insurance.

Self-storage.

It's a stucco, five-story building filled with ten-by-ten units.

I park my car and go inside, as if I don't see her pulling into the lot. As if this heart, the one I didn't realize I possessed until I saw her, is about to shatter.

The door to the main building is open, only the inside units are locked, so I enter quickly and wait below the first stairwell. It's not lost on me that I'm treating my wife like one of my targets and it fills me with self-loathing. So much that I slam my head into the cinderblock wall while lying in wait, welcoming the rush of pain. The blood that wells up and trickles down my forehead—and then, there she is.

Stepping carefully into the humid hallway, her beautiful eyes searching for the husband she should have been able to trust. She walks down to the end of the first floor, clearly searching for an unlocked storage unit, but when she doesn't find one, she returns, approaching the staircase to try the next floor.

Her lilac scent hits me on her way up the stairs and I breathe it in hungrily from the shadows, before emerging and coming up behind her quickly.

I clap a hand over her mouth to cut off her scream.

"Hi honey." I kiss her neck. "If you're looking for my unit, it's on the second floor."

She starts to shake and I don't blame her.

I'm a monster, after all.

One she's unknowingly been feeding with her body, her love, her trust.

I walk her up the stairs and guide her into my unit, pressing the code on the wall, a mechanical whir filling the air as the metal door peels open and reveals what must look like her worst nightmare. My theory is confirmed when she makes a sound inside my cupped palm and starts to struggle. "Jolie, please." Her fear of me makes my chest feels like it's caving in. "I'm not kidnapping you. You have nothing to be scared of from me. I would fucking die before hurting you. If nothing else, you have to believe that, okay? Please."

I try to see the room from Jolie's eyes. The pictures of her taped to the wall, shots of her leaving the supermarket. Hundreds of photos of her sleeping, showering, exercising. There are news clippings regarding her kidnapping. Some pieces of her clothing, including panties that I've stolen so I could touch them unseen. Hold them to my face. Use them on my cock.

And then there's the guns.

A wall of them, neatly lined in racks. Ammunition, silencers, ski masks.

She's gone eerily still and that scares me more than anything.

Explain. You have to try and make her understand.

"I saw you on the news. I saw you, so brave and beautiful, and I had to get closer. Had to make contact. Know everything. Protect you. And then...we met and I was right. This fire, this love between us is real. You feel it too. I never expected it to move so fast. I thought we would date and I would make myself change. That maybe I could learn to feel for you the normal way men feel about women, but every second..." I exhale roughly against her temple, draw her back more securely to my chest. "Every time you breathe, I grow a little more obsessed. It's something I can't stop."

Jolie whimpers. Which tells me nothing. Nothing.

"Can I take my hand off your mouth?"

She nods.

With a deep breath, I drop my hand away.

My wife turns and punches me in the face. Hard.

Her knee jerks up and comes within an inch of my groin, before I block it.

Even with my head buzzing with pain, I'm so proud of her. One self-defense class and she's already confident enough to fight back when she feels threatened. If I was some average joe on the street, she might have succeeded, too, but I'm a hit man with ten years' worth of military training.

There's a thin length of rope within reaching distance and I use it to bind her wrists, throwing the end over one of the ceiling rafters, triple knotting the bindings and leaving Jolie's hands tied in the air above her head, captured.

"I don't want to do this," I say through my teeth. "I just need you to listen."

"I've heard enough." Her eyes are bright with unshed tears. "You are no better than Joseph Hynes."

My head jerks back like I've been slapped. She's right. Of course she's right.

This was my greatest fear all along. Being the thing that scares her the most.

"I love you. All I can say is that's real. It's the realest thing I've ever felt."

"Well I don't love you," she chokes out. "I don't even know who you are."

My heart lurches, sinks, sinks all the way down. "Don't say that. Yes, you do. Every moment was genuine, I was just holding back the full extent of what you do to me." I step closer to Jolie, breathing into the crook of her neck, cradling her hips in my hands. "But when I'm inside you, when we're close to finishing and I'm going for broke, that's me. You've met me, felt me and you've loved it."

"No," she whispers, but I catch her hesitation. "No, you played me. Made me feel safe—"

"You were always safe," I growl.

She ignores me. "Why do you have so many guns?"

"Work."

Stark horror dances into her expression. "Oh God. What do you do?"

I swallow my trepidation. There's nowhere to hide anymore. "I'm a hit man."

Surprisingly, her features don't register shock, but there is so much happening behind her eyes and goddammit, I would give anything to crawl inside and read her thoughts. "The other night...you weren't coming back from the kitchen, were you?"

I shake my head slowly.

Her head tips back on a watery sniff. "You kill people for a living, you've tied me up in a storage unit full of pictures of me—my god, you've been stalking me—and you expect me to believe I'm safe right now?"

"Yes."

She pulls on her restraint, slumping when it holds fast. "You're a psychopath."

The accusation hits me like a spray of bullets. I've always thought this was the case, but a psychopath doesn't love like this. Doesn't have regrets or guilt or attacks of conscience. But if I tell her any of that, there is no way in hell she'll believe me. This storage unit has damned me. My lies have fucked me over. I do not have a chance with this woman any longer.

I'm a criminal to her.

A stalker.

A crazy person.

If I really love her, I have to put my money where my mouth is.

I...I have to release her.

If for no other reason than she'll know my feelings are real. Because I don't think I can go on living if she believes the last perfect, beautiful month of our lives was some sick, perverted fantasy I played out at her expense. That would haunt me forever. If I choose to go on living without her. The jury is out on that one.

I bring our foreheads together. "I'm going to let you go. I'll untie you, let you out of this room and disappear. You'll never have to see me again." Her breath hitches, her eyes searching mine. I watch them closely, so closely, as I drag my fingertips up the inside of her thigh, pressing them to the silk material of her panties and massaging gently right over the top of her clit. "Please, just let me come inside you one last time."

"No," she breathes, shaking her head, yanking on the rope that secures her to the rafter.

It kills me, but I start to remove my touch…until she makes a breathy sound of protest, reluctant lust wafting into the gold of her eyes. Her thighs cinch around my hand before I can fully take it away, and hope lights up my entire system. Our uneven exhales mingle in the darkness. I should let her go now. I shouldn't fuck her. Because I can see she's confused by the fact that her body still craves mine, even though she surely hates me.

But I can't. I can't walk away when I have the chance to be joined with Jolie.

It's an impossible feat.

My hands go to my zipper, pulling it down and springing my cock free. Of course I'm hard as a rock. Because as much as I love this woman, I can't help but also love having her restrained and horny, her tits rising and falling with growing anticipation.

At my mercy, one last time.

I reach up beneath her dress and tug down her panties, wincing a little when they land on the filthy floor of the storage unit. She deserves so much better than this, but here we are. If this is the only way I can have her, so be it.

Looking into her conflicted but turned on eyes, I cup her tits.

Mold them in my palms, before dragging my fingertips slowly down her ribcage, squeezing her hips and that supple ass, smoothing my touch down and up her thighs, then delve a finger between the soft folds of her pussy, groaning when I find her soaked.

"Ah, honey." I push my finger deep, pumping it in and out, memorizing the feel and texture of her. "Does being the object of my mania make you a little too hot? Don't worry, you can enjoy getting fucked by your stalker as much as you want and I won't tell a soul. Your secret is safe with me."

Her eyes spark ominously, but I don't give her a chance to respond.

I yank her thighs up around my hips and plow my cock deep into her tight channel, relishing the sound of her stunned moan. How it echoes around the small room where I've fantasized about fucking her so many times. With the rafter supporting most of her weight, she's lighter than usual, so I take hold of that claimed-wife ass and ride her up and down my dick. Fast. Without mercy. I bounce her like a little fuck toy the way she likes it, listening to her try to refrain from whining in my ear and losing the battle. Calling my name. Wailing it.

"Christopher. Oh my God. Oh my God."

I slap her ass. "Going to miss this Daddy cock, aren't you?"

She bites her lip to keep from answering, her eyes squeezed shut, as if ashamed of herself for enjoying what I'm doing to her so much.

"When I'm gone, when you're in bed at night, trying to satisfy this pussy, you call for me by the right name. Evan." Hating the way she stiffens and this newly revealed truth, I latch onto her neck with my teeth, raking that sensitive flesh and licking away the sting. I fuck her harder in some deluded effort to make her forgive me. "Matter of fact, you do it right now. Call me by the right name before I go. I want to see it on your beautiful lips."

A beat passes. "Evan," she murmurs brokenly.

"Louder."

"Evan!"

I growl, wrapping my arms around her, mashing my lips into her neck, kissing, sucking, jacking my hips up and impaling her hard, rough, over and over, until she starts to whimper, her thighs trembling around my waist. "Good little girl. Come for Daddy one last time."

Her scream is the sweetest music, her cunt gripping me, releasing, gripping, releasing, warm moisture aiding my final pumps, and I peak with a bellow, grinding up into her heaven and filling her with my hot spend. "I love you, I love you, I love you," I chant into her hair, clutching her ass, using that grip to work her pussy roughly against my spewing dick. "I will love you forever, Jolie. My wife. I leave you with my heart."

We both go still a moment later, our harsh breaths bouncing off the walls of this cave where I've obsessed hour upon hour over her. And I will always obsess over her, miss her, pine for her breath on my skin, but the real version of that is over now. It has to be. I've hurt her—scared her—and that is unacceptable.

Wordlessly, I untie my wife, rubbing her wrists to bring the life back.

She takes her hands back quickly, looks at me, looks around at the room. With tears brimming in her eyes, she edges toward the exit, as if expecting me to stop her.

I almost do. God, I almost do.

A beast growls inside me, telling me to tie her back up.

Hold her captive here. Possess her. Feed my obsession.

But I let her go. I let her run, because my love won't allow me to do anything else.

And the farther she runs, the more painful my heartbeat gets...until I feel nothing at all but torturous agony.

CHAPTER EIGHT

Jolie

Two weeks later

I LOOK UP from my sketchbook and see it's dark outside.

With a gasp, I fumble for my phone and turn the house lights on, breathing through the nerves. Willing them to abate. They do, finally, but I continue to stare at nothing, like I'm half asleep or in a trance.

It has been two weeks since Christopher…Evan disappeared. Poof. Without a trace.

I keep expecting him to show up. To be standing in the kitchen when I come out in the morning. Or to roll over in the middle of the night, straight into his welcoming arms.

But that hasn't happened.

It hasn't happened.

I've thrown myself into self-defense classes. Therapy, too—after a thorough sweep of the office. I found a microphone taped under the desk. I stared down at it in the palm of my hand, waiting for the outrage to hit. It did, but so briefly I almost missed it. Yes, it was wrong of Evan to intercept my personal thoughts. They are sacred. And mine.

But I can't help but consider what he did with the information.

I healed thanks to myself. He took the fears I voiced in therapy and found roundabout ways of lessening them. Rearranging furniture in our bedroom and living room so there would be fewer hiding spots. Attaching a whistle and pepper spray to my keys without me asking. Encouraging me to do self-defense classes.

I'm not an expert on psychopaths, but I know a little, after being kidnapped by one. And they don't care about the needs of others. It's not in their DNA.

Meaning, Evan can't be one.

Meaning...there is a strong possibility he might genuinely love me.

In a very twisted way.

Swallowing the lodgment in my throat, I close my sketchbook and stand, looking around the apartment. At the stillness where there used to be laughter. Moaning. Companionable silence. It's so empty without him. I'm...

No.

I refuse to be empty over the loss of him. He stalked me. Lied to me about his name, his job, where he was going every day. Listened to my most personal thoughts.

He murders people for a living, for god sakes.

A long time passes before I realize I've been standing in the middle of the living room, unmoving. With a huffed breath, I start to pace. I need to put Evan behind me. Not to mention, all of the embarrassment that comes from being fooled again into thinking someone was normal. So embarrassed that I couldn't bring myself to contact the police and tell them I'd been stupid enough to marry a man who was lying about his identity.

I don't want to admit it to myself, but there's another reason I didn't call the cops.

Evan would never hurt me. I know it in my soul.

My eyes burn and I scrub at them with the heel of my hand. I need to continue to focus on my recovery and my self-defense classes. I even sent in an application this afternoon for a ground floor position at a design firm. I'm making strides.

I'm just so…bereft.

I miss him.

There, I admitted it.

I think he really did love me.

It was in every touch, every hug, every action, the vibration of his voice. And I loved him, too. Even in the storage unit, I looked at him, at all of his lies and deceptions and I felt a crazy, untamed, singular kind of love. It teems inside of me now, too, stronger than ever. I ran away from him. I accepted his offer to never see him again. But I would do anything to have him walk into this room and overwhelm me with his affection, his touch, his kiss.

Before I can talk myself out of it, I take my car keys off the peg and drive to the storage unit. I've driven by a couple of times over the last two weeks, but never gone inside. Perhaps I should be scared. Perhaps it's unwise to come here alone after dark, but the urge to be near Evan in some way is so undeniable, I'm walking into the building without a backward glance.

I recall the code he punched into the security pad for the unit because it was my birthday. My throat feels tight at the memory, but I swallow and enter the four digits, wringing my hands as the door trundles open.

Nothing.

It's empty.

No...wait. There's a large box pushed into the far back corner, hidden in shadows.

I advance on it quickly, like it might disappear, using the flashlight from my phone to illuminate the surface. There's nothing distinct about it. Just a plain, cardboard box.

But when I open it, I find hundreds of light bulbs. All sizes and shapes and brands. Filling the box all the way to the brim. And there's a note on top.

So you'll always have light.

I go down on my knees in front of the box. The tears that have been threatening to fall for two weeks finally erupt, pouring down my cheeks in heavy torrents of grief.

When I turn the note over, I'm expecting a way to find him. There's nothing, though. Not an address or phone number. He's left me no way to reach him. What am I supposed to do? I made a decision after finding out he'd lied and now I have to live with it forever? There are no qualifications or second thoughts? That's it? He just vanishes and leaves me to reel without him? I just want to see him one more time. Just one more time.

I pull my knees up against my chest, rest my head on my knees and sob.

I'm not sure how long I sit there pressed beside the box of light bulbs, aching for my husband's arms around me, but I start to hear his voice. It comes to me in snippets of past conversations. I think of the first time we met, the first night we spent in bed together and something pops into my memory. Something I haven't thought of since he said it.

This is where it begins, angel eyes. Listen to me. It begins here. If you ever feel lost, come right back here to the beginning and find me. I'll always be right here.

I can feel his body moving inside me as he makes that vow.

What did he mean, though? Or was he just saying words in the heat of the moment.

No.

No, that isn't like Evan.

He's purposeful and organized and thoughtful.

He built an entire persona so he could make me his.

He planned. A lot. And executed.

I'm standing before I realize it, running out of the storage facility toward my car. I peel out of the parking spot and break the speed limit to get home. I fumble with my phone to get the house lights on and push through the front door, sprinting to the bedroom. I waste no time flipping over the mattress and…

I stumble backwards.

A map has been drawn on the bottom of my mattress in black marker.

On one end, a house has been drawn. On the other end, connected by a long, squiggly line is water, boats, all set to a backdrop of cliffs.

There's a lighthouse, too. It's the only part of the drawing with color—red.

Is Evan telling me this is where I'll find him?

It has to be.

And it's not lost on me that he's chosen a beacon of light to await me, to bring me back to him, because he's always thinking of me and my needs. In this case, my affinity for light at all times. If I needed any further proof that there is so much good in this complicated man, I've just gotten it, and I can't stay away any longer. I want my husband back.

After a quick internet search, I find the lighthouse. And I go. I just go to him.

THE BEACON IS on when I arrive at the red lighthouse.

There doesn't seem to be any technical need for it, because the moon is full in the gray night sky, not a cloud to block its beams. The ocean spreads out at its feet, empty of boats.

Somehow I know he left it on for me.

Somehow I know it has been on every night for two weeks.

Just like the drawing on the bottom of my mattress, there is a house attached to the lighthouse. It's modest, rustic and beautiful, surrounded by a rambling garden. The sound of waves crashing against the cliffs helps soothe the ripped edges inside of me, but not enough. I'll never be soothed a moment of my life without him.

It's a truth I accepted on my hour-long drive to the coast.

This love between me and Evan might have dark shades, might have nuances that people wouldn't understand. It might even be wrong. But it's right for us.

This man held me up, reminded me I'm strong, showed me love.

I'm not leaving him deserted.

My gaze is drawn to the very top of the lighthouse and I make out the outline of a man's body. Not just any man's body, though. It's my husband. Tall, powerful...forlorn. I can read the anguish in his stooped shoulders as he looks out at the ocean.

A sob rises up in my throat and I move quickly toward the lighthouse, tears blurring my vision. I have to circle the base to find the entrance. When I do, I pull open the door, letting the ocean wind carry it and climb the spiral staircase, my heart starting slamming against my eardrums.

When I'm a few steps from the top, his voice, a mere scratch of sound, reaches me.

"Who's there?"

I reach the top. There is a circular railing separating us, an opening in the center where the huge, rotating light is positioned. Evan hasn't even turned around to see who is coming. His big hands are pressed to the glass, his head bowed forward.

"It's me," I manage.

It doesn't occur to me until that moment, when he doesn't turn around, that maybe I've lost him. I called him a psychopath. He poured his heart out to me and I walked away. Maybe I've broken him. Or maybe he's hardened his heart—

Slowly, he pivots, his expression one of disbelief. "Jolie?"

A miserable sound leaves me at seeing him so haggard. His eyes are bloodshot, rimmed in dark circles. He hasn't shaved in weeks, black whiskers occupying his cheeks, jaw, chin. He's lost weight, his skin is sallow. He's lost.

"I found your map."

He grips the railing, knuckles white. "I can't believe…you went looking for it."

I go toward him with measured steps, traveling the curve of the lighthouse. "You found me the biggest light possible," I murmur. "How could I stay away from a man who loves me that much? A man who loves me so much he'd change his name, his life, spend his days watching and protecting me? Listening to every word out of my mouth so he can please me?"

His eyes burn. "Some might say you should be terrified of a man like that."

"They're wrong," I whisper.

Something inside of Evan snaps and he barrels toward me, catching me up in his arms, sinking down to his knees with me wrapped around him. With us wrapped around each other, inhaling the scents of one another's skin, clawing to get closer. Closer.

"I'm dying without you," he rasps into my neck.

"You don't have to be without me anymore."

"Jolie...I'll never be normal when it comes to you. I'll never be a husband who waves goodbye while you go shopping or out on some girls' night. It just won't fucking happen."

"I know," I whisper. "I want every part of you."

"Forever?"

"Forever."

That wild light comes on in his eyes. The one I've only seen glimpses of before. But this time it's not fleeting. It doesn't go away. And I know it's going to be there permanently. My body responds with a swift surge of lust, my heart expanding, pounding, my existence narrowed down to the man who looks at me like I'm the ultimate treasure.

"Then bring me back to life, angel eyes." He lays me down. "So I can spend a hundred years keeping you in my sights."

EPILOGUE

Jolie

Five years later

I GLANCE IN the rearview mirror and a thrill rides over my skin.

Where is he?

I've been out shopping and haven't caught sight of my husband once, but I know he's there. He's never far. Always watching. But today he's being extra cagey. His car is nowhere in sight. The narrow road to our lighthouse by the sea usually has very few cars, so I can spot him trailing me, but all that stretches behind me now is an empty dirt lane.

Rain begins to pitter patter on the windshield of my car, the smell of salty ocean air winding in through my cracked driver's side window. I can hear the sound of my pulse in my ears, feel the answering call of the one between my legs.

I'm craving Evan, as always.

All those years ago, I think deep down I knew he was stalking me unaware. It was why I spent entire days in a turbulent state of arousal. Those eyes on me. Those thoughts being projected at me constantly. As they are now…though I can't see him.

We moved to the house beside the lighthouse five years ago and life has been a dream awash in ocean mist ever since. Our relationship has changed in the sense that there is no longer only one obsessed party. There are two. I am a fiend for this man who watches me in the night, trails me with a knife strapped to his ankle, ready to protect, makes love to me like he's conquering the world. Like he'll only get one chance.

Evan retired from being a hit man, having made enough money to live very comfortably, operating the lighthouse at night. Illuminating the darkness on my behalf.

When I returned to him, we spent weeks, possibly months, lost in each other. But he recognized my need to be productive, so he encouraged me to start designing again. I started with our own home and discovered my purpose. Designing homes for single women who feel a need for extra security. I design with an eye toward eliminating hiding spaces, shedding light on dark corners and providing safety. It's fulfilling in a way I never dreamed.

What about my life isn't fulfilling, though?

The means of getting here, to this state of bliss, might be far from normal, but the means are for me to decide. I love a man who has an unhealthy fixation on me, one that seems to grow more potent as time goes on and that will never change. No matter how many times I wake to find him staring at me in the darkness, my discarded clothing clutched in his hands. No matter how many times he inks my name onto his skin. No matter how many storage lockers he fills with pictures of me in private moments.

With the lighthouse coming into view, I run a hand down my throat. I fondle my breasts, imagining they're his capable hands. My eyelids flutter briefly and when I open them to look in the rearview mirror...

Evan is sitting in the backseat.

My heart flies up into my throat and I swerve slightly on the dirt road, though there is no danger since there are stretches of grass fields on either side.

"Pull over," he says gruffly.

The rain is starting to fall hard now, the sound of moisture hitting the roof drowning out my harsh breathing. I do what Evan says, pulling the car onto the side of the road, my fingers trembling when I put the vehicle into park.

"Turn off the ignition."

I gasp at the sheer depth of his voice, fumbling to follow his instructions.

And then I feel his breath on my neck. He's close.

So close.

His lips graze my ear when he talks. "Unbutton your dress." I flick open one button and his breath begins to saw in and out. "Faster."

I undo them quickly, though it's difficult when I'm shaking.

"You stayed gone too long."

"I'm sorry," I whisper. "Were you at home, missing me?"

His laugh is dark. "Oh, I was following you the whole time. But I can only stand watching so long without…having." He rips my dress open the rest of the way, yanking down the cups of my bra to knead my breasts in his strong hands, and the car fills with my breathless whimpers. "Get in the back seat."

Damp with excitement, I start to open the driver's side door, but he doesn't allow it. He wraps an arm around me and pulls me over the console. It's rough and a little violent. Desperate. It's us. The way he throws me down on the back seat and shreds my panties in his hand…it's us. The way he braces a hand on the window and drags his panting open mouth down my throat, across my nipples, back up into my hair, like we haven't been together in months…it's us.

"You've had me hard all day, little girl." I hear his zipper being pulled down. "Open your fucking legs."

"Yes, Daddy," I breathe, dropping my thighs open, savoring the flare of primal lust in his eyes when he looks at my sex. Every time is like the first. He runs cherishing fingertips over the mound of it, down the damp slit.

"My God," he moans, shuddering. Groping for his erection, he fists it and fills me with a strained grunt. Thrusting crudely once, twice, his mouth falling open. "Oh Jesus it's so sweet."

I drag my nails down the front of his shirt, twisting the material around my fingers, pulling him closer, sobbing when he pins me, giving me the full effect of his dominance, his muscles, his obsession. "You feel so good," I say through my teeth. "Mine. You're mine."

"That's right," he rasps against my mouth, his eyes wild. "Claim me while I'm claiming you. You know I love that. Tell your Daddy all about it."

"I need you."

"Yes."

"I feel sick without you."

Lips peeled back, he pounds into me now, our bodies straining, our heat fogging the rain-dappled windows. "Good girl. More."

"I love you."

His big body quakes at that, his mouth consuming mine, his body bucking into me mercilessly. "Jolie," he grates, his hand fisting on the window above me. "I love you. I love you."

And he does. He never lets me doubt it for a second. Not in all the decades that follow, our mutual obsession growing, our love flourishing in the lighthouse by the sea.

THE END

Step Stalker

CHAPTER ONE

Vale

I STEP ONTO American soil for the first time in four years.

The lights of the airport are bright, but they're nothing compared to the flashes that go off around me. Camerapeople wielding digital Nikons and pushing microphones into my face. It wasn't supposed to be this way. The media was never supposed to find out my identity, but an intelligence leak means my face has been all over the news.

I'm the Navy SEAL who killed the world's most wanted terrorist.

Civilians are cheering for me as I pass, calling me a hero. In my head, I know I did the right thing. Saved countless lives by taking a madman's. But the last four years is a blur of blood and explosions and near drownings. The kill they are cheering for was just a split second buried under a mile-high pile of harrowing shit. And I don't want the credit or the accolades or applause. I just want to get somewhere quiet and finally take a deep breath.

Is that going to be possible?

On the fight back to California, I kept waiting for

the relief to kick in. I'm no longer going to be active duty, thanks to a fistful of shrapnel buried in my calf, courtesy of the very same terrorist I took down in a firefight. There will be no more live battles for me. I'd be lying if I said I wouldn't miss it. The heat of the fight is in my blood now. But I was looking forward to letting my guard down for one fucking second—and it's not happening.

Even in this sterile airport, the adrenaline is surging in my veins.

I'm searching the crowd for a sniper, my palms itching for the gun in my bag.

The smiles on people's faces seem distorted. False. Their voices ring in my ears.

Somewhere above me, "The Star-Spangled Banner" begins to blare from a speaker and everyone sings along as I pass, taking pictures of me with their cell phones. The reporters shout questions over the din. *How does it feel to be a hero? What will you do now?*

As if I just won the Super Bowl, instead of taking a human life.

They don't understand.

They've never been there.

I feel like a fish out of fucking water, gasping for air, just trying to get out.

Get to my family.

Up ahead, I finally see my father, but instead of relaxing, I straighten my back automatically, harden my jaw. My limp is pronounced, thanks to my injured right leg, but I do my best to walk normally. No weaknesses have ever been allowed in front of the man. When I reach him, I hold my hand out for a shake, not a hug.

"Welcome home, son," my father booms, his chest puffed out. "I knew you'd return a hero just like your old man. Well done."

I nod once, transferring my attention to the woman beside him. "Ma'am." I take her hand and shake it gently, the bones as fragile as the rest of her seems to be. I'm worried if I grip too hard, I'll break them. There is nothing fragile where I've been. "You must be Vanessa, my new stepmother."

"That's me," she beams, smoothing her hair when a cameraperson sidles close for a better shot. "We're so glad to have you home." Vanessa looks around, a frown creeping between her arched brows. "Now where did Lula disappear to?"

Lula.

My stepsister.

At the mere mention of her name, my muscles lose some of their tension. Out of everyone back home, I'm most interested in seeing her. Meeting the girl for the first time in person. She's been writing to me since our parents got married a year ago and those letters…some nights they were the only thing keeping me sane. Tethering me to the real world.

I scan the teeming crowd for a young girl, beginning to worry again. All these people. Is it safe for a young girl to be alone in a sea of people like this?

"Oh, there she is. Lula!" Vanessa reaches behind a

pillar—

And pulls a female out into the open who is *definitely* not a girl.

This is Lula?

No. No, it can't be.

I've been picturing some gawky high schooler in braces. This is a *woman.*

Young, yeah. But her body leaves no doubt to her maturity.

Unlike when I shook my stepmother's hand, I wouldn't be afraid of breaking Lula. No. She's a curvy little beauty with hips I could grip, juicy breasts that would spill over in my hands. A plump, beautiful ass that would cushion a rough ride.

Oh my God. Why the hell am I thinking of my stepsister like this?

Every ounce of blood in my body has rushed south at the sight of her, turning my cock stiff and achy in my briefs. God, those wide green eyes of hers are pretty, too, surrounded by thick lashes. I almost choke on my tongue thinking of the welcome home I'd like from that feminine mouth. How soft and pliant her lips would be around my dick, all that reddish brown hair tangled around my fingers.

These are not the thoughts of a hero.

These are not even the thoughts of a decent human being.

Everyone in this airport has placed me on a pedestal and it's up to me to remain there. All my life, I'm going to be the man who killed the world's most hated man. I'm a representative of the Navy. The son of a general. I cannot be lusting after my stepsister. It would be wrong even if I was a regular old Joe, but I'm not.

I'm Vale Butler, a decorated Navy SEAL.

I'm going to be a commander at the naval base, training recruits.

There is no room for slip-ups.

But lord, she radiates comfort. The same brand of sweet care her letters gave me.

Those lavish lips spread into a smile, eyes sparkling like emeralds, and she springs forward to hug me. *Fuck.* I almost groan the word out loud as her curves mold to my strength, her gorgeous body plastering to mine, soft on hard. She smells lightly of incense and I inhale greedily, closing my arms around her. Holding on tight.

And all of the noise around me disappears, leaving only Lula.

There's only the sound of her breathing against my throat, her heart rapping against my abdomen, on account of our height difference. She's the lighthouse in a storm. I've already been holding her an inappropriate amount of time, especially for a stepsister I've never met before, but I can't seem to pry my arms from around her.

"Welcome home, Vale," she murmurs, the husky notes of her voices hardening my shaft even more, pressing it to her belly. But when she looks up at me, I can see she has no idea I'm erect. No idea that this instantaneous attraction is burning me alive. That I'd like to drag her into the nearest available room and work out this raw lust in a frenzy.

On top of being my stepsister, she must be a virgin.

Don't even think about it, Vale.

I'm not. I can't.

Still, when I finally manage to step back from Lula, the chants of my name sound like a mockery. An accusation. I'm obviously not the true-blue hero they think I am.

"I'm so glad you're safe," Lula says, her cheeks flushed from my too-close attention.

I'm staring. I'm holding her by the elbows, worried she'll get away. Or someone will try and hurt this sweet girl who has been sending letters to basecamp for a year. Letters that were witty and kind and didn't pry. She talked about herself a little, but mostly she spoke about nature and beautiful things happening around the world. Things that aren't war. Those stories transported me and I appreciated them, but damn, now I wish she'd talked more about herself.

I want to know everything.

"Thank you for writing to me," I manage, my voice sounding unnatural. Almost predatory. In need. "Your letters...I don't know what I would have done without them."

"Really?" She breathes huskily, causing velvet bolts to twist in my balls. "I didn't bore you with flower life cycles and meditation techniques?"

"God no. I only wished they were longer."

"Oh," she says, the stain deepening on her cheeks.

Jesus Christ, she's too sweet. Too good for the world I've been living in. And yet I want to rip her out of that flowery dress she's wearing and lick her pussy until she screams.

I'm not even sure she's legal. We never exchanged ages. I've been imagining her younger this whole time. No matter what, she's a damn sight younger than my thirty-two years. Add our age difference to the list of reasons I shouldn't be rock hard right now. I'd like to fall on the excuse than I haven't been laid in a couple of years. That has nothing to do with this, though. It might make my need for relief more urgent, but I've never reacted to a female like this in my life.

Christ, not even close. I'm *starving* for her.

"All right," my father says, sounding somewhat uncomfortable. "I think the vultures have seen enough of our reunion. Let's go home."

Home.

The house where I grew up. I'll only be staying there for a few nights before heading to Coronado where I'll be stationed at the naval base going forward. As a commander. But for the next three nights, I'll be in close quarters with Lula. My stepsister. And I have no idea how I'm going to survive without feeling her naked body beneath mine.

Vanessa and my father turn and hustle through the crowd toward the exit.

Lula seems concerned when I remain rooted to the

spot. Going home with her is going to be my salvation and my doom. Five minutes around this girl and I'm already infatuated beyond belief. It's taking an immense effort to control myself. To keep my hands at my sides. To keep from acting as her human shield against threats—they're *everywhere.* If something happened to her, I would go off like a fucking bomb.

When she reaches out and threads our fingers together, giving me a patient, coaxing smile, I follow after her as if in a trance. "Our rooms are right next to each other," she murmurs back at me. "I hope you don't mind the adjoining bathroom."

I'm screwed.

CHAPTER TWO

Lula

H E'S EVEN MORE perfect in real life.
At least, on the surface.

I've been looking at pictures of Vale since our parents married. His image is framed all over the house. Graduating from the naval academy, receiving commendations. The front page of last week's *New York Times* has been laminated and magnetized to the refrigerator.

California SEAL Fires the Kill Shot Heard Around the World reads the headline.

Another picture is there, too. Vale in his starched uniform covered in medals, his jaw firm, eyes serious. Back at the airport, though, I got a glimpse of the man beneath the tough military man exterior. He didn't like the attention and definitely wasn't comfortable in the large gathering of people. I could almost feel the nerves running roughshod through his system.

What has this man been through? I can't even imagine.

Every time I pictured our reunion with Vale at the airport, I saw him striding toward us confidently. Extending a hand to his father and slapping the older man on the back, making a jocular joke for the cameras. I never expected Vale to be stoic, limping, eyes tortured. Holding the bag over his shoulder in a white-knuckled grip. There is more to him than a granite-jawed hero—although he is definitely that, too.

I've never met someone in real life with so much *presence*.

So much outward strength.

In this town, he's considered a god. The paragon of male perfection. Rife with muscle and power and intelligence. He jumps out of helicopters into foreign oceans, dismantles bombs, goes for days without sleep. He towered over everyone in the airport, his arms so thick with muscle they could barely be contained in his jacket. His blue eyes are riveting. Intense. His brown hair cut short, along with his trimmed beard. He's polished to a shine, while on the inside, I can almost hear the broken pieces of him rattling around. I know it's odd to hold my stepbrother's hand, but I couldn't help it. He needed someone to steady him. And he held it all the way home from the airport, connecting us across the backseat, those blue eyes fixed on me the entire drive.

Which leads me to my problem.

Letting out a breath, I close myself in my bedroom and lean my forehead against the door, willing the dewy heat plaguing my skin to subside. What is happening to me? Am I simply nervous from meeting Vale, a world-renowned hero? Or is it something else?

On the drive home, I turned wet between my legs.

Embarrassingly slippery.

Meanwhile, my mouth is dryer than desert sand.

I've read about female arousal. Of course I have. I'm going to school in the fall to study Eastern medicine. Meditation. Alternative therapy. I'm well-acquainted with how the human body should behave. I just never could have planned for my first ever sexual, feminine response to come courtesy of my stepbrother. Highly inconvenient.

You. Are. His. Stepsister.

Sure, he might have held my hand tightly, occasionally brushing his thumb over my knuckles. Sure, his gaze might have meandered down to my breasts on the ride home, remaining there long enough to create the damp sensation between my thighs. But he's just a solider who has gone a long time without female companionship. It isn't like we grew up together. Nor are we related by blood. Obviously, *nothing* can happen between us, but I don't blame a man with that much masculinity for feeling lust over the female form.

Even if I'm surprised he feels it for *me*.

My mother has been talking for weeks about all of the women she's going to introduce Vale to. All kinds of debutantes and daughters of their successful friends. And all of those women have one thing in common. They're rail thin. Svelte. A very different body type than my own—and my mother loves to point that out. She always has. Clucking over my jean size or suggesting I go for more walks. Truth is, I do go for a lot of walks. I love being outside and I *want* to love my curvy figure. It's just really hard to fully enjoy my extra padding when I'm constantly being told it's a negative thing.

There's a muffled click and I lift my eyes to the door that leads to our adjoining bathroom. Vale's shadow moves underneath, followed by the running water of our shower. My pulse picks up at the image of Vale stepping beneath the spray, water coasting down over his thick pectorals, dampening the dog tags hanging between them. The soap suds traveling down in rivulets to his buttocks, so high and firm. And in front...

His sex would be waiting. Long. Thick. Neglected.

"Oh my God, would you stop?" I whisper, shaking myself.

The cops should come arrest me for having these thoughts about someone I'm related to by marriage. I can't even imagine what my mother and stepfather would say. They are all about image. All about maintaining the perfect reputation of a four star general and his doting wife. She never makes a misstep. She would be mortified if she knew I was changing my panties right now because my stepbrother turns me on. How am I going to make it through the next three days without totally embarrassing myself?

At least I have that camping trip tomorrow.

A break from whatever is happening to me.

I finish tugging on the white bikini-style under-wear and smooth my dress down over them, flopping down on my bed and looking around at my room.

Speaking of my mother, she could not hate my vibe any more than she already does, so maybe there is no point in trying to keep her pleased with me? Just this morning she came in filing her nails and eye rolled the multi-colored hanging tapestries and strings of mini lanterns. But I love my space. I love the rich scent of incense and the invitation to stretch out in the cool darkness. And okay, I'm seriously trying to distract myself from the fact that Vale is fifteen yards away, naked, in the shower.

Although…he *has* been in there a long time.

That shower basin usually creaks, too. Under a man his size, it should definitely be making some noise, right? Is he okay in there?

When steam begins to curl out from beneath my door, I rise from the bed and cross to the bathroom, knocking tentatively, concern curling in my breast. "Vale?" I call. "Is everything all right in there?"

A long pause. Then a muffled, "Yeah."

His tone of voice tells me he's not fine.

"Do you need something? A towel?"

There's no response this time.

My fingers tap on the door handle. Do I dare go inside? There's a churning in my chest telling me there's something wrong. After the haunted look I saw in his eyes at the airport, I'm even more worried. "You are studying mediation. The human body is a temple. Nothing more," I whisper to myself, shifting side to side on my bare feet. "It's *just* a body."

I open the door and step into the steam, waiting

for it to clear and yeah…

It's not just a body.

Vale sits in the basin of the shower with his legs bent and raised, forearms resting on his knees, back pressed to the tile. He's soaked and glorious and muscular in the extreme, wearing nothing but dog tags and a far-off expression on his face. Which is what prompts me to set aside my admiration of his form, allowing my concern to come rushing back in.

"*Vale,*" I say, opening the glass shower door and stepping inside, hesitating only a few seconds before kneeling down in front of him, staunchly keeping my eyes averted from the flesh between his legs. The warm shower spray rains down on top of me, soaking my dress instantly. "What's wrong?"

He snaps out of his trance and shakes his head. "I'm fine. I just…" His throat works in a rough pattern. "Everything is so fucking quiet, you know? I'm not used to it. Where I've been for the last four years, quiet means something bad is about to happen. Logically, I know there's nothing happening outside on the street. No tanks or landmines, but I can hear them in my head. It's like I'm still there, Lula, but I have none of what I need to protect you."

Before I register what's happening, he wraps me in a bear hug and pulls me onto his lap, pushing my face into his wet, corded neck.

"I don't want anything to happen to you, princess," he rasps, stroking my hair.

Oh my God.

I knew Vale was tortured by the things he'd experienced, but I had no idea his trauma was so severe. Heat presses to the backs on my eyelids. There's nothing I can do to stop myself from snuggling closer, wrapping around him and holding tight. I sense he needs it, needs the contact from another human being. Badly. "Nothing is going to happen to either of us."

"Don't say that, Lula." He's crushing me to his chest now, his mouth moving against my ear. "Those are famous last words."

My heart lurches. How many friends and fellow soldiers has he lost? "Vale, you're home now in California. Look at me." I press my forehead to his, waiting for his blue eyes to meet mine, almost sobbing over the torture in them. "Focus on your breathing. Do you feel it in your stomach and chest?"

After a moment, he exhales, take a long pull of oxygen and nods. Just a subtle tip of his head. "Yeah."

"Good." On impulse, I slide my fingers into his hair and he groans, eyelids shuttering, pressing his scalp into my touch. His vulnerability is so real and honest, it packs such a punch, I can hardly catch my breath to continue. "In and out. Feel your abdomen expand. Focus on it. And we're going to let that breath out into the rest of your body slowly. Let it wash into all of those places where you're locked up."

"God, Lula. I've needed your voice." His parted mouth dips to my neck and he gathers me closer on his lap, like a man holding on to a lifeline. "Keep talking to me, sweet girl."

I can't pretend I don't feel his erection growing underneath me. It's quite huge and impossible to ignore. The hard flesh presses up against my panties, the material of them soaked from the shower spray still raining down upon us both. I've never been in any kind of sexual situation, but the impulse to rock myself on that bulge is fierce. Instinctive. Somehow, I manage to hold myself back, however. Vale is definitely not thinking clearly. God forbid we do something that he'll regret when he's back to his calmer self.

"O-okay," I whisper, my fingers luxuriating in his hair, head tilting to the left so I can feel his breath more fully on my neck. I'm not a saint, apparently, and these things are too intoxicating to pass up. "Now become more aware of your body, Vale. Feel your arms and feet and shoulders. Come back into yourself, letting your breath expand into every region. Your body is the only world that matters right now, there's nothing outside of it."

My stepbrother turns his head, his lips dragging across my cheek to my mouth, hovering a breath away. Remaining there for several heavy breaths. "There's you." His lips graze mine, those blue eyes hot and intense, cutting through the dimness of the shower. "Your letters saved me. Now here you are, saving me again. My princess."

"Vale."

"I know. I know we can't do this." A low rumble takes place in his chest. "But God, I'd love to put you flat on your fucking back right now." A muscle jumps in his cheek. "Make those titties jiggle for Daddy."

I don't know what happens to me.

One second I'm caught between burgeoning hunger and surprise that this flawless man wants me—and the next I'm being run over by release so potent, I can only sob and shake, my sex clenching madly inside my panties, his erection stiff and pulsing along with my climax, even though neither one of us dares to move and create friction. I'm having my first orgasm right on top of his rigid length—and he only had to say the right word to unlock me, make it happen.

Daddy. He said Daddy.

His eyes are bright with surprise and lust. "Goddamn, Lula. Is that your first?"

I drop my face into his neck and whimper, nodding. Shaking head to toe.

"Ahhh Jesus." He rolls his hips beneath me and stars prick the backs of my eyelids. "Fuck it. Give me that mouth, princess. Give it over *now*."

Is this really happening?

This famous, battle-hewn warrior is so desperate for me?

But he's not merely a warrior right now, is he? At this very moment, in my arms, he's Vale. He's the lonely soldier I've been writing to. He's a man who is facing a very different reality than the one he's been living and it overwhelms him.

Maybe he only wants me because I'm convenient. Because I'm compassionate and he's reeling. I don't care, though. Not right now.

I only want to soothe him.

Be what he needs.

All it takes is a slight incline of my chin and his mouth is on mine, unruly and wet. His kiss is like being transported. My life is now divided into before my stepbrother's mouth and after. It's animal and desperate, lips twisting and taking, his hips lifting beneath me, his hands fisting in the sides of my dress. I've never been kissed before, but it wouldn't have mattered if I had, because no one could compare. He's male, unquestionably in command and yet somehow humble, groaning brokenly as he sinks his tongue into my mouth and rubs it erotically against mine.

"Lula, I can't slow down. I'm sorry." He surges forward, lifting me and dropping my back to the shower floor, his hands shoving up the hem of my dress and wrestling with my panties, jerking the sodden material down to my knees. Water from the above shower is dripping off the ends of his hair, the sharp blade of his shoulders. "Have to get my cock inside you—"

There's a loud knock coming from somewhere.

We both go still, except for our sides which heave from exertion.

"Lula, dinner is on the table," calls my mother's voice. A few seconds pass, followed by another knock in a different location. "Dinner is served, Vale. I'm sure you're starved for a home-cooked meal."

Vale seems to come out of a trance, swallowing hard and throwing himself back against the tile wall.

Dragging a shaky hand down his face. The shower spray is landing directly on me now, so I sit up and turn it off, trying to piece together what just happened. "Be right down, Mother," I call back, hurriedly pulling my panties back on. "I-I…better go change," I whisper, positive I'm blushing to the roots of my hair. "I know you didn't mean for this to happen. I know it's just been a long time since y-you've been touched. Probably. I don't know. Maybe you just needed comfort. But I'm not going to make a big deal out of it."

"Lula, it is a big deal. I'm your stepbrother. I'm older and know better. I'm…"

"Living under a microscope," I finish for him. "I get it."

And I also know he probably regrets getting caught up in the heat of the moment. I just happened to be here when he needed a distraction. When his male needs were—and still are—at a fever pitch. There's no way I can let him think I've gotten the wrong idea. That he likes me. How humiliating would it be if he was forced to let me down easy? That has always been my greatest fear. That I would misread a guy's interest and force him into telling me sorry, I'm just not his type. I'd rather be alone than have that happen. To find out my mother is right and my body is going to prevent me from living life to the fullest. From being happy.

"I'll see you at dinner," I say, scrambling to my feet and booking it out of the shower, thankfully without slipping.

"*Lula*," he grits out, coming to his feet.

But I'm already closing the door and working my way out of the wet clothes, a pain in my chest forming when I realize that might be the first *and* last time I kiss Vale. It's obvious that I formed an attachment to him through our letters and now meeting him in person? There's a whole new dimension to the breathlessness he inspires in me. The sense of right-ness.

There's nothing I can do about it, though.

So I better just pull my head down out of the clouds.

CHAPTER THREE

Vale

SITTING AT THE table with my father and step-mother with a dick that could shatter glass is uncomfortable, to say the least. There is no help for it with Lula sitting across from me, however. She's changed into another dress, and this one is tight, short and white of all colors, as if I need a reminder I almost fucked this innocent virgin on the floor of a shower. No condom, no foreplay. I would have burst her cherry and ridden like hell. After she was kind enough to fight my demons with me. Christ. I should be ashamed of myself. I should be more ashamed that I wish to God we hadn't been interrupted.

I can already feel this getting dangerous.

I'm a man with lethal capabilities and the ability to surveil someone unseen. I'm already planning on watching her while she sleeps tonight, this sweet, loving angel who happens to be related to me by marriage. I'm itching to get my fingertips on her things. To go through her laundry and find the panties in which she had her first orgasm, so I can drag them all over my body, tie them in a knot around my dick.

I'm almost too horny to eat, but my father is

watching me closely, as usual, so I manage to chew and swallow, my attention straying to Lula's juicy tits. That dress is tight and worn, like she's had it forever. Molding to her soft skin and making me insane. That mouth of hers closing around her fork and dragging turns my cock into a pulsing trunk, jammed up behind my fly.

You can't have her.

I know I shouldn't even be looking at Lula with these eyes that have witnessed so much horror. I'm too fucked up to be in her presence, let alone lay a finger on her. I haven't even bothered being diagnosed with PTSD because it's obviously one of my main problems. No doctor's note required. What is the point of addressing what's wrong with me when I know it can't be cured? Nothing can erase the images from my head. Nothing can rip the shouts for help out of my head. Or this feeling of being useless now that I'm a civilian again.

She makes me feel normal. When I read her letters, when she held me in the shower, the storm inside my head devolved into a tranquil lake. But that's not okay. It's unacceptable. I'm not going to make this girl—and that's what she is at *eight-fucking-teen*—with a normal life ahead of her become my cure. I have to stay away from Lula for the next three days and hope like hell I can overcome this growing infatuation once I leave for Coronado.

Yeah right.

She's already gotten to me.

At this point, all I can hope is that I'm as noble as everyone believes me to be. Noble enough to keep my hands off my teenage stepsister and walk away without ruining her life.

"So, Vale…" Vanessa sips from a glass of white wine and sets it down. "I know you've only been back for less than one day. And your father made me promise I wouldn't ask right away, *but*…some of my local friends have daughters your age. Some of them slightly younger. Career-minded girls who haven't had time to date until recently." She winks at me and my stomach turns. "I know they'd love to meet a certain celebrated war veteran."

It doesn't escape my notice that the fork suddenly becomes too heavy for Lula, her hand falling to rest beside her plate. She must be embarrassed by her mother's inappropriate timing. Even my father, who is clearly enamored with Vanessa, seems irked. "Let the man have one day of peace before ringing the dinner bell, would you?"

Vanessa winces, but there's no remorse in it. "Excuse me for wanting to present this heroic SEAL with a lineup of stunning women. They might be professionals, but every last one of them could pass for a pageant girl. I am *very* discerning."

Lula is no longer eating and it takes every bit of my willpower not to march to the other side of the table, settle her on my lap and start feeding her bites of truffle mashed potatoes. "Thank you for thinking of me, ma'am," I say politely as possible. "But I'm not interested."

God help me, I can't imagine a set of hands on me that don't belong to my stepsister.

The thought of anyone else touching me turns my stomach.

A memory accosts me. Lula mewling around my tongue, her pussy shifting in my lap and I have to reach down and adjust myself roughly, barely able to keep from panting.

Vanessa isn't ready to quit, unfortunately, and her next comment sets my teeth on edge. "I can see it now. Someone with captivating looks to match your own. A graceful disposition. Long legs like a ballerina..." She smiles into her glass of wine. "Are you convinced yet?"

"No," I reply, sharply, the handle of the fork digging into my palm. "And trust me, the last thing I'd be interested in is someone exactly like me."

I'm being too abrupt. Too disagreeable. This is not how the media darling is supposed to act. I'm meant to have a humble attitude and a funny rejoinder for every question. Everyone's ideal Captain America. Even in front of my father. Especially in front of him.

Forcing myself to swallow a bite of chicken, I search for a way to soften my irritated response to Vanessa. "Two people exactly like me would be a lot of baggage for one relationship, Vanessa."

"Baggage?" she asks.

An uncomfortable itch forms on the back of my neck. I'm suddenly restless, but when I find Lula's eyes across the table, the beginnings of an earthquake inside me become manageable. "You don't leave combat without it," I murmur.

My stepmother starts to ask another question, but she's cut off abruptly when my father slams a fist down on the table. "None of that complaining in my house." Once upon a time, I would have jumped sky high at one of his outbursts, but I'm a man now. A SEAL. I've been in countless battles and even spent a few weeks being tortured in a POW camp. Nearly had my leg blown off. I don't flinch in the face of his temper anymore. "We show gratitude *only* in representing this country. If you want to take that honor and turn it into something to cry about, do it somewhere else. At least you got to live when so many others didn't."

I might not flinch at his anger anymore, but this rhetoric was repeated so often to me growing up that I can't prevent the stab of guilt. He's right. I should be grateful to be home. I should be strong and unshakeable like I was taught. I definitely shouldn't be brought to my knees in the shower by flashbacks. My father and I hold each other's gaze for long moments, neither one of us willing to lose the staring contest.

Vanessa clears her throat. "Um…Lula. Are you all set for camping tomorrow?"

That question splits my focus right down the middle. "*Camping?*" I practically shout at my stepsister. "Where? With who?"

She raises an eyebrow, clearly thrown by my reaction. "I'm going with two of my girlfriends, Santana and Jess. We're heading up to Prairie Creek for the night."

I'm genuinely doing my best not to spiral into a panic attack at the table. Mainly because it wouldn't be a good look in front of our parents if they knew I'm already protective as hell over the stepsister I only met this afternoon. Doesn't she know how many accidents can happen in the wilderness? She could misstep and fall from a cliff. She could be attacked by wildlife. Hit her head and fall into a body of water. The list goes on and on. Are they out of their fucking minds letting this young girl take off alone like this?

"You're sure that's a good idea?" I ask, stabbing the tines of my fork into some chicken. "Who is chaperoning you?"

Lula wrinkles that adorable nose at me. My cock swells so swiftly, I have to grit my teeth. "No one is chaperoning us," she enunciates. "Since we're all legally adults."

"Yeah? Well bears don't check ID, Lula," I fire back.

And she laughs. It starts out as a snort. She tries to muffle the sound with her hands, but the giggle bursts out of her and the craziest thing happens. I start laughing, too. I can't recall a single other time in my life that I've laughed at this dinner table. No, I've been lectured and shouted at and reprimanded. There was no mirth whatsoever until now.

Until her.

"I'm sorry," she gasps, fanning the tears of laughter in her eyes. "I'm just thinking of a bear on his hind legs asking to see my driver's license!"

She doubles over and Jesus, is that my own laugh booming through the dining room?

I mean, there is *no way in fuck* she's going camping without me there to protect her. But even I have to admit, a bear checking identification is too funny for me to stay pissed. And that's when I notice that my father and stepmother aren't laughing along with us. In fact, my stepmother seems more annoyed than anything over Lula's giggling fit.

Me? I'd like to seal the sound into a jar. Save it forever.

"Lula will be fine. She's a frequent camper," drones Vanessa. "She finds balance in nature or something. I don't know where she gets it. Certainly not from me."

"It's the simplicity of wildlife," Lula says hesitantly, as if she's not sure her opinion will be welcome at the table. "I can't teach people how to find their quiet place if I don't stay well acquainted with my own."

My father rolls his eyes. "Generation Z and their all-important self-care. Lula thinks she is going to make a career out of it."

"Then she *is* going to make a career out of it," I snap, gripping the fork until it hurts. "She's good. And I'm pretty sure her methods are better than bottling up your aggression for decades until you're nothing but an angry prick all the time."

We square off, my father and I, him chewing his bite slowly, jaw grinding.

This is not how I was taught to speak to my father. As a child, a statement like that would have earned me a backhand across the mouth. But it will be a cold day in hell before anyone speaks to my sweetheart stepsister that way and gets away with it. And it feels good, too. Not saying the exact right thing. Saying exactly what is on my mind, instead of following the humble soldier script that seems to have been written for me.

My father laughs unexpectedly, slapping a palm off his knee. "Looks like the SEALs did their job and put some fire in him. He's definitely not quiet and introverted anymore, is he?"

"No, certainly not," Vanessa agrees quickly, visibly happy to have the mood lightened. "We have blueberry pie for dessert. Then I thought we could all watch a movie in the den. Won't that be nice?"

CHAPTER FOUR

Lula

AFTER DINNER, I go upstairs to brush my teeth and put on a pair of fuzzy socks—a required movie viewing accessory, since it's cold in the den—and when I come back down, everyone has already taken their spots. My mother is curled up on the love seat with her mini poodles, Tamsen and Boo Boo. My stepfather is reclined in his easy chair, frowning down at the remote controls. And Vale is on the couch, watching me beneath hooded eyelids.

The only available spot in the room is beside him.

Truthfully, there is no other place I would rather sit. I'm just so confused by what's happening between me and my stepbrother, the idea of two hours beside him turns my stomach into a trampoline for nerves. After what happened in the shower earlier, I thought I had the situation figured out. Vale is lonely and starved for affection after being away so long. In such perilous circumstances.

I'm still pretty sure that's the case. I'm just convenient.

A warm body to slake the urges of a big, testosterone-laden warrior.

But the way he stood up for me at the dinner table, the protectiveness he displayed for me when he found out about camping...it doesn't add up. Is it possible there is more happening here than meets the eye?

Swallowing hard, I cross the floor of the den and sit down on the couch to Vale's right.

He's leaned back, one elbow resting on the arm of the couch, his magnificently thick and corded thighs spread in the pose of a man who can and does handle hard situations. After his shower, he changed into sweatpants and it's an effort not to look *there*. At the apex of his thighs where there is a clear outline of his manhood, fat and *definitely* not contained by underwear. Oh yeah. My stepbrother is one hundred percent free-balling it.

Vale runs his tongue along the inside of his lower lip when he catches me staring. I notice the flesh in his sweatpants rise quickly, pushing at the seam, bigger than I could have imagined. He mouths a curse and grabs a blanket from the back of the sofa, throwing it over his lap and hiding the evidence of his arousal. And we both stare straight ahead at the television, both of us breathing faster than before.

As the movie begins—a comedy about a dog and its scatterbrained owners—I begin to wish I'd worn pants. The simple act of sitting this close to Vale and knowing he has an erection is making my sex warm and achy. Wet. So wet that my panties are sodden by the time the first scene is over. A hot shiver passes through me. And another.

"Lula," my mother calls from across the room. "You're freezing. Share some of that blanket with Vale."

"I'm fine," I say quickly. Too quickly.

Vale grunts, lifts the edge of the blanket, his eyes almost black when they meet mine. "I see you shivering. Come here, Lula."

If I protest now, it's going to be weird. My resistance might even draw attention to the fact that I'm attracted to Vale, thus wary of getting too close, and that's the last thing I want to do. "Um...okay. Thanks." I slide closer to him on the couch, my tummy flipping over when our hips meet. The outsides of our thighs press together, softness to ample muscle.

Vale leans over and tucks half of the blanket around me, his brow furrowed in deep concentration. As if he takes my warmth very seriously. "That better, princess?" he whispers, right against my ear. And all I can do is nod vigorously, training my eyes on the television, praying I won't have another spontaneous orgasm like I did in the shower. When I climaxed after barely being provoked. It's him. This man. He has a crazy effect on me, and I don't seem to have much control over it.

My nipples are stiff, my inner thighs buzzing with sensitivity. Every part of me that connects with Vale is rejoicing happily, wanting to snuggle and luxuriate in his power and masculinity, but I force myself to remain stock still.

At least until, beneath the blanket, Vale hooks his pinkie finger around mine.

Smooth and slow. Clutching possessively.

My clitoris throbs in response.

Head to toe, I'm sensitive. I'm physically aware of every single movement my stepbrother makes from the scratching of his eyebrow to the slow lift of his hips—and of course I see it. His bulging shaft beneath the blanket. He lowers his hips again afterward, but I know it's there, mere inches from my left hand—which he is holding now.

I'm *holding hands* with my stepbrother, his thumb brushing side to side on the small of my wrist. He can almost definitely feel my racing pulse there. There's no hiding it.

To our right, my stepfather begins to snore in the recliner, head tipped back against the cushion. My mother laughs at the sound and hits a few buttons on her phone, lowering the lights in the den even more. To almost pitch black, except for the flickering television screen. "To help him sleep," she explains in a conspiratorial whisper, going back to petting the dogs. She's on her third glass of wine, though, her own head beginning to nod on the pillows.

A few minutes later and she's unconscious, too.

With both of our parents sleeping, the awareness between me and Vale is multiplied tenfold. He squeezes my hand and lets it go, but I'm not given a second to mourn his touch, because he slides that arm around my shoulders, tugging me more securely up against his side.

"You'll be warmer this way," he says, lips grazing my temple. "I'm sorry about dinner. My father being dismissive of the career you want."

"There's nothing for you to be sorry about," I whisper back. "You stood up for me. It was...nice. Someone having my back. Thank you."

"No one should have to stand up for you. Not in your own house." His upper lip curls. "I'll make sure to put an end to that before I leave for Coronado." The reminder that Vale is only here on a temporary basis makes my throat feel clogged. That reaction must be showing on my face, because he frowns, leaning down to roll our foreheads together. "Ah, princess..."

Our mouths open and release a breath, bathing each other's lips in warmth, preparing to launch into a kiss that neither one of us can prevent, but there's an eruption of snoring from my stepfather. Vale and I put a few inches of distance in between our mouths as the man shifts in the recliner, turning slightly away from us and resuming his nap once again.

I study Vale's chiseled face in the flicker of the television, feeling closer to him than I ever have with anyone. I felt that way the moment he walked out into the open at the airport, the emotion only increasing with every passing hour. Every exchange of knowing eye contact. I'm eager to know more about this man. What other chance will I have if he's leaving soon?

"I was surprised when your father said you used to

be quiet and introverted," I breathe for his ears alone, barely checking the urge to touch his chest beneath the blanket. "I mean, you came across thoughtful in your letters. But the media has portrayed you as kind of…"

"A confident man's man with the perfect answer for every question?" He chuckles quietly, but the sound holds no humor. "The press has given me this persona to make everyone comfortable with celebrating the kill. I've been coached by the Navy on how to respond. No one wants to hear it was a low-down and nasty business. They want to think it was something like they might see in a movie. Now the hero just has to look pretty and wave for the cameras."

My heart gives a long tug. "How are you feeling on the inside?"

He blows out a breath. "Isolated. Displaced." That muscular arm tightens around me, pulling me closer, his brow knit in thought. "I don't feel that way right now, Lula. With you."

Pleasure washes over me, warm and potent. I can't let the confession go to my head, however. He's been on US soil for a matter of hours and I'm the only person who is willing to show him some comfort. Even among his own family and friends. At least, that's what I seem to be telling myself so I don't get far-fetched ideas in my head about this hunky, heroic man developing an interest in me. "What about the other men on your team?"

A line hops in his cheek and he looks down at his lap. "They're good guys. The best. We were closer before all of this happened, though. I'm getting credit for something that was a joint effort. They say they're fine with it, that they don't want the notoriety, but it's hard to stay happy for someone when the president is thanking them in a speech without a single mention of anyone else. And now that I'm injured and my identity has been leaked…"

"There's was just no time to make any of it right," I finish for him in a whisper. "I'm sure that's unsettling. Not even having that foundation of your friends."

He gives me a dazzling half-smile, his white teeth flashing in the darkness. "Are you sure meditation is your jam and not psychology?"

I bite my lip to contain a laugh. "I've always been great at recognizing issues in other people and knowing how to correct them. But when it comes to my own, it's a different story."

A wrinkle of concern forms between his brows. "Anyone would have issues growing up in this house, but I don't like knowing you have them. Talk to me."

I've always tried to minimize my problems. It's just a knee-jerk reaction. Logically, I know they are just as valid as anyone else's. But when I start to talk about them out loud, I find myself rushing through the details and saying *it's fine it's fine it's fine* a lot. "Nothing, really…"

He tips my chin up and gives me a stern look. "Lula…"

God, he is so handsome. No wonder good-looking

people always seem to be in positions of power. Telling them no when they want something is extra hard. Not to mention, his worry is genuine. I can feel it radiating from him in waves.

"Well, our parents have everything figured out, at least on the surface. They always have a plan and a goal, whether it's organizing a charity or rallying people around a political cause. And they seem kind of bewildered that I need to think and meditate before making most decisions. It's not just my career choice they think is frivolous and silly...it's me." I struggle through a swallow. "I'm an outsider in my own house." Somehow I find the courage to echo his earlier words. "I don't feel that way right now, Vale. With you."

I've just seriously put myself out there by admitting that. It's so unlike me to take risks, especially with the opposite sex. But Vale doesn't give me a chance to dangle on the line or feel self-conscious. No. He dips his mouth to mine and takes a long, slow pull of my lips. "To think my original plan was to go directly to Coronado from the airport. What if I'd missed out on you, princess?" In one smooth move, he lifts the blanket and drags me onto his lap. Effortlessly. I'm facing the television, my bottom wedged tightly against that bulge, the bare backs of my thighs resting on his clothed legs. My feet aren't even close to touching the ground.

We're in a room with our parents and I'm sitting on his lap.

If they woke up, there would be no mistaking what's happening or explaining it away.

Especially when Vale winds my hair in a fist and gently tugs, bringing my back flush to his broad chest, his heart pounding against my spine, his breath feathering my neck. "There is nothing frivolous or silly about you. The way you help reach below someone's surface just makes them uncomfortable, because they're afraid what they'd find under their own."

Emotion makes the tip of my nose sting momentarily. "Thank you."

"I'm only telling the truth, Lula." He exhales roughly, shifting his hips, his teeth grazing the sensitive skin beneath my ear. "You're a fucking treasure. Don't ever doubt it. Okay?"

"Okay," I breathe, my nipples puckering painfully, my nerve endings waking up and dancing like they've been dormant, waiting for this man to arrive and touch me.

"You do have one serious problem, though," Vale says in a gruff voice beside my ear, his chest rising and falling heavily underneath me. "And we need to discuss it."

"I-I do? We…do?"

He unwinds my hair from his fist, trailing that hand over my shoulder, collarbone and down to my breasts. Kneading the left one once through my dress, before sliding his hand down the front of my bodice, dipping those long fingers into my bra and fondling me, skin to skin. "I've only been here half a day, Lula, and I can see...you've been parenting yourself. Isn't that right?" He unsnaps the front of my bra, groaning deeply in his throat when my breasts tumble free into his waiting hands. "They live in their own world, don't they? Letting you disappear into crowds at the airport. Camping. You're not getting the attention you need. Or the protection."

There is so much truth to what he's saying.

Of course, I'm able to camp and handle myself in public alone.

But. There's no denying that I do feel like I'm fending for myself all the time.

There's no denying how isolated I am in my own home. Isolated just like Vale.

My stepbrother lifts his head briefly, his lips leaving my neck as he glances around the room, making sure we're not being watched. He pulls the blanket over the top of us more securely, covering us from neck to feet. When he's finished with the task, his hand doesn't return to my breasts, though.

No, it cups my knee, squeezing. Slowly. Then his fingertips climb beneath the hem of my dress, traveling higher, higher up my inner thigh. Knowing instinctively where he's heading, I bite my lip and squirm a little in Vale's lap, earning a *"shhh"* from his gorgeous mouth.

When he's halfway to the juncture of my thighs, he seems to lose patience and grips my sex roughly, his breath releasing in a rush. I have to throw my head back against his shoulder and concentrate on holding back my climax. The very act of him touching me there is enough to blow my hormones sky high. His hand is warm and strong and possessive, his palm perfectly curved to my mons, his fingertips digging into the giving flesh of my femininity. "I mean what I say, Lula. You need more attention. Better care. My father obviously isn't qualified to parent you way you need." He begins to massage me gently, teasing the flesh inside my underwear. "This pussy needs a Daddy, doesn't it, princess?"

A seismic ripple passes through me, my thighs jerking closed around his hand, and it's everything I can do to keep from panting in the too quiet, too crowded den. I never would have expected my body to react to that sentiment so eagerly. But it does. I *do* want this capable man to care for me. I want to soak up his attention like a sponge that has been left out and forgotten too long. I've never had a strong male support figure in my life. Not one that made me feel safe. Not one that took an interest in me.

Even if Vale's presence in the house is only temporary, I can't help but gravitate toward it. Wanting to hear more. Wanting to live inside this feeling of being cherished and secure.

This pussy needs a Daddy, doesn't it, princess?

"Yes," I finally answer, as quiet as a mouse.

I might as well have shouted it based on his reaction. He groans long and guttural into my shoulder, his shaft growing impossibly large beneath me, pressing up into the split of my bottom. Unfettered now, I open my thighs back up and rub against him, waiting in breathless anticipation to find out what his touch will do to me next.

I don't have long to wait to find out.

Those thick fingers slip into my panties, delving into the ample wetness, parting my folds with a slow, purposeful stroke. "Fuck. That is sweet." His middle finger drags up and back in the valley of my flesh, making me whimper. "Actually thought I could leave in three days without a backward glance, but that's not going to happen, is it? This needs to be guarded at all costs. Needs to be raised right. That's what I'm here for now, Lula, you get me?"

There is no way to process the meaning behind what he's telling me—or if he means something more serious than my brain can currently grasp—I'm too caught up in the maelstrom of sensation. The winding up of storm clouds in my tummy. Especially when the pad of his middle finger grazes my clit for the first time, then moves faster and faster on the small, sensitive bud, shooting lust and urgency straight down to my toes.

"Never been a Daddy before, but I was yours the second I stepped off the plane, wasn't I? You knew it. And so did this pretty virgin cunt." He pushes his middle finger inside my drenched entrance, both of us gasping, the sound of damp flesh barely drowned out by the sound of the movie. "And what does that make you, my too-tight princess?"

The answer is somehow obvious. "L-little girl.

Your little girl."

How do I know this? No idea. It's instinctive. Like slipping on a new, second layer of skin that is infinitely more comfortable than the first.

"That's right," he rasps into my neck, his hips starting to roll beneath me. Quickly. Desperately. "They want to slack off on parenting duties? *Fine.* I'm stepping in. I'm the one who gives permission and advice and buys your clothes now. Vale is Daddy. Say you understand."

We're getting too loud. Our breathing is out of control, the rasp of our clothing seems magnified in my ears. I can hear every slick stroke of his fingers through my sopping wet flesh. So I nod, instead of answering, tipping my head back so he can see the affirmation in my eyes. And whatever he sees in my expression riles him up, brings his mouth down on mine, kissing me over my shoulder. Now I'm being ridden in his lap, his middle finger pumping in and out of my previously untouched channel, his tongue sweeping into my mouth with ownership.

My orgasm sinks its teeth into me, and I whimper into the kiss, struggling through the tumult of sensations, my butt grinding down into his lap, my womanhood clenching and pulsating around his finger. *Oh God. Oh God.* This is far more intense than the release he gave me upstairs in the shower, because I'm being pumped full—and because he's coming, too, this time. I'm still at the apex of my climax when Vale twists to the right and throws me face down on the couch, his hips jackhammering mine through my panties and his sweatpants. The springs of the couch creak underneath us and the blanket has been discarded on the floor. If our parents opened their eyes right now, they would see my stepbrother on top of me, humping me violently on the couch—and I still don't think we'd be able to stop.

"Do you have any idea how fucking hot this lush, round ass makes me? Those big, juicy tits? *Jesus Christ.*" He thrusts against me even harder, his fingers burying in my hair, twisting the strands. "You were built for me. Built to get it rough. Built to take Daddy's pounding."

My mouth is open in pleasure, in sensual overload on the couch cushions. A moan works its way up my throat, but I turn my head at the last second to bury the sound. And that's when my panties are yanked down, great, glopping wetness striping across my cheeks. My stepbrother's spend lands audibly in the still, dark room, his strangled groans muffled in my neck, big, huge body jerking and jerking, over and over again on top of me until his release runs down the split of my bottom, all the way to my sated sex, mixing with the proof of my own pleasure. Only then does Vale collapse on top of me.

Almost instantaneously, there's a shift across the room, my mother changing positions on the couch. With a frustrated curse, Vale eases off me and adjusts his sweatpants, wiping me clean with a sweep of his T-shirt and tugging my panties back up into place quickly. We're in the process of sitting up, both of us still catching our breath, when my mother yawns loudly.

"Oh my goodness, don't tell me I fell asleep just like your father."

Neither Vale nor I have the wherewithal to answer. I can barely *think* straight, let alone speak. I just hooked up with my stepbrother. On the couch. Mere feet from our parents.

Was it a one-time thing?

It didn't sound like it. It sounded like Vale was claiming me...permanently.

But it's hard to trust that when I've been conditioned to be insecure. What if he was just saying words in the heat of the moment? Santana and Jess are always complaining about guys who make promises in the dark but ghost them the next morning. Is it fair to hold Vale to anything he said to me? Maybe things will be clearer in the night of day?

Again, my mother yawns. "Lula, you're leaving early for camping, right? Maybe you should head upstairs and get a good night's sleep."

A muscle flexes in Vale's cheek and I get the distinct impression his willpower is the only thing keeping him from pinning me down again. His blue gaze is fastened on my mouth, even more intense than I've seen it since he arrived. Those big fists are bunched on his thighs, that upper lip on the verge of peeling back. What does his demeanor mean? Does he want to touch me again or—even more likely—is he annoyed at himself for getting carried away?

With a hard pinch in my chest, I get to my feet unsteadily. "You're right, Mother. They're going to be here early and I haven't even packed." Briefly, I meet Vale's glittering eyes. "Good night."

I go upstairs to my room and close the door, listening for Vale to follow—and he does, a few minutes later. His footsteps move in a pattern on the other side of our adjoined bathroom, giving me the impression that he's pacing.

If he's worried about my holding him to his promises, he doesn't have to. I won't.

A lump slides up and down in my throat when I swallow.

I'll go camping in the morning and give him some space, maybe a chance to...go out. See other people besides me. After all, I'm the only woman he's had any contact with.

You're convenient.

Right before I go to bed, I turn the lock on my main bedroom door, as well as the bathroom bolt. I'm not sure why I do it. Maybe as a way to maintain the little pride I have if Vale, in fact, feels he made a mistake. It takes me a while to fall asleep, but I do eventually, intense blue eyes haunting my dreams.

CHAPTER FIVE

Vale

I'M IN THE driver's side of a car, the seat reclined all the way back so I can't be seen from the road. I watch Lula exit the house across the street carrying a pillow and sleeping bag, a backpack slung over one shoulder. A low, animal growl leaves my mouth at the sight of my delicious stepsister, her soft skin glowing in the morning light. It takes every ounce of self-control not to throw open the door of this car—which I broke into with ease—and storm across the street to demand to know why she locked me out last night.

Yeah right. If I do that, I'll end up buried in her pussy in broad daylight.

Right there on the sidewalk. However I can get it. Get *her*.

Aware that I'm sucking in ratting breaths, I drag a hand down my face and order myself to rein in the hunger. The obsession that has grown into something uncontrollable literally overnight. I returned to my bedroom last night after the movie and forced myself to take some time and get my possessiveness under control. After damn near fucking her on the couch, I was almost unhinged with purpose.

I'm not leaving this house without her. Not going to Coronado unless she's at my side.

I'm going to be what she needs at all times. Going to take care of her. I wanted to hold her down last night and demand promises. I wanted inside of her so I can start working on getting her pregnant and locked down before someone steals her from me.

What man worth a damn *wouldn't* try?

She's a fucking light in the darkness, so sweet and compassionate and understanding. She's got an adorable sense of humor. She's astute. Smart. Knows what she wants out of her future. And *Christ*, that body. My dick is standing straight up already just watching those titties shake inside her tank top. The palms of my hands itch like crazy to grip those wide hips, hold her steady while I rock deep, my stomach slapping up against the perfection of her ass. God-*damn*, I'm going to make myself come thinking about being inside of her for the first time. Going to get my sperm so deep, it'll take a week for a single drop to escape.

A car pulls up at the curb near Lula and I reach for the gun at my hip, adrenaline firing on all cylinders, making every hair on my body stand up. I relax slightly when my stepsister smiles and waves at whoever is in the vehicle. They park and get out. Robotically, I register their facial features like I was trained, noting that one of them is blonde, tall, fair-skinned while the other has dark hair in a bun, a sepia complexion and two eyebrow piercings. That's all it takes.

Two seconds with my eyes off Lula and I'm starved for the sight of her.

The friends are forgotten as I zero in on her, watching with rapt attention as she loads her things into the back of her friend's car, chatting happily about how great the weather is for camping. Once she's finished putting her things in the trunk, she glances back at the house. Hesitates. It's wishful thinking that she's hoping to see *me* before leaving, right? Obviously I scared the living hell out of her last night. I went way too far too soon. For godsakes, she only met me in person for the first time yesterday and there I was, humping her like a beast and explaining that I'll be her Daddy going forward. No wonder she locked the doors.

I need to be more artful. More patient with her. She's a virgin. Inexperienced.

If she knew how high this inferno inside me has already built, she would probably never come home from camping. She'd take her chances among the bears.

I'm not taking any chances with her surrounded by wildlife, however. As soon as Lula gets into the backseat and her friend pulls away, I follow. I keep an inconspicuous distance for hours, even allowing other cars to get between us, reasoning that I know the name of the campsite and I won't lose her. I know exactly where Lula is going to be—and I plan on knowing her location at all times in the future.

Yeah, there's no way to douse this fire she's lit in me. I'm going to have her, damn the consequences. She's mine. She's fucking *mine* and no one is going to take her away from me.

I covet this responsibility to follow her on the camping trip and keep her safe. The privilege of being her man, her protector, is like air in my lungs. I'm not sure how we're going to deal with my parents, the military brass or the press, but whatever their reaction, being with Lula is worth it. By a damn sight. Bring it on. I've never needed anyone or anything so much in my life.

Mine she's mine she's mine.

After a long stretch of driving up a winding, mountain road, the car carrying my stepsister pulls off into a parking lot. I drive past just to be safe and circle back, driving into the lot behind them a few minutes later. Parking at the opposite end and watching them unload supplies from the trunk, wishing I could carry Lula's load. God, I would give anything to be the one going camping with her. The wilderness is a perfect setting for the animalistic things I want to do to her.

Eventually they start hiking down a path in the direction of the apparent campsite—and I follow, keeping to the trees, moving without a sound. Inhaling her incense scent from the air and dragging it into my lungs greedily. I'm still hard as a rock in my jeans. So stiff it's painful. But I refuse to stop long enough to jack myself off. I've come on Lula's perfect skin. Now anything else will be inferior and I'll be hard again in seconds. There's no point.

They stop ahead and begin pitching their tent, organizing chairs around a stone ring. They've picked a nice spot with a bubbling stream not too far away and a dense canopy of trees that give them ample shade—and allow me to easily remain unseen. I perform a silent perimeter check of the area to make sure there are no recent animal tracks or venomous creatures that might sink their teeth into my Lula. Once I'm satisfied that she's safe, I rest a forearm on the trunk of a redwood and listen to their conversation.

"I'm seriously considering quitting this whole dating business," says the blonde one. The back of her nylon chair is embroidered with the name Jess, so the other girl must be Santana. "The guy I went out with the other night was a disaster. Word to the wise, if he's asking for anal after one date, run for the freaking hills."

"No. He didn't," Santana groans, leaning forward. "Did you do it, though?"

There's a long pause, then Jess says. "Yeah, it might have slipped in."

The three girls erupt into laughter, but I can see my stepsister is shifting uncomfortably in her seat, playing with the beads on her bracelet. If I was within reaching distance, I would have already pulled her into my lap. "How did it feel? Weird or good?"

"Oh, definitely weird," Jess laughs. "It's kind of like…satisfying, I guess? Guys are so turned on by it, they only last like, two seconds."

"It's kind of flattering," Santana pipes in, sipping from a mug.

"Why do they like it so much?" asks Lula.

Jess shrugs. "It's just tighter." She gives Lula a sly look. "Although you're still hanging on to your virginity, so you're probably tight no matter what."

"Lucky me," Lula responds with a smile. "Is that, like...really important to a guy?"

"Depends on the size of his *you know what*," Santana answers, nodding sagely.

Any other time, I would probably be pretty amused by this conversation. It's obvious that teenage boys are just as clueless as they always were—not that Lula will ever have to worry about that. It's also obvious that these girls have a lot of affection for my stepsister. She's obviously innocent as hell, but they don't seem to be judging her halting questions.

"Why are you asking, Lula?" Jess asks, leaning over the elbow Lula. "You never ask us about sex. Do you have someone specific in mind?"

Lula picks up her own mug and takes a hasty sip. "What? No. I'm...no."

Santana perks up. "That wasn't very convincing."

"Yeah," Jess agrees. "You've got your stepbrother staying with you now after all."

Lula's cheeks turn pink. "What do you mean by that?"

"I *mean*..." Jess draws out. "Did he introduce you to a hot Navy SEAL friend or something?"

"Oh," breathes my stepsister, understanding dawning. "No, he…he didn't. Introduce me to anyone."

Goddamn right I didn't.

If that ever happens, check on hell, because it's frozen the fuck over.

"It's only Vale staying at the house. No friends. Nothing l-like that." She's back to fidgeting and it's like I can read her mind. She's thinking of my finger pumping into her cunt, my tongue sweeping the sweet cavern of her mouth—and God, now I'm not just hard, I'm dripping. "I'm only asking about sex, because…well, if there's ever an opportunity, I want to be prepared."

"I'm not buying it!" Jess says, jabbing a finger toward the sky. "Come clean, girl. Who are you thinking of blowing?"

"Nobody!" Lula insists. A pause ensues. Then, "But if I was…what would you consider the proper technique?"

Santana and Jessa throw up their hands in victory. "Knew it!" crows Santana. "Hey, listen carefully. You need to worry less about your blow job technique and more about his cunnilingus skills."

Lula nods, wide eyed. But her head slowly starts to shake. "Yeah, I don't know about that. I don't think I would like it."

Jess chokes on her drink. "What? Why do you think that?"

"I think I would just be self-conscious, you know?" She laughs, as if trying to make light of the statement.

"My mother is always saying men don't like…the extra weight. On a girl."

I almost blow my cover right then and there.

Almost march down and demand Lula get on her back, so I can devour her like it's a pie-eating contest and she's strawberry-rhubarb. How can this girl not realize she's a smoke show? She's insecure about her weight? I've never had a type, but as soon as I saw Lula, my type became her. Exactly what she is. If that's heavier than whatever people deem normal, then this is how I want her to stay. My favorite things about her body are its softness and resilience and mouthwatering curves. My fingers are fucking *miserable* without touching her.

"Lula," Jess says hesitantly. "If I man doesn't think you're sexy, he's an idiot."

"*And* dead wrong." Santana adds.

"Thanks, guys," Lula says, splitting a smile between her friends.

It's slightly stiff, though, as if she's not totally convinced.

Her friends seem to notice she's uncomfortable talking about her body, trading a look with each other, before Jess says, "Let's break out the s'mores and talk about blow jobs."

Subject changed, they start rooting through supplies for marshmallows and chocolate.

But my mind is stuck in one place.

That pussy.

Burning her self-consciousness to the ground.

As soon as she gets home, I'm going to put my tongue to work.

That's what I should have done last night, instead of grinding on her ass cheeks. I was just in such a frenzy at the time, I wasn't thinking straight. Next time, I'm going to spread those legs apart and lick until she realizes she's a goddamn bombshell.

For the next hour, I groan into my fist, watching her lick melted marshmallow from her fingers. I swore I wasn't going to beat off, but she makes it nearly impossible just by being Lula. By being mine. Her sweet laughter drifts up through the trees and starts my heart thundering in my chest. I'm full of her, head to toe. Consumed.

So when she excuses herself to go wash off at the stream, of course I follow.

Keeping to the shadows. Licking my lips. Starving for the taste of her.

Will I make it through today and tonight without coming out of hiding to touch her?

I know I should. This level of obsession could terrify Lula. Put her out of my reach.

I'm stalking her—there's no other word for it.

But when she strips out of her clothes, my will rapidly begins to deteriorate…

CHAPTER SIX

Lula

I DIDN'T COME to the stream to clean off.

Well, I *did*. The s'mores are sticky little guys. But I also snuck away to do a little communicating with nature. Santana and Jess are well used to my spontaneous meditation sessions—they just aren't aware of my preference to have them in my underwear.

With a smile curving my lips, I lift my face to the sun and hike to the waterfall. It's my favorite spot, thanks to the grassy knoll on the other side. It's a little hidey hole, away from the world. Quiet, dark, curtained by water. The white noise is perfect for blanking my mind, letting the beauty of my surroundings soak in.

All right, it's going to be pretty hard to blank my brain today when I can't seem to stop thinking of Vale—his eyes, his voice, his body—but I'm going to try. I can't let myself get too carried away with this infatuation or I'm only going to be disappointed. Already, I've gone way too far by asking my friends specific questions about sex. They're going to be relentless now. What would they say if they knew I'd hooked up with my stepbrother?

What would *anyone* say?

Maybe I won't have to worry about it? Maybe it was a one-time thing?

When I ponder that possibility, my chest aches even worse.

Determined to enjoy the beautiful day, I look around on the off chance someone else is hiking through. Then I unfasten my jean shorts and drop them down to my ankles, groaning in delight over the warmth of sunshine on the backs of my thighs, my butt. Wanting to experience the heat everywhere, my tank top comes next. My bra. I'm in nothing but a pair of black bikini-cut panties now and I turn to the sun, raising my arms up so its rays can reach out and touch me. I focus on my breathing, inhaling the splendor of nature and releasing gratitude slowly—

A twig snaps.

My arms drop abruptly to cover my breasts, alarm prickling at the nape of my neck.

"Santana?" I call. "Jess?"

There's no response.

It's not totally unusual to hear twigs and branches and leaves falling from the trees. The forest floor is littered with debris from above, so it's a common occurrence.

But the sudden electricity racing up my skin is not common.

I narrow my eyes and scan the trees, my gaze lingering on the shadows.

There is no one watching you. Don't be paranoid.

Taking a deep breath, I wade into the stream toward the waterfall, concentrating on the water licking at my thighs, then eventually my panties. How the cool, crisp quality of it climbs my belly and refreshes my senses. When I reach the waterfall, I don't hesitate to position myself beneath it, letting the water cascade down the front of my body, down my breasts, back, legs. My hair is gloriously drenched in seconds, the dull roar of falling water drowning out the forest sounds, leaving only my heartbeat—

And memories of Vale in the shower.

How water pooled in the valleys of his collarbone, how his hair sagged low on his forehead, dripping. How his harsh breathing echoed in the shower stall, mingling with mine.

I don't realize my fingers have dipped into my panties until the pad of my middle one grazes my clit and I shudder, my moan absorbed by the waterfall's rush. My toes curl into the smooth pebble floor of the stream, the waterfall caressing me everywhere—my nipples, the sensitive insides of my arms, my neck. But it's not the waterfall I'm picturing in my head as I rub myself faster, using my middle and ring finger now. I'm thinking of my stepbrother in sweatpants trying to hide his erection from our parents.

There's a slight chance of Santana and Jess following me here and I really don't want to get caught masturbating. Although they would probably high five me and inquire about my technique. Truthfully, I don't have one. I've never felt the pressing need for release until meeting Vale. Now my body is on edge. Sensitive and starved. And I have to appease it.

In the interest of privacy, I duck beneath the waterfall and walk on my knees to the center of the hidden grassy knoll, flopping down on my back. Letting out a long, low moan, knowing I'm the only one that can hear it. And that freedom makes me twice as hot, makes me tease the ring of my entrance and press a finger inside of me, my heels digging into the earth, hips lifting, my gasp loud in my ears—

There's a break in the sound of water hitting the stream and my eyes fly open.

I see the outline of a man and terror grips me.

I open my mouth to scream, but I never get the chance.

He moves like lightning, springing forward, through the waterfall, landing heavily on top of me, his big hand covering my mouth, catching the sound before it escapes. I buck and twist, my instinct to fight kicking in immediately. But it becomes obvious right away that there is no point. His arms are made of steel and there's a precision to his movements that tells me I'm not the first person he's had to silence in a cave. Oh God oh God—

"Lula, it's Vale. You're safe," he rasps in my ear. "You're safe, princess."

Shock renders me motionless beneath his muscled body, my breath racing in and out of my nose. There is still a scream lodged in my throat, my claws out, ready to scrape. But now...now I'm just confused.

Vale is here? How? I'm a hundred miles from home.

What is going on?

Keeping his hand sealed over my mouth, he looks down at me with glittering eyes—and I feel it. His hard shaft against my inner thigh. He was watching me. He was watching and being turned on by me. That was him snapping a twig out in the forest. Wasn't it?

I know one thing for sure.

I shouldn't be feeling relief right now because this man is Vale and not a stranger.

It's actually more alarming to think my stepbrother might have followed me all this way.

Right?

So why is my fear ebbing? Why do I have the urge to let my thighs fall open?

"Good girl," he whispers, nuzzling my hair. Still covering my mouth. "You don't want to fight me, do you?"

How am I supposed to answer that? I *should* be fighting him.

Right?

"If I let go of your pretty little mouth, are you going to scream?"

I shake my head no, because what would be the point? He'd have my mouth covered again in a split second. And no one who came to my rescue would be a match for my stepbrother, the ruthlessly trained Navy SEAL.

His lips skate down the side of my neck. "I can't

kiss you if you're screaming, can I?"

My clit throbs in response to that barely breathed question, my eyelids fluttering, trying to stay open. But his tongue bathes my throat, his teeth grazing the edge of my jaw and clamping down on my ear and oh lord, there's a rush of wetness between my thighs. I'm confused and aching and appalled at myself, but that last part is fading. Fading under the inundation of need for this man, no matter how he got here. Or why he came.

Vale takes his hand off my mouth, immediately replacing it with his lips.

His male groan fills my head, his taste coursing through me.

His urgency.

My hands are slowly manacled above my head, his powerful body settling more fully against mine, his hips in the cradle of my thighs, that long, hard part of my stepbrother pressed to my sex. Ready. Demanding placation. I'm trying to stay afloat. Trying to make sense of what is happening, but he won't let me. Won't allow me to think. His tongue invades my mouth over and over and over, fuzzing my thoughts and heightening my arousal until I'm fully participating.

As soon as my resolve slips, Vale grows more aggressive, angling his mouth right, left, raking his lips down my neck, then back up, capturing my mouth before I can breathe a word.

"I was only going to protect you, Lula," he says

hoarsely against my jaw. "I was only going to keep you safe. But you went and got naked, didn't you? You went and fingered your virgin pussy. *My* virgin pussy. Didn't you?"

"I thought I was alone," I gasp, not even sure if I'm making sense.

"Oh, you're never going to be alone again." He rams his hips up into the juncture of my thighs, making me whimper. "Meet your permanent chaperone, princess."

His mouth stamps back down on mine, his lips urging me to open so he can tangle our tongues together. He keeps my wrists imprisoned with his left hand, his right one stroking down the side of my face to my breast, squeezing, rubbing the knuckle of his index finger against my nipple until I start to whine into the kiss, his tongue muffling the sound.

"Nod your head if you understand I'm about to fuck you, Lula." His tongue licks over my ear, his hips rolling roughly. "First with my mouth. Then it's all dick."

A finger of tension traves down my spine.

He's going to put his mouth on me there?

I mean, I was going to meditate about it for a while. Get used to the idea before I ever let it become a possibility in my life. With anyone.

But it's going to happen so soon? With *this* man?

As if I need a reminder that he's a bronzed, battle-roughened god, Vale sits back enough to whip off his shirt, revealing a wall of rugged muscle. Scars. A dark forest of hair. He's the definition of a man. Built for battle. And his blue gaze is fastened on my wet panties like they are earth's greatest offense. A second later he's ripped them clean off.

Because he's going to perform oral on me.

Oh my God. I'm suddenly hyper aware of every dimple on my stomach and thighs. How I'm going to look from below. Everything. "I...I..."

"God*damn*, princess, look what you've done to me," Vale grits out, unzipping his jeans, that long, hard appendage swinging up through the opening, curved and heavy. I bite my lip to keep from moaning when he fists it without gentleness, squeezing it up and down.

Still, I try to close my thighs, shield myself, some evil voice—that sounds an awful lot like my mother—whispering in the back of my mind that he must be mistaken. "Vale, I don't think—"

I have no time to prepare before he lets go of his sex, flipping me over onto my stomach, a hard slap delivered to my bottom. So hard it makes me gasp. "This body of yours makes me stiffer than I've ever been in my life." He comes down hard on top of me, his harsh breath in my ear. "I'll take a fucking bite right out of this perfectly plump ass if you ever close your thighs to me again. The pussy belongs to Daddy. Do you understand me?"

My self-consciousness starts to take a knee, but I'm still not sure.

Is *he?* Really sure about me?

Before I can voice my concerns, I'm flipped back over and he gets in my face. Uses his knees to shove my legs open and slaps his shaft several times against my damp, feminine flesh.

Smack smack smack.

"You see this cock, Lula? Hurts so bad it's dripping come, begging for what you've got between these sweet-ass thighs. But not until I eat every soft, juicy inch of you alive. Understand?" He kisses me hard, tunneling his tongue into my mouth, groaning jaggedly, breaking away to speak in a rush against my lips. "Just so we're clear, I'd fight another hundred wars for a shot at this tight little cunt. You're built like a fucking woman. You're built like what I *need.* Now spread your legs and take this tongue. Daddy's starved."

Whatever reservations I had are swept away on a tide of need so forceful, I actually shove him downward by those rock-hard shoulders. Needing to be pleasured. Needing his mouth. I am staring up at the rock ceiling of the cave but seeing nothing. Sucking in air. And that's before he even licks me the first time. Once the tip of his tongue wiggles open the sides of my flesh and mashes against my clit, rubbing it up and down, his groan vibrating my thighs, I start to sob and twist, my thighs falling wide, fingers clawing into the earth.

Oh Jesus.

Oh God.

Was I really going to pass on this?

Vale looks almost drugged, his pupils blacking out the blue, that incredible back rippling as his mouth works, tongue flashing pink in the cave. He pushes a long finger into me, twisting it, then drawing it in and out faster, faster, with more pressure. It's a relentless assault. A thin layer of discomfort over a treasure trove of pleasure. *Just have to get there. Get there.* And it's easy when his tongue continues to bathe my clit, loving it side to side, up and down, Suckling it lightly while he adds a second finger, fucking me now with them. Hard.

Something inside me gives way and I choke on a scream.

Because on the heels of that gentle rip, a new tide moves in. It's huge and frothy and overwhelming and there's no way to escape it. I look down into his wild eyes and see the animal hunger there. The encouragement to accept whatever is happening.

Pleasure that is so intense it's almost painful careens through me, coiling every muscle I possess, squeezing my loins, and I watch through fevered eyes as moisture from my body lands on his face, leaving his mouth and cheeks and chin wet. Dripping. He licks it off with an expression of rapture, wiping his face off on my belly as he prowls upward. Up my body until we're face to face, me gasping for air, him darkly satisfied with the outcome of what just happened.

"My little girl squirts just like I knew she would. And she's fucking delicious." He comes down on top of me hard, pressing me down into the earth, lips flush against mine. "Now. Are you ever going to close your legs to me again?"

"No," I whimper, my fingers sliding into his hair. That's where they belong. His breath catches at my touch and my confidence grows even more. More. *He wants me to touch him. He's dying for it.* "N-no, Daddy."

"I didn't think so."

With a roar, he buries his sex inside mine.

"Vale!"

"Ah fuuuuuck." His eyes are delirious, jaw slack. "That's tight as *hell.*"

I'm coherent enough to know he brought down the barrier of my virginity with his fingers and I'm grateful for that now. Oh God, I definitely am because there's no time for acclimating. He ruts me like he's dying. I was aware of his raw strength before, but it's so much more obvious now when he doesn't hold a single ounce of it back, grunting into my neck, his hips powering between mine in quick, brutal pumps, raking me up and back on the grass like a ragdoll. I've never felt more feminine in my life. Never felt so sexual or attractive or alive.

"Thought a girl was writing me those letters. Then you show up with these big, round titties and an ass that can take a good long pound. A fucking *woman.* That's what I need." He jerks my legs up around his waist and his pace turns bruising, his thickness squelching in and out of my channel, his balls loudly rebounding off my buttocks. "A woman who still needs a Daddy, though, doesn't she? A Daddy. A brother. An obsessed stalker who watches you finger your little, wet pussy from the trees. I'm all of those things to you now. Hear?"

"Yes! *Yes!*"

"Going to protect you." His voice is like gravel in my ear. "Going to keep what's mine."

A tingle chooses that moment to start beneath my belly button, sinking lower, lower and building in intensity, so I can't speak, I can only nod unevenly.

"Couldn't find any birth control pills in the bathroom cabinet. You hiding them somewhere else? Tell me now."

What is he asking me? My tummy is starting to ripple, the sensation carrying to my mons now, and when that delicious throb starts in my clit, I know it won't be long. It won't be long before another orgasm hits me and *I want it.* With every cell in my body, I want to climax while he's slapping in and out of me, our bodies slippery with sweat and stream water.

"Answer me. You on protection or fertile for me, princess?"

"I'm...I'm..." I whine, pushing up my hips to meet his thrusts, crying out when the thick base of his erection saws wetly against my clit, again and again and again. "No pill."

A great shudder goes through him and he groans, flexing every one of his many muscles and he bears down, flattening me between his big body and the earth, my knees shoved open wide as possible in his hands. His drives are so forceful, so thorough, I scream from the sheer brute strength of them, the fact that I'm being unquestionably claimed.

"I found you, Lula. I found my woman. And I'm not fucking around." He licks his thumb and brings it between our bodies, teasing my clit side to side, fast, jiggling it—and I come apart, screaming into his kiss, our teeth bumping because his hips are still rutting me at an unruly pace. I'm mid-orgasm, can't see anything but sparks, my sex constricting violently around him and I can only picture what we're doing. How it looks. This strapping soldier in the prime of his life on top of a curvy young girl, his stepsister, doing his best to nail her into the ground. And the image, the forbidden nature of it, takes me higher, makes me bite his mouth, makes my claws bury in his back, earning me a sound halfway between a gasp and a growl.

"Goddamn right I'll get my little girl pregnant," he grinds out, thrusting once more, the movement jagged. Grinding high and deep. "People will talk, but we know it's right, don't we?"

"*Yes*," I moan, eager beyond belief to provide him with pleasure. Whatever he wants.

With a wince, he starts to shake, his warmth spilling inside of me.

He starts pumping again, but there's no finesse to the movements. He's just a desperate creature trying to get rid of the physical lust. It's an animal all its own. His mouth finds mine and we wrap our arms around each other, my legs locking around his waist, anchoring him as he comes, that soldier's body quaking, sticky heat overflowing my channel and sliding down the cheeks of my backside. He moans long and loud into my neck, his shaft flexing and jerking inside of me, until he loses all power in his muscles, falling on top of me, breathless.

"Mine," he whispers reverently, licking salty sweat from my shoulder.

I move on autopilot, offering him solace because my soul commands it, dragging my nails up and down on his scalp, kissing the side of his face. I'm not sure when my insecurities start to pile up again, but they do. One by one. I wish I didn't have them. I wish they didn't exist. I've grown up with them, though, and they're a part of me. They've gotten worse since my mother remarried and I live with two perfectionists who obviously don't approve of anything about me.

There's still a part of me that worries I'm just what Vale needs *right now*. Someone who will care for him unconditionally. Someone close and convenient while he gets used to civilian life again. What happens when he suddenly looks around and decides he can have someone different? Someone of his stature and swoony good looks?

Of course, he did drive a hundred miles to stalk me.

There is something to be said for that.

But he's a protective man. A tracker by trade. Maybe following me was simply him remaining within his military comfort zone? Maybe—

"Lula." Vale's mouth slants over mine, his tongue invading my mouth for a long, thorough kiss. "You're getting tense on me. Let my seed work, princess. Don't fight it."

"Your seed?" My eyes fly open and everything he said to me in the heat of the moment comes rushing back to the fore. "Oh my God, you…you didn't use a condom!"

Vale raises an eyebrow. "We've established that." He cups and kneads my breast, wetting his lips. "Condom? You might as well forget that word even exists."

"But…"

Oh no. His need to establish roots, his need to carve himself out a safe place, runs more deeply than I thought. So deep he's willing to get me pregnant over it. What if he regrets tying himself to me, though? He's only been back one day.

"Vale," I breathe, scooting out from beneath him and sitting up, covering my breasts with one arm. "You…are you sure you don't want to explore your options?"

Blue eyes grow sharp. Even sharper than usual. "What does that mean?"

"I mean…you haven't even started living your new life as a discharged SEAL. You can't just…you shouldn't just make hasty decisions—"

"Lula…" His tone holds a stark warning. "I don't know what puts these doubts in your head, but I meant what I said. I found my woman and I'm not fucking around."

There's a clattering of hope in my chest, but I'm apprehensive about trusting it. To fling caution to the wind and believe this could be real. That this gorgeous hero wants me. *Only* me. The girl her mother calls a "chubby hippie" when she thinks no one can hear. "I just think you should take some time to make sure this is what you want. I don't want you to regret settling down so fast—"

"I've lived a lot of life in my thirty-two years, Lula." His voice is firm. "I've met all kinds of people. Women? Sure. I've been in a few short relationships that didn't have a fucking speck of the magic we make. I know this is right. I know what I want and need—and it's you. If I'm moving fast, it's only because I'm worried someone will steal you out from under me." He swallows. "Someone who doesn't have panic attacks in the shower."

I suck in a breath, caught off guard by his show of insecurity. I'm not the only one. "That doesn't make you *less*. That makes you more. It means you have a heart and a conscience and the capacity to feel."

"If you believe that, then *trust* what I feel."

My hands wring together in front of me, my heart begging for me to take a chance.

Vale comes closer and threads his fingers through my hair, tipping my head back and devouring me whole with a groaning kiss, his shaft hardening once again between us—

"Lula!"

I freeze at the sound of Santana's voice, followed by Jess's. "You better not have gotten eaten by a fucking bear, dude."

My eyes lock with Vale's.

There's a question in his. It's very clear.

He's letting me make the decision about what I want to do. Do we walk out of here together and own this thing between us? Or keep it hidden? More than anything, I want to step through the waterfall holding his hand, but once that cat is out of the bag, there's no putting it back in. He'll have no chance to think this over. To be sure about us. How can he make such life changing decisions when he doesn't even know what his new life will look like yet?

"Go back to your friends," he says gruffly, kissing me. Stroking my cheek with a knuckle. "I'll be watching you through the night. And we're going to talk when we get home. As soon as possible." He lifts my chin with the tip of his index finger. "Do I make myself clear?"

"Yes, Daddy," I breathe, as if it's the most natural response in the world.

Maybe it is.

I just don't know if it's the best thing for Vale.

His eyes darken with pleasure, nearly impossible to walk away from. But I do.

With my heart in my throat, I slide into the water beneath the falls and wade out into the sunlight to a round of cat calls and whistles. "Lula! Where are your clothes?"

"What were you doing in there?"

"Naked yoga," I breathe, flushing to my hairline and searching the ground for my clothes, heading in that direction. "It's totally a thing."

It takes every fiber of control not to glance back and search for Vale behind the waterfall as we return to camp. And every step of the way, I pray I made the right move.

CHAPTER SEVEN

Vale

MY HANDS TWIST on the steering wheel, my gaze locked in on the back of Lula's head. She's riding in the car ahead of mine, halfway home from camping. It's murder not having her in my passenger seat where I know she'll be safe. The girl driving my precious stepsister is more concerned with changing the radio stations than the road ahead. Every time she swerves, I swear my heart is going to jump out through my mouth.

For the time being, I have no choice but to keep a distance.

Lula's hesitance to be with me is my fault.

I knew. I fucking knew I shouldn't have revealed myself at the waterfall.

Revealed myself as her stalker.

But the sight of her tasty body in the sunlight was too much to resist. There was no stopping me. I had to possess. Had to claim what's mine.

And she will be mine.

There's no maybe about it.

I have some work to do first, though, and I've had the night to think about it. Hours of sitting in the darkness, guarding my girl. Replaying over and over again the way her pussy clenched around my dick, her eyes losing focus, her teeth snapping at my mouth. All those sweet curves welcoming me home, her thighs struggling to get wider.

Hearing the way she sobbed for Daddy.

I exhale shakily into the car's interior.

I've been trained to be patient. Sometimes it takes days, weeks or months for a target to appear. To step into my sites. But Lula isn't a target and this isn't war. She's a female. The most important one. And her feelings are what I have to aim for. She thinks I need time. That I'm making a hasty decision to be with her, when that's simply not the case.

Like I said, I've done and seen a lot in my lifetime. I know brightness like hers isn't just available everywhere, especially for a weary soldier like me. It's unique and perfect. Like walking through a sandstorm and finding shelter. During my service, I saw the worst of humanity. Enough to know when I've come across the best—and I'm holding on to her.

Come hell or high water.

But apparently she's going to need...courting. Some convincing.

Since I can't take her out on a date in a stolen vehicle, I ditch the car in the airport parking lot and rent a luxury sedan. My plan is to buy a permanent car at a dealership near Coronado when I'm getting settled on base. For now, a rental will have to suffice. My instinct is to find something black, but I think of

Lula's brightly colored energy, the lively pink and yellow fuzzy towels in the bathroom. Her aqua sandals on the shoe rack by the front door of the house. With that information, I go with a cerulean blue Jaguar and head toward the house.

When I walk into the kitchen, my father lowers his newspaper. "Well there you are, son. If I wasn't positive you can take care of yourself, I would have been worried."

Vanessa breezes into the kitchen with a clinking glass of iced tea in her hand. "I'm sure we can guess how a red-blooded man spent one of his first nights back on US soil…" She winks at me, stirring the drink with her index finger. "I'll forgive you for not letting me fix you up. Maybe it's better you went out and blew off a little steam first."

"Always with the innuendo, Vanessa," my father grouches, going back to the paper.

"You knew what you were getting into when we started dating," she laughs.

Lula walks into the room and my senses are turned up to full wattage. I have to shove my hands into my pockets so I won't reach for her, settle her butt somewhere, wedge myself between her thighs. *Jesus*, she looks edible. The camping trip has been showered away leaving behind tan lines that peek out from beneath the straps of her purple tank top. She's barefoot, wearing these tight yoga pants that make her backside look like a meal and I have to grind my jaw to keep from growling.

Her eyes go soft when they see me, but then awareness moves into them.

Heat.

Curiosity, too.

As if she's wondering whether or not my intentions have changed overnight. They haven't. They're *never* going to change. And I try to communicate that to her with my eyes. I must get at least some of my point across, because she crosses quickly to the fridge and stands in the cool opening, fanning her neck.

"How was camping?" Vanessa asks Lula, trading an eye roll with my father.

"Oh, um..." Lula's throat works, her gaze drifting to mine briefly. "Beautiful. Peaceful. A family of deer walked right through our campsite this morning."

"Wow," Vanessa says, absently, reading the newspaper over her husband's shoulder.

I wait for them to ask her more, but they don't.

They don't encourage her. Their mild interest isn't even convincing.

Yeah, I need to get her moved out of his toxic environment as soon as possible. I grew up in it. The pressure to conform, to be a certain way—like my father—is immense. Having offbeat interests, like Lula, has made her a target for their disdain at the worst of times, indifference at the best. There is no way in hell I'm going to let them dim the light shining inside of her.

Not happening.

"I was thinking we could do something together

tonight, Lula," I say into the quiet kitchen, an even heavier silence ensuing. She straightens from the fridge, a glass of orange juice in her hand, eyes wide on me. "Get to know each other better. Since we're family now."

"O-oh," she breathes. Then, comically, downs the entire glass of juice, because she obviously doesn't know what to say. It takes an effort not to laugh. "I would like—"

"Are you sure, Vale?" Vanessa gives a skeptical laugh. "I have a network of beauties on speed dial—"

"Vanessa, I don't know how many ways I can say that I'm not interested," I growl, holding my step-mother's startled attention for several beats, irritation making my fingers flex. "Do not bring it up again."

I'm up against enough skepticism from Lula. I don't need Vanessa making it any worse.

There is only one woman I'll ever want. If it was up to me, I would tell our parents everything right now. But I've pushed Lula enough in the last twenty-four hours. Now it's time to have a little patience while she gets used to the fact that I'm not going anywhere.

After a moment, Vanessa nods reluctantly, dropping heavily into one of the dining room chairs. My father watches me curiously, like he wants to say something but chooses to read the sports page instead. As for my stepsister, she bites her lip and leaves the room, subtly indicating I should follow after her. As if I'd do anything else.

We meet at the base of the staircase, her incense and orange juice scent making my mouth water, along with her plump tits. Hell, every inch of her makes me hot. How in God's name am I going to wait until tonight?

I shoot a glance toward the kitchen to make sure we're not being watched, then I lean down and kiss her mouth, sliding my tongue in to pet hers once, twice, my cock unfurling in my jeans, in dire need of Lula's pussy.

She pulls away with a scandalized expression, but she's breathing fast. "Vale," she says in a furious whisper, looking over her shoulder. "You can't just d-do that."

"I could if we told them you're mine. They will eventually have to get used to it."

Lula hedges. "I'm…I'm still not sure—"

"You're not sure I'm thinking straight. Or that I know what I want." I tip her chin up, trace her lower lip with my thumb. "Don't worry, I'm going to clear it right up for you, princess."

After a moment, she nods and relief settles in my gut.

"I didn't sleep last night, so I'm going up to grab some now."

I press my thumb into her mouth, groaning when she sucks on it reflexively, seeming to surprise even herself. Her eyelids turn heavy, her nipples pebbling against the front of her tank top. It's on the tip of my tongue to order her upstairs into my bed. I'd love to spend the whole day there, riding her in every position known to man, but I need patience. She's an emotional soul. And didn't she tell me she has to meditate on decisions? Rushing Lula could only hurt me in the long run and I refuse to take chances with someone so important.

"Be ready to leave at seven." Reluctantly, I slide my thumb back out of her gorgeous mouth, using the wetness to coat her lips, leaving them glossy. "Wear the skimpiest pair of panties you own. Enough skirt to keep other men from seeing what's between your legs—what's mine—but not enough I can't yank it up when I need to."

When I speak her to like this, commanding her gently, Lula gets the same expression on her face she had in the woods. When she took off her clothes and let the sunshine warm her bare skin. It's an expression of belonging, relief, anticipation. Being my little girl is right for her in the way it's right for me. In the way *she's* right for me.

Tonight I'm going to make sure she realizes it fully.

LULA WALKS DOWN the stairs that night and tension ripples in the air.

Our parents might not realize there is something going on between us, but they aren't entirely comfortable with us going out together, either. Maybe they sense the truth. Maybe they could feel my arousal all the way downstairs throughout the day. Sleep never hit me. Every time Lula's bed springs creaked on the other side of the bathroom. Every time she murmured into her phone or laughed or *breathed*, I had to restrain myself from charging into her room, pinning her down, getting the release only she can provide.

Not too much longer and I'll be alone with her again. *Finally.*

Next time I'm inside of her, I'll have her promise. She'll be confident in my intentions.

I'm dressed for a date in black jeans, boots and a button-down shirt, which throws our parents even more. But they're extra thrown when Lula descends the stairs in a plaid skirt, a low-cut black shirt tucked into it. Knee high black socks.

I'm erect in seconds.

My fierce sudden arousal makes it necessary for me to turn from the room and adjust myself, back teeth grinding. Next time Lula tries to imply she's not sexy, I'm going to throw her over my knee and paddle that delicious ass, so help me God.

"You look…" *Fuckable. Hot. Like a little girl who's horny for a second round of dick from her stepbrother.* "You look very nice, Lula."

"Thank you," she says, turning pink beneath her camping tan.

"Where are you going?" Vanessa inquires, her smile slightly brittle. "When will you be back? Lula is only eighteen, you know. She might legally be an adult, but she still has a curfew."

Lula giggles, but sobers when she realizes her mother is serious. "I do? Since when?"

"Since now." My stepmother waves a hand, as if conjuring an appropriate time. "Midnight sounds good. Please be home by midnight."

"She'll be with a goddamn SEAL, Vanessa," my father says with forced casualness. "No safer place to be, right?"

Is there a warning in his eyes?

It's hard to tell. I might be projecting because my feelings for Lula are so wild and untamed and possessive, it seems unrealistic that I'm keeping them hidden. I'd like to tell Vanessa that I'll keep my future wife out as long as I damn well please, but that could cause a scene, and right now? I just want to get Lula out the door.

Without a word, I gesture for my stepsister to precede me out of the house and down the front walkway. I watch wolfishly as her ass bounces in that schoolgirl-style pleated skirt. If no one was watching us right now, I'd wrap her hair in a fist and push her face down over my car, flipping up the rear of the skirt to inspect her panties. But we're definitely being watched. A glance over my shoulder confirms our parents are eyeballing us from the porch.

"This is your car?" She clasps both hands under her chin. "I love the color."

Pride moves in my belly. "Good. That's what I was hoping for."

I open the passenger side door for Lula, watching her thighs settle on the seat. Inhaling the scent of her. Itching to run my hands everywhere. Up her thighs to that round, generous ass. Down her tits to her soft belly. I'm not going to make it very long before the need to be inside of my stepsister—*fucking* her—overwhelms me.

Trying to even my breathing, I cross in front of the car and enter the driver's side, firing up the engine before I'm fully seated. Before I pull away from the curb, my possessiveness gets the better of me and I reach over, sliding my right hand between her thighs and cupping her lush little cunt, waving at our parents with my left hand. "They don't tell me when to bring you home. I decide that, don't I, princess?"

"Yes," she whispers, her head falling back against the seat. "You decide."

I hook a finger in the thin strap of her panties and rub her clit with the pad of my middle digit, slowly, once, twice, eliciting a gasp. "Wave at our parents."

She raises a hand and I press down on the gas, pulling into traffic.

I continue to stroke the little bud at the apex of her sex, making her hips writhe, until we reach a stoplight. Then I draw up the plaid material, adjusting the pretty blue material back into place over her pussy, giving it a final squeeze. "Going to bring this home dripping."

A rush of sound leaves her. "Where are you taking me? A…hotel?"

Pulling through the intersection, I glance over at her in surprise. "If all I wanted from you was sex, Lula, I'd have been in your bedroom all afternoon."

"I was kind of hoping…"—she fidgets with the hem of her skirt—"…you *would* visit."

I cock an eyebrow over her obvious nerves. "Why is it so hard for you to admit that?"

She searches for the right words. "I don't have a lot of experience flirting. I've always had this nightmare about guys…rejecting my interest, I guess?"

I'm torn between shock and jealousy over the fact that she's ever wanted to flirt with another male in the first place. "You must have grown up with a lot of idiots."

"Yeah…" She bites her lips and smiles a little. "Yeah, I think maybe you're right."

That's when I notice there's something different about Lula. I noticed it when she came down the stairs but was too horny to put my finger on the change. Now I know. It's confidence. She's wearing a short skirt, her eyes are bright, her smile coming easier. Those tanned shoulders are thrown back. Is it possible I broke through to her yesterday beneath the waterfall? Did her friends' encouragement help?

Is she starting to realize what a fucking catch she is?

God, I hope so.

With hope rising in my chest, I reach over and hold her hand, guiding us on to the highway. "If I remember correctly, there's a bar about half an hour up the coast. Live music." I bring her hand to my mouth, rubbing my lips over her knuckles. "I don't care who sees us together, but I figured you might want some privacy for now. There shouldn't be anyone who knows us there. Knows...how we're related."

Lula nods. "For now, I think that's best." Her nose wrinkles. "But won't people know who you are, no matter where we go?"

I jerk my head toward the console where I left a black baseball cap earlier. "Brought a hat. Plus, it's nice and dark inside this place. And that's a damn good thing, princess..." My gaze roams over her lavish set of tits, the blood in my body rushing south to my groin. "Because there isn't a hope in hell of keeping my hands off you."

CHAPTER EIGHT

Lula

VALE BRINGS ME to a bar called The Coyote.

I don't have a fake ID, but the bouncer takes one look at Vale and doesn't question him leading me inside. He was right about it being dark in here. Comfortably so. There are flickering hurricane candleholders on every table, lit in a pale yellow glow. A cover band plays at the back of the expansive space, the sound of a harmonica pleasing to the ear. On the left, there is a scattering of tables occupied by couples and groups of friends. To the right is a long bar and that's where Vale brings me, all the way to the corner where he positions me against the wall, blocking me in with his big body.

It takes me a moment to realize he's pinning every customer at the bar with a steely glare. "Vale." Laughing, I tug his elbow. "What are you doing?"

"Letting them know you're mine. That you're leaving with the same man you walked in with." Out of sight, he settles a hand on my bottom, shaping it roughly. And after a moment, his intense blue eyes find mine through the low lighting. "Never felt like this, Lula. I'm worried what I'll do if someone looks at you. *Mine.*"

I play with the middle button of his shirt, surprised how easily I'm flirting with Vale. I wasn't lying
when I told him I've rarely flirted in the past, but
now…now I'm not worried he'll be uncomfortable
with my intentions. He's made it clear he's attracted to
me. That he finds me desirable. And I'm starting to
feel that way. I never would have worn this outfit
before yesterday, but I love the way it makes me feel.
Feminine and sexy and a little naughty. As if being out
at a bar, illegally, with my stepbrother isn't more than
enough naughtiness for one night. "How about you
look only at me, Vale, then you won't know what
anyone else is doing?" I bite my lip and twist the
button of his shirt. "And it won't even matter."

His breath releases in a rocky rush. "Fuck, you
were tempting before, but now…Lula, you're
blossoming. You're going to bring me to my knees."

I can hear Santana and Jess in the back of my
mind, cheering me on. "Maybe you'll bring me to *my*
knees," I murmur, heat racing up my cheeks. Who am
I anymore?

"*Lula,*" he moans, dropping his forehead to mine.
"Don't do this to me. Don't hint that you might suck
my cock when I promised myself I'd give you a proper
date."

"Okay," I say, breathlessly, my confidence growing
at an exponential rate, excitement filling my tummy
with fizzy bubbles. "I guess I'll just think about it," I
say teasingly, dragging a finger down the thick slope of

his muscular chest, continuing downward, scratching my nails against his belly button. "How it'll taste. How deep I can take—"

His mouth cuts me off with a growl and I'm backed into the wall, his fingers burrowing into my hair, his tongue licking deeply, past my teeth, stroking, stroking, stroking. He curls a hand under my left knee and jerks up my legs, notching his hardness flush to my sex, rocking roughly, his hard exhale bathing my wet, swollen moth. I'm up on my tiptoes and he lifts me higher now, off the ground. Are we going to have sex in this dark bar? It certainly feels like it—and knowing I made this powerful man lose control is a heady feeling. Exhilarating.

"Can I, uh…" A man to my right clears his throat. "Get you two a drink?"

We break apart, breathing hard. Vale looks almost delirious, and for some reason, I cannot keep the smile off my face. *Look what I can do!* Unfortunately, my smile also seems to harden Vale's resolve. He plants a solid kiss on my forehead and throws a nod at the bartender. "I'll have a beer. Whatever pilsner is on tap. And she'll have…"

"A dirty martini, please," I say brightly.

When the bartender walks away to fix our drinks, Vale lunges at me, growling into my neck, and a laugh bursts out of me. "I'll give you a dirty martini."

He tickles my ribs and I squeal. "I wish you would."

"*Lula*. I'm hanging by a thread." Suddenly, he

picks up me up by the waist and drops me into a stool. I'm still reeling from the utter delight of being manhandled with such ease when my stepbrother hits me with a stern look. "Behave."

"For now?"

His lips twitch with mirth, and my God, he's so mind-bogglingly hot with that baseball cap pulled low on his forehead and dark blond hair sticking out at the sides, I have to sigh.

"For now," he agrees, kissing me softly. With promise.

A few minutes later, the bartender drops off our drinks. Vale stands between my thighs, his left hand resting on my hip, his back to the rest of the bar. He hands me my drink with a skeptical light in his eye. A second later, I found out why. I sip the mixture of vodka and pickle juice, immediately wanting to spit it out. Vale chuckles, taking back the martini and setting it on the bar. Then he tips his beer to my lips to get rid of the after taste.

"Is this your first time drinking?" he rumbles, right up against my ear.

"Besides the wine coolers that Santana steals from her mom's fridge? Yes." I wince. "I thought it sounded like something a cool adult of legal drinking age would order. But if this is what the cool kids drink, leave me out of it."

His grin makes my stomach flip. "I'll order you something different."

"No rush," I say, making him laugh, before a worry occurs to me. Leaning forward, I drop my voice to a whisper. "Hey Vale, could you get in trouble for bringing me here?"

He lets out a rush of breath. "Technically, yeah. I could." A beat of silence passes. "Wouldn't mind some trouble, though. Maybe everyone would stop..."

"Stop what?"

The muscles of his throat shift up and down. "Expecting so much of me. Putting me up on this pedestal, because of what I did. I never asked to be the face of an entire military branch and there's just no way anyone can live up to the image. I love being a soldier. A lot of that love came from being anonymous, though. Now I'm this symbol of...I don't know. Hope. And hope isn't a bad thing, but it can't come from a stranger."

"No, it can't. As a soldier, you want to make things right for the people. You want to do what the brass is asking of you, because you follow orders. But you're only one person out of billions. All you have is the light in yourself. You're allowed to guard it. You're allowed to take healthy steps to keep the light burning." I pick up his hand and thread our fingers together, using my thumb to rub slow circles into his palm. His pulse is tripping over itself in fast beats at the base of his wrist, so I lay my lips there and hum until it slows and Vale can take a deep breath. "And there's no pressure here. Not right now. Focus on that."

"God, Lula," he crowds closer between my legs,

whispering into my hair. "Look how good you are for me. No one can do what you do. You put me on solid ground."

"Eventually you'll learn to do this for yourself."

"Maybe. Maybe I'll learn to stop a panic attack before it starts, but knowing I have you on the other side is what's ultimately going to bring me through it. You *are* my light, Lula." His mouth traces over my temple, planting a kiss. "Let me be yours. Let me take you out of that house where you're not being appreciated and make you happy." He pulls me close, locking us together in a way that is indecent in public, his erection flush to my sex, my thighs hugging his hips, his hands creeping up the back of my skirt to massage my backside. "We'll have a family together. Our first child might be forming in your belly as we speak."

A fog bank of lust is beginning to roll in, obscuring my inhibitions. Blotting them out into mere smudges. And it has a lot to do with his tongue dragging up and down the side of my neck, his hips rocking me on the stool. Of course, I've considered the fact that I might be pregnant. It seems so unlikely. I'd never even had sex before yesterday. But I remember the feel of his hot seed flooding into me, that determination on his face, and I know it's more than possible. "What are people going to say, Vale? You're my stepbrother."

"All you have is the light in yourself. You're allowed to guard it. That's what you told me, Lula, and that's what I'm doing. I'm keeping you. Yesterday, I thought the most important thing in life was meeting expectations, but baby, all I want to do now is meet yours." His mouth finds mine and he French kisses me in a blatantly sexual way, his tongue provoking mine in an erotic dance. It feels scandalous to be kissing my stepbrother like this in plain view of the bar, our bodies simulating sex. My panties are sodden against the ridge in his jeans and he continues to hump me, the legs of the stool bumping on the wooden floor of the bar. Finally, he stops moving, both of us breathing like we just finished a marathon. "All this talk of light, princess…" he says choppily. "But right now, I need to give you some attention in the dark. Can't wait anymore."

With that, Vale throws some money on the bar, picks me up off the stool to settle me on my feet and hustles me toward the front of the bar, favoring his injured leg. The crowd has multiplied since we arrived and Vale keeps a protective arm around me, the ball cap pulled extra low over his eyes.

"Oh my God. Is that Vale Butler?" someone says as we pass.

My stepbrother's muscles tense against me. "That's him. That's the terrorist killer. Holy shit." Some murmurings go through the crowd. "Vale! Yo, Butler! Let us buy you a drink."

A hand claps him on the shoulder. "You're a hero, man."

Vale curses and slows us to a stop. "Lula…"

"I know. You can't just walk away and ignore them." I squeeze his hand and give him a smile. "And I know it bothers you, having to maintain this hero image in front of people who don't really understand what you've been through. But here's the thing. While you smile and be kind and let them take pictures, your thoughts and your feelings remain your own. They can't touch them. It's okay."

An intense expression transforms his face. "I'm going to marry you."

Before I can answer, he drapes a protective arm across my shoulders and turns to face his admirers. He waves like the humble solider he is, blinking against the sudden onslaught of cell phone flashes. "Evening, folks. I'll pass on that drink. I'm bringing my girl home for the night. But if anyone wants a picture...?"

I don't expect it when Vale keeps me glued to his side in every last one of them, his fingertips brushing up and down my arm. Occasionally, he leans over and kisses the crown of my head or my lips while everyone watches with growing interest. And with my heart in my throat, I realize the cat is most definitely out of the bag...and Vale ripped it wide open on purpose.

Maybe I should be nervous about the fallout to come.

Maybe I should be calling my mother to warn her.

I don't, though. I can't break the spell Vale is weaving over me, stealing my fears and worries with every glance, every whispered word of affection. He's making me believe this relationship between us is real and lasting.

It is.

My heart is pounding with that knowledge.

Deep down, I've known it since our eyes met for the first time. We're supposed to be together. A connection runs between us that can't be undone or subdued. I need him and he needs me. By the time he finishes taking pictures and signing autographs, he's touched and kissed me dozens of times, propelling my awareness to new heights. The knowledge that our relationship will probably be public by morning makes my core thrum with heavy heat.

Everyone will know he's been inside of me.

The act of claiming me publicly has turned on my stepbrother as well.

Even more than before.

We don't even make it to the car.

CHAPTER NINE

Vale

I HAD VISIONS of bringing my princess to a hotel. Laying her down in soft sheets and making love to her slowly, but that will have to wait for another night. I'm too goddamn horny. My dick is like a crowbar in my jeans, my loins in a fucking knot. Even walking the two blocks to my car is unacceptable. I need inside of her now. Need under that plaid skirt. Immediately.

As soon as those pictures start circulating on the internet, everyone is going to know I'm the man who has the privilege of riding Lula. The possessive animal inside of me loves that. Craves the title of Lula's man. The father of her children. Her husband. The one who shares her bed and keeps her tight pussy satisfied. Fuck yes. I can't wait.

My reputation is going to take a hit and I'm sure the Navy is going to come down on me like a ton of bricks, but they can bring it on. I know what I need to be happy now. To be normal. And it's this girl beside me, her hand curled trustingly in the front of my shirt.

Maybe I'm not quite earning that trust by dragging her around back of the Coyote, into the dark end of the parking lot, but these are desperate times—and she wants it, too. She wants this dirty hot fuck behind the bar, doesn't she? Yes. God yes. Our mouths are wet and desperate, tongues engaged in a sensual battle, her fingers fumbling with my belt.

I have to break free of the kiss to groan, the potency of having Lula undo my pants is such a stroke to my heightened senses. "Look how badly you want to get to that cock," I push through my teeth, tilting my hips up blatantly. "One fuck and you're a little fiend for it, aren't you? Aching for Daddy's ten inches."

She nods, biting her lip, finally getting my belt unbuckled. Going to work on my button and fly next—and I somehow forgot about her teasing me earlier. About giving me a blow job. But I remember pretty fucking quickly when Lula kneels on the asphalt, her gorgeous tits nearly spilling out of her top, my hard dick in her hand. Mouth glossy and ready. My balls twist up and I almost ejaculate all over her beautiful moonlit face.

"Oh *fuck.*" I fist the hair on the back of her head, guiding her closer to my lap. "I can't believe I'm letting you suck me off in a parking lot. I just need that mouth so bad."

"I want to give it to you so bad," she whispers, her tongue flicking my engorged head. Rendering me speechless, my lungs pressurized with the breath I'm holding. I let it out in a growling rush when she runs her tongue through my slit and takes me between her lips, half of my thickness sinking into the warm, wet cave of her mouth.

"Jesus Christ," I pant, my eyes rolling into the back of my head when she starts to bob that pretty head, fucking me with her mouth, the suction and grazing of her teeth straight out of heaven. "Paid real close attention to that lesson from your friends, didn't you? Goddamn. You were born to suck cock, little girl. That's it. Deeper. Deeper. That's my best baby girl."

Lula moans around me, scooting closer on her knees, as if I'm a water tap and she's dying of thirst. She cages my length in her fists, dragging them up and down along with her mouth, turning me inside out. It's the thorough, sloppy, enthusiastic suck job of every man's dreams.

"Going to fuck you so hard for this. Going to make you come like a horny back-alley girl," I say on a gravelly exhale, my upper lip starting to perspire, along with my chest. My forehead. The smooth, sexual treatment from my stepsister's mouth is making my clothes stick to my body, my balls humming with seed between my legs, aching to be empty. I could easily drain my spend into her perfect little mouth right now, but it has to be inside of her. In that hot, young cunt. We made a lot of progress tonight. She's starting to trust the promises I'm making her. But a soldier always has a back-up plan. If she hesitates to become my wife or gives me any more nonsense about taking time to think, to settle into my new civilian life, I'll damn well make sure she's pregnant. Unable to escape me.

Lula is mine.

I'll spend my life with her by fair means or foul.

Yeah, my release isn't going anywhere but straight to her womb. Problem is, the girl is enjoying the shit out of my cock. It's an incredible sight. One that makes me hotter than sin. The way her eyes are squeezed shut, the way she makes a savoring sound every time she sinks down on that fat johnson. Have to stop. I have to stop soon. But my fingers move of their own accord, wrapping themselves in her hair, pumping my dick into her suctioning mouth, precome firing from my tip and landing on the back of her throat, making her choke a little bit, a tear rolling down her cheek from the pressure of my growing length, the way I prod her gag reflex. And even those details seem to make her more eager, her hands jerking me harder, faster, saliva on her chin.

Jesus, she's perfect, perfect, perfect.

I'm on fire with lust, my climax beginning to peek over the horizon, an ominous tingle wrapping around the lower half of my spine. "Lula. Lula. You suck Daddy so good," I groan, rocking my hips. "But baby, baby, baby, you have to stop before I nut. *Christ.*"

Subtly, she shakes her head, taking me even deeper. Nearly collapsing my knees.

My nostrils flare, pleasure spearing me—and I can't stop myself from tunneling to the back of her throat, holding her face against my lap and grinding once, before using my grip in her hair to tug her off me. She coughs once, whimpers my name and tries to slide me between her lips again. God almighty. If I allow that, it's game over, so I yank my stepsister to her feet, capturing her incredible mouth with mine, distracting her with a kiss while I gather the material of her panties and rip them clean off.

I look her straight in the eye and shove two fingers up into her cunt, making her cry out in pleasure, her arousal dripping into my palm, sliding down my knuckles. "Fuck yes, there's my wet princess," I growl against her mouth. "Get up here on this dick."

Some of the haze clears in her eyes and she glances down between us. "You mean just…" She gestures between our bodies. "How?"

"How what?" I'm too worked up to discern what she's trying to ask me. I wrap a forearm around Lula's back and lift her up, shifting my hips, searching for friction. Her friction. The perfection I never knew existed until her. "Get those hot-ass thighs around me. *Now*, Lula."

Her eyes widen and they snap up, locking around me and I can't wait, I can't wait. I'm about to come from the warm pillowing of her legs perching my hips, those delicious breasts that swell with her every breath right in front of my face. No, I can't go another second, so I rocket my cock up inside of her and bounce my tight little girl up and down, the wet slaps of our sex loud in the parking lot. "Y-you're holding me up so easily…" she whimpers, her fingers curling into my shoulder.

"Of course I am, princess," I grit out, pumping, pumping, reveling in the incredible tightness of my future wife. "I'm a fucking SEAL."

Lula climaxes with a shaky sob, shocking the hell out of me. Making me roar into her neck with male pride. I'm not sure what I said to give her such a quick orgasm, but I'm grateful as hell. To feel that rippling contraction, the spasming of her spread thighs, the drip of her moisture onto my balls. The innocent face I fell in love with on sight is flushed and rosy, her eyes glazed over, her tits no longer contained inside her shirt, more than halfway out of her bra. They jiggle with every upward fuck of my hips, the sight of her big nipples pushing me to the breaking point.

"Say it. Say you'll *be* with me forever," I groan raggedly, kissing her, our mouths hot and urgent. "Say the words and I'll give you Daddy's milk."

"I want to be with you forever," she whispers, her eyes sparkling.

My heart goes wild in my chest, making me short of breath. Making my blood swim with pure joy. The tide is rising faster now that I've been given the ultimate gift. Now that she's admitted out loud that I'm her man. I've claimed my female. Mine. Mine. Mine.

I try to be gentle, but she's made me into an animal and I can't stop myself from slamming her up against the wall of the bar and going for broke, my dick hammering up into her dripping little pussy, her cries filling my ears.

"*Daddy*," she whines, clawing my shoulders, my back, her knees digging into my sides—and it's her enjoyment of my brutal fuck that gets me off. Knew it the second I saw her that she could take it. That she would love my lethal soldier's nature coming out to play, holding nothing back. And here's my proof. The fact that my violent thrusts push her into another orgasm at the same time as mine, that tight channel closing up around me like a vise, drawing out my seed like cannon fire.

"*Lula.*" I rail her against the wall, driving upward several more times, fast and hard, then I hold deep, shoving her knees open and pinning her with my hips. "Look at it. Watch my seed coming up." She does what I ask, moaning at the sight of my cock's base flexing, flexing, rippling with the emerging semen. "Going right where it belongs, isn't it, princess? Right into to that fertile fucking pussy. God yes. Right into the woman I love."

Lula gasps, her eyes flying to mine.

I didn't mean to make the confession like this, behind a bar while I'm in the throes of a climax, but it's the truth that's written on my soul, so I let her look into my eyes. Let her see how much I mean it. "I love you, Lula."

"I love you, too," she breathes unevenly, throwing her arms around my neck.

Did she really just say that?

Oh God. This is real. I'm home. I'm finally home.

Those four words out of her mouth set off another round of spurts and I have to grind her into the wall to set those final drops free, bucking and grunting until we are both fully sated and I'm holding my stepsister as close as possible, breathing her in, the love I have for her threatening to swallow me whole. Maybe it already has.

I've pushed our luck taking her behind the bar. The last thing I want is her to be pictured in a compromising position. I'll protect her at all costs for the rest of my life. The need to do that has my chest in a cage. So I fix her clothing and mine, taking her hand and walking her to the car. I'm barely able to take my eyes off her the whole ride home. As soon as we're upstairs in the house, I'm going to walk straight through that adjoining bathroom and take her again, slower this time. Going to eat that pussy like a man at his final meal.

My intentions show on my face, too. I assume so, since she can't stop blushing, making my cock even harder. Even more eager to get upstairs and fuck. We only have a matter of hours before those pictures of us together at the bar start circulating, but honestly, it's the last thing on my mind. I just want to forget about the outside world and lose myself in this girl every day for the rest of my life. I don't want to think about anything else.

Tomorrow morning will be soon enough to deal with fallout. We'll have to speak to our parents and that discussion isn't going to be easy, but I'll shield Lula. I'll protect her from unfounded criticism and outside forces, because that's my job now and I crave it.

My father is in the living room when we walk inside. He nods at us over the top of his book, his eyes lingering on our proximity. Maybe he already knows there's something serious between me and my stepsister. Maybe not. But I want another night of making promises to Lula before she has to face their ugliness.

Reluctantly, I kiss her soft mouth and leave her outside of her bedroom door, wanting so badly to walk through it with her, to have no secrets from anyone, let alone our parents. However, I console myself with the fact that she'll be back in my arms in a matter of minutes.

Where she belongs.

Unfortunately, those outside forces that could keep us apart are much closer than I imagine.

CHAPTER TEN

Lula

WHEN I WALK into my bedroom, I might as well be floating on air.

I lean back against the door and press my fingers to my freshly kissed lips, smiling with such abandon it actually hurts my cheeks. Tonight was a fairytale and an erotic sex dream all rolled into one...and I get to have this all of the time. I've finally accepted that I'm going to be with Vale because a relationship is what we both want. He wants me and I want him. Badly.

Any self-doubt has been thoroughly scrubbed from my brain by his promises, his lovemaking, the way he treats me. If he cares enough about me to face heat from our parents and the Navy, how can I doubt his intentions?

Now that I've stopped worrying about him regretting getting involved with me, my own feelings have blossomed. When I told Vale I loved him, I've never meant anything more in my life. Yes, I love the heroic SEAL. But I love the honest, passionate man under the surface even more—and I'm the only one who gets to have him.

Me. Lula Butler. Hippie, occasional nudist, high-pitched giggler.

Twirling toward my dresser, I mentally go through my wardrobe. Ooh, I have those purple silk panties. Maybe I should surprise him in nothing but those? Internally squealing, I click on my hanging lanterns.

Something moves behind me and I gasp, turning to find my mother sitting on the edge of my bed. There is an empty wineglass lying sideways on her lap and her phone is lit up beside her thigh. Enough to see the picture of me and Vale on the screen. It was taken tonight at the Coyote. In it, he's kissing me full on the mouth, my face cradled in his hands.

There's no mistaking the less than platonic nature of how we're touching.

I'm surprised when a calm settles over me. We expected our parents to find out. I'm almost relieved our relationship is out in the open, so we can deal with the fallout and move forward. "Mother—"

"How drunk did you have to get him to kiss you?" She finds this question infinitely funny, but the sound of her laugh is ugly, embedding under my skin like a splinter. "God, Lula. How desperate do you have to be to throw yourself at your own *step*brother?"

My skin smarts like I've been slapped. My *mother* is saying these things to me. I've always kind of accepted her criticism, but now I see so clearly how wrong it is for her to treat me so poorly. I deserve better. Remembering there is a man on the other side of the bathroom who wants me to be his wife, I raise my chin. "I'm sorry you have such a low opinion of me. Vale wasn't drunk when he kissed me and I didn't throw myself at him. That's now it happened at all."

"*It?* What is it? Certainly you don't believe you're in a relationship with him."

"Actually, I do," I say softly. "I am."

She snorts, followed by a long pause.

Her eyes turn calculating and my skin starts to feel clammy, my pulse picking up.

"Well, well, well. I would be impressed if I didn't find your actions incredibly selfish and short-sighted."

My heart starts to pound in my ears. "What do you mean…selfish?"

She comes to her feet slowly. "Right now, Vale is the perfect American hero, but by morning, he's going to be a pervert who sleeps with his barely legal stepsister. Do you have any idea how this is going to look? He'll be lucky if he gets to keep his job!"

By the time she finishes, my mouth is dry and I'm feeling slightly dizzy. Could my relationship with Vale really threaten his position on base in Coronado? "We…haven't gotten that far yet, but Vale isn't worried—"

"If that's what he told you, he lied." She shrugs a shoulder. "Then again, men lie all the time when they need a quick lay. Is that what you provided him, daughter? You must have, since he's been home all of two days. You made it really convenient and easy, didn't you?"

Of all the things she could have said, this one hits the lowest below the belt.

From Vale's very first touch, I worried my proximity made me attractive to him. The fact that I was close and…accessible. I shake my head, trying to fight off the doubts that are slowly climbing from the graves where I buried them. Coming for my newfound confidence with sharp, gleaming teeth. "No," I breathe, hating the moisture that pools in my eyes. "That's not true. We love each other. I don't need you to believe me. Our opinions are the only ones that matter."

"Oh yeah? You should see the snide comments on this photo," she drawls, holding up her phone. "Do you have any idea what people are saying? What they think when they see you two together? Such…" She eyes my body pointedly. "Opposites."

"I don't care."

That's what I say out loud, but my confidence is skating on thin ice.

"Well you can imagine," my mother snaps. "How long is he going to put up with that? He's in the public eye, Lula. You're forcing him to deal with laughter and criticism and taunts. You're forcing him to do that by being with him!"

"No, I'm not," I whisper, backing away from her until my back hits the dresser.

But is what she says true? If Vale was pictured with one of the society girls my mother wanted to introduce him to, wouldn't people be more satisfied with his choice? Wouldn't it make more sense and invite less negativity? And with one of those girls, he wouldn't face any potential discipline from the Navy, either. Is being with me bad for Vale? I don't want to hurt him in any way—I love him too much.

"You're obviously beginning to see reason," sneers my mother. "Good."

There's a knock on the door of the adjoining bathroom.

Quickly, my mother crosses my room toward the entrance. "Sometimes the hard thing is the right thing," she whispers—and then she's gone.

Sometimes the hard thing is the right thing.

Those words play over and over in my head as I unlock the bathroom door with partially numb fingers, my throat clogging up at the sight of Vale's grin. In sweatpants and bare feet, he's shirtless, his abundance of muscles highlighting our differences. He's carrying a plate of sandwiches that he must have put together in the kitchen while I spoke to my mother.

One look at my face and his smile crumbles.

"What the hell happened?"

I can't look him in the eye. "Nothing."

"Bullshit, Lula." He pushes into my room and sets down the plate on my dresser, turning in a quick circle to survey the room, his sharp movements reminding me he's a SEAL to the bone. When he spots the discarded wine glass on my bed, he holds it up, dread and irritation beginning to creep into his expression. "Your mother was here. What did she say to you?"

All I can do is shake my head.

There's a hole in my stomach and I can't stop

myself from speculating on those comments. What are people saying? I'm no longer in doubt that Vale loves my body. And *I* love my body. It jiggles in a lot of places. It also camps and meditates and goes to school and makes friends and lives life. I'm not defined by how I look. Nobody is.

But other people can be so cruel and thoughtless and *vocal* about things that strike them as different. Not typically done. Vale and I are one of those things. Do I really want to subject him to people who are constantly going to point out the difference in the ways we look? Or that I'm his stepsister? Fourteen years younger? The list goes on. He might be able to salvage his American hero image without me. Am I being selfish if I don't let him go?

I take a deep breath and look him in the eye. "Vale, maybe…maybe it is for the best if you take some time to think. In Coronado. Alone?"

His jaw looks like it's about to shatter, his muscles rigid.

Blue sparks snap in his eyes.

"I've had enough of this," he growls, storming toward me—

And right past me.

Out the door of my bedroom and down the stairs.

I run after him down the hallway and watch as he leaves the house, slamming the door behind him hard enough to rattle the hinges.

That's it then. I've finally pushed him away.

He's gone.

In a trancelike state, I pace back to the bedroom and crawl into my bed, pulling the covers tight around me. I lie very still for long moments before the crying starts. A huge, hiccupping sob wracks my body and I release the sound into the pillow, curling in on myself. I know I should try and slow down my breathing and center myself before this crying jag gets out of control, but I don't want to find peace or be calm. I want to rage at the unfairness of what's just happened.

Because it *is* unfair. We're two people who found love with each other. Isn't that supposed to be a beautiful thing? Aren't people supposed to celebrate that, not try and tear it down?

As an hour ticks by, I think back to the people in the bar.

How they didn't seem judgmental at all. How they were kind and welcoming.

I think of Santana and Jess, instinctively knowing they'll have my back no matter what.

And Vale…

God, I love him so much. He won't give a crap what anyone says. He never wanted the squeaky-clean image, because it's not real. He's a soldier who has had to do hard, traumatizing things. And me…I'm his lifeline. Didn't he tell me that?

You put me on solid ground.

Vale wants me because I'm good for him. He cares about me. Enough to guard me overnight while camping and defend me to our parents. I make him happy. And he doesn't want to be with me in *spite* of my body type. This is simply the body of the woman he fell for. In turn, he's fallen for every inch of me.

He loves me.

He loves me like crazy. When it comes down to it, the only person who is making me feel terrible is my mother. Am I going to let her continue to do that to me? She's been doing it my whole life. *She's* the wrong one. Not me—and not us.

I sit up in bed, wiping the tears out of my eyes.

I can't believe I let him leave. After telling Vale I wanted to be with him, I stumbled and possibly hurt him. That knowledge is painful and unacceptable. I have to go find him.

Wiping my damp cheeks with more purpose, I swing my legs off the side of the bed and speed walk out of the room, down the stairs. Vale is probably long gone, but I have to try and find him anyway. I have to tell him I'm sorry and demand he forgive me for losing faith.

I throw open the front door of the house—and there he is.

Striding up the walkway, still shirtless and barefoot in sweatpants. Only this time he's not carrying a plate of sandwiches, he's holding a small black box in his right fist. There's a determined expression on his face and he's such a welcome sight, he's so gorgeous that all I can do is sniff loudly and say, "I'm sorry."

"No," he rasps, coming to a stop in front of me. Towering over me by several inches, his eyes the most intense shade of blue. "I'm sorry, Lula. I should have stayed and reassured you. I shouldn't have stormed out like that. I just thought actions would carry more weight than words." His throat works with a heavy swallow. "You're mine. All mine. And I *need* you. I don't give a damn what the world thinks or what our parents say—we know this is right and good and perfect. We know this was meant to be." He kisses my lips softly and goes down on one knee, snapping open the ring box, bringing a choked, happy sound past my lips. "There was only a pawn shop open this time of night, but I'll get you a better one. I just need to get a ring on your finger. I need you to know I'm positive about us and I'll never need time to think or consider it. I *know.* My heart knows. I only need time with *you*—every second, every minute, every day. Will you please give that to me, Lula?"

"*Yes.*" Not a single beat passes between his question and my answer. I throw my arms around the man I love and we hold each other on the top step of the house, rocking together, the ring box still open between us. When he finally slides the diamond onto my finger and kisses me, I let the happiness blanket me and my heart. I let it cover the holes that were punched in my insides earlier and seal them up tight.

Never to be reopened.

EPILOGUE

Vale

Five Years Later

I'M NOT SUPPOSED to be here. But I can't stay away from my wife.

Across the street from where I'm parked, she is having an outdoor potluck with some of the other SEAL wives. She's in her element in the outdoors, lifting her beautiful face to the sunshine, laughing along with the other women. Christ, I can't take my eyes off her. When I met her, she was perfect to me. I had no idea she would get even better with time.

How is that possible?

How am I even more obsessed with her than I was in those first few days? How is my body holding it all together without imploding?

I manage to seem normal, going about my duties as a commander of the new recruits. Training them. Preparing them for combat. But I never stop counting the seconds until I'm back in her arms, where I feel like myself. Where I feel loved and happy. With my wife.

Our parents never accepted our relationship and we've come to terms with that. Truthfully, I think we're better off without their negativity in our lives. It took me a while to coax out of Lula the things her mother said to her that night in the bedroom. Forgiving Vanessa would have been impossible for me anyway. She almost lost me the light of my life.

After a few weeks of awkwardness when we moved to base, people here started to accept our relationship, along with the annoyed military brass. I'm not their golden child anymore, which is great, because I never wanted to be. Lula and I are stepsiblings who fell in love, and our new friends are not only used to it five years later, they would defend us to anyone. They adore my wife—rightly so—and she has many champions in her corner.

None bigger than me.

I'm Lula's number one fan. I marvel over her on a daily basis. While still in school and raising our first child, she started an outdoor meditation business that meets all over Coronado now. At the beach, in the parks, sometimes in our house. They do camping trips, too, of course. And I'm always there, quietly watching her from a distance. As I am now.

Over in the park, Lula takes a sip of lemonade and lies back in the grass, closing her eyes. Stretching her toes. Feeling the nature around her, I know. Communicating with it. Feeling totally uninhibited and comfortable in her perfect skin.

Normally I love to watch her meditate, but at the angle she's lying, I can see down the top of her shirt to those full titties and my dick stretches the fly of my pants. My groan of her name is loud in the quiet car, my mouth dry with need. There's always a need for her. It's incessant. I banged her on the kitchen table this morning before our son and daughter woke up, my hand over her mouth to muffle the screaming, but it wasn't enough. I need her pussy on a constant basis. I need it *now*.

She's been planning this potluck for the last couple of weeks, though, and I can't just interrupt the damn thing because I'm hard up for a Lula fix. Although it wouldn't be the first time I've gotten impatient and stolen my wife from her friends. They all laugh about it, saying they wish their husbands gave them the same level of attention. They think it's romantic—and in a lot of ways, I suppose it is. What they don't know is that sometimes I have to bite down on a leather belt when I'm fucking Lula so I don't sink my teeth into her precious skin, instead. They don't know I lie awake at night watching her, counting eyelashes and freckles and breaths. They don't know I track her phone and beat off to pictures of her in my office.

I'm out of control. I know that.

There's just no way of reining in this passion for her.

She's my princess.

The savior who brought me out of the darkness, helped me control the panic attacks and flashbacks. Lula urged me to meet with a therapist and I did—still do—employing a combination of psychology and meditation to feel steadier as a civilian. My therapist doesn't know about this, though. How I stalk my woman.

How I unzip my pants, as I'm doing now, and slowly slip a hand inside, fisting my erection. Licking my lips at the sight of Lula's tits. Teasing my cock up and down, imagining it's her giving little mouth. She loves sucking me off. Especially when I'm in uniform. And now I think of the last time it happened. When we came home from a gala last week and she got down on her knees in that red dress, her matching lipstick smearing on my cock with every hungry suck of her mouth. How she whined and whimpered at the taste of me.

I'm breathing hard in the car now, my hand beginning to move faster.

I'm still watching her, wishing I was on top of that sweet body. Riding it.

My actions pause when she rolls onto her belly in the grass and sends me a pinkie wave.

Loud breaths echo in my ears.

I've been caught.

Hell, maybe I wanted to be caught. I barely hid my location.

I hold my breath when Lula stands up and says something to the other women. Then she walks to the far end of the park where way less people are congregated. Where there is no sunshine and dirt instead of grass. Big, towering trees that provide shade.

And cover. For what she's obviously going to let me do.

Merciful princess.

With my heart rapping loudly in my chest, I drive out of my parking spot and leave the car much closer to where she's now disappeared. I follow her with my dick huge and heavy in my pants, a single-minded need to fuck, my limp doing nothing to slow me down. Up ahead, I catch a flash of her yellow shirt, tucked into a white skirt, and pick up the pace. I'm aroused and sweating and desperate by the time I reach Lula. Her eyes are sparkling with love, and Jesus, she's so beautiful it hurts, but there's no time for flirting or greetings. Nothing.

I simply spin her toward the closest tree and yank up that skirt. Ripping the daisy-covered panties to her knees and burying my dick as deep as it'll go. "*Fuck!*" I bellow into her neck, already rifling in and out of her tight wetness, my stomach smacking up against that round, juicy ass that drives me insane. "Hold on to the tree and tilt your hips for Daddy, baby. Come on. I'm hurting. I'm hurting so bad."

"It's all for you, Daddy," she whimpers. "Take it."

I'm a tenacious fiend for this woman and I let her know it, fucking her with unleashed possessiveness. Violent need. Obsession beyond belief. I tunnel my fingers into her hair and draw her head back, fucking her mouth while I take her body, raking my free hand down over her bouncing tits, lower to her pussy where I play with that pretty little clit. She's wet as hell, dripping all around my thrusting flesh, down her inner thighs. All over my fingers while I stroke her, listening to her staccato breathing so I know when she's ready to pop.

As is wont to happen, I'm suddenly overcome by a wave of affection for this woman. My best friend, my wife, the mother of my children. My stepsister. Love crowds into my throat and expands in my ribcage until I'm gasping for air.

"You look so fucking pretty lying in the grass," I choke out into her neck. "I just want to be in bed holding you all day. Doors locked so you can't get out. I want that all the time, princess. Is that bad? I want to be with you, inside you, looking at you all the time. *All the fucking time.*"

Her breath is starting to get choppy, her thighs trembling.

Close, close, close.

I crave her orgasm like a drug. More than my own.

"I love you looking at me. I love you inside of me." Our mouths mate over her shoulder, wet and nasty and raw. "I just love you so much," she finishes on a whisper.

And that's always what does me in.

Hearing she loves me releases the hold on my balls and I start to grunt, stooping forward and pumping, pumping, pumping into her pussy like a lion impregnating his lioness. Isn't that exactly what I'm doing? Isn't getting her pregnant always the goal? Yes. Yes. I want more babies with her. A big, happy house full of laughter forever.

Lula is my heaven.

"I love you, too," I ground out, stroking her clit as fast as I can so she climaxes with me—and thank God she does, back bowing, her channel tightening up and milking my length in that magical way of hers. I soak up the sounds of her cries, my own release ripping my stomach to shreds with its intensity. It's like this every time I fuck her. Like it's been years since the last time, when in reality it may have only been hours.

I'm insatiable for this woman. Always will be.

And as she turns in to my arms and sighs happily, looking up at me with unabashed love, I settle my mouth against her ear and let her know it.

THE END

Truck Driver

CHAPTER ONE

Tatum

IT'S A TUESDAY night and it's raining. I've only made $13.50 in tips since my shift started at four o'clock and the parking lot of the truck stop diner is empty, so I guess I'm not leaving here a millionaire tonight.

"Maybe tomorrow," I murmur, using my breath to fog up the window, etching a little heart into the condensation with my pinkie finger. Humming to myself, I lean my forehead against the cool center of the heart and let myself drift, green neon blurring where it reflects in the expanding puddles on the other side of the glass.

I close my eyes and think of the panel I'm working on, envisioning a pencil in my hand, the lead tip scratching along the surface of the paper, adding details to worlds I create in my own imagination. My sketchbook is in back of the diner, tucked into my messenger bag where it hangs on the coat hook. My boss doesn't like me working on my comics in the diner, but surely he'll make an exception when there isn't a single customer in sight.

A little buzz of excitement zaps my fingers and

they twitch, my butt already scooting toward the aisle of the booth where I've been daydreaming since sunset. I chew my lip in anticipation of where I'm going to take the scene next. Maybe I'll make myself a chocolate shake to *really* get those creative juices flowing—

Blinding lights sweeps across the interior of the diner.

I shield my eyes until it cuts off, then scoot back toward the window to peer out, already knowing it's going to be a rig. The diner is located on the edge of the interstate, so almost all of my customers are truck drivers, hauling goods from point A to B. Passing through. They're stopping for a cup of bottomless coffee to help stay awake. Maybe some conversation to remind them they're alive after fourteen hours on the road with no one to keep them company. My boss is always saying this is the perfect job for me, because I'm a chatterbox and truck drivers are the only ones who don't mind someone else's voice nattering on about everything from the latest celebrity gossip to comics.

The door of the rig slams in the parking lot and I reach for my apron, but my hand pauses in mid-air, my breath catching at the sight of the figure slowly cutting toward the entrance through the rain. It's a downpour and he's not even hurrying to get out of the wet. His slow stride is purposeful and measured, head down, rain soaking into his gray T-shirt and jeans. As he gets closer, I spy the rivulets of water snaking down his forearms like veins, the droplets hanging on the ends of his dark brown hair.

Why do I feel anchored to the leather seat?

I'm supposed to be up already, preparing a menu and a mug of coffee, a greeting on my tongue. Instead, my mouth is dry, stomach clenched while I wait for the bell to ding over the door. Rain pounds harder against the window and I swallow heavily, my pulse picking up when the lights flicker overhead, signaling the potential for a power outage. Maybe I'm naïve, but I've never been nervous to be alone in the diner before. Sure, the cook is in back watching television on his overturned bucket, but I almost never see his face. He cooks and goes home. Not really someone I would rely on for protection.

The bell rings over the door, seemingly louder than usual.

I jolt to attention in the seat and whisper, "Move," to myself, inching my butt toward the aisle, attempting to put my apron back on at the same time. My fingers are incapable of securing the tie behind my back, though, because he's inside now, stopped dead in his tracks just inside the door, and his eyes...they pierce me like a bullet.

My lord, he's big and thick.

Handsome in a weathered way. Like he started off pretty but saw some things along the way and lines were etched on his face, features turned a little weary. My fingers twitch, wishing to put those unique lines on paper. To replicate the sinew of his shoulder in my sketchbook.

That drenched shirt is stuck to muscles I don't typically see on my regulars. He must be a new driver. Hasn't gone soft from sitting for long hours and existing on road food yet. This man appears to be in his early thirties, too. Younger than my usual crowd. And about ten times as intense. His jaw pops while looking me over, his attention tracing down and over the generous curve of my hips, down to the tips of my sneakers. Back up to my dark, messy ponytail.

He makes a low groaning sound and drags long, blunt fingers through his wet hair, slicking it back from his face—and then he's picking toward me, slowly, leaving wet footprints in his wake. I have the strong urge to run and I don't know why. Maybe I have an undiscovered sixth sense like so many of the superheroes in my comics. Mine is knowing things are about to change. That's what this man's eyes are telling me. Nothing is ever going to be the same.

I snatch up a laminated menu from the closest table and hold it in front of me like a shield. He watches me do this with an amused flick of his brow, stopping when his boots are two feet from my sneakers. "Hello," he rasps in a voice like smoky midnight.

"Hello," I whisper, tilting my head back to maintain eye contact. This man is well above six foot three and I'm a full foot shorter. "Are you here to tell me I'm a long-lost descendant of a revered warrior and I have to come with you to fight in a battle between good and evil?"

Three ticks of the oversized neon wall clock go by. "No."

"Oh," I breathe, realizing I just said all of that out loud and my face is turning beet red as a result. "Just here for coffee, then?"

Blue-black eyes track a path down the center of my breasts. "Something like that."

I'm usually launching into my third topic by now, but this stranger has me completely tongue tied. I've never been so aware of the tight fit of my white blouse or the high hem of the black skirt it's tucked into. I'm still making a feeble attempt to tie my apron and with my hands behind my back, the blouse is stretching over my breasts more than usual—and he's watching. Jaw clenched, he's watching—

And then he moves so quickly, I gasp in alarm.

I'm being turned around by his strong, impatient hands. Before I know what's happening, he has taken hold of the apron strings, yanked them tight enough to jerk my hips back, and tied them soundly into a bow. It's such an intimate—and let's face it, inappropriate—gesture coming from a stranger that I don't know how to respond. I should probably call the police, but I can only stand there and breathe, goosebumps decorating every inch of my skin. The heat of his breath ghosts over the back of my neck and I whimper, my loins constricting for the first time in my life. I'm...aroused. By a man. For the first time in my twenty-one years.

My eyes fly wider than they already are.

I was beginning to think it would never happen.

But why is my body responding to a man I also seem to...fear?

Maybe I'm fearful *because* I'm turned on? Because the feeling is so new?

His breath turns hot on the side of my neck, his body heat permeating the thin layer of my blouse and heating my spine. My shoulders. If I lean to the right, my ear will touch his mouth. What is happening here? Am I still sitting in the booth daydreaming?

Or has the moment where I explore physical pleasure finally arrived?

"Where do you want me?" he scrapes out.

A shiver almost violently over the forward question. "I don't understand...d-do you mean l-like...which position? Because I don't know anything about this sort of thing." I drop my voice to a whisper. "About *sex*. If you told me I'm supposed to hang from the ceiling fan, I would probably believe you. Or are you asking me where do I want you, as in, a location? Like a bed or—where else *can* it be done beside a bed?"

"I'm asking you where I should sit, Tatum."

"Oh."

I'm on the verge of dying from embarrassment when alarm captures me in its grip, my temples pounding. "H-how do you know my name?"

Thunder shakes the windowpanes while I wait for his response. "You're wearing a name tag," he drawls finally, his lips making the barest yet potent contact with the side of my neck. Dragging up to the spot behind my ear. "Now show me where to sit, baby, before I decide to educate you on just how many locations there are to fuck besides a bed."

CHAPTER TWO

Hoss

GOD HELP ME, the picture didn't do her justice. I've never seen lusher, more dramatic curves on a female and my hands are desperate to grip them, trace them, memorize every mind-blowing inch. We're alone in this godforsaken truck stop and she's so horny she's tripping all over herself, flushed, picking up coffee mugs and setting them down with a rattle, as if she's completely forgotten how to do her job. Virgin. No doubt about it. My dick is hard as stone for the innocent waitress—

And I'm here to traffic her.

I'm here to drug and smuggle this beautiful creature across the border to Canada before she's taken to parts unknown. Sold off. Never to be seen or heard from again by her loved ones. Used to slake the lust of sick, depraved men for the rest of a severely shortened life.

At least, that's what I've been hired to do.

What I will do? Another story entirely.

Finally, she sets down a steaming mug of coffee in front of me and it's everything I can do not to knock it aside and reach across the counter, haul this gorgeous girl into my lap and pop her cherry right here on this rusty stool. I've been sick with hunger since my boss showed me Tatum's picture, a candid shot of her cleaning her clothes at a laundromat, leaned over a folding table, her brow furrowed in concentration while she drew in a sketchbook.

I'm not a man who has ever been absorbed by lust. Women are occasional entertainment. I don't remember their names, faces or anything they say to me. But hell if there isn't something about *this one*. A picture of her has kept my stones in a chokehold for a week. I've dreamed about her. Imagined her in stores and in passing vehicles. Everywhere. Actually seeing her in person, though? There's no comparison. If she touched me, I swear to God, I'd lose my grip on whatever control I have left. She's soft and blushing and sweet and everything I've always thought was a myth.

And if my boss gave this job to someone else, I might never have known about her.

I drain the scalding hot coffee to distract myself from that horrifying thought.

"Would you like something to eat…" She looks at me expectantly, a smile flirting with the corners of her incredible mouth, no idea that I'm the big bad wolf. "That was your opening to tell me your name," she quips, sliding a menu in my direction. "Seems fair, since you already know mine."

Is it unwise to tell her my name? Absolutely. Does my will to hear her say it in that musical voice override any concerns? *Christ yes.* "Hoss."

One of her brows ticks up. "Hoss?"

I grit my teeth to combat the rush of blood to my cock. "That's right," I growl.

Her throat works with a nervous swallow. "What would you like to eat, Hoss?"

You. Whole. Now.

I need to get a hold of myself or she's never going to trust me. I *need* her to trust me, so I can help her. That means being patient. Putting my burning need on hold until I've done what is necessary. "Do you have any pie?"

She nods toward a row of clear cases. "Cherry and apple."

A pained laugh almost escapes me. "Cherry."

The lights flicker overhead while Tatum is cutting me a slice of pie, adding whipped cream and bringing it back, setting it down in front of me. "It's a bad one tonight," she murmurs, adding a fork to my plate. "The roads must have been terrible."

I grunt in agreement, sinking the fork into the flaky crust and carving out a huge bite. Watching her pupils dilate as I carry it to my mouth and slide it in. "Let's just say I like it much better in here." I swipe my finger through the cream and lick it off, imagining I'm tonguing it out of her pussy while she gasps and squirms. "I thought it got lonely out on the road, but you're pretty isolated in here, too, without any customers."

She glances over her shoulder toward the back of

the diner. "I have my sketchbook to keep me company."

Sketchbook. The one she was drawing in at the laundromat. I've been dying to know what she was drawing. Been dying to know everything about her, really. All I know so far is her name, age and address. Plus the location where she's supposed to be delivered in a week's time—not that it matters a damn bit. "What do you sketch, Tatum?"

Her lashes sweep down to hide her eyes. Shyly. "I'm a comic book artist. Or…aspiring, anyway. I'm still saving up for art school." She gives the empty rows of booths a wry look. "Tonight isn't exactly going to put me over the top."

Art school. Comics. This girl has a whole future planned out, but my boss takes none of that into account, does he? She's just a number. A payday.

Not to me, though.

"Why comics?"

"I can't imagine wanting to do anything else," she whispers, growing animated, eyes sparkling. Gorgeous beyond words. "There are no rules. And so much of the worldbuilding can be done in photos. For someone like me who doesn't like a lot of description, but loves dialogue, it makes the story so much more compelling. My…"

I realize I've been holding my breath listening to her talk. "You what?"

"My favorite series is called *Comeback Girl.* The heroine is this underdog, all the odds are stacked against her, but she fights back every time." The sound of pouring rain fills the diner, but my heartbeat is louder. "Sometimes when I'm bored and there are no customers, I think of what Comeback Girl would do. And this place becomes my secret lair where I plot world domination. Or at least, plot to take down the bad guys."

I'm a bad guy, aren't I?

Technically, yes. I'm one of the worst out there.

That fact sticks in my throat and stops me from responding.

When her words have been hanging in the air too long, she grows visibly self-conscious. Twin spots of red appear on her cheeks and eyelashes fluttering, she looks away quickly. "I'll leave you to y-your pie," she stammers. "Just signal me if you want a refill on that coffee."

She turns to leave and my fork is already clattering down to the plate, my hand shooting across the counter to trap her wrist. "Stay," I rasp, unable to hide all of the desperation. "I'm sorry, I'm not...great at making conversation."

Sympathy makes her eyes go from brown to honey colored. "Most truck drivers aren't. I usually talk enough for the both of us."

"Why aren't you doing that with me?"

"I don't know. You're different."

"How?"

"Drivers usually remind me of my corny uncle Pete," she explains, slicking her lips with that pretty pink tongue. "You don't remind me of my uncle at all."

My cock pounds in my jeans. "Good."

"Why is it good?" she breathes—and I realize my grip on her wrist has tightened.

I'm guiding her through the opening of the counter and dragging her around to my side, despite my better judgment. All the way into the V of my thighs, her belly stopping an inch away from my bulge. Jesus, I want to yank her closer. All the way. But I rake my knuckles up and down the curves of her sides instead, listening to her soft, surprised expulsions of air. "It wouldn't be appropriate to stand like this with your uncle, Tatum."

Her gaze travels to my mouth and lingers. "If we're getting technical, I shouldn't be standing like this with a customer, either."

I flick a glance at the kitchen. "Is the cook going to rat you out?"

"No. I don't know." She's getting flustered. Her nipples are in hard little points and she knows I can see them, clear as day, and it's causing her to shift around in between my outstretched thighs. Making me want to trap her, hold her down like a fucking predator. "I-I've never done anything bad enough to test his loyalty," she adds.

"Maybe we should."

"How?" she asks.

"Tell him you're closing early and let him see us leaving together." I drag her an inch closer, my hands flexing on her full, perfect hips. "By morning you should know whether or not he squealed to your boss."

"So it would just be an experiment?" she says quietly. "I wouldn't actually go to your truck."

"Yes, you would. We have to make it believable." I lean in and inhale against the side of her neck, letting my chest press to her tits. "Once we're in my truck, of course, we're just going to play Monopoly, but he won't know that."

She giggles.

A full-on, girlish little giggle and God help me, my world tilts sideways.

I grow so stiff behind the zipper of my jeans that my vision triples and I start to sweat. Oh shit. Shit. That giggle. I need to hear it again. I'm aching for a replay, my balls drawing up tight to my undercarriage. What the hell is wrong with me?

"Do that again," I order thickly, my mouth open on the slope of her shoulder. "Laugh like that again, baby. Come on."

"I...can't do it on command. You have to give me something to laugh about."

My fingers move of their own accord, tickling her sides—and that giggle fills the air again and I don't know what comes over me. Teeth on edge, I crush her against my chest and continue to wriggle the fingers of my right hand into her side. She thrashes around, letting loose that sweet, innocent sound and I want more. *More.* My hand drags down over her plump, sexy ass to her bare thighs and I squeeze them in turn, making her squeal and dance around, her tits jiggling around between us.

"You like that, baby? You like when I tease and tickle you?"

"Stop!" she cries. "It's too much. I can't breathe!"

"You love it." I surge to my feet and drop her ass down on the nearest stool, leaning back a little so I can witness the effect of what I'm doing. The way her skin is turning rosy, her eyes glassy—*and that giggle.* It's like angels singing. Only it's not having a heavenly effect on me whatsoever. My dick is throbbing in time with her tinkling laugh. And this stool is not good enough. I need her *beneath* me wiggling around like this. I'm fucking panting for it. My cock is swollen and my breathing is ragged, my hunger becoming rawer by the second. I don't know what the hell is wrong with me, but I'm too revved up to care. I want her naked and tittering beneath me, all flushed and breathless, calling me...

Calling me...no.

Am I sick in the head and never realized it?

Or is it Tatum alone making me need something I never could have imagined?

I don't have a chance to answer that question, because a horn beeps twice in the parking lot and Tatum gasps, pulling out of my grip and off the stool. She stumbles a little, trying to catch her breath, and all I can do is sit there and reel at what almost happened. I almost blew this whole operation.

She straightens her skirt and tucks loose hair into

her ponytail, her cheeks on fire when she looks over at me. But then, oh hell, she gives me a wobbly smile and my heart slingshots up into my throat. In that moment, I remember why I was sent here. To traffic this sweet girl so some faceless monsters could make a profit from her pain. I won't be worthy of her until I've made her safe. I won't deserve her until the threat has been eliminated. The need to commit violence against anyone who would think to harm her is teeming in my chest. Multiplying.

I will begin tonight.

"Tatum," I bark, before she can greet the incoming customer.

She blinks at me. "Yes?"

"You will be here tomorrow night."

It's not a question, but she answers anyway. "Yes. My shift starts at four."

I have a week before she is expected to arrive in Canada. I have time. That's how I reassure myself on the way out the door of the truck stop diner, everything inside of me screaming to go back in, collect the girl and lose myself in her.

Soon.

CHAPTER THREE

Tatum

A NOTHER QUIET NIGHT.
Not totally dead, at least. There are two customers seated at the counter eating burgers and discussing truck routes. Near the window, there is a lovestruck teenage couple that I'm pretty sure are runaways. They paid me in quarters and their feet are resting on duffel bags beneath the table.

Everyone has paid their check, so I'm leaning on the counter, pencil in hand, working on my latest panel, which is basically just *Comeback Girl* fan fiction. In this scene, she is charming the devastatingly sexy truck driver, totally robbing him of his common sense with a bat of her eyelashes. She's pretending not to know he's evil and, of course, he has underestimated the underdog at his own peril.

This scene is nothing like what happened last night. Hoss gave me no indication that he's evil. As far as I know, there are no villains in history that tickle their victims to death. Maybe he was simply a gorgeous figment of my imagination and I lost my chance to see him again by giggling like a deranged toddler. *Of course* he couldn't get out of here fast enough.

With a sigh, I flip my pencil over and erase a way-ward strand of Comeback Girl's hair. I put lead to paper again a moment later with the intention of fixing my error, but the tip of my pencil breaks off. "Shoot," I mutter, ducking down to look beneath the counter for a new one.

What I see instead has my jaw dropping.

Sitting amidst the waitress supplies is a glossy comic book covered in plastic.

Holding my breath, I pick it up and make a short, punctuated sound that halts the conversation between the truck drivers. "This...this is the first issue of *Comeback Girl*. This is literally number one. *One!*" I can't breathe. All I can do is stare down at the item in my hands, afraid to damage it. "Where did this come from?"

And how long has it been sitting here?

There are tears in my eyes. I hold the comic to my chest as carefully as possible, hugging it like an old friend. I'm probably dreaming, but this is the best one I've ever had. Almost as amazing as the truck driver dream from last night, which I'm positive now must have been my overactive imagination trying to entertain itself. Only...

I told Hoss about my *Comeback Girl* obsession, didn't I?

Does that mean this number one issue is an extension of the dream?

Or does that mean last night was real?

With a frown, I turn toward the kitchen, planning to put the comic safely in my purse where it won't get damaged. *Comeback Girl* isn't a popular comic and this won't be worth a fortune or anything, but to me, it's pure gold.

As I start to turn, a new figure appears out of no-where at the end of the counter and I jolt back, nearly dropping the glossy magazine in my hands. Hoss.

Hoss is back. Sitting at the end of the counter.

He's here.

Chocolate-brown hair in disarray. A black eye. Cut lip. Lounged back casually.

His expression is anything but casual, though. His eyes are twin blue beams that could burn a hole right through a superhero's body armor. That jaw is bunched, his right hand in a fist on the counter. He is making the other customers uncomfortable, obviously, because they throw a tip on the counter and skedaddle toward the exit without so much as a thank you in my direction.

A lot like last night when I was in the presence of the trucker, my belly starts to feel funny, flexing in odd places that make me uncomfortable and curious at the same time. My shirt goes from professional to indecent in two seconds flat, my bra too flimsy to hide the way my nipples harden with awareness. I suddenly have the urge to play with my hair. I can feel his big fingers in my side last night, searching out spots that made my womanhood clench, made me strain to keep from peeing my panties.

I assumed my loud laughter turned him off.

But he's back. Does that mean he liked it?

Liked...tickling me? Liked touching me, period?

"You don't have that one," he says, voice gravelly. "Do you?"

Disbelief steals over me. Even though I had a suspicion Hoss left me the comic, I can't quite wrap my head around the gesture. What it means. "You...this was you?"

His fingers drum once on the counter. Slowly. One fingertip at a time, one by one. "It had better only be me leaving you presents, Tatum."

Oh. Oh my.

Is he my boyfriend now?

Am I too dense or inexperienced to know what's going on here?

"You are. Mostly. Someone brought me a little Route 66 sign once with my name on it. You know how they have those turnstiles in gift shops with a whole bunch of names on key chains or refrigerator magnets? They never have a Tatum, so that was a nice gift to receive. Just knowing it's out there somewhere on a turnstile for other little Tatums to find. You know?" My heart is walloping in my chest as I go toward him. "This is the best gift I've ever, ever received, though. Where did you find it?" I study the damage on his chiseled face. "And did you have to beat somebody up for it?"

"No." He touches a tongue to his split lip. "This was a separate job."

Swallowing, I glance toward the parking lot. "Did you have an accident with your truck?"

"No."

Alarm bells are beginning to clang in the back of my head. "Do you have a second job? Something besides driving a rig?"

He stares at me for long, silent moments before inclining his head slightly. "Yes, Tatum. I do."

The front door of the diner opens and closes. The teen couple is gone.

Now it's just me and Hoss in the diner, no sound except for the oldies playing. The ticking of the giant neon clock. The rush of the interstate in the distance. And my pulse. I can hear that pounding like a fist on a door. "This second job involves you getting into fights?" His jaw ticks in response. "Should I be...nervous?"

At this, he shakes his head without hesitation. Slowly. "Everyone else should be fucking nervous, baby. Not you."

"I thought my manic giggling freaked you out."

He huffs an incredulous laugh. "You have no idea how wrong you are." He leans in, forearms flexing on the counter. "Give me the chance to prove it. Come to my truck."

A tremor runs through my inner thighs, turning my juncture hot and confusingly damp, making it necessary to squeeze my legs together. "But I'm working."

"The way you make me ache, Tatum..." He shifts

in his seat, something hot and desperate blanketing his features. "It doesn't give a shit about the rules."

"I make you ache," I repeat in a whisper.

All other sounds around me fade out, except for his voice. "You make me do a lot of things."

"Like what?"

"Come over here and I'll tell you."

My feet are trapped in quicksand. I can't move. Do I want to circle the counter and experience this man's incredible hands on me once more? Yes. More than I want this comic book in my hands. More than I want anything. But there is a voice in the back of my mind warning me that I'm about to get a rude awakening. Warning me that there is more to this man than meets the eye. "I should probably stay over here," I murmur, wetting my lips.

A dangerous light comes on in his eyes.

He crooks a finger at me. "Come here, Tatum."

"Uh…"

"I can come back there, if you like."

"Customers aren't allowed back here."

"Like I said, there are no rules when I'm aching like this."

"Oh."

My head is growing more muddled by the moment in the presence of his gruff intensity, but I'm thinking clearly enough to remember that if my boss comes in and there is a customer behind the counter, I will get fired. "No, I'll come to you," I eek out, setting down the comic carefully and brushing the wrinkles from my skirt.

Slowly, I start to make my to the opening in the counter—but I only make it three steps when Hoss lunges to his feet with a growl and strides there faster. "Can't wait that long."

I stop dead in my tracks and watch the human equivalent of a bull bearing down on me. I tilt my head back at his approach, stumbling back until my butt hits the metal refrigerated cabinets—and then he's pressing me against it. Hard, with his hips. He's gripping the sides of my skirt and yanking me up on my toes, his hips pinning me to the metal barrier. "Quit my job and made a lot of dangerous enemies to get back to this pussy, Tatum," he rasps into my hair. "To get back to your giggle. Your beautiful face. Your soft skin. Don't tease me."

I can barely speak around the heart in my throat. "I'm not teasing," I whimper.

"You tease me just by standing there. Crossing your legs and squeezing, like maybe you think I don't notice, baby? I can see every one of those little goosebumps around your nipples. I can feel you wiggling around beneath me, laughing and squealing." He fists my hair and draws my head back, baring his teeth against my lips. "God, you're so deep in my head already and digging deeper, deeper, by the fucking second. So don't tease me. *Don't do it.* When I ask you to come here, please understand I'm on the verge of dying if I don't touch you."

My skin is made of molten lava, knees weakening.

"I-I didn't realize…"

"You didn't realize I'm a lunatic? Neither did I. Not until I saw your picture. Now you're day and night. You're my *day*. You're my *night*."

"Picture?" In my mind, pages are flipping. We've gotten to the twist. I had an intuition in my stomach that I wasn't seeing the full picture and now…now I've stumbled upon a clue, haven't I? Comeback Girl would be slowly removing the hidden dagger from her bot. "What picture, Hoss?"

Clearly, he didn't mean to let that slip. His nostrils flare and he slams his fist down on the counter behind me, rattling my nerves. "Goddammit, Tatum."

I try to push away, but he hauls me even closer, bringing our mouths an inch apart. My toes are barely scraping the tile ground. "You are going to come out to my truck and listen to me. Calmly."

"Like hell I am."

"You are in no danger from me." He tilts his hips, groans, then rams my hips up against the waist-level refrigerators. A hard protrusion is pressed up against the seam of my panties, and despite my well-founded fears, I can't help wanting to rub my femininity all over it. "I don't want to harm you," he growls. "I want to *worship* you."

"Maybe you say that to all your victims."

"Victims? *Jesus Christ*."

The next thing I know, I'm being thrown over his shoulder and he's stomping through the diner, my comic book dangling from his free hand. I'm so stunned that it doesn't occur to me to scream until we've almost reached the door. I twist around, frantically looking toward the kitchen, but the cook isn't there. He's probably out back, having a smoke. But I scream anyway. I scream as loud as possible before the glass door closes behind us, the tinkling of the bell fading into the night.

I need to fight. I need to get away.

He saw a picture of me. Where?

Has he simply been trying to charm me out to his truck?

Why would he do that when he's strong enough to carry me there against my will?

"Let me go."

"Never."

A truck door opens and I'm being drawn off his shoulder, lifted, crowded through an opening by his big body. Frantically, I look around at the tiny room. It's located behind the front seat of the rig and it's only big enough to hold a twin-sized mattress, the bedding messy. A small refrigerator. A desk lamp in the corner. "Oh God, how many people have been killed in here? Some luminol would light this place up like a Rorschach test, wouldn't it?"

"Enough," he says through his teeth. "No one has been killed in here."

I lunge for the lamp and swing it at his head. "Save it for the judge!"

He catches the neck of the lamp in mid-air and smashes it against the wall, the bulb shattering onto the floor, leaving us in the barest bit of light coming in from the front seat. For long moments, we stare at each other, breathing hard. I'm shocked to find out I'm still severely attracted to this man, even though he's about to make me a future cold case. And that attraction only amplifies when he takes a step in my direction and slowly strips off his shirt.

Oh lord. He's like a sculpture. A sculpted work of art that has been graffitied on.

"Lay down, Tatum."

CHAPTER FOUR

Hoss

CHRIST, SHE HAS so much spirit.

So much life inside of her, it makes me feel alive, too.

I almost wanted her to succeed in clocking me with the lamp, just so she could be proud of herself. I'm fuck-starved and starry-eyed for this girl—and thanks to my slip-up, she obviously thinks I'm a murderer or something equally terrifying. Yet when I toss aside my shirt, she blinks several times and starts to breathe faster, because no matter what incorrect assumptions she's made about me, she's still horny as hell and I'm going to have to use that. I have no choice. If I don't distract her, if I don't use every weapon at my disposal, she's not going to let me keep her safe. And her safety is paramount.

If something happened to her, this world would never recover from my rampage.

"Lay down, Tatum."

"Did you get those tattoos in prison?" she blurts.

I point at the mattress. "Down."

She shakes her head.

I move like a shot, catching her around the waist

and wrestling her down onto the mattress, careful not to hurt her. She tries to knee me in the junk, but I get her pinned down roughly beneath me, wrists trapped above her head. "Now, you're going to listen."

"You can't make me. My ears are closed."

"My cock is hard."

"What?"

"So you *are* listening."

"You villains and your sneaky tricks."

"I am not a villain." I bring my forehead down on hers and brush my lips side to side over her softer ones, memorizing the way her thighs turn pliant around my hips, almost against her will. "I work for a man who *is* a villain, though, Tatum. All right? I got in deep with him growing up. I had no family, no education. He gave me a job driving a rig, smuggling medical supplies across the Canadian border, selling them at more affordable prices in the States. I lost both of my parents to illnesses when I was real young and…listen, it might be illegal, but it's a cause I believe in."

She's not breathing, just searching my eyes. At the very least, I have her attention.

Thank God.

"But this man I work for…his operation has been changing over the last few years. He started moving stolen merchandise, possibly weapons. He never asked me to do any of that. Maybe he knew I wouldn't. I don't know. But last week…" The rage starts to boil up inside of me. "Last week, I overheard a meeting between my boss and a man I didn't recognize. They were talking about trafficking women. I was going to call the FBI, Tatum, but then I saw your picture. I saw it on the screen of my boss's laptop and I knew I couldn't leave it to chance. The FBI could take months to get evidence and arrange a sting, but I don't have to deal with the red tape. So I convinced my boss to cut me in. He thinks I'm bringing you across the border."

She starts to tremble. "Are you?"

"No, baby. God no." I lean down and kiss her, initially as reassurance, but her taste is like a warm wave rushing through my head, my chest—and I can't stop. I groan and press her mouth wide, sweeping in with my tongue and moving it in and out, in and out, deeper each time, showing her what it's going to be like to fuck. Her taste is a mixture of cherry cola and innocence, turning my dick into a pulsing rod. "Tatum, I'm not waiting for law enforcement to stop this man. His plans have advanced too far and he's too smart. Maybe if he hadn't targeted you, I would let the FBI handle it. But he made a very big mistake, threatening what's mine. Didn't he? He's *not* getting away with it." I slant my mouth over hers and lick the whimper from her tongue. "Going to kill for you. Going to burn the whole operation the fuck down. It's the only way I'll ever sleep at night. I need to know they'll never come for you, Tatum. That they'll never even think about you again."

When we break for air, she scans my face with a mixture of wariness and concern. "How did you get the black eye?"

"Last night, I drove down to Indiana for the comic. I found a man selling it online." I let go of her right wrist and reach down, slowly gathering her skirt higher and higher on her thighs. "I also arranged a meeting with another driver. One of the others who has been hired to kidnap the women on the list." Memories of bones breaking and a mouth gasping for a final breath float through my mind. "He won't be completing the job, let's just leave it at that."

"Did you kill him?"

"Don't ask me questions like that, Tatum. Not unless you want the answer."

Her heart is fluttering beneath me. "I can feel you lifting up my skirt," she whispers. "You villains and your sneaky tricks."

"I'm only a villain to anyone who fucks with you." I drop my mouth to her neck and lick a path from shoulder to ear, sinking my teeth into her sensitive skin. "I saw the picture and you became mine. Then I met you in real life and found out what the word *obsession* means." Looking her in the eye, I roll my hips, grinding my cock against her little white panties, rejoicing in her stutter of breath. The way she's beginning to pant like she's excited despite her nerves. "I'm a good decade older than you. I've done bad things. Every night, when you laid your head on your pillow and started to dream, I was out committing crimes." I hook a finger in the waistband of her underwear and start to draw them down her thighs.

"I'm violent. I'm cynical. I'm mean. But you will be my fucking princess. You will be my…"

"What?" she whispers.

I leave her panties mid-thigh and stroke my finger-tips up to her pussy, slipping my middle one up and down between her wet folds. "God help me, you'll be my little girl. The only one I've ever wanted. The last one I'll ever need."

Her expression verges on confusion, but the gush of moisture onto my fingers tells me she likes what I'm saying, even if she doesn't fully understand. Yet. "I'm not a little girl, though," she whispers, her eyelids struggling to stay up, thighs growing restless.

"And I'm not a Daddy. But I think you want me to be yours." Securing our mouths together, I slip my pinkie finger into her tight little hole, drawing it in and out. "I think you want to be tickled and fucked by Daddy in the back of his truck." She clamps around my pinkie so hard, I couldn't tug it out if I tried. "Don't bother answering. Your pussy just did it for you."

I've never been like this. Burning alive for anything or anyone.

My back and chest are prickling with hot sweat, my nuts are throbbing with the weight of my semen. I can smell the sweet flesh between her thighs and possessiveness rattles the inside of my skull. I've got her naked from the waist down, but I need her nude. Immediately. Taking hold of the sides of her white blouse, I rip it down the center. "I want you naked.

The way you came into this world. Because you're about to enter a whole new one, Tatum. Our world. We do what makes us hot and we don't give a fuck about right and wrong. Answer me how you should. How it feels good."

Her lashes flutter down, briefly hiding her eyes. "Yes, Daddy."

Oh my God.

I spoke of her being reborn, but with that single word, I've been renewed, as well. My life has a new purpose and she's on a mattress in the back of my truck, silver in the moonlight, her trust in me expanding by the moment. Because her instincts tell her it's right.

Triumphant, I dive down and close my teeth around the front snap of her bra, attacking the final barrier like a rabid animal, tearing side to side until the clasp gives way and her tits come bouncing out, big and supple and creamy. *Mine.* "God*damn*, you're beautiful. You're my princess, head to toe." I drag my mouth down the valley of her breasts, licking side to side, up and over her nipples until she's squirming, gasping, then down, down toward that place between her legs where we both need me to be. "Yeah, head to toe, you're a princess. But tits to pussy, Tatum, you're going to be my tormenter, aren't you? You're going to make me crazy with this soft, sexy body. I've already ridden it a thousand times in my head and I'm about to have it for real. *Finally.* Right after I wet up your tight, little fuck pocket."

Wedging my cock good and tight to her heat, I reach down and tickle her ribs.

That sweet giggle bathes my ear and I groan uncontrollably. I feel a click in my stomach, a rush down lower. My whole life, this is what I've needed. This girl to laugh and wiggle around beneath me. Perhaps it's perverted, but I'll never be able to live without it again. When I find the backs of her knees and tease them with my index fingers, that's when she really lets loose, bucking and filling the truck cab with girlish squeals that ruin me and make me a god at the same time. "Yeah, you like that don't you?"

More laughter. "I...I don't know!"

"Maybe we should try tickling you with my mouth, baby," I mutter thickly on my way down her body. She's shoving at my shoulders because she doesn't understand what's coming. Or maybe she's self-conscious, because she's never had a man give her oral—and no other man ever fucking will. But despite her half-hearted protests, I press my mouth against her cleft and wiggle my tongue between her folds, releasing some trapped moisture and letting it coat my tongue. Getting my chin and lips as wet as possible, lubricated for her pleasure, and I use everything I've got, licking and nibbling and raking my mouth up and down her pulsing, swelling clit, savoring her shocked intakes of breath, the way her thighs open and close, as if she doesn't know what to do in the face of such an overwhelming sensations. But finally, she gives into it and lets me dominate that pretty nub, groaning and stroking it with the tip of my tongue until her body starts to tremble and she's saying words that don't make sense.

Time to claim her.

Time to *fuck*.

My throat is choked with emotion as I give her perfect pussy a final lick and reach down to unzip my jeans, letting out my rigid dick. "It's our first time," I whisper against her gasping mouth, jacking my cock in my hand. "I'm making you mine, baby. This is the beginning of our lives together. You will never, ever get away from me as long as you live." I bring my shaft to her opening and drag it side to side over that sweet, wet hole, teasing it into accepting me. She tries to look down at what I'm holding, but I nudge her head back with my forehead, not allowing her to see, knowing my size will only scare her. I can't afford another delay when I'm this primed. This desperate to make her mine. "There's going to be a little pressure, baby, but I promise you this." I sink in the first third of my cock and watch her eyes flare with a mixture of panic and excitement. "I promise that after you bleed on it, you're going to come on it, too. Do you believe what I'm telling you?"

Only a second ticks by before she nods. "Yes."

"Good girl," I praise, giving her a long, winding kiss. "You want my cock."

"Yes," she sobs, gripping my shoulders.

"Best girl. Best girl," I mutter into her neck, rocking my hips forward, filling her, almost losing my seed over the first slap of my balls against her big, beautiful ass. Then, oh fuck me, I can't process anything but how tight and tiny she is, her hot, sodden pussy wrapped around my inches and squeezing the life out of them. Her breath saws in and out against my ear, our heartbeats rapping in perfect sync. I'm home. I've found heaven, right here. She's the end game I didn't know my whole life was leading to. "Open your legs," I grit out. "Show me trust."

Slowly, the muscles of her inner thighs lose tension and they fall sideways onto the mattress, the release of nerves turning her wetter. More pliant. But she's still whimpering, obviously struggling to get used to me being inside of her.

"Listen to me, Tatum," I whisper into her neck, reaching up to fist her hair, my hips dying to buck. To nail her into the mattress. Patience, though. I have to have patience with my future wife. "This is the first and last time I'll ever hurt you."

Those words calm her down and she looks into my eyes, nodding, shifting her hips—

She gasps. "*Ohh.*"

"What?"

"I th-think it's better now." Her death grip on my shoulders eases. "I think I like it."

"Oh, you're going to like it, little girl," I growl, using my grip in her hair to tug her head sideways, exposing her neck for a long lick. A bite and a rough suck. "You're going to fucking love it. Just tell me when you're ready for Daddy to start pumping."

"There's m-more?"

"There's so much more."

"Show me."

The leash is off. My hands leave her hair and slide beneath her ass, holding it in two firm hands—and I hit her with six quick drives. Just enough to make her scream. Then I tilt my hips to bring the trunk of my cock up against her slippery clit and I grind on it gently, catching her breath, making her gorgeous eyes roll back in her head. And I stay right there, riding that pretty pink source of pleasure, watching color climb her face, feeling her nails sink into my back.

"Oh…please. Hoss. Don't stop. Don't—"

"I'll never stop," I grunt. "My job is to make you come. Your job is to fucking let me."

"*Daddy.*"

"That's right. I'm Daddy." I apply a little more pressure, hips dropping slightly, and she whimpers, her back arching involuntarily, her hands sliding through sweat on their way down to my ass—and hell yeah, those little hands grasp at my flexing cheeks, nails scraping, her hips beginning to roll and lift in time with my grinds. "Horny girl. *Knew* you'd be a slick horny ride."

She cries out, her core beginning to clench.

My cock throbs painfully in response, dying for a rough-as-hell ride, but not until she finds pleasure. Not until her body understands that my dick is a tool and she knows how to use it. "Almost there," I murmur, studying her, sweat dripping down the side of my face. "Going to give you a little more pressure. You can take it. Don't be scared of it."

When I release my weight and bear down on her clit with more purpose, more friction, her nails sink into the flesh of my ass and she screams, her pussy tightening around me like a fucking belt, her moisture sluicing down the thick trunk of my johnson—and I go for broke after that. I pin her down to the fucking mattress and I pound her like a piece of meat. Her whimpers of pleasure fill the back of the truck, almost drowned out by my harsh groans, the shit that's coming out of my mouth. Promises to treat her like a princess and fuck her like a whore.

My Tatum doesn't take offense to the filth, though. No, she's the opposite of offended. Never felt anything more tight and eager in my life. If she was strong enough, I swear to God this horny little hellcat would flip me over and ride me—and it's only our first time in the sack. By this time next month, she's going to be sucking me off on the highway, begging me to pull over and get her pregnant.

Get her pregnant.

That mental demand has me bellowing brokenly into her neck, my lower body rifling up and back, dick smacking wetly into her hole. Putting a child in her belly didn't occur to me until this moment, but Jesus, that's what I want. Do I even have a choice? I didn't even consider putting on a rubber and I've got a sack full of come that I've been saving up just for Tatum. Her pregnancy might be a foregone conclusion—and hell if that doesn't make me goddamn wild.

I slide my hands out from beneath her ass and grip the edge of the mattress above her head, riding rougher than a virgin can take, but can't do anything about it. Her pussy is wet as fuck and she's hollering for me to keep going, so I do. Keeping my grip on the mattress with my left hand, I spit on the fingers of my right and bring them down to her clit, massaging it in circles. "If you can come while I'm fucking you this mean, baby, I'm going to have you on your back day and night. You perfect princess. You perfect girl. Mine. I'm banging the shit out of what's mine. Say it. Tell me who this pussy is wet for."

"My Daddy."

"Louder."

"*Daddy!*"

Jesus save me, that's what gets her off. Screaming my shiny new title loud enough to hear on the interstate. She's coming on a thin mattress in the back of a rig in the parking lot of a truck stop, getting railed like I paid for it, but we might as well be in the finest hotel on our honeymoon, because that's how it feels to be with her. To be together. My chest wells up with a crowded feeling right before I come, leaving me unable to breathe, my heart going a million miles an hour. I'm too choked up to say another damn word, so I simply flatten my girl and bellow brokenly, my hips shaking through three final drives, pressure being driven from my balls into her body where it belongs. Where it'll breed my future wife. My life. My Tatum.

"Oh my God," she sobs. "It's so hot. There's so much of it. I can feel it everywhere."

She's talking about my semen. Out loud. Praising it. And it makes me pop off harder.

Longer.

I'm panting and boneless by the time I'm finished, collapsing beside her like a man who has just been baptized, razed by the holy spirit. I pull her into my arms and she comes so sweetly, so trustingly, I know I'm finding a church tonight. I'd sell my soul to be her husband. She's my everything. Today, tomorrow and always. "Tatum—"

The sound of car doors slamming out in the parking lot is followed by the sound of clipped voices, raising my hackles. Men. They sound familiar—and they shouldn't. Not here, so far from home. From the headquarters of the freight company I work for.

They're here for Tatum.

My boss knew I was bluffing. That I could never traffic a human being, let alone this one. This fucking angel on earth that belonged to me the second I saw her photograph. Mine.

Mine.

If they touch her, I will slaughter them like dogs.

"What's wrong?" she whispers, looking up at me, drowsy. Beautiful.

There are at least half a dozen men out there. I can't take chances with those odds.

Fuck. Being apart from her now is going to be like ripping the heart out of my chest, but I don't have a choice. Keeping her safe is my priority. "Tatum, listen to me very carefully," I tilt up her chin. "I need you to take the truck and go. Drive somewhere safe, then switch to a train. Travel at least a hundred miles west, then find a motel and wait for me there. I'm going to give you my phone, so I can call you and find out where you are."

"But…why? What's happening?"

The voices are getting louder. Approaching the truck. They recognize it. "I don't have time to explain, baby. I have to protect you. Please just do as I ask."

I'm in love with her. I realize that when she nods and jumps into action like a badass, fixing her clothing and climbing into the front seat. Starting the rig, even though she has no experience driving one. We give each other one long, final look.

"I'll find you, Tatum," I vow before I jump out, still shirtless.

And take on the six violent men approaching me with everything I've got.

CHAPTER FIVE

Tatum

Three months later

I WALK ACROSS the dark campus, holding my nightly ginger ale in my hand...but this time I'm surprised to find I don't need it. Glory hallelujah, the morning sickness has passed. Honestly, if I wasn't so exhausted from attending a full day of art school classes, I might even dance a jig, right here in the darkness.

After stopping long enough to stow my ginger ale away in my backpack, I continue across the empty pathway, traveling beneath streetlights, darkness, then back into the light. A pattern I've grown familiar with since I finagled my way into art school in Minnesota. Dark, light. Night, day. Work, sleep, repeat. But at least I'm safe. At least I found a way to follow my dream, despite having my life knocked over like a house of cards that night three months ago.

Up ahead, on one of the benches, there is a couple making out. The girl is all but straddling the boy and I'm pretty sure they're up to no good inside his overcoat. Not wanting to disturb them, I consider my alternate routes. There is a narrow alleyway between two campus buildings that leads to the street, but it's pitch black, so I usually only take the shortcut during the day. Still, when the girl whines and fully seats herself on the boy's lap, I veer toward the alley, trying not to think of the one and only time I truly lost myself like that.

On reflex, I curve a hand over my belly, which is only beginning to swell with signs of life.

Hoss never came for me. Never called his phone.

I did exactly as he told me. I drove the rig several miles down the interstate and left it at a truck stop near a train station. Using the money he gave me, I booked a train ticket to Wisconsin, found a motel room and waited, leaving only for food and to buy clothes, toiletries. I waited for weeks, sketching comics on the surfaces of motel notepads. Somewhere around the beginning of the third week is when I started to throw up. And I realized my period was late.

What would Comeback Girl do?

I asked myself that so many times.

But until I saw the two red lines staring up at me on the pregnancy test, I never really, truly answered the question. If Comeback Girl was pregnant and on the run from possible human traffickers—would she sit around and wait for a man to show up and make everything okay? No. She would pull up her big girl panties and start over. She'd make her own comeback.

And the terrible truth is that...

Is that...

Hoss could be dead. Those men I watched approach him in the rearview mirror might have killed him for helping me escape.

I have to stop walking because the pang in my chest is so severe. I prop a hand on the wall of the building and breathe in and out. This happens every time I think of Hoss, but the pain is slowly starting to get easier. It has to. Because I have a mission now. He or she is growing in my stomach and I'm going to do what's necessary to take care of my child. Our child. And that includes making money, putting myself through art school and becoming a steady provider. I will give this baby the stable life it deserves. I'll be their superhero. And my own.

I'm halfway down the alley when footsteps approach me from behind.

My blood instantly turns to ice, my sneakers halting mid-stride.

I exhale, watching my breath curl in the air.

Slowly, I turn, praying it's just the make-out couple hunting for more privacy.

But I don't see anything.

There is a dumpster pushed up against the wall, some trash dancing around on the asphalt. My fingers curl around the straps of my backpack and I start to walk faster, mentally cursing myself for not spending some extra money on pepper spray. Comeback Girl would never be caught out at night without a weapon.

With one more glance over my shoulder, I start to jog—

And I run smack into a man.

I stumble backward and fall. My backpack breaks my fall, but alarm is racing down my spine, a shriek building in my throat. This man doesn't belong here. On a college campus. Bald and hulking, he looks like he should be checking identifications at a biker bar or something. "Come with me."

"No way," I spit out, crab-walking backwards until I have enough distance between us to lunge to my feet, spin and run in the opposite direction.

Another man steps out from behind the dumpster, blocking my exit from the alley. "Hello, Tatum." His smile sickens me. "You didn't think you could run forever, did you?"

Oh God.

Oh God, it's them. The traffickers.

My hand wants to cover my stomach protectively, but some instinct warns me calling attention to my pregnancy is a bad idea. "Why me? Why go to all of this trouble to track me down? I don't understand."

"At first, you were just convenient. A girl with a deadbeat family who wouldn't bother looking for you. Working alone at night on a truck route. One of our scouts happened to stop in for coffee one night and knew you'd be perfect. No muss, no fuss," says the bald man, licking his lips. "And let's not forget about those big bouncy titties. They definitely helped your cause."

"Or hurt it," quips the second man. "Depending on how you look at the situation."

They're so casually confident, I can't help but be

terrified. I'm strong and smart, but these men have the air of professional criminals. They probably have guns.

"Yeah, that's how it started," says the second man. "But then...the boss became convinced you know too much. We couldn't just leave you in the wind."

What am I supposed to do here? I don't know. But I'm *not* going quietly.

I throw my head back, open my mouth and scream as loudly as possible.

So loud that my own ear drums start to throb.

Not three seconds passes before a hand clamps over my mouth and I'm dragged back against the bald man's chest. The other one pulls his gun and advances on me, murder replacing the jocular quality of his expression. "Scream like that again and I'll—"

A hand snakes out of the darkness and lowers the gun, twists the man's wrist, making him cry out. Then an elbow flies up, sending blood and teeth scattering onto the ground.

What...the heck?

I barely have time to process Hoss stepping out of the darkness. Or how different he looks. Deranged, really. Homicidal. Scarier than these two men on their best day. And righteously angry. So full of rage that even though I know he's here to help me, I'm scared of him. There's a feral quality in his eyes that wasn't present before.

He brings the edge of his hand down in a concise chop of the man's shoulder and he cries out, the gun dropping to the ground...only to be caught by Hoss.

Two clean shots are fired into the man's forehead, a silencer making the shots sound like quiet zings. The gun is leveled at the bald man before the other one even hits the ground. As the lifeless corpse slumps sideways onto the asphalt, a scream lodges in my throat, horror burning a path up my esophagus. "Hoss…" I whisper.

If he hears me, he gives no indication of it. His face is a mask of malice.

No humanity to be found anywhere. Where has he been for the last three months?

I don't know. But I don't think it was somewhere good. That is fast becoming obvious.

"I'm giving you five seconds to let her go," Hoss grinds out. "Or you're going to end up like your friend."

"You're the one," the bald man breathes. "You're the one who has been killing us off."

A sinister smile transforms Hoss's face. "They should have shackled me a little tighter. Or bumped me off, instead of keeping me prisoner. There is nothing, there is *fucking nothing*, that could have kept me from her. And your five seconds are up."

Hoss cocks the gun. He can't fire, though. It's too risky. I'm being used as a shield.

That hesitation costs us, because my captor has time to reach for something.

Now there is a gun pressed to my temple, as well.

Every ounce of color drains from Hoss's face.

"It's going to be all right, baby," he says, voice

strained.

"She's coming with me." The bald man begins to back up, taking me with him. "The boss is adamant. We leave her alone, it means you win. And she's a loose end. He can't allow that."

"When was the last time you spoke to the boss?" Hoss asks.

My captor hesitates. "Last night." A tremor goes through him. "Why?"

A muscle pops in Hoss's cheek. "That tracks. Since I killed him this morning. You're the very last of the vermin." A glint flashes in Hoss's eye. "Let. Her. Go."

"Fuck you. You're bluffing," sputters the bald man.

"Am I?"

The man holding the gun to my head is distracted. Caught off guard. This could be my best opportunity for escape. Without hesitating another second, I drop my weight. Completely allow my knees to collapse. It's a move I learned from *Comeback Girl*—and it works. The bald man is so startled by my sudden plunge that he can't hold on. Hoss is already surging forward to get between me and the man. "Don't kill him," I blurt, reaching for Hoss's leg. "Just let him go. Please. No more—"

A shot is fired into the center of the bald man's forehead.

He drops lifeless to the ground.

And then there is only Hoss, seething in the evening fog, his arm muscles bunched and rippling in the sleeves of his T-shirt, his broad back tensed. Eyes still carrying that wealth of homicidal rage that scares me. When I met him, he was a truck driver. Now he's a murderer.

You're the one who has been killing us all off.

"Tatum," he whispers, kneeling in front of me. Dropping the gun and taking my face in his hands. "Ah Jesus, you're even more beautiful than I remember."

My heart dances in my chest.

He's alive. So solid and gorgeous and reassuring.

But there is blood all over his face and that terrifies me. How casual he can be about the fact that he killed two men seconds earlier. Still, I allow my heart to operate my actions because I have no choice. I'm throwing myself into his arms before I can guess my own intentions. His thick arms crush me to his chest and he makes a strangled sound, running his hands everywhere. Up and down my back, over my hair and sides and hips.

"Baby. Oh God, baby," he says, helping me to my feet. "I've been sick without you. Every day has felt like a goddamn year." His mouth finds mine, his lips dragging mine wide with a gruff intake of sound, his tongue sweeping in to taste me. Sinking in to claim me more fully, his large body swaying into mine. As if the taste of me has sapped him of tension. "Everything is okay now. I'm going to take you from here. We're going to leave tonight and I'm going to bring you somewhere safe."

Everything inside of me wants to nod, to let him take my hand and guide me wherever we can be together. But...no. I can't. I can't do that. My new life is here. I've struggled every second of the last three months to build this new foundation and I'm not giving it up. There is no way I'm just going to walk away. And furthermore...

I have my baby to think about.

My child is going to need stability.

Normalcy.

And this man...Hoss. When I pull back and look into his eyes, I can see that he's changed. He just murdered two men without batting an eyelash. He's cold and ruthless. I know he would never hurt me or our child, but...he could bring trouble to my door. He could kill again. Even if this trafficking ring has been eliminated, I could see him bumping off a man for flirting with me. Whatever he's been through, he's not in his right mind now. My instinct is telling me that. There are too many red flags when all I want is a peaceful life for my baby.

"I can't go with you." I sink back onto my heels. "This is where I live now. My life is here." I'm not sure why I decide not to tell him I'm pregnant. Maybe because I don't think he'll allow me to remain behind if he knows I'm carrying his child. I don't know, but I tuck my secret down deep and guard it like only a mother would. "I've worked really hard to carve out this little routine. This life. And I'm staying here."

"I see how hard you've worked to make a life in

this place without me and I'm so goddamn proud of what you've done all by yourself, baby. Those comic book heroes don't have anything on you. But we can't stay here, Tatum," he says, beginning to look concerned. "The ring has been eliminated, but I just killed two men. We have to move. Tonight."

"I can't," I whisper. "You did these terrible things in order to protect me. As much as I'm grateful for them…they scare me."

"No." He searches me eyes, a realization seeming to dawn on him. "*I* scare you."

My throat starts to ache. "Yes."

All at once, he seems to realize there is blood on his face—and in kissing me, the red substance has transferred to mine. Looking horrified, he strips off his shirt and uses it to clean the smears of blood off my face. "Let me take you home, Tatum. We'll talk about this. I'm not leaving without you." He drops the shirt and takes my shoulders, shaking me gently. "I've barely been able to fucking *breathe* for three months."

I'm not going with him.

But we can't stay here.

We need to leave this crime scene now, before we're discovered. I'm surprised I'm able to think this clearly when he's pinning me with those intense, imploring eyes.

"Come on," I whisper. "Come to my place. Get cleaned up. I'm not far from here."

He keeps hold of me, like I might run away or disappear. "Tatum…" All at once, he lunges, flattening me against the wall of the alley. "I need to fuck," he rasps into my hair. "You going to let me fuck you in your bed? Tell me yes. I'm half insane—I know that. I know, baby. Being away from you did this to me. Tell me I get to have your pussy tonight or I'm going full-blown mad. I need that hot little pussy. Need to *wreck* it."

"I d-don't know," I stammer, lust sneaking in like a summer heat wave and wafting its way through my middle. Lower. Tickling my loins into a twist. "Won't that only make leaving harder?"

His frustrated curse peppers the air. "Every time you suggest we're going to be apart, I go a little more insane, Tatum," he says in a warning tone, his body pressing me tight, tight, tight to the wall. *"Please stop."*

I swallow hard, my fear sensors ringing over the unnatural light in his eyes. "Let's go home. For now, let's just focus on getting cleaned up. Okay?"

He's hard.

Between us, there is a thick ridge trapped between our stomachs and I can see how badly he wants to use it. Right here in the alley. His fingertips are tracing the waistband of my jeans, ready to yank them down. "Not in front of...th-the bodies..." I whisper.

"But later?" Hoss says against my mouth. Urgently.

A hot full-body shiver passes through me. "I don't know."

He presses his forehead to mine and lets out a rocky exhale. "Tatum...don't punish me. I did what I had to do."

With my heart in my throat, I take his hand and guide him from the alley. "So did I."

CHAPTER SIX

Hoss

I ALREADY SUSPECTED I'd gone a little crazy without Tatum.

The way she peers up at me confirms it. I've become a beast.

Look at me. Walking down the street shirtless, my hands covered in gunshot residue and blood, walking beside this innocent creature. My princess. My reason for living when the walls were closing in and I hadn't seen daylight in weeks. I'm starved for her breath on my skin, her body beneath mine. I scared myself back in the alley, because Jesus, I almost ripped off her pants and took her, despite her denials. Despite her obvious nerves in my presence.

We stop in front of a boarded-up restaurant and she guides me to an outdoor staircase climbing the side of the building. It leads to a beaten-up door—and no, no, please don't tell me this is where she has been living. There isn't another soul out on the street because it's largely deserted. The perfect place to prey on a female.

Did I get to her just in time?

Or am *I* the animal preying on her now?

I don't know. My head is so fucked. I'm broken and restless and desperate to find solace between her thighs. In her arms. I miss her voice and scent and sense of humor. And as she lets me into her little apartment, perhaps against her better judgment, I toy with the notion of boarding the door and never letting her out.

That's how I know I'm bad for her.

She's right.

She's right—I should leave.

I've murdered and suffered so much since the last time we were together that I am not fit to be around this sweet girl. I also know damn well I won't leave her alone until my pulse stops beating. That's a dead certainty, more reliable than the tide.

"Are you hungry?" she asks, setting down her messenger bag.

When I see the sketchpad sticking out, I find it hard to swallow. "Yes."

My growl turns her cheeks pink. "I'll make you something while you're in the shower." She walks to the kitchen sink, opens a cabinet and bends down, stretching the jeans across her gorgeous ass and I automatically unzip my jeans, because I'm swelling so fat, the goddamn thing no longer fits inside the denim prison. When she straightens, holding a garbage bag in her hands, she gasps at the sight of my cock jutting out from the V of my fly. "Um…"

"Tatum…"

"We should put our clothes in this bag and get rid

of it, right? S-so there is no, um…evidence…"

"Baby. Come get this cock."

"I don't think that's a good idea."

"It's the only idea." I stroke myself a few times and watch her eyes turn glassy. "Horny as ever, aren't you?"

"I haven't been. Not until now."

"Because I wasn't here."

She wets her lips. Nods. Thank Christ. I knew she wouldn't let another man touch her, but I don't even like the idea of her being wet unless I'm here to take care of the problem.

"I've never been…" She shakes her head. "Never mind."

I surge forward, desperate to hear what she was going to say. "What? Tell me."

When I tilt her face up so she can't avoid eye contact, she confesses her secret in a whisper. "I've never wanted to be with anyone else. Like we were…in your truck. I thought there was something wrong with me."

"There is nothing, not a damn thing, wrong with my princess." I jack off while looking at her mouth, those swollen pillows that were made for kissing me. "You were just waiting for your king."

"Don't you mean my prince?"

"No. I mean your king." I snag her hand and place it on my throbbing dick, hissing through my teeth at the softness of her palm, the mere fact that I'm with her and she's touching me is almost overwhelming enough to make me ejaculate on a dime. "I'm the king and you're the princess. You remember how we play, baby."

Her eyelids flutter closed and she fists me, finally, the soft circle of her hand giving me a gentle pump, then a rougher one. "Yes. I remember."

"Good girl," I whisper beside her ear, licking the lobe crudely. "Show Daddy your bed."

Her hesitation causes a roar to build in my throat. I look around for something to put my fist through, frustration welling inside of me. The need to be destructive. I'm bad for her. I've lost my mind and she knows it. The knowledge is right there on her perfect face. I'm lucky she even let me inside her apartment.

"I shouldn't..." she says quietly.

"Yeah," I return in a hoarse tone. "Maybe you shouldn't." I take her wrist and drag her along behind me to the bathroom. "Shower with me, Tatum. You've got blood on you, too. And Christ, I can't let you out of my sight. I'm already teetering on the fucking edge. I need eyes on you or I'm going to lose whatever sanity I have left."

"Shower?" she squeaks when I lock us into the small bathroom. "Together?"

"I've seen you naked before, Tatum," I say, shoving down my jeans, stepping out of them, along with my socks. "I see you like that every time I blink."

Again, I'm made painfully aware of how thoroughly I've lost my mind, because the fact that she's shielding her body from me starts a vein ticking behind my eyes. A growl builds in my throat and I have to concentrate on not ripping the garments from her body. *Calm down. Calm down, she's scared of you.* I settled for backing her against the door and, as calmy as possible, unfastening her jeans and pushing them down her hips.

"Show me what I need to see," I demand, lips to her forehead. "Show me those big tits and that luxury pussy, before I starve to death from missing your skin on mine."

Her head falls back and she's dazed, denials growing weaker, weaker by the second.

I waste no time getting her jeans all the way off, ripping open her blouse and fumbling with the snap of her bra. Those lavish tits spill out and I almost spray my seed everywhere.

"God, you are so fucking perfect, baby." I lean down, guiding one of her tits to my mouth in a gentle hand and suckling that little raspberry tip, my balls pounding with a riotous pulse, dick begging to be planted between her curvy thighs. "My lush little girl," I breathe, licking my fingers and trailing them down her stomach toward her...

I stop.

My heart seizes in my chest.

There is something different about her shape.

Her belly has a subtle swell, a barely noticeable difference to the naked eye, but I remember every square inch of this girl. I've thought of nothing else for months.

"You're pregnant."

Tatum's alarmed gaze flies to mine and I have my answer.

I'm immediately winded. With hope. With relief. And...pain. I'm in terrible pain.

"You weren't going to tell me?" I fall to my knees and press my face to the bump, incapable of swallowing, my hands roaming over her hips, her belly, memorizing the changes in her, small though they are. "You were going to send me away. Keep this to yourself. Weren't you?" My vision doubles from the agony ripping through my chest. "That's not happening, Tatum," I wheeze. "Leaving you would have ended me. Hollowed me out for life. Leaving you and our baby? Might as well chain me up in hell. You think I could leave my family unprotected?"

"That's just the thing, Hoss. We don't need protection anymore. Not from anyone but..."

"But me?"

I ask the question to her belly, pressing my lips there.

Kissing her. Kissing our child.

"Yes," she whispers.

And I know she's right. I'm not normal. I've been reborn in blood and mayhem. I'm fueled by anger and hunger and desperation right now. I have no place around this perfect girl and this innocent child. But there is no way in hell I can walk away. *Ever.* And the pain of Tatum keeping this secret from me, when all I want is to cherish her, is too much to bear after everything else I've been through.

Pressure builds inside of me, expanding, pushing outward from all sides, my temples pounding, heart rioting out of control. I'm in such a fucking state of need and pain and love, I don't realize I've carried her out of the bathroom until we're already entering her bedroom and I'm pressing her down onto the bed. "I'll be better, baby," I grunt, coming down on Tatum's sweet body, quelling her struggles with my weight. "Kiss me. Open your legs. Let me remind you how good it is when you trust me." I rake my mouth up the side of her neck. "Heal me."

For some reason, those two words seem to register with her more than anything else I've said. She goes still beneath me, our breath mingling together, her eyes searching mine. Slowly, her hands come up and her fingers thread through my hair.

I moan, long and loud and shamefully, at the caring gesture. I've never been cared for. I've never had someone look at me the way she is right now. Like I'm a wounded animal and instead of kicking me or closing the door, she's considering bringing me inside and bandaging me up. "Please," I say hoarsely, urgently. "Please."

"What happened to you?" she whispers.

I swallow, bury my face in her neck. "The night you left, I fought them in the parking lot, but there were too many. The two men who were still standing at the end took me to the boss and he locked me up. For a month. In the basement of some warehouse, barely any food. Constant darkness. Daily beatings.

They thought I was an undercover fed or an inform-
ant, since I helped you that night." I press down
tighter to her body, wanting to absorb her warmth and
goodness, use them to battle the bad memories.
"Finally, I got free and...Tatum, I killed my way out.
I've been killing ever since to make you safe. Killed
every last one of them. And I'd do it again." I trail my
lips up to her mouth and snare her in a kiss. A hot,
promissory one that makes her gasp, her back arching
beneath me, her plush tits on display. "No one touches
Tatum," I growl, feasting on her nipples. Sucking
them one by one. Licking at the peaked sweetness with
hungry strokes of my tongue. "No one but me."

"Th-thank you for defending me," she chokes out,
starting to tremble. "I'm sorry for what you went
through. It must have been terrible. But—"

"Shhh." I kiss my way down her body, nibbling at
her swollen belly and hips, hands pressing her knees
open. "Like I said, I would do it again." She's still
wearing her panties, but they are thin and easy to rip
off with two hooked fingers—and then, there it is. The
pussy that I've been thinking about nonstop since I
first walked into her diner. It's as perfect as I remember. Soft and juicy, her slit glistening in welcome,
leaving no doubt that she wants this cock. The
evidence is right there in front of my face and it's on
my tongue, too, because I'm already lapping at her.
Kissing the split of her sex, tracing it with my thumb.

I'm using my fingers to make a V and gently parting her flesh, revealing that slick, private place and the

quivering little bud that's going to push her over the edge. Not only into orgasm, but into needing me. Allowing me into her body, even though I'm an animal now. I lock eyes with her up the front of her body and I keep eye contact while jiggling my tongue against her clit. I do it without cease, seconds going by while she grows more flushed, hips restless, eyes unfocused. But I keep on looking at her and applying more pressure, more, jiggling until she's panting, palming her tits and rubbing her nipples. *Fuck.* Hottest sight of my life. Knowing I'm tending to the pussy of the woman carrying my baby fills me with pride. Lust. Love.

Need her. Need our connection. The deepest one I can get.

Desperate for it, I do something that makes me a bastard. I wait until she's right on the verge of coming and then I retract my tongue, savoring her sugary taste inside my mouth. I prowl back up her body with she shakes her head in disbelief. "No, please…just a little bit longer, Hoss. Please."

"Be with me. Be my *wife*. I'll lick you down every night of the goddamn week. I'll sell you my tongue in exchange for one hard fuck, baby. You can do whatever you want with it." I notch my cock firmly between her thighs, rubbing it in the stickiness of her arousal, gliding the trunk of it up and down between her damp lips, listening to her gasp when I ride over her sensitive clit. "Heal me. Let me in. Let me fucking love you."

Emotion crests in her eyes and she pulls me down for a kiss. I feel the barrier give way between us, feel permission in the way she gives me her tongue, her inner thighs perching on either side of my hips.

With a ragged sound, I reach down and guide my dick to her entrance, struggling to get it inside for several seconds, before grinding it deep, deeper, all the way to my balls, my harsh expletive loud in the small, dark room. "Mother*fucker*. Baby's even tighter than I remember." It's a wonder I don't flood her right then and there, but I can't. Not when she's already so wary of me, her trust so hesitant. Thank God for her attraction to me or I wouldn't be buried in the sweetest pussy on earth—and I show her I'm grateful for that. I scoop my hips up and twist them, stroking her inner walls on all sides, giving attention to her G-spot.

"*Hoss*," she moans, her head beginning to toss on the pillow.

"Touch me," I beg her, angling my hips and keeping them arrowed in the direction that makes her whimper. "Touch me everywhere while I tickle you on the inside."

Her hands twist in my hair, fall to my shoulders and glide down my pecs, back up my arms. Everywhere she touches becomes her property and I get harder, harder, my balls wrenching tighter at the rasp of her fingertips and palm. My nerve endings are baying like dogs when their master has come home.

"You own me. *Feel* that. You own me, Tatum." I

kiss her hard, sweeping my tongue in and making love to her pretty little mouth, kissing her while life grows between us. While she feels every ounce of the life she gives my dick. I'm driving her up the bed with every nasty thrust, the mattress creaking below, flesh smacking off of flesh. "Tell me I'm hitting your spot. Tell me my cock is rubbing it right."

"You are," she sobs, slapping and pushing at my shoulders, drawing them closer, writhing beneath me. Confused by how much pleasure she's getting after so long without it. "Hoss. Hoss. Oh my God."

"That ain't my name when you're getting drilled by this cock, little girl. And you know it. You call me Daddy when it's fuck time."

"Daddy," she whispers, eyes glazed—and her pussy screws up into a spasm, throbbing, the tightening and loosening of those little muscles making me bellow into the pillow beside her head. Jesus Christ, this tight fucking goddess. This perfect, beautiful creature. Thank God I've found her again. "Feels so good. So good."

With her pleasure achieved, there's no other word for what I do to her after that but one. Rutting. "In the future, baby, you're going to get more than one orgasm, but I've been without this pussy for months. I need you to hang on tight while I filthy fuck you and get my nut. Can you do that for me?"

Still dazed, she nods, gripping my shoulders.

Not expecting me to pull out, flip her over face down and yank her ass up to my lap. Dick in hand, I spit on her asshole and watch the moisture snake down over her pussy, giving me the additional wetness I need to enter her from behind and pound her little pink pie. Hard. I grip the headboard with my left hand, taking her throat in my right, and I lose touch with reality. I can hear the smack of hips meeting ass, can hear her crying out with pleasure—*oh, Daddy*—but the beating of my heart is the loudest. *Finally mine. Finally mine again.*

"Tatum," I choke, my mouth moving through her hair. "Need to give you my come."

"I want it," she whines, clenching around me.

I can hear the pout in her tone. She's baby talking on her hands and knees, as if I needed any more proof that this is the last women I'll ever need. The only one I'll ever love. The one I'm obsessed with down to the marrow of my bones. My Tatum.

"You want Daddy's sperm?" I grunt in her ear.

"*Yes.*"

"Are you sure? It's hot and nasty." I lick up the center of her back. "So much of it."

She looks back at me over her shoulder, pushing out her bottom lip. "Please?"

Come rockets from my balls so fast, I don't have time to prepare. I fuck her in a blur, trying to get rid of the insane pressure that isn't ebbing nearly fast enough. My vision blurs and I ride that tight gash until it's filled, until my spend is splashing everywhere, squelching onto her thighs and my stomach because I can't stop grinding and thrusting like an animal.

Somewhere in the middle of it all, she crests again, too, constricting around me and pushing my lust to another level, sending me into another lengthy round of spasms, until finally I drop face down on the bed beside Tatum, gathering her tight to my body before she can leave. Or disappear. She's pliant and boneless, rolling up right against me.

But instead of falling asleep, she fights the unconsciousness.

She battles the drowsiness, keeping a wary hand wedged between us.

My girl doesn't trust me. I make her nervous. She won't let down her guard.

That's how I know I have to be a better man for her.

For my child.

I'm a feral animal right now. I want to take Tatum and go on the run, but she wouldn't be happy. She doesn't want to leave this place. So I have to work with that. I *will*. I'll do anything it takes to remain at her side. I'll do anything it takes to make her love me, trust me. It's going to take a lot of work, but I welcome the chance to prove myself to her. That I can give her the normal she seeks. That we can be a family.

I'm sick over having to leave, yet I know there is no choice. The bodies have to be taken care of if we plan to remain here—and that's only the beginning of the work I'm going to put in to earn this girl's affection. I lean forward and kiss her temple, her lips.

"Sleep now, Tatum," I say gruffly, my chest

packed tight, close to bursting. "I'm going to make everything better. You'll see."

Finally, she gives up the fight and falls asleep.

With one final look at her, I leave the apartment with my chest in shreds.

CHAPTER SEVEN

Tatum

Two months later

I TAKE OFF my backpack and plop down on the bench, taking out my peanut butter and jelly sandwich from the front pocket. I'm in between classes and starved after eating only a fistful of Cheerios on my way out the door this morning, due to sleeping through my alarm. I've been doing that more and more lately. Not only because the baby growing in my belly is making me tired, but because...I think I messed up really bad.

I'm sad.

It's hard to get out of bed when I'm sad.

I'm doing my best to be upbeat for the baby's sake, but every time I close my eyes, I see Hoss's face. His mask of pain and adoration and need. I trust myself to remember that I was truly afraid of him the night he returned. How could I not be when he killed two men so easily? When all of his movements were so sharp and raw and alarming?

I told him I couldn't go with him.

That I needed to stay.

But I didn't know I would be left feeling so hollow

once he vanished.

I'm losing my mind a little, too, in his absence. I swear I feel him everywhere. Even when I'm sleeping at night, there is a sort of electric presence in my apartment. As if he left a piece of himself behind to haunt me. Haunt my decision to let him go.

I miss him.

I miss the way he looks at me, like I'm the ultimate treasure. I miss the way my heart trips over itself at the sound of his voice and the cherishing manner in which he kisses me, strokes my skin. I read somewhere that pregnant women get really aroused as the pregnancy wears on and I can now attest to that. My nipples are so sensitive that I am flushed by the time I finish fastening my bra in the mornings. I'm waking up wet and achy on the regular—and I can't seem to get the same relief that Hoss gives me. What I manage to do with my fingers pales in comparison to the consuming rush I get with him inside of me.

Why didn't I ask him to stay? Why didn't I ask for time to get used to the new, rougher edges of his personality? It would have been worth it to feel his love right now.

To give my love to him in return.

Because I do. I love him.

It gets stronger and more obvious with every day that he's gone.

I bite into my peanut butter and jelly sandwich, chewing even though it tastes like dust in the wake of my troubling thoughts. Where is Hoss? Is he all right?

Does he still think and worry about me? Am I imagining the tingle at the back of my neck when I'm walking home at night? Or switching classes during the day? Maybe. Possibly. I don't know, but I always, always feel safe now, no matter where I'm going. Or what I'm doing.

It's like I've been surrounded in a protective bubble.

Last month, I started working as a campus tour guide to make some extra tuition money, so I could cover the extra costs not included in my student loans. After one day on the job, I was toast. Pregnancy and three hours on my feet did not mix well. I went home that night sore and frustrated. The next day, I was let go from the position—with six months' worth of pay. My supervisor told me they wanted to help out a single mother in need, but I didn't quite believe him. Still, it's crazy to think Hoss had anything to do with my unexpected windfall, isn't it? If he was near, I would know. Wouldn't I?

I take a second bite of my sandwich and start to reach for the caffeine-free iced tea in my backpack, but something across the street from campus catches my eye. A new shop. The sign is colorful. Bright. Why does something about it feel almost familiar?

It takes me a moment to grasp why.

The font used on the sign is the same one used on the cover of the *Comeback Girl* covers. And the name of this new shop is Comeback Comics.

I drop my sandwich. "What…the heck?"

Before I know I've moved, I'm on my feet, back-pack dangling from my fingertips as I walk through the crosswalk, drawn to the shop by a magnetic force. The font, the name...it has to be a coincidence, right?

Only, when I walk through the door, there is a scent in the air that immediately wakes up all five of my senses. There is the smell of musky comics mingled with fresh ones, yes, and that is enough to make my fingertips tingle. But underneath that is a dangerous frosted pine aroma that my body would know anywhere. My mouth salivates at the introduction of it and I make a small sound in my throat.

I spin around in the center aisle, my vision a kalei-doscope of color. "Hoss?"

There's no answer.

There is nobody in the store, except for me, mak-ing me wonder if I'm imagining all of this. Like some weird pregnancy hallucination?

Seconds pass with nothing but the sound of my breathing and then I hear it. Rummaging coming from the back room. I turn in that direction, drop my backpack and start jogging, almost crashing into the very prominent Comeback Girl display.

Not a coincidence. This can't be a coincidence.

"Hoss?" I call, running into the back room.

A man is bent over a stack of boxes, a ballcap pulled down low over his face.

"Hoss," I sob, tears rushing to my eyes.

I expect him to drop the clipboard in his hands and open his arms. Embrace me. But he doesn't.

Instead, he takes several steadying breaths and lifts his head, looking at me briefly out of the corner of his eye, his knuckles turning white around the clipboard. "Not Hoss anymore. Daniel." His chest rises up and shudders down. "Don't come any closer. I thought I was ready to see you, but I just…I need a minute to get myself under control."

The last part of that sentence is spoken in a rasp, his hand pressed to the center of his chest, rubbing furiously. What is going on here? I don't understand. "Get yourself under control?" I sob, wiping at my eyes.

"So I don't scare you again," he explains, dropping the clipboard and bracing his hands on the cinderblock wall. "I can't fuck this up."

I'm trying to process everything at once. His words. The changes to his appearance. He has bulked up, become huskier. Grown a beard. Instead of his usual T-shirt, he's wearing a button-down that strains around the swell of his muscles. My panties turn damp just looking at him, remembering the pleasure that body gives mine. Relentlessly.

But he isn't touching me now. Why?

I can't fuck this up.

My heart twists at the realization of what's going on here. He scared me last time he arrived without warning. For the last two months, he's been planning this. He's been transforming himself with a new identity, preparing this shop in my honor, trying to get himself normal again so he could be right for me and the baby.

Now he's afraid of breaking.

He's holding parts of himself back because I wasn't ready before and he doesn't want to drive me away again. But I'm ready now. Not only have I been given the time and distance to know I don't want to live without him, I know he would never be anything but good for me. For our child. The kind of man who would make this grand of a gesture is a king.

That's how I want to treat him.

Like he's the king to my princess.

"Daddy," I whisper. He buries his mouth in the crook of his elbow and groans. Great shudders pass through him and he pounds a fist into the wall, but I'm not scared of him. Not anymore. I advance on Hoss...no, Daniel now. And I fit myself in between him and the wall, framing his face with my hands. "You did all of this for me?"

"I'd do anything for you," his breathes raggedly.

I trace his cheekbones with my thumbs, along with his bottom lip. "You've been watching me."

"I keep my Tatum safe."

"You got me fired with six months' pay."

"When you walked home that night, I could tell your feet were hurting. I had to...drink myself unconscious to keep from breaking down your door and making you better. It wasn't time yet. I had to learn how to be normal again. For you." His hands lift and cradle my stomach. "For the baby."

My chest is packed so full, I can barely draw breath. "I missed you. Every second."

His eyes betray his inner turmoil. "I could say I missed you, too, but that wouldn't even begin to cover the hell I've been living in without you."

"I'm sorry. I'm sorry. The name is perfect. Comeback Comics. It's perfect."

"All for you," he says, kissing my forehead hard. "Everything for you."

My fingers go to the button of his jeans, unsnapping them. Carefully lowering his zipper over the part of him that is already huge and hard. Ready. I reach inside the opening and mold my hand to his thickness, massaging it while he moans, his hips rolling into my grip.

"No, baby," he grunts. "Not yet."

What? My brain refuses to understand. "No?"

Teeth gritted, he circles my wrist and tugs it away from his lap. "Please, I have to show you the rest before I lose myself in you, Tatum. Having a plan and sticking to it...that's how I've learned to keep my hunger for you leashed. To control my rage at the world for having the nerve to be dangerous while you're living in it. I'm barely holding on, but I can do it for you. I'd do anything for you. I just need you to trust me. Feel safe with me."

"I do—"

"No. No, you'll see the home I made for us first. I need to show it all to you. I need you to understand how much I love you, so you don't send me away again." He reaches down and cups my womanhood beneath the loose skirt I'm wearing. Encompasses all of me in his calloused grip. "Because the next time I'm buried in this, I want you to have confidence in me. I want you to be fully aware of what I'll do to make you happy. You'll be proud to have me as the father of your child."

"I am." The regret that has been building up inside of me for months breaks free, along with my tears. "I should have held on tight to you. I will now. Just let me."

"I'll let you do anything you want with me," he breathes, cautious hope flaring in his face. "As soon as we're home. I want you to see everything I'm offering before you give yourself to me. Your body. Your heart and future. You need to be sure." A light of madness flickers briefly in his eyes, reminding me of the night he left. "Because God help me if you ever change your mind, Tatum. God help everyone in my path. Do you understand?"

Yes. I do. He needs me to commit completely.

I already am. I'm ready to be his. I never want to be apart from him again.

Maybe he needs me to understand the full scope of his love, the deep, the dark, the magnitude, before I throw myself to the wind. So he can always be sure I knew what I was getting myself into.

"Take me home, then," I whisper.

DANIEL LOCKS UP the shop and we walk hand in hand

for five blocks, the trees growing denser, the houses larger. Kids play in the street and the sound of traffic grows more distant. Every time we reach a stoplight and have to wait for the crossing signal, Daniel pulls me into his arms and kisses my forehead, my cheeks, my mouth, whispering fervently how much he's needed me. More than once, we miss the signal completely and have to wait for the next one.

I'm sensitive everywhere. My breasts are heavy, the back of my neck is hot.

I want to be laid down and ravished by this long-lost man.

But the set of his jaw speaks to his determination and I have no choice but to ignore the swelling desire and keep walking, until finally, we stop in front of a house.

It's robin's egg blue. The windows are trimmed with fresh white.

Shade and sunlight dapple the yard, a hammock swaying lazily in the breeze.

It's private and cozy and exactly the house I would have picked if I'd had a choice of every single residence on the block. It's perfection.

"This…is…"

"Ours," he says, unlatching the gate and pulling me through. "It's ours, Tatum."

The daisies planted on either side of the brick path blur with my tears. Wiping away the moisture with my shoulder, I watch Daniel unlock the door with capable fingers. It pains me to know this wonderful man who loves me has been living in this dream house without me, but never again. I'll never let him leave again.

We step into a small entryway and I can see the entire first floor from there. The brand new, rustic kitchen to the left. Living room furniture gathered around a fireplace to my right. A staircase traveling upward from the center of the space. But instead of leading me up, he takes me past the stairs, toward a small door. When he pushes it open, I give up all hope of stemming my tears, because there is a desk bathed in sunlight. Framed *Comeback Girl* comics on the walls. A portable crib folded up in the corner. A big, thick, round rug on the floor covered in pillows of all shapes and sizes.

"You've been doing so well in school," he breathes against my ear, his hand sliding along the back of my neck and taking hold. "This is where you'll study. Where you'll sketch." His hand scrubs down my spine. "Right where I can see you. Right where you're safe."

"It's incredible. The whole house…is incredible." I make a choked sound. "You did all of this for me?"

He bares his teeth at my temple. "There is no end to what I would do for you."

Love and lust are snaking through me at such a rapid rate, I can barely remain standing. I'm…worshipped by this man. He's showing me the proof. Now I need to feel it.

Moreover, I want him to feel the proof that I worship him back.

I am done being waylaid. I need to get…way laid.

Thank God I didn't say that out loud.

"I love it, Hos—Daniel." I glide my palms up and down his pecs, listening to the growl kindle in his throat. "I want to live here with you forever. You, me and the baby." I unfasten his jeans again, both of us already starting to breathe faster. "But right now, it's just you and me…"

Unexpectedly, his left hand circles my throat, his hold firm, but gentle. He searches my eyes long and hard. "You making me a commitment, Tatum? Because if you are, it's forever. No exceptions."

"Forever," I say, trembling under the onslaught of need, the wet rush between my legs. "Forever," I echo, kissing the notch of his throat.

"No matter what, Tatum." His jaw ticks. "Even when I'm a little insane?"

"Yes." I lick the stubbled curve of his throat. "Because I know your love is stronger."

A hoarse rendition of my name is his only response.

I trail my mouth down his chest and stomach, landing on my knees on the soft rug. I force myself to be careful unzipping over the large protrusion even though I'm desperate to get the taste of him in my mouth. He's never been there before, but somehow my body already knows what his exact texture and size and flavor will be.

Perfect. Smooth and hard.

Beating veins and a thick tip.

His fingers sink into my hair like he owns me, my

mouth—and he does. I look up at him like a servant while I bring him repeatedly to the back of my throat, lavishing attention on the bulbous head of his erection with my tongue, watching it turn more and more purple every time I break for air, stroking him in a tight fist, wet friction noises filling the room.

Nostrils flared, he looks down at me and groans my name, over and over again, one hand leaving my hair to massage his balls until I've learned enough to take over the task. He unbuttons his shirt with shaking hands and tosses it down on the ground.

Looking up at his broad, muscular form, the hair and tattoos and wounds, I suck harder. I suck like a woman in awe of a warrior, because I am. I'm shaken by my gratitude and appreciation for this man. My need to please him. My love. My relief that he's back.

"You missed your man's body, didn't you, baby?" He takes hold of my head, beginning a slow, crude thrusting rhythm into my mouth. "Turns that hole slick and willing, doesn't it?"

I moan a *yes* around his arousal, rubbing the underside of him enthusiastically with my tongue, his balls growing harder in my palm.

"You should feel what your body does to mine. There's no comparison." He grits his teeth, head tipping back to face the ceiling. "I can't even believe you're sucking my cock right now. I'm...maybe this is a dream."

Wanting to convince him otherwise, I open my throat and bring him another inch deeper, swallowing, the walls closing in on him, earning a stripe of salty spray on the back of my throat and a shouted expletive from Daniel.

"Fuck!" He guides his erection out of my mouth with a wince and reaches for the leather office chair, dropping down into it heavily, pulling me off the ground with desperate hands. "Sit on it, little girl, and ride. Need some of that pregnant pussy. *Now*." He hauls me between the V of his thighs—and Lord, he is such a marvel of masculinity and lust that I'm straddling him in the middle of his hoarse instructions, both of us yanking my panties to the left so I can sink down, down, down on his thrumming inches.

Before I can roll my hips, his fingertips settles on my ribs...

And I'm being tickled.

The high-pitched notes of my giggle fill the office and I squirm on his lap, gasping when he grows harder, his eyes flintier. His touch digs more firmly into my sides and I jerk up and back while he hisses expletives, my womanhood turning damper around his impaling erection. "Fuck yeah," he growls, slapping my ass hard. "Wiggle around on it, baby."

I do as he says. I wiggle and squirm while he tickles me, giggling uncontrollably.

Until he bares his teeth and rams his hips upward, bouncing me on his lap several times, rattling my molars. My scream splits the air, an orgasm that has been building for months careening through me, pulling every one of my muscles taut, dropping me into an endless round of spasms. Tight, release, tight, release, moisture flooding down where our bodies join and dripping to the rug. "Daddy, Daddy, Daddy," I chant, writhing as close as possible, grinding my womanhood against the base of his hardness, the rub of my clit making the climax fuller, longer, so overwhelming that my vision triples.

"Broke into your apartment while you were in class. Every fucking day. Jacked off with everything you own. Stroked my cock with your pillows and scrunchies and panties." His hands take my backside in a bruising grip and he starts to pull me up and back, impaling me again, again, again on his hardness, his hips thrusting up to add to the impact. "Even broke in a few times while you were there, sleeping like a little princess with these buns up for grabs." He spanks me roughly, one cheek after the other. *Smack. Smack.* "Licked in between them once, couldn't help it. Had to get some sugar, baby, and your legs opened right up in those sheets, wanting more. Never come so hard in my life. Right there on the shitty carpet." The rhythm of his body entering mine grows jagged, urgent, his breathing erratic. "Until now, huh? You're about to fuck me up so bad with that tight little brat hole, aren't you? You know what Daddy needs. That wet cram. Those hips hitting just right. Fuck. Fuck. *Fuck.*"

I'm picked up and laid down on the floor, pinned, his hips giving one final drive before he begins to shudder, his body straining, flexed. Getting deep as he can before letting go, his jaw slackening, thick semen filling me almost instantly and seeping down around the connection of our bodies, his body jolting with aftershocks, more releases of moisture, for long, fraught moments, our hands clinging, eyes locked. Looking into one another's souls.

"I love you, Tatum," he rasps.

"I love you, too. Hoss. Daniel. Whoever you are, whoever you'll be."

He can't speak for long moments. "One of these days, I'm going to get the girl of my dreams into an actual bed," he finally says into my neck, his mouth worshipping me with kisses.

"How about today?" I whisper, bringing his forehead down to mine, letting him see how much I adore him. Accept him. Always and forever. "We have nothing but time."

EPILOGUE

Daniel

Five Years Later

I'M LATE FOR back to school night.

I hate running behind. Hate knowing Tatum is waiting for me, wondering where I am. The very thought of her being disappointed has me wiping sweat from my brow while crossing the street toward the elementary school our son attends. I don't disappoint my wife—not fucking ever. But thanks to a shipment arriving just as I locked up Comeback Comics for the day, the delay was unavoidable. I'm fifteen minutes behind.

When I reach the front of the school, I'm about to jog up the steps to the main entrance, until I realize I can see our son's classroom from the street. It's lit up, full of parents. No kids. They're all home with grandparents—or a babysitter, like Daniel Jr.

I step onto the grass and peer through the window, my gaze seeking out my wife immediately, my cock growing the moment I find her in the back of the room, leaning against the wall in her pretty blue dress, listening intently to the teacher. Her purse is at her feet, sketchpad sticking up out of the top, as usual.

God, I'm so proud of her.

She doesn't know it yet, but today's shipment contained her very first edition of her first published comic—*Truck Stop Idol.* It will be waiting on the front window display when we arrive for work in the morning and I can't wait to see her light up. Can't wait to tell her how proud she makes me. To be her best friend, her husband, the father of her child. Her lover.

Yeah. I'm her lover. Although that word doesn't really describe what we do together in bed. Not completely. I'm her lover at times, yes, when she wants it sweet and slow. Usually when she's getting close to her period and feeling emotional. I stroke deep, look her in the eye and tell her she's perfect, because hell, that's what she is. Other times, I'm the man who holds her throat and fucks her face down in the storage room of the shop. I'm the man who takes her home on our lunch break and licks her clit until she breaks, sobbing and shaking and lacking in any filter. Those are my favorite times. When her guard is totally down and she admits to being obsessed with me. The way I'm fucking obsessed with her. Endlessly. Madly.

I've got a hotel room booked for tonight. After back to school night ends. I'm going to rip her pretty blue dress to shreds to get at those big, beautiful tits.

Just as I'm willing myself to look away from the perfection of Tatum and join the rest of the parents, I notice a man behind her. Notice him leaning forward to say something in my wife's ear, brushing a strand of hair out of the way in order to do it. And I see her shoulders stiffen, eyes going round with alarm. My heart drums uncontrollably in my chest, rage turning my blood to boiling. What the fuck did I just witness? Did that man just make a pass at *my* wife?

Yeah.

He did.

I can tell by the way Tatum moves to a different part of the room, hugging her elbows. Searching the entrance of the classroom for me.

I'm running before I know I've moved.

On the way to the room, I know this is bad. I know damn well how capable I am of violence. After all, I slaughtered a dozen men to keep Tatum safe five years ago. I made positive back then that no danger could ever touch her—or our family—again. I've managed to bottle the intensity and let it out only in doses, but it threatens to erupt now.

In one fell swoop, I could ruin everything.

I'll get arrested. That's the only way my fingerprints or DNA could be linked to any of the murders. If that happens, I'll be taken away from my family, found responsible for the kills I made as Hoss.

Unless I'm careful.

Outside of the classroom, I manage to get myself under control, schooling my features before walking in with an apology, going to stand near Tatum. Since I'm the local comic book shop owner, everyone knows me and I receive several waves. Very deliberately, I don't look at the man who dared touch a strand of my wife's hair. I don't look because I know I won't hold it together. Instead, I thread my fingers through Tatum's and tuck her against my side, shielding her from view of the man I plan on…speaking with tonight.

"I'm sorry," I whisper into her hair.

"It's okay," she says back. "You wouldn't be late unless it was important."

My chest swells with so much love, I have to focus on breathing in and out. I love this woman so damn much. I love her trust in me. That she knows I can be counted on. I'm the luckiest man alive to have her. To be this woman's protector—and protect her I will.

Half an hour later, I've let go of Tatum's hand long enough to let her converse with some of the other mothers. And that's when I finally let myself look at the son of a bitch. I smile at him and tip my head at the hallway. After a slight hesitation, he follows, probably reassuring himself that I couldn't have seen what he did. That I didn't witness him taking the biggest risk of his life. But he's about to find out he's wrong.

As soon as he joins me in the hallway, I wrap his necktie around my fist and drag him to the closest stairwell, kicking the door shut behind us while he chokes in alarm. "What…what the hell are you doing?"

I don't bother answering. I simply tighten my hold on his tie and pull down with all of my strength, bashing his nose into the metal railing. Hard. Teeth clenched, pulse hammering wildly in my temples, I lift his bloody face back up to mine and look him dead in his terrified eyes. "If I ever see you so much as look at my fucking wife again, I swear to God, they will institutionalize me for the things I do to you. Do you understand me? I will walk around this town with that slimy hand dangling from my belt. Your death will be so painful, you'll be begging for it by the time it arrives." I slam his face into the railing twice more, satisfied by the crunch of bone. "Do you understand me, motherfucker?"

"Yes," he slurs, blood pouring from his mouth.

"You're lucky I'm leaving you alive this time." I twist his tie another time around my fist. "I'd love to snap this neck like a twig."

"No. Please."

"It's a shame you were hit by a car in the parking lot. They kept right on driving, didn't they?"

He nods vigorously. "Yes."

"Keep your mouth shut about me. And don't ever, ever, ever breathe in my wife's direction again or I'll pay you another visit. I'll be a lot less lenient."

"I won't tell anyone," he heaves raggedly, slumping to the stairs when I finally let him go. "Hit by a car. Fine."

The man stumbles to his feet and lurches down the stairs, out an emergency exit.

I remove my own tie and use it to clean the specks of blood from my face and hands, breathing through the rage until I'm together enough to rejoin Tatum. But when I turn to pass back through the stairwell door, I find my wife standing there. Watching. Waiting.

For several seconds, her expression is blank. Unreadable.

Fear of her reaction threatens to topple me. No. No. No. I've been so careful not to show her the dark side of me for five years. She feels safe with me. And I've ruined all of it, all of those incredible trust building moments with her in one fell swoop—

The sound of her swallowing reaches my ears and I notice…her nipples are hard.

At first, I'm confused.

But she lets out a shuddering breath. A sound I recognize well. It's one she makes when she's turned on. Or I've done something that inadvertently made her hot, like planning a surprise weekend trip or getting our son to bed while she sketches in front of the fire. Is it possible that she liked me defending her with my usually leashed violence?

"Tatum…" I approach her with caution, scared to death she's going to run from me. Say she doesn't feel safe with me. "I'm sorry, baby. But…I'll never be capable of letting another man touch you and get away with it. He's lucky I didn't kill him."

"I know," she breathes, setting down her purse, reaching for me. "I'm lucky too. Aren't I? To have someone who loves me so fiercely."

Inundated by shocked lust, I pin her hard to the stairwell wall. "You don't even know the fucking half of it," I rasp against her mouth.

"Yes I do. You show me every day." She chews her lip a moment, glancing toward the hallway. "You can't be inside me now. I'm…too worked up. I'll be too loud." She turns around and presses her palms to the wall, angling her hips back, her ass curving right into my waiting hand. "But I need you to erase the memory of anyone but you. Remind me who I belong to." she whispers. "Please, Daddy?"

God yes.

I love this woman so much it's criminal.

And I know we're reached a new level of understanding about each other. I'd kill for her and she's not just okay with it, now that she trusts me. She *wants* it that way.

Craves me in all forms, the way I crave her with my very soul.

My teeth pull back in a snarl and I ruck up her dress, pulling her panties down. Taking a moment to groan over her hot little jiggle, I slap the pretty, round cheeks of her ass, the sound echoing through the stairwell. *"Mine,"* I growl into her ear, already planning the many ways I'm going to take her tonight. "Forever."

"Yours. Forever."

THE END

In His Custody

CHAPTER ONE

Brody

THE YOUNG BLONDE troublemaker I've been fantasizing about for months walks out of the juvenile detention center and stops abruptly, cocking a light brow behind her sunglasses.

"Who are you?"

"Your stepfather. Brody." I hold out my hand, silently begging her to take it. "Nice to finally meet you, London."

Even though her eyes are shielded by Ray-Bans, it's impossible to mistake the hurt that streaks across her face before she hides it. "I should have known my mother wouldn't come to pick me up herself." London breezes past me toward the parking lot, tight backside twitching right to left in painted-on denim. "Let me guess, she's on a cruise with a new best friend who is trying to convince her to invest in a pyramid scheme disguised as a makeup company."

My lips tilt as I follow her. "Something like that."

"I didn't even know she'd gotten married." London flashes me a sassy smirk over her shoulder. "Again."

"It's a good thing she did or you'd be taking the

bus home."

Her smile slips a touch and I immediately regret the harshness of my words, but I sure as hell don't take them back. I'm a former Army captain turned police chief. Coddling isn't in my nature. Thanks to a lack of parental guidance, London has been in and out of juvie since she turned fifteen—and that shit ends now. Her mother might have been incapable of laying down the law, but that is not the case anymore.

She's too goddamn perfect to spend another day locked up.

It's up to me to put her on the right path.

I unlock the doors of my Range Rover, watching through the window of the driver's side as London boosts herself into the seat in a huff, tits jiggling around in the low neckline of her white tank top. My cock is already stiff as a board. Seems like it has been this way ever since I met her mother, Kelli, in a bar and I saw that picture of a kiss-blowing London on her phone. It's been like this, rigid and swollen and starved. Waiting.

Planning.

This might be the first time my stepdaughter is meeting me, but I'm well acquainted with her. I've been paying the guards at the detention facility for information. For video. Photos. Access. Anything I can get my hands on. Until I can have the real thing.

When I settle into the driver's side of my vehicle, it takes every ounce of self control not to reach over and slide my hands down the front of her tank top. To test the weight of her braless tits in my palm. See if her nipples can already get hard for me…or if she needs some seducing first. Either way, I'm going to have her.

I *need* to have her.

With a discreet adjustment of my belt buckle, I start the car and pull out of the parking lot, heading in the direction of my house. "I bet you're relieved you never have to go back there, huh?"

"Oh, yes." She crosses her delicious legs and gives a little shimmy. "Next time, I get to go to big girl prison. It's like the grown up table at Thanksgiving. Just with handcuffs."

I'm already shaking my head. "You're done getting locked up, London. As long as you're on my watch, you'll be staying out of trouble."

London snorts. "Please. You're going to be part of my life for a week, then I'll never see you again. Just like all the other boyfriends and husbands. Don't act like you care."

"How about I prove it to you, instead?"

Momentarily, she seems caught off guard. "Yeah, um. Good…good luck with that." I can feel her curious eyes roving over me, turning my balls to lead. "What are you? A cop or something?"

"See that? You're too smart to spend your life in a cell."

"Oh my God. You *are* a cop?" She tilts her head back and groans—and I swear to Christ, I almost pull the car over and pull that bratty little mouth down to my lap. "Seriously, just take me back to juvie. It's better than living with a police officer."

I clear the desire from my throat. "How so?"

"There are a hundred other girls in juvie! The guards' attention is divided." She crosses her arms and flounces back against the seat. "At home, I'll have to deal with your authoritarian nonsense all by myself."

"That's right." I slow to a stop at a red light, keeping my tone mild. "By the time your mother gets home from her business trip, I'm going to have you on the straight and narrow. No more running your mouth to cops, stealing cars or disturbing the peace. No more drunken dancing in fountains or chaining yourself to government buildings, either."

"Okay. So you've done your research."

"I always do." *When it comes to you.* I don't say that part out loud, but I would love to. I'd love to tell London everything right now. That I'm obsessed with her. That I've spent the last few months orchestrating this moment. When I'd bring her home and have her all to myself.

I can't come clean this soon, though. She doesn't trust me yet. And earning my stepdaughter's trust might be one of the most difficult feats of my life, considering she's been abandoned, over and over again, since she was a child.

Never again, baby. I'm here now.

"When is my mother coming back from her..." She does air quotes. "Business trip?"

My fingers flex on the steering wheel. "About a month or so."

That's a lie. I doubt London's mother is ever coming back.

The girl sitting in the passenger seat of my car is my sole priority now.

My sole…everything.

"How did my mother hook up with a cop? I can't wrap my head around it. She is just as resentful of authority as I am. Last time I saw her, she was trying to kick a coke habit and failing." London gestures at me. "How did this happen?"

The truth?

I'd had a shitty day at work and needed a drink. I lost an officer in a gun fight that afternoon and gave myself permission to numb some of the pain with whiskey. Rare for me. To give in to weakness like that. But there I was, replaying the moment over and over again, wondering what I could have done differently, when Kelli stumbled to the bar beside me.

Crying. Drunk.

If I hadn't seen the picture of London on her lock screen, I would have asked her to go bother someone else. All it took was one glance, though, and I was done for.

"We met at a bar," I say simply. "The rest is history."

"I can't see you in a bar." She tilts her head, the ends of her blonde hair brushing against her nipples. "Maybe you should take me to one now, so I can get an accurate picture."

"Funny."

"It can be a welcome home gift." Leaning across the console, she walks her fingertips up my bicep, dragging up the sleeve of my T-shirt. "One little drink. Come on, Daddy."

I groan behind my teeth, coughing quickly to disguise the sound. My dick is straight and solid as a flagpole, come dribbling from the tip to soak into my fly.

Get yourself together.

She only called me that title as a joke, so I can't take it seriously, as badly as I want to. As badly as I want to pull over to the side of the road, throw her facedown over the backseat, yank her panties to her ankles and fill her to the fucking hilt with Daddy.

"No bars," I bark. "Not until you're twenty-one."

Maybe not even then.

"You've had no structure. No guidance. But that ends now, London. You're going to live under my roof and follow my rules. You're eighteen. An adult now. It's time to act like one. We're going to figure out what you want in life and get it together."

London is pouting at me. "Look, I appreciate you wanting to turn me into a respectable citizen and all, but you don't have to take responsibility for me. I've been taking care of myself for a long time. You are hereby absolved of any obligation."

"I don't want to be absolved."

Her panic is turning more and more palpable.

She's grown so accustomed to being deserted that my interest is probably terrifying. To London, getting attached is probably the worst thing she could do, because getting abandoned will hurt all the worse when the time comes. She has no way of knowing I'll never leave her as long as I live, so I'll just have to show her.

"You know…" She licks her lips nervously. "There are other ways I can get you to back off."

"Impossible."

"Oh yeah?" She unhooks her seatbelt and turns, coming to her knees on the passenger seat. Placing her hand on my thigh, she presses her open mouth into my neck. "I could seduce you." She's trembling like a leaf. "Bet my mother wouldn't take too kindly to her new husband lusting after her daughter."

My cock almost breaks my zipper. "And you would tell her, is that right?" I manage.

"Every detail. So I g-guess you better stay away," she purrs, her hand sliding to my inner thigh and inching higher. "Keep a heathy distance, Brody. I'm bad news."

"Oh yeah?" I turn my head, bringing our mouths less than an inch apart, watching her cornflower-blue eyes widen. "You ride good cock, little girl?"

She gulps. "The best."

Don't ask her to prove it.

Not yet.

Not this way. When I get her beneath me for the first time, I want it to be because she's hot for it. Because she feels something for me. Not to drive a wedge between us.

I put my mouth to her ear. "Liar. You think I can't tell that your pussy's been sealed up tighter than a vault?" Finding her eyes with mine, I reach down and stoke a finger down the seam of her jeans, making her gasp. "You might be wild, but you've kept your panties on, haven't you? And before you lie, London, understand that I've gone through your medical records. Several times."

She pulls back slowly, twin pink circles decorating her cheeks. "Who are you?"

"I'm your stepfather—and I'm in charge now." Her mouth is calling to me, but I force myself to plant a kiss on her forehead instead. "Breakfast is at eight o'clock sharp."

CHAPTER TWO

London

I WAKE UP at six-thirty after a measly three hours of sleep and resume pacing at the foot of my bed. Who is this guy? He is not like my mother's usual conquests.

He's got a job, for one.

Two, he's a cop.

Three, he owns property.

Brody actually has his life together. My mother tends to date or marry men who are in the same financial straits as her. One of them hits the number or gets a lucrative gig, they tie the knot, then everything goes to pot when they inevitably party too hard and hit a downswing.

I've known Brody for less than a day and already I know this man doesn't know the definition of downswing. Case in point, he's already awake and exercising downstairs, as evidenced by the clanking of weights and hum of the treadmill. The fact that he's working out doesn't surprise me. I would be lying if I claimed not to notice he's in incredible shape. He's in his late thirties, a little silver around the temples, tall, stacked with muscle.

Hot.

There, I admitted it.

This douchebag who thinks he can control my life is extremely sexy, in a hard, brooks no disobedience kind of way. Men usually turn me off simply by being men.

Thanks to my mother's revolving door love life, I've been around enough of them to know they're needy and immature and gross. Which is why I've played keep away with my virginity. There isn't a single member of the opposite sex that deserves it. Or me.

I go solo.

That's the way I like it.

People come and go, so I have to have my own back.

You've had no structure. No guidance. But that ends now, London. You're going to live under my roof and follow my rules. You're eighteen. An adult now. It's time to act like one. We're going to figure out what you want in life and get it together.

There is no way Brody meant that.

That he wants to help me achieve something with my life. He made it sound like we're on the same team, which is ridiculous. Why would he care what I do in five minutes or five years? I'm nothing to him. His future ex-wife's daughter.

And I feel the pressing urge to prove that.

I want him to be a scum bag, like all the other men I've met, from my father all the way down to some of the security guards at juvenile hall.

The alternative—that he really cares—gives me too much hope. Hope is the enemy. It almost always lets me down and I've been burned too many times to let it happen again.

A feline smile curves the edges of my mouth.

I might not have a lot of experience with men— okay, none—but I'm sure I can make Brody crack. I learned a thing or two about sex appeal by listening to my fellow offenders. If I can seduce Brody and film the entire thing on my phone, I can blackmail him into leaving me alone by threatening to show it to my mother. I'm sure he'll opt to save his own skin. Men always do. Then I can put my worries to rest that he might be different.

Skipping to my dresser, I open the top drawer, hoping to find some old clothes of mine.

This house is not where I was living last time I offended and got sent to juvie. Oh no, my mother and I were in a one-bedroom in a far worse section of town. I know it's a longshot that she brought my clothes here and put them away, but, holy wow...she did. Not only that, there are new clothes. Nice ones, with the tags still on!

With a breathy laugh, I go through them all, rubbing the expensive fabric on my skin, until I remember my mission is to seduce Brody this morning.

"Right. Game face." I dig until I find the shortest pair of shorts I can find and put them on. Without underwear. Next, I tug on a sports bra and a cropped tank top, leaving my stomach bare. After rubbing my fingers against my scalp to give my hair that sleepy look, I pad downstairs to the home gym. I wasn't given a tour last night. No, I kind of ran inside and hid in my room after that whole surprising exchange in the car. But I can hear metal hitting metal on the other side of the door, so I know I'll find my new stepfather here.

I roll my neck a few times, then push open the door, strutting into the small gym.

I'm working it like a runway model—

Until I catch sight of my sweaty, shirtless stepdad and run smack into a pillar.

"Jesus." He drops the barbell he's pressing overhead and comes toward me, visibly concerned. I try, I really do try, not to notice the way his thighs ripple in the navy blue sweatpants, but it's impossible. Once I notice the thighs, I can't help but become highly aware of the thick pendulum of manhood swinging between his legs. Holy mother of God. "Are you okay, London?" he asks, tipping my chin up. "Looked like you bumped your forehead."

"It's fine." I'm staring desperately up at the ceiling, forbidding myself from checking him out again. Honestly, I don't even need to. His chiseled, glistening upper body is branded on my brain forever. But— wait. Wait. Why am I avoiding looking at him? Is this how a seductress would behave? I'm never going to get what I need at this rate. "I'm really fine," I murmur, meeting his eyes for the first time. Gathering my courage, I let my attention travel down the front of his chest to his navel. "Don't let me interrupt your work out."

He tucks his tongue into the corner of his mouth. "Baby, you're dressed to interrupt."

"Oh this?" I twirl a strand of my hair around my finger. "I couldn't find any other exercise clothes."

"Is that what you came down here for?" His knuckle grazes my belly, slowly traveling up and down, stopping at the waistband of my shorts. "Exercise?"

"I love working out."

Lie. Huge one. I hate it. Satan invented it.

But I need to buy myself time so I can set up my phone to record the seduction.

"Well, don't let me stop you."

"Thanks." I turn around, celebrating when I feel his attention glue itself to my nearly bare butt. "I'll just hop on the stair climber."

"Be my guest," he rasps, adjusting himself.

I make a meal out of getting on the machine and beginning to climb, exaggerating every movement and watching his jaw flex in the wall of mirrors. "So, Brody…" Discreetly, I slip my phone out of my sports bra, setting it in the cup holder of the stair climber, facing it in the direction of the squat rack. "Do you work today?"

"Yes," he growls, tearing his gaze off my bottom, walking to a shelf near the door and chugging a full bottle of water without coming up for air. The thing between his legs is no longer a pendulum. Ah, no. It's pushing against the front of his sweatpants like an extended fist. "I'll be back for dinner. You're going to stay out of trouble while I'm gone."

"There go my plans," I quip, sending him a teasing look over my shoulder.

The water bottle pauses on its way back to the shelf. "You're in a playful mood."

"I think we got off on the wrong foot yesterday." I arch my back and really give him a show, feeling the shorts ride even higher. It's not the most comfortable thing in the world, but he's even less comfortable. His Adam's apple is tucked up under his chin, his chest rising and falling in quick succession. "Maybe we can try again?" I ask cheerfully.

"Try again," he repeats gruffly. "Yeah. I'd like that."

"Great." Continuing to climb, I peel off the tank top and toss it away, leaving me in nothing but the tiny shorts and sports bra. "Any ideas how to…achieve it?"

In the mirror, I watch his jaw firm. "You can start by telling me about your fascination with roller coasters."

I almost fall off the stair climber. "What? My what?"

He raises an eyebrow. "You heard me."

"Of course I did, but…how did you know that?" I start to climb faster. "I know Kelli didn't tell you. I've barely spoken to her about it."

"When your things were brought here, I noticed

several notebooks full of sketches." Finally setting down the water bottle, he moves to the squat rack and settles the bar on the range of muscles that make up his shoulders. "You've been interested in designing them since you were pretty young. Some of those sketches were even in crayon."

"The colors make me feel more imaginative," I blurt, before I can stop myself. "Hey, you shouldn't have been going through my things. A lot like you shouldn't have been reading through my medical records." I watch him drop into a squat, his thick ass pushing out, thighs flexing, and my mouth turns utterly dry. "Why were you interested, anyway? In the medical stuff, I mean."

"I wanted to make sure you were being taken care of in juvenile hall."

"It took you several reads to determine that?"

Our eyes lock in the mirror, his unreadable.

He doesn't respond.

"You know, most stepfathers aren't this interested in their stepchildren."

He replaces the bar on the squat rack with a metal rattle. "I'm not most stepfathers." He swipes a hand down his sweaty face. "So. Roller coasters."

"You're telling me," I mutter. "If you're thinking of encouraging me to become an engineer as part of your Fix London Plan, you're crazy. I'll never get into a good school with my kind of past."

"Your juvenile records are sealed," he points out, his attention once again zeroing in on my butt.

Darkening. "You're young, London. People have started over a lot later in life. It doesn't hurt to fill out an application or two." Once again, our eyes find each other's in the mirror. "You can make it happen."

My heart is sprinting in my chest and it has nothing to do with climbing fake stairs.

This guy doesn't look at me like everyone else.

Like I'm just another screw up who will end up with nothing. A nowhere life.

His expression is...optimistic. That's not something I've had associated with me before.

It's dangerously close to hope.

I'm suddenly desperate to change the subject. To prove to me and this man that he doesn't really care about me. That he's not willing to put in the work. No one else has. Maybe I am a lost cause. Why can't he just accept it like everyone else?

With a lump in my throat, I hit record on my phone's camera and hop off the stair climber. I make my smile flirtatious, adding a side-to-side bump in my walk, slowly approaching my increasingly wary stepfather. This man who is probably double my age, but...attracts me. I can't deny that. The closer I get to him, the more my nerve endings jangle, the weight in my tummy growing heavier and heavier.

When I reach Brody, I trace a line down the center of his chest with my fingertip, my breath catching at the way his pectorals bunch in response. "You must spend a lot of time in here." I bite my lip, letting my finger dip into his belly button, unable to ignore the stiff rod protruding from between his thighs. "If I was committing a crime—and I've done my fair share of that—you'd be the last cop I'd want to chase me."

Blazing eyes trace the slopes of my breasts. "Why is that?" he rasps.

"Maybe…just a little…" I move in close and whisper in his ear, his erection pressing against my hip. "I'd like getting caught."

He fists my hair, tugging my head back. "What are you up to, London?"

"A challenge," I gasp, shocked to find myself enjoying his aggression. My scalp prickles with a twist of his hand and my nipples bead, the air evaporating from my lungs. "If you can squat me twenty times, I'll apply to one engineering school."

Did those words just come out of my mouth?

Am I really thinking of setting myself up for that kind of rejection?

But what if I don't get rejected?

See? That little voice of optimism is already whispering in my head.

I knew he was dangerous.

"Squat you," Brody repeats, his dark brows pulling together. "You mean, with you on my back?"

"No." I shake my head and move in closer, winding my arms around my stepdad's neck. I have a momentary crisis of conscience. I'm making a move on my mother's husband! But then I remember she's probably already moved on to someone else and will inevitability be married ten or fifteen more times before the decade is over...and I hop up, wrapping my legs around Brody's waist, sucking in a breath over the huge bulge I encounter against my sex. "With me on your front."

Brody closes his eyes, that enormous part of him pulsing and growing. "London..." he warns hoarsely. "It's not polite to tease."

"Is that what I'm doing?" I breathe against his neck. "I thought I was helping you stay in shape. And getting off...on a better foot with my new stepdad."

His hand slides down the small of my back, hesitating, before pushing into my shorts and gripping my right butt cheek, kneading it roughly. "You're doing the opposite. You're trying to shove me in some category." He tilts his hips, yanking me higher and tighter in one move, grinding me to his thick ridge of flesh—and I moan brokenly. "I won't go."

"It feels like you are," I breathe, nails digging into his shoulders.

"Twenty squats and you apply to school?" he pants.

I would say anything right now to get another dose of friction. His erection is a living thing, swelling and beating against my slit, so close I can feel every ridge of his sex through the thin material of my shorts. "Yes, yes." I climb higher, whimpering when he swats my backside with a firm palm. Twice. Three times. "Please."

"God help me," he mutters thickly, bending his legs and coming up with a thorough roll of his hips, riding me on the fatness of his manhood, his head falling back to let out long groan. "One."

I watch our reflection across the room in the mirror, my eyelids drooping to half mast. I look like a horny sexpot, my thighs open around Brody's hips, my toes dangling several inches above his knees. Clinging to him, tongue bathing his sweaty neck. His buttocks straining every time he dips low, then punches up. Yes, he's punching now. Thrusting. Dropping down and driving up with a pump of hard male between my legs. My legs shake with the force.

And we're only on six.

We have to stop.

I didn't realize. I didn't know I could have an orgasm so easily. But there's something about this man. It's as though he has a direct line to all of my nerve endings and sensitive zones. Places I have a hard time finding myself. His fingers are creeping between the split of my buns, his middle finger pressing tight to that pucker and I whine his name, sucking the skin of his neck like some kind of maniac, razing him with my teeth. And he bounces me up and down, making me cry out every time I land on that hard rod, the length of it rubbing my clitoris.

"Stop." I tighten my legs around his hips, contradicting my order. "I...think. I think..."

"Did your plan to tease Daddy backfire, you horny little cock tease?" He presses his fingers tighter to my back entrance and grunts, rifling his hips up and down. "Are you about to come in those tiny fucking shorts you put on to torture me?"

"Y-yes. Yes. Stop."

He jiggles that forbidden pucker and I see stars. "But we have five more."

"I d-don't want them."

"Are you sure? Your claws are in my fucking back, baby. You're soaking through your shorts *and* my sweatpants." He bends his knees slowly. "I'm pretty sure you want the last five."

"No." I scramble to hold on. "I don't know."

Brody rams his hips upward and I scream, right there on the verge of something earth shattering. Every coiled muscle in my body is poised to implode. "Four more," he groans. "But I bet you only need one, huh, little girl? One more from who? Call me by name, London. You know the one."

"Daddy," I scream through clenched teeth.

And with a growl, he goes for broke, humping me through our clothes, grinding up into me, dropping low and doing it again, again, again, his moans pushing me over the finish line, pleasure tearing through me like a juggernaut. "Fuck. You can't help it, can you? Born to make me fucking crazy, weren't you, little girl? Parading this pussy around and daring me to take it. I will. I'll have it so many times, you'll ask me for permission to take a piss."

I'm reeling from the crudeness, the glorious wrong and right of everything that's happening here, when Brody drops me to my feet, pulls down my shorts and spanks me hard. I think it's going to be over after one slap, but he keeps going. Bringing his palm down soundly on my buttocks until I'm bracing myself against one of the mirrors, making a low keening noise, pushing up for more. Begging for the punishment I didn't know I needed.

"Now. Enough." He pulls my shorts back on over my smarting flesh and spins me around again, clasping my jaw and holding me steady so I'm looking him in the eye. "Now, you're going to send me the video you just took on your phone. Then you're going to erase it like a good girl. Aren't you?"

Wow. Caught. "Yes."

"And when I leave for work, you're going to fill out the application."

I nod, no idea what's happening inside of me.

I thought I hated authority. I've bucked it my whole life. Resented it.

But having this man ask me to fulfill promises in such a firm, but…loving way. It's like the nectar I've been trying and trying to suck from the flower is finally flowing into my veins.

It's hopeful and right and kind of twisted.

But looking up into his golden-brown eyes, I'm instantly addicted.

What am I thinking?

Not only am I tempted to trust this man I met yesterday, but he's my stepfather and he just gave me an orgasm. Didn't even take his own, just shook me like an earthquake and maintained his authority. Even now, I want to kneel in front of him and return the pleasure. I'm so eager to do it, I'm shaking.

It's terrifying.

He's too close. I'm too eager to trust.

Whatever hold Brody has on me, I have to sever it now before it becomes too strong.

It's why I run out of the gym, taking the stairs back to my room two at a time and locking the door, sliding down to the floor and reeling over what just happened, rocking side to side. How he…got to me. Made me want to trust and obey. I can't let it happen again.

I wait in my room for Brody to leave for work, fill out an online application for the closest engineering school as fast as possible—after all, I never go back on a bet—and blow out of the house with the intention of finding my old self. Or trouble. Whichever comes first.

CHAPTER THREE

Brody

I T TAKES ME a goddamn hour to get through the station.

Phones are ringing off the hook and everyone needs paperwork signed off or a fresh set of eyes on their case. By the time I finally make it to my office and close the door, I'm so anxious for the scent of London, I almost rip the drawer clean out of my desk.

I take out the steel box and place it in front of me, unlocking it with the combination only I know, flipping open the lid to take out a pair of her panties. Cost me hundreds to have these taken from her things in juvie, but they're the only thing that's been getting me by without her.

Pressing the lacy black underthings to my nose, I inhale deeply, my dick already at full mast from her lavender scent. I've never had a hard-on like this. My breaths echoing in the quiet office, I unbutton my jeans, tear down the zipper and shove her panties inside the opening, raking them up and down my rigid cock.

"Oh, fuck, baby. You like rubbing your pretty cunt on Daddy?"

In my head, I can see her as she was earlier in the gym. Flushed and wide eyed, scared to feel the pleasure we were generating, titties bouncing. Thighs open for Daddy. Now, she answers me in a whiny voice: "Yes. I love it. Please don't stop."

"I won't. I'll never stop." I drag the lace over and between my balls, winding the material around my erection and jacking myself off. With my free hand, I open my phone and pull up the video. The one of me squatting with London wrapped around me in the gym. Biting down on my bottom lip to muffle a groan, I watch my hand slide into her shorts and take hold of that hot, young ass. I watch myself fuck her through our clothing, her thighs clinging to me even as they shake, our mouths raking each other's bare skin hungrily.

Her breathy voice fills my office and I lean back, beating off with my teeth clenched, praying for the end. Imagining she's straddling me now, my cock buried deep between her legs, her hips working up and back, her pussy hot and drenched around my flesh, releasing it and impaling herself on it again, again, again, her oncoming climax making her clumsy.

"I'm going to blow, little girl. Take it deep and grind. Grind down on that dick hard. Pout that little lip out at me. Make me come so good."

On my phone, I've tugged down her shorts to spank her and now there's no way my balls can hold back. Not at a beautiful sight like that. They drain with such force, I strain the muscles of my throat trying to contain the shout. Her lacy black panties catch the majority of my spend, but some of it seeps out and rolls down my knuckles. And I just keep jacking, jacking, trying to get the kind of relief I need, but it's never enough. God knows, masturbating is better than I could have imagined now that I can picture the girl of my dreams, but it's never good enough when I know she exists out there with that little wet hole between her legs.

Waiting for Daddy to claim it.

Finally, the last drop of semen ekes out and I shudder, my fist dropping to my side, my cock still half-hard where it protrudes from my lap.

I take a moment to clean myself off and open a different app on my phone. The one that connects to the camera system in my house.

There she is.

My heart thrums at the perfect vision she makes in my home. Lying in the bedclothes I picked out for her. She's sprawled out, looking at the screen of my laptop, graceful fingers tapping at the keys, still wearing those indecent shorts that don't cover half of her ass cheeks.

No shirt or bra.

That smooth slope of her back is on display, right down to the top of her backside.

Underneath my desk, my cock starts to harden again, but I ignore it and focus on what she's doing. Zooming in, I can see that she's filling out the application and I breathe a sigh of relief. When I left the house, I worried I came on too strong.

Hell, I *did* come on too strong.

Spanking her. Speaking to her the way that I did.

Urging her to call me Daddy.

It's just that I've been waiting so long to have this chance with London. Seems like forever I've been waiting for her to be discharged from the juvenile offenders' program. To be home with me where she belongs. Under my watchful eye, being cared for. The good kind of caring she's been deprived of for far too long—that's what I'll give, day in and day out.

God knows I'm a pushy bastard. My means aren't ethical. But I know this girl. I've read her transcripts with her juvenile hall therapist. I've watched every video of her on Kelli's phone, several times. I've read through her diaries and notebooks and watched her on juvie surveillance cameras. Her exterior is tough, but on the inside, she's aching. Her soul is that of an angel. She wants to be loved and accepted, but she's scared. Pushing her is my only option. Pushing her to follow her dreams so I can support her and prove I believe in her, until she's strong enough to believe in herself.

Getting physical wasn't supposed to happen quite so soon. After all, I'm her stepfather. If she knew I'd orchestrated the whole marriage just to get close to her, it could scare her away. Is there a hope in hell of reigning in my lust now that I've felt her legs around my waist, though?

On the screen of my phone, she rolls over on the bed and presents her tits, arms raised over her head. She sighs and stretches, forcing me to wrap my hand around my stiffening dick, stroking it tightly and thoroughly. "Baby wants to play again?" I say, my breath quickening. "Open your legs and rub that beautiful clit. Show me where it aches."

Instead of obeying my will, however, London sighs and bounds off the bed, crossing to her dresser and taking out a jean skirt, shucking her shorts and pulling the denim on hastily, followed by a T-shirt and flip-flops. Where is she going?

Instantly on alert, I shove my throbbing cock back into my jeans and zip up, following her progress from room to room around my house. And when I see the stubborn set to her chin and desperation in her eyes, dread invades my stomach. She might have followed through on her promise to complete the application, but she's onto her own agenda now—and it's up to me to stop her before she does something destructive.

I once asked Kelli why she gave her daughter the name London.

Because she's meant for grander things than me! And doesn't London sound grand?

That was one of the only things Kelli was ever right about. London is meant for more. She's wily and intelligent. Funny. Beautiful. Creative. Some of the sketches in her notebooks look like they could have been done by professionals. But after a lifetime of being left in her mother's dust, she doesn't realize how much she deserves better. How capable she is of achieving it. And if she continues to follow the pattern she's been on, London is probably going to do her best to get locked up again so she doesn't have to try—and face the disappointment. It's easier to her than failing. She's protecting herself.

But she doesn't have to do that anymore.

She has me.

I'm not letting her fall.

Coming to my feet, I watch the dot moving on the screen, letting me know she's on the move, thanks to the tracking device I put in her phone last night when she finally fell asleep.

When I realize where she's headed, I mutter a curse and snatch up my keys, running for the door.

CHAPTER FOUR

London

THE DEVIL'S DEN is the place to go in town when you're looking for trouble.

I should know, since most of my youth was spent in there, beneath the freeway overpass. From a distance, I can see that it's the same old characters leaned up against a beat up Chrysler, passing around cigarettes and something stronger. My most recent stint in juvenile hall was six months after helping fence some stolen iPhones, so I haven't seen these idiots in a while.

That's exactly what they are. Idiots.

The definition of insanity is doing the same thing over and over again, expecting a different result—and that's what they do. Committing petty crimes, thinking they won't get caught. At least I know I'm going to get caught. I'm well aware that the cops are going to come straight to the Devil's Den and pull us in for a lineup as soon as the crime is committed.

I've had a lot of time to think over the last six months. Knowing I will be put in real prison next time I do something illegal has made me pretty introspective. And I've started to ask myself, *why?* Why do I continually let these criminals include me in their activities when I know it's only going to land me in a cell?

Growing up, I was always shuffled to the side. Pawned off on neighbors, friends, the barest acquaintances, while my mother vamoosed with new boyfriends. For so long, going to juvenile hall was my way of controlling where I ended up. Instead of being put somewhere, like a sack of useless sand. Like someone who only gets in the way.

Now, though…I'm an adult. I can still control where I end up, but I no longer have to find refuge from my mother's whims and her sketchy boyfriends behind bars.

What if I can actually make something of myself?

I've never allowed myself to wonder, but dammit, Brody got in my head.

I think that's why I'm here, across the street from the Devil's Den, trying to psyche myself up to make my triumphant return. Because I'm scared.

Shit. I hate admitting that.

This is what I know, though. I know how to mess up, get sent away, continue the pattern. It's been my safety net for so long, but I'm not a kid anymore. The consequences are more severe. Am I really willing to chance prison so I don't have to expect more from myself?

You're young, London. People have started over a lot later in life. It doesn't hurt to fill out an application or two. You can make it happen.

Brody's voice stops me from taking the first step across the street.

Unbelievable.

My stepfather's encouragement is actually working on me. How pathetic.

What would he gain from my success, anyway?

What is his angle?

I've never been anything but a burden to my mother's significant others. I don't understand why Brody is different. Or how he could want so much for me when we've only just met for the first time.

With that thought weighing heavily on my mind, I decide to put off my return to the Devil's Den for another day, and turn to head back to the bus stop—

"London!"

Someone calls my name from across the street and a loud cheer goes up from the dozen or so teens and twenty-something's loitering beneath the freeway overpass. I can't help but feel a spark of warmth in my chest over their earnest reception. Despite their mental shortcomings, these people were here on the days and nights when I had no one at all. So despite the tug of foreboding in my stomach, I execute a sweeping bow and pirouette across the street to a soundtrack of thunderous applause.

"You're back. How was the slammer?"

"Looking hot, as always, blondie."

"Did you bring us presents?"

The unofficial leader of the group is Lurch, thanks to his height and slightly curved upper spine. He steps forward and ruffles my hair now, leaving a cigarette dangling from the corner of his lips. "Hey, London," he drawls, giving me a speculative once over. "You're just in time."

That seedling of trepidation in my belly grows roots. "For what?"

A couple of them trade looks.

Lurch tosses down his cigarette, grounding it out with the toe of his boot. "We're going on a run. Nothing major."

"Yeah, nothing major," a girl to his right echoes.

I keep my expression neutral, but I'm wishing I'd just stayed home. Maybe filled out another engineering school application. Not that I expect to be accepted anywhere, but I have to admit...it had felt good to complete the form and send it. Felt good to try. "What is nothing major?" I ask, blithely.

"You always were a good wheel woman, weren't you, blondie?"

"London," I say tightly. "And I'm not really...prepared for a run. Not today."

There's a shift in the energy around me. I know how this goes. Once you're in this world, you're completely in. Or you have to get out, free and clear. There is no in between and that's where I'm standing right now. "It's just a beer run," Lurch says, holding up his gloved hands. "The weekend is coming up and we're low on supply. Tommy and Grinch have a contact at Walmart. He's going to open the exit door, so we can get in and out without a problem." He claps me on the shoulder and a shiver runs down to my wrist. "You drive."

They don't need me. There are plenty of options for drivers.

This is just their way of pulling me back in.

"Ah…" I plow my fingers through my hair and back away. "You know, actually, I have plans this afternoon. I really just came by to say hey—"

"What are you…going straight?" Lurch laughs while lighting another smoke. "Aren't you the girl who drove a stolen police car into a lake on her sixteenth birthday?"

It's on the tip of my tongue to tell them it was an accident—at least the lake crashing part—but everyone is already laughing and I have no choice but to laugh, too, or look salty. Yes, I did steal the police car. I was desperate. My mother was getting ready to leave me with her ex-boyfriend's sister, who I'd never met. And I was scared, angry, young and reckless.

"Yeah…" Someone else pipes up. "Didn't you once chain yourself to the door of city hall to protest the circus coming to town?"

"Then take a swing at the mayor when he tried to unlock the chains?"

More laughter.

I don't tell them that the mayor groped me while trying to unfasten those chains, his clammy hands roving beneath my belly button and over my breasts, squeezing until I cried.

The words die in my throat because I realize…I

am one of these idiots. A lot of the times I was taken into custody, I was acting out so they would take me out of my mother's care. Other times, like protesting the circus, I really cared about the cause. But none of that matters. What matters is that every stupid thing I've done is a stain on my reputation.

Lurch holds out the keys to the Chrysler, raising an eyebrow.

Waiting for me to take them.

They're right.

I was crazy to think I could overcome my past now, wasn't I?

Still, Brody's voice in my head makes me hesitate, my fingers pausing over the keys. Maybe…maybe if I call him, he'll help me? He's so confident. Bossy.

He'll know exactly what to do and—

They all start pushing me toward the car, playfully, but I can't get away. I laugh and push back, but I'm already being nudged into the driver's seat, keys tossed into my lap. The door slams, Tommy and Grinch piling into the back seat, Lurch in the passenger side.

Okay. One run and I'll never come back. I'll try. I will.

I'll fill out applications and let Brody convince me I have potential.

What's the worst that can happen?

Oh. A lot, apparently.

CHAPTER FIVE

Brody

WHEN THE CALL goes out from dispatch, a pit opens in my stomach.

Five suspects in custody.

Robbery.

The more I listen to the chatter between the dispatcher and the responding officers, the more I learn. An employee of the store is also being held on suspicion to aid and abet the robbery. The entire offense was caught on CCTV. No mention of London, but I know she's among the five suspects. I know it.

I'm driving like a bat out of hell from the other side of town, hitting the gas through red lights and turning corners on two wheels. She must have left her phone at the Devil's Den, because I tracked her there only to find her gone, a bunch of punk kids in her place, none of them willing to talk. More than anything, I just want to concentrate on getting to her and making everything okay, but I refuse to take her safety or freedom for granted. Picking up the radio, I bark into the receiver. "If one of the suspects is London Allen, keep her at the scene until I get there."

A crackle comes from my dashboard mounted radio. "Copy that, Captain." A long pause, followed by a snicker. "It's London, all right. Didn't know she was back in town. Girl's always been trouble—"

"Don't question her. Don't even look at her." The muscles in my throat are strained. "Do you copy?"

His tone changes abruptly. "Yes, Captain."

I slam the radio back into its perch and peel into the parking lot where the robbery took place. Red and blue lights flash in the alley behind the Walmart and with a squeal of tires, I'm parked and exiting the vehicle, ignoring shouts of my name and storming toward the row of suspects lined up on the curb.

There she is.

Handcuffed in the middle of street scum, like a diamond mistakenly dropped among ashes. Her cornflower eyes find me immediately, then zip away, her chin turning stubborn. The tip of her nose turns red, though, giving her away—and my heart turns over.

Goddammit. This is my fault.

I came on too strong.

Didn't give her a chance to trust me before I started asking her to consider the future. My poor girl probably got scared to death. Of course she fell back on bad habits. It was too much, too soon. *Fix it.*

Clearing my throat hard, I turn to the closest officer. "I'll bring London Allen down the station and take her statement myself."

"Keep a close eye on your keys," warns the officer,

smirking. "She's been known to steal cop cars and take them for a swim." He turns his back to the row of suspects and lowers his voice. "I wouldn't mind taking her for a little joy ride, if you know what I mean."

Rage makes my eye tick. "She's my stepdaughter."

The color drains from his face. "Jesus, I didn't know—"

"Go near her and I'll saw your dick off with a butter knife. Are we clear?"

"Yes, Captain."

My hands shake with the need to wrap around his throat. "Get the fuck out of my sight. And if I hear that kind of filth out of you again, about anyone, I'll have your badge."

Head down, he scurries away and I waste no time approaching London. Though she's stiff as a board, I help her stand and walk her to my police car, loading her into the backseat. I'm desperate to get the cuffs off her wrists, but I'm already putting myself under speculation with this personal treatment of my stepdaughter; releasing her too quickly would put me in jeopardy with internal affairs. I have no choice but to bring her to the station and take her statement. But it'll be a cold day in hell before I let this angel spend another second behind bars.

On the drive to the station, the car is silent, thanks mostly to the thick partition between us. I suspect she would have stayed quiet no matter what, but I can't tell if her pride has been stung or if she's pissed over getting caught.

Minutes later, I lead her through the back of the police building into a private interrogation room and finally allow myself to touch her. Making sure the room is locked and there is no one on the other side of the glass, I grip her waist and lift her onto the edge of the metal interrogation table, curling my fingers into fists before I give in to temptation and skim them up her smooth thighs.

"Are you okay?"

"Fine," she bites off, still refusing to look at me.

I'm not having it. I capture her chin and lift, giving her no choice but to look me in the face. "What happened?"

She rolls her eyes. "You know what happened."

"I want to hear it from you."

Puzzlement shifts her features. "Why?"

It pains me that she seems genuinely confused. "You don't think your side of the story matters?"

"It never has before."

"It does now." I brush my thumb along the curve of her jaw. "It matters with me."

She searches my face. "Why?"

Because I'm going to love you, make you mine, keep you forever. You don't know it yet but you're looking at the man who is hungry for you every second of the fucking day. It's too soon to spring any of that on her, though. Look what happened the last time I got impatient. She hauls off and robs a goddamn Walmart. "It matters because you're my stepdaughter. That makes you my responsibility."

"Is it your responsibility to touch me like you did this morning?" she challenges, huskily.

I fist the sides of her jean skirt and yank her closer to the edge of the table, making her gasp. "You wrapped your legs around me, little girl, if you remember."

"I remember," she breathes, quickly shaking herself. "What's the point of telling you my side of what happened if you're not going to believe me?"

"What makes you so sure?"

"No one ever does. Ever." Pink climbs her cheeks. "I heard that officer laughing about the time I drove the police car into a lake. It was a stupid thing to do. I know that, but…there was a deer in the road. That's why I swerved and ended up…never mind."

"Keep going."

"That's why I drove it into the lake. Not to destroy property. I barely made it out of the car in time myself." That nugget of truth pulls a choked sound out of me. For a moment, all I can see is London crawling out through the window of a police car, water pouring in from all sides, and it rattles me to the core. "I've done some reckless things, but I meant well some of the time."

Her voice cracks on the final word and I can't help it, I trace her temple with my open mouth, planting a kiss on her hairline. "Of course you did."

"I just wanted to be in control of something. Everything, my whole life, every second of it, felt so…changeable. At a moment's notice."

I pull her close and she rests the side of her face on my chest, relaxing against me completely when my hands start to trace circles on her back.

"If you really want to know what happened today…"

"I do."

She lets out a slow breath. "I fell back into my old pattern. There I was again…pawned off on another one of my mother's men. Sometimes it feels good to be self-destructive when the alternative is sitting there and acknowledging how terrible I feel. You know? But…"

My palm slips under her T-shirt and drags up her spine, causing her to shiver against me. "But what, baby?"

Her nipples turn erect against my chest and she tries to draw her thighs together, but I block their progress with my hips, slowly urging them wider by stepping closer, resting the ridge of my cock against her lacy pink panties.

London draws back slightly, looking up at me, dazed. "I tried to say no and walk away, because I thought of you. I wanted to call you to come help me. I've never even thought of doing that before with anyone." Moisture swims into her blue eyes. "I didn't want to do it. I changed my mind, but I got stuck. And then everything happened so fast—"

"I believe you," I say without hesitating.

And it's not just a line. I do.

It's about time someone did.

About time someone took a look at the setbacks she's been facing since birth and marveled over how bright she's become despite it all.

"You...do?" London whispers.

"Yes."

Her eyes briefly stray toward the door. "But they won't. I'll still have to get booked and go in front of a judge. Tried as an adult—"

"No, London. I won't let that happen." I wrap her long blonde hair around my fist and tug lightly, watching her perfect lips puff open. "Repeat after me. My stepfather is going to take care of it."

Her tits rise and fall quickly, her back arched thanks to her hands still being cuffed behind her, pushing those little globes against the front of her thin T-shirt, displaying her puckered nipples like works of art. "My stepfather is going to take care of it."

God help me, I told myself I'd take this slower, but she's so sweet with tears in her eyes, her body opened to me like the petals of a flower. We're alone in this darkened, locked room and she's just shown me the first sign of trust. Her admission that she almost called me, that she second guessed her actions, might not seem like a big deal to anyone else, but it's a huge step for us. It's a foundation.

I can't stop myself from lowering my mouth to hers, brushing my lips side to side on top of her gasping ones. "As your stepfather, I should comfort you in times like this, shouldn't I? When you've been upset?"

Slowly, she nods. "Yes."

I push closer, pinning my hard dick between her panty-covered cunt and my belly. "Are you comforted by kisses, little girl?"

She whimpers. "I don't know, I've never kissed anyone."

A moan kindles in my chest. "If you want your first, you better offer me your tongue."

Her breaths are racing now, but that tongue does sneak out to wet her lips, remaining perched there on her lower lip, her eyes on me obediently.

This is exactly what I imagined when I saw her picture for the first time.

I saw her just like this.

Asking for pleasure. Trusting me. Surrendering.

I've never been a man who goes in search of female companionship. I've dated throughout my life, but the military won most of my focus. I'm an aggressive man. Dominant. Never once has it crossed over to the opposite sex, though. Never once have I needed so badly for a woman to look up at me just like this. It's only ever been London. She called to me through a picture, woke something up deep inside of me and it's clawing to get out.

With a low groan, I lick our tongues together, twisting my lips on top of hers so I can sink deep, pulling at her flavor, the kiss wet and nasty from the get-go. London's head is tipped all the way back, her hands still imprisoned at the small of her back—and Jesus Christ, having her completely at my mercy makes my cock thick and heavy in my jeans. I rock against her and she whines into the kiss, opening wider so I can devour, tongue fucking her sexy little mouth while she mewls and writhes around on the table in front of me.

I am not fucking her in an interrogation room for the first time.

Not a chance in hell.

But if I don't quit grinding on her virgin pussy, that's exactly what's going to happen.

Going to have her pregnant within twenty-four hours of coming home.

"Wait," she blurts, pulling away, her lips swollen from my treatment of them. "Brody...y-you're married to my mother. We shouldn't be doing this."

Of course, she's right. According to what she believes is reality.

Is she ready to know how deep my obsession with her runs?

Fuck. I don't know. And I'm not taking a chance. I'll never play fast and loose with London or our life together. "You're right," I manage, dropping my forehead down to hers, out breaths mingling hotly between us. "I'm sorry. I was worried about you and got carried away."

She nods, her eyes soft and drowsy, hips restless.

Horny. God, she's worked up. Can't sit still for a second.

Giving in to temptation, I lift up the hem of her soft denim skirt and look between her spread legs, finding her panties drenched, molded to her unfucked slit. Lord above, she's exquisite. Every golden inch. "We'll take care of this." I drag my knuckle up through the center of her pussy and she cries out, coming off the desk. "Then we'll behave. Sound good, London?"

"Yes," she says quickly, her head falling back with a sucked-in breath when I slide my fingers beneath the waistband of her panties, tugging them down her thighs. Her neck is so inviting, I'm powerless to do anything but lick the smooth column from throat to earlobe, removing her underwear in the process and dropping them to the floor. And with my hands free, they find her tits immediately, dragging up the hem of her shirt to her neck and acquainting my palms with the supple weight of them, the greedy nipples begging for attention.

"Gorgeous girl," I rasp, leaning down to close my lips around one of the rosy buds, drunk from the taste of her in seconds. So intoxicated, I don't know how I'll be able to tear myself away from the innocent peaks. Especially when she's at my mercy, restrained. Unable to do anything but accept the pleasure. "Do you like me being in charge, London?"

Her nod is cautious, but her eyes are ablaze. "Yes."

That word out of her mouth, the confirmation that she feels this intense bond between us, too, sends my pulse into a gallop. "Did you enjoy your spanking this morning?"

"Yes," she whispers, her nipples plumping against

my palms.

"I didn't do it because I was mad at you. I need you to know that. I'd never lay a finger on you out of anger."

She peers up at me, like she can see right through me. "I…know."

"Do you?" My voice is thick with emotion. "Why do you think I spanked you?"

"I'm not sure," she whispers. "I only know that it made me feel…grounded. I'm always kind of lost and floating. Treading water in the system, no idea what'll happen in the future. But when you s-spanked me, I was present. There was someone holding me down and keeping me from flying away."

Jesus. My heart climbs up into my throat.

It's on the tip of my tongue to tell London that I'm in love with her.

That I knew it the second I became aware of her existence.

This bond between us is only beginning, though, for the love of God. She's only been home for twenty-four hours. One step at a time.

"I've got you now, baby," I say, raking my hands down her thighs, pushing open her knees, wider and wider, exposing her pussy even more, drawing her feminine lips apart slowly, revealing the pink paradise beyond. "I won't let you fly away. Ever."

My obsession won't allow her out of my sight, more accurately.

Ever.

When I go down on my knees in front of her, she sobs, the handcuffs clinking behind her on the metal interrogation table. "Brody, I...I've never..."

"Shhh," I breathe against the inside of her thigh. "You have no secrets from me."

I clutch her ass in my hands and draw her to the edge, inhaling the peachy scent of her cunt, kissing the parted flesh, once, twice, before sliding my tongue through that wet valley. Her gasp of surprise rings in my ears, the delicious taste of her causing my cock to leak against the fly of my jeans. I moan roughly and suction my lips over as much of her pussy as I can, dropping my tongue down on top of her clit and bathing it in fast strokes.

"B-Brody."

London falls backward on the table, her cuffed hands keeping her back arched and her hips rear off the table helplessly, her thighs restless on either side of my head. She's sensual and nervous at the same time, lifting her flesh to my mouth eagerly one second, hesitantly the next, until she finally gives in and begins pumping her hips up toward my tongue, broken moans falling from her lips, wetness releasing and coasting down my chin.

Christ, I can't get enough. She's smooth and sugary and hot, her clit swelling with every drag of my tongue, her sharp intakes of breath telling me when she's on the verge of an orgasm. Her virginity is only inches away from my mouth right now and a savage, possessive part of me wants to stab my tongue deep and pop her little cherry, but I command myself to have patience, appeasing myself with the reminder that no other man will ever get near it.

"Oh. Oh my God." One more lick and her pussy starts to quiver, her legs stiffening where I've rested them on my shoulders. "Brody."

I close my lips lightly around her clit and apply careful suction, increasing the pressure until she's crying out. "What do you really want to call me, little girl?"

"Daddy," she heaves, then the storm breaks.

My tongue remains on her clit, polishing it determinedly while she finishes, her body shaking with beautiful spasms. Her tits are still out and they grow flushed, juicy in the rush of pleasure. My plan was only to give London relief, but she's too beautiful. Too tempting. And I've been hungry for so long that I can't help but wrap her hair around my fist and guide her down off the table to her knees, settling her in a kneel with her hands restrained behind her back, her eyes drowsy from her climax, her nipples in two, tight puckers.

I can't get my dick out fast enough. I'm grunting and panting, my balls drawn up into my body, prepared to release. No sooner do I have it in my hands than does the come spear up, hot and thick, from my balls. With a groan of her name, I stroke my cock once and paint a stripe of white across her face. And when she opens her mouth and sticks out her tongue, her expression unmistakably excited, I unload the rest in hot, greedy spurts, my groin straining under the intensity. The perfection of the moment. Putting my claim on this girl.

Making her mine.

Finally, the throes of my climax ease off and I cup her chin, dragging a thumb through some of my spend and glossing it over her lower lip. "That's a good girl." I slide my thumb in and out of her mouth, my breathing still labored. "You know what comes next."

My words make her tremble so violently she can barely get to her feet, even with my help. But she does. She does and she bends over the table eagerly, moaning excitedly as I yank up the back of her skirt and crack my palm across her ass. Several times. Watching her glistening pussy lips shake with every slap.

"Daddy," she whimpers. "Daddy."

"That's right." I kick her feet wider and deliver a resounding smack, one on each cheek. "I satisfy the front, then I remind the back who all of this belongs to. Understand?"

"Yes," she shrieks into the table. "Yes."

"Are you going to behave now?"

"Yes, I promise."

"Good." I soothe the stinging flesh on her ass with a slow, gentle massage that slows her breathing and loosens her tense muscles. "So very good." I slide her panties back up her legs and fix her skirt, finally uncuffing her wrists, standing her up and turning her around.

God, she's a vision, visibly dazed, teeth marks on her bottom lip.

"Are you going to take me home now?" she whispers.

"I have a better idea."

CHAPTER SIX

London

B RODY BRINGS ME to an amusement park.

Even after he buys our tickets and leads me through the massive entrance, I still can't believe it's happening. The sounds of children screaming on the roller coasters awakens hope and excitement that has lain dormant in my belly for so long. I want to go watch the brightly-colored cars fly down the tracks and loop upside down. I want to watch for hours.

And Brody seems content to let me, sitting beside me on a metal bench, the two of us unmoving in the midst of the chaotic crowd.

He doesn't say anything when I gape, tracking the progress of a car full of people as they are slowly cranked to the top of an incline and dropped, picking up enough momentum to complete a sideways spiral. My pulse races, my fingers itching for my notebook. So much time passes that I don't realize it's fully dark outside until Brody brings me a soft pretzel and a Coke.

"Are we actually going to ride one of the coasters or just stare at them all night?" he asks me playfully, biting into his own pretzel.

I'm momentarily distracted by the sight of his straight white teeth burying in the dough, his muscular throat working to swallow the bite. Even the hand holding the pretzel is hypnotic, because I remember what it feels like on my skin. On my bare knees, my cheek, my backside.

What exactly is happening between me and my stepfather?

We are seriously attracted to each other. That much is very, very obvious.

But it runs deeper than that. Even now, I want to climb up onto his lap and have him stroke my hair. I want to tip my face up and get a kiss. I want to whisper that forbidden D-word and feel him grow aroused. And it would feel like the most natural thing in the world.

It's not, though.

It's not.

I have to remember that.

This man is married to my mother and he's already given me two orgasms.

We've kissed. He's used his mouth between my legs, on my breasts.

My body is already desperate for more. Not only for the physical release, but the emotional comfort I get from his touch, the connection between us.

"What are you thinking about?" Brody asks, lowering the pretzel to his thigh.

Until he asks the question, I don't realize I've been staring at him.

Specifically, his magical mouth.

Behave. He told me to behave.

What happened between us shouldn't happen again. I might have a non-existent relationship with my mother, but I'm not the kind of person who wrecks a marriage. It's definitely time to start reigning in my behavior.

"Um." Sitting up straighter, I push my fall of blonde hair back and smile. "N-nothing. I was thinking we should definitely go ride one of these suckers."

His smile crinkles the corners of his eyes. "Let's go."

We walk through the busy park, the flashing lights glowing in the darkness around us. He lets me choose which one we're going to ride and I pick one of the more classic, older rides in the park. "I always wanted to ride it when I was young, but never got the chance," I say, as we take our place at the back of the line.

"You drew this one a lot in your notebooks." He settles a hand on my shoulder, shooting a tingle straight down to my toes. "But you made some improvements to it. Added a waterfall and some lighting effects."

Surprised pleasure fills my chest. "You remember that?"

His thumb massages circles into the back of my neck. "I remember everything."

Am I imagining it? Or is the subtext that he re-members everything about me?

Wishful thinking, London. He told you to behave, remember?

"Yeah, the one thing I always think is missing from roller coasters is atmosphere. What about the music and strobe lights and smoke? There should be a storyline."

Another long stroke of of his thumb up into my hairline. "You're going to do it yourself one day."

His touch is causing an answering clench between my legs. The fact that we're being pushed into such close quarters by the people behind and in front of us really isn't helping matters. My nipples are hard, tingling. We're standing side by side, hips touching, but without the support of a bra, it's impossible for him not to notice the points pushing up against the cotton of my T-shirt. The only indication he gives is some increased pressure from his massaging touch.

More than anything, I want to turn in to Brody's hard body and have his arms wrapped around me. He towers over everyone in line, his posture that of a man in control. A man who holds the reins to the universe. He's left his police badge in the car, but he might as well be wearing it for the amount of authority rolling off his broad shoulders.

I'm attracted to a lot more than his body, though. The way he keeps encouraging me…it's the first time anyone has ever done that. And I'm actually starting to believe him. I'm growing hungry to set goals, professionally, and try and reach them. Back in the interrogation room, he trusted me. Believed me. It's making me want to believe in myself and my abilities.

"We've only talked about me," I say, eager to know more about this man who has become a giant fixture in my life, literally overnight. "What about you, Brody? You haven't been a cop in town long or I would have met you before. Where did you come from?"

He seems a little caught off guard by my interest. "Baltimore." He clears his throat. "That's where I grew up. When my tour with the army ended, I applied for a job with law enforcement. Transferred south when the captain position opened."

"Of course you're military." I grin up at him. "It's right there in how you stand."

His eyes narrow, lips twitching. "How do I stand?"

"Like a drill sergeant." My body turns toward him naturally, flirtatiously, the toes of my flip flops meeting the hard front of his boots. "Mean."

Brody takes a slow step closer, forcing me to tip my head back...and the move grazes our hips together, sending shivers of delight to my nerve endings. "Am I mean to you, little girl?" he asks, sliding a finger into one of the belt loops of my jean skirt.

I pout up at him. "Uh-huh."

"Really?" He dips his head to speak beside my ear. "I might be a little mean when I want to get a point across, but ah, baby, it makes you so fucking wet, doesn't it?"

Heat spreads between my legs. "You said to behave."

"You make it hard to follow through when I can see the shape of your nipples through that shirt and you can't stop looking at my mouth." With the use of my belt loop, he tugs me up against him, making me gasp. "You thinking of how well it licked your pussy?"

Stepdad.

He's your stepdad.

Behave.

If I don't figure out a way to put out this fire he's lit inside of me, I'm going to climb him right here, in line for this roller coaster. There is something about the anonymity of the theme park. No one here knows how we're related by marriage. No one knows us at all. We're a man and his much younger girlfriend. A little unusual, but nothing illicit.

If only they knew.

Biting my lip, I turn so I'm facing away, but Brody clutches my hips and yanks my backside into the curve of his lap. Still, I try to overcome the flames licking at my inner thighs. "D-do you still have family in Baltimore?"

"A sister." His mouth falls to my neck, skating up the side. "You'll meet her one day."

"Will I?" I breathe, shuddering when his right hand travels from my hip to my stomach, slipping beneath my shirt to rest there, right below my belly button. On my bare skin.

"Yes, London. You will."

There is no mistaking the erection he presses to my backside, or the way he rocks against me, his breath hot against the crown of my head. We move with the flow of the line, stepping together, our bodies tightly pressed. My panties are soaked to the skin, my breasts heavy and aching. In this place, this park that doesn't feel like real life, my inhibitions are fading into nothing. Maybe they never existed at all when it comes to this man, because it's as though he was made for me. As though we were made for each other, drawn by a magnetic force.

I don't realize my eyes have closed, my body lost in the rhythm of his grinding movements, until Brody's chest muscles flex and stiffen behind me. His fingers dig into my stomach slightly and there's a wealth of possessiveness in that touch—and when I tip my head back and look up at Brody questioningly, I notice he's looking at something up ahead. Following his line of vision, I see a group of guys my age leering at me.

We're in a dark part of the waiting area now, bathed almost entirely in black by an artificial rock overhang. No one is paying attention to us, save that pack of rowdy idiots, but the last thing I expect is for Brody to slide his hand further into my jean skirt and grip me intimately between the legs. At the same time, his teeth sink into the side of my neck, his hand massaging rhythmically, at such a perfect pace and strength my eyes roll back in my head.

"Show them I'm your Daddy, London."

I'm wrapped in the pleasure, the friction, but there's something inside me that can't help but obey him. That wants to obey him, because it will give him satisfaction as well as me.

Without hesitation, I drop my head back and let my stepfather molest my mouth.

Let him sink his tongue deep and wind it together with mine, his grip turning almost bruising between my legs, the pleasure/pain almost pushing me toward a climax. Almost, almost, but he breaks the kiss and walks me forward once more, breaking the spell. The group of guys walk ahead quickly, muttering to each other, eventually moving out of sight. And there's no more behaving. Not after that.

I turn in Brody's arms and find myself yanked up on my toes, our mouths feasting on each other, his big hand beneath my skirt, roughly kneading my butt cheeks, his huge erection wedged between our bellies.

"We're going to ride this ride, little girl," he rasps, tracing the split of my backside with his calloused middle finger. "And then I'm going to take you to the parking lot and fuck you silly in the backseat of my car. Tell me you want it, too."

"I want it," I whimper, letting him lift me up into his hold, my toes rubbing against his shins, our mouths interlocked and breathing, breathing.

"Please step into lane three," someone calls behind us. "You're in the next car."

We both laugh, Brody managing to set me down, but he keeps his arm around my shoulder, his lips grazing my temple periodically, as we take our place to wait our turn.

As excited as I am to ride this roller coaster—I've

been waiting since I was a child—I can barely focus on anything but the man beside me and what's about to happen.

I'm going to have sex with him and there's nothing I can do to stop it.

My conscience is no match for the gravity between us.

How safe I feel with him. How wanted.

On the way down the steep drop, everyone around me screams and I throw my arms up in the air, screaming along with them, letting the night air cool my flushed cheeks, the wind sending my hair in a hundred directions. And when I reach the bottom and I'm laughing, more exhilarated than I can ever remember, Brody is watching me with an emotion in his eyes that I can't name, but it echoes inside me, substantial and undeniable.

He takes me hand and helps me off the ride, leading me out of the park.

CHAPTER SEVEN

Brody

I T SEEMS TO take hours to reach my Range Rover, but in reality it's only minutes. I have to keep stopping to kiss London's sweet mouth, my hands running all over the delectable curves of her body. A few times, I swear we're not going to make it to the relative privacy of my vehicle, that I'm going to back her into the shadows and fuck her standing up in plain view of anyone passing by, but we make it somehow, my finger stabbing the button on my key ring to unlock the door.

As obsessed as I am with my stepdaughter, I underestimated how much. I was shortsighted to think I could take this slow and work on bringing us close when I love her so much. When I need to be inside her more than I need the blood in my veins. She is magnificent. She is mine. And I can't wait any longer to make that truth real in every sense.

Even though we've only known each other one day, I have to believe she will not get scared and run away when I reveal the full truth of how I found her. I have to have faith.

Confidence intact, I pull open the back door,

watching London clamber inside on hands and knees. She turns to me, wide eyed and excited, and there's no more waiting. Her thighs are parted, showing off her panties, offering me her cherry on a platter. I'm going to take it. I have to. With my cock straining painfully behind my fly, I lunge in behind her and slam the door, locking it, turning and flattening her on the backseat.

"Daddy is done waiting," I growl, ripping her T-shirt down the middle.

The street light comes in through the tinted window to play on her pale, trembling globes, the peaked nipples in the center of them.

"Fuck," I snap, unzipping her jeans skirt and tearing the thing down her legs, throwing it over my shoulder. "You've driven me to the edge, little girl. It was hard enough having you wiggle that tight ass around in my lap without coming. Then I see other males looking at you?" I yank down her panties and discard them in the foot well. "For that, I'm going to pump so deep, you'll see stars."

"How is that my fault?" she whispers, watching me unzip my jeans, quick breaths expanding her ribcage.

"It's not, baby." I take my cock, groaning over the freedom, the space it has now to grow. "You're just the one who pays for my jealousy. It's not fair, is it?"

She shakes her head, moving her long blonde hair around her shoulders.

I push her legs apart and pin her, dropping my heavy dick down on top of her mound and rolling my hips. At the same time, I shove my mouth up against her ear and say, "No, it's not fair, but those are the breaks when you've got a sweet little hole between your legs that fits a man's cock, London. It's where seed goes. And the seed builds and builds every fucking second of the day in a man." I ram my dick up against the juncture of her thighs, capturing her gasp with my left palm. "When I see another man looking at what's mine, all I can think about is getting my seed inside you first. Your tight, wet pussy does that. It drives me goddamn crazy, so I can only imagine what it's doing to every other man in the vicinity. When that happens, you get fucked, hard and raunchy. End of story. Fair is the last thing on my mind."

Maybe I should be holding back the harsh truth of my possessiveness, but I can't. With her cornflower eyes blinking at me over the top of my hand, everything comes tumbling out. She's got me too horny and jealous to temper my words. Or my actions. That must be why I take my left hand off her mouth and take rough hold of my cock, guiding it between her thighs. Rubbing a path up and down within her folds to gather dampness, before working it into the impossibly narrow entrance to her body.

"Come on, baby," I grit, managing to get the head inside. "Let Daddy in."

"I'm trying," she hiccups.

God, she's so beautiful, naked beneath me on the seat. With her cunt lips parted around my shaft, I almost shove the rest of the way in. But I love this girl.

I love her in a way that goes beyond reason and sanity—and she's a virgin. Whether she did it consciously or not, she saved herself for me. I won't squander this gift.

Bringing our mouths together, I soothe her with a long, unhurried kiss. I tongue her deep in that pretty mouth until she starts to mewl, her hips getting restless. Moisture rushes to the place where I've only managed to get an inch deep, the slickness allowing me to push in more. And more. Until I'm about halfway. I keep working my mouth over the top of hers, swallowing her little anxious sounds. Waiting for a sign that she's ready for the rest of my cock. And I get it when she digs her nails into my ass and makes a sound of frustration.

"More, Daddy."

I go fucking blind for a minute, the pleasure of those words is so intense. Then, desperate as a beast in heat, I grip the door handle, prop my right foot against the opposite side of the vehicle and shove—hard—ripping through the barrier of her innocence.

London's whine fills the car, clashing with my growl.

"Are you okay?" I ask raggedly.

"Yes," she gasps, her knees raising, hugging my sides.

I'm already stroking. Ferociously. I can't stop.

She's tight as hell and drenched. Perfect.

The Range Rover rocks around us, the windows fogging from our hot breaths and the aggressiveness with which I'm mating my stepdaughter. There is both pleasure and pain in the act. Pleasure from looking at her, having our sweaty skin slide together, our mouths locked and fucking in their own way, my cock being squeezed rhythmically, being taken to heaven. There is also pain in keeping the semen from spewing out immediately, in honor of her perfection. In honor of my obsession. There is pain in my cramped belly, my weighted balls slapping off her supple backside, over and over, reminding me how badly I need to lighten them.

The sexual frustration, the effort it takes to keep from ejaculating, sends my teeth into her shoulder, burying there with a roar. Her cries are gratified, her fingers tunneling into my hair and holding me there, even encouraging me with whimpers to bite down harder.

I have to stop.

I cease my hurried pumps, all too aware that five more and I'm done.

"Lasting until you come is going to be the death of me," I rasp, my lips moving over her mouth. "But I'll wait every single time." I nip at her chin. "No relief until you're shaking."

"I don't know how," she says in a rush. "Th-there's a ticklish feeling but it's different than the one...than when you did it with your mouth." Pink climbs her neck and I fall in love with London a hundred fold. No, a thousand. "It's b-bigger."

"Damn right it is, baby. My cock is filling you this

time." Keeping eye contact with her, I grind the base of my shaft against her clit, only thrusting a few inches in and out of her entrance. "Let the feeling get even bigger. I've got you."

London nods, looks at me through her lashes. "The feeling is in my chest, too." She claps a hand down over her heart, her tits bouncing around it with my punctuated drives. "H-here. I can't help it. I know this has to be a secret—"

"No." My heart shoots up into my mouth. "Don't you dare try to help that feeling, London. It's safe. You are safe with me." I pick up my pace, driving her up the seat with every slap of my hips. "Let the feeling get bigger everywhere. In your tummy and in your chest. I have the same ones."

Her back arches on a moan. "You do?"

"God, yes, baby. Do you think I'd be able to keep you a secret?" I drop my mouth to the slope of her neck, raking a path up to her ear. "If we're in the same room, my hands are on you. No other way I can live."

"But—"

"I'll worry about the hard stuff. Right now, your job is to come." I groan into her neck, gripping her knees and shoving them up until they're touching the seat and she's folded in half, my hips pounding furiously, the seat creaking beneath us, the car rocking on its wheels. "Daddy's meat can't take much more."

Two thrusts later, her breath catches, her pussy cinching up tight around me and she wails in my ear, her knees shaking against my pressing shoulders.

"Brody." She slaps her hands down on my humping buttocks and digs her nails in, screaming up at the roof of the car. "Daddy."

Nothing could keep me from releasing now. It tears out of me like a pack of wild dogs, shredding my stomach and knitting it back together tightly, harsh shudders taking me over. Everywhere. My thighs, my straining balls, my throat. Months of lusting and fantasizing are pumped between her thighs, my much larger body flattening her on the seat, my final drives savage, an assault on her tempting body and sweet, wet cunt.

"Mine." I grip her around her throat, looking her in the eye. "Mine."

"Yes," she gasps, eyes unfocused. "Just for Brody."

"That's right." A hard shudder wracks me as the final drop of come is expelled. "Forever, little girl," I say, kissing her hard. "Consider your fate sealed."

I go boneless on top of her, my mouth moving against her temple, whispering her name, promises, praise for the way she took me. But when I catch her eye, she looks like she wants to say something.

"What is it, London?"

The color on her face deepens. "I was wondering if…well. What about the rest?" She crooks her finger and I come eagerly, my dick getting hard again when her lips graze my ear. "I want my spanking, Daddy."

The words have barely left her mouth before she's flipped over, face down on the seat, the sounds of my slaps and her answering whimpers echoing in the dark car. It has never been more obvious that this girl was made solely for me. That she is the love of my life. My soul mate and obsession. We are two sides of the same coin and nothing will ever come between us.

And that means it's time to tell her everything.

As soon as we get home, London is going to find out exactly how deep—and twisted—my feelings for her run. Not to mention, what I was willing to do to have her.

CHAPTER EIGHT

London

I 'M DEPLETED OF energy. Feel like I'm flying, even though I'm a lump of limbs on the passenger seat of Brody's Range Rover. I can't seem to stop mooning at him, either. Everything about him steals my breath. The way he drapes his wrist over the steering wheel, making capable turns, reaching over to stroke his thumb down the side of my face every so often.

What am I going to do?

What is happening here?

Am I in a serious relationship with my stepfather? It certainly seems that way, especially when he's throwing around words like fate, forever and mine.

And Daddy.

I'm not sure what's happening inside of me—or if there is something a little twisted between me and Brody—but I can't help the rush of emotion attached to that title. It makes me feel coveted and safe and treasured. Like our attachment is permanent and not fleeting, not temporary like I'm used to. When he uses that word, or even when I do, I feel special. And this thing between us becomes more permanent.

Right?

A touch of worry creeps in. I've been fooled before. My mother tried to put down roots a few times when I was young and I got my hopes up, made friends in school, thought this might be the time she finally stuck around longer than a few weeks. But that was never the case. There was always that afternoon when I came home from school and found someone else in her place. Or a note explaining that she was gone and a non-family member would be watching out for me until she returned.

This thing with Brody feels incredibly different, but that just means it will hurt hard if I'm wrong, doesn't it?

My pulse is firing when we turn the corner down his block—and it skyrockets when I see who is standing in the driveway of Brody's house.

It's my mother.

She's leaning against the bumper of her Jetta, studying her nails. Tan, but visibly exhausted in a teal Cancun sweatshirt and pajama pants. I've arrived home to this scene more times than I can count and there used to be a spark of joy and hope when she came back. This time, though, there is nothing.

At first.

Dread starts to creep in slowly—and I realize in that moment how attached I've gotten to Brody in only a single day. Stupid. That was a stupid thing to do. My mother is home now—his wife! He'll have no choice but to set me aside. Abandon me. It's even the right thing to do, isn't it? I'm the interloper here. I'm the betrayer.

"Goddammit," Brody mutters through his teeth. "I don't believe this."

"It's fine. I understand."

His sharp gaze zips to mine. "You understand what?"

"That you have to…that this c-can't happen again." My throat feels like it's closing up. I don't believe it, but I think I fell in love with this man. I was right, this hurts worse than any other time. He can't keep me. No one ever keeps me and this time is the worst it's ever felt. A hundred times worse. I yearn for the safety of juvenile hall where they could lock me in and I could lock out the hurt and the people who did it to me.

"London, I'm going to explain everything," Brody says firmly, pulling the Range Rover up to the curb and putting it into park. I look out the passenger window toward my mother, whose expression is blank, her face obscured by the raindrops that are beginning to land on the windows of the vehicle. "Stay right here, okay? Do not move until I come back."

I nod, even though I have no intention of listening.

My whole life has been about outrunning the hurt, trying to get as far as I can away from it before it sticks to me. This time, it's already stuck, but I'll keep going and hope my feelings for this man go away.

As soon as Brody gets out of the car and approaches my mother, I throw myself out of the passenger door and book it across the street, holding my ripped T-shirt together and cutting through the darkness. Brody shouts my name, alarmed, but I continue to sprint, cursing my choice of flip flops from this morning. The sky opens up overhead and the rain gets worse, dampening the asphalt, thunder rolling in the distance. Tears are blurring my vision, making the streetlights look like little balls of fire. I ignore the burning in my lungs and keep running, needing to get away from the vision of Brody walking away from me, just like everyone else.

There's a park at the end of the street. Blindly, I run toward it, hoping to find somewhere to take cover long enough to think of a plan. But I've only gotten halfway through the park when I'm dragged to a stop by an immovable object. An arm bands around my middle and I'm elevated off the ground, legs still moving in mid-air, my back meeting a hard chest.

"I told you not to move until I came back," Brody bellows above my head. "Don't you ever run from me again. You could have gotten hurt, London."

"Put me down," I scream, fighting his hold, panicking. "Please don't make me come back. Please just let me go!"

"What part of forever don't you understand?" He stomps us toward an overhang of trees, putting us out of sight from the houses on the other side of the street. "I am never letting you go. Don't even say those words out loud."

"You have to. She's back and now you have t-to

leave me. Or move on." A hiccup wracks me. "It happens every single time and you're not going to be any different."

"Oh, I'm not?" He sets me down on the dampening earth and spins me around, taking my shoulders in his big hands. "I know you've been hurt, baby, and that you're scared. But you need to trust me."

I'm already shaking my head. "No. No—"

"Dammit, we were supposed to have time." He squeezes his eyes closed. "I thought the money I gave your mother would keep her gone, but I underestimated how irresponsible she is."

"Money?" I sniff hard, wiping tears and rain off my cheeks. "I don't understand. What are you talking about?"

Brody sighs unevenly, his hands dropping away from my shoulders. He paces away, hands on hips and comes back. And I gasp when the moonlight catches his face, because...he's more intense than I've ever seen him. His eyes are so penetrating that my pulse tumbles end over end. "I paid her to leave so I'd have you alone when you came home. All to myself. I met your mother in a bar. She was going on and on to the bartender about needing some medical procedure, a cist removed, but she didn't have the insurance coverage. It wasn't any of my business. I wasn't interested in the conversation. But then...she unlocked her phone and I saw you on the screen." He takes a step closer. "God help me, I was done. I knew you. I looked into your eyes and you were mine."

"What?" Confusion floods me. "But you…married my mother."

"I married her so she'd have the benefit of my insurance. But she never had me, London. Not once. I'd never lay a fucking finger on her. There's only you." He advances on me further, but I take several steps back, unable to breathe, trying to get a handle on what he's telling me. Trying to puzzle my way through. Is this real? Or a dream? "We had an understanding, she and I. She gets medical coverage and some money to occupy her…and I get to be the one who welcomes you home. Feeds you and puts a roof over your head. She wasn't supposed to come back so soon. Not before you and I had trust between us. Not before I could explain—and I was planning on telling you everything tonight."

Rain is dripping unchecked down my face now. I'm in too much shock to wipe it away. Since yesterday, I've been living in an alternate reality. None of my beliefs were based in fact. "Did she know you would…sleep with me?"

"We never said it out loud," he says hoarsely.

"But it was understood."

His throat works with a swallow. "I suppose so. It was very hard to keep my feelings hidden. And eventually, one of the administrators called her and she discovered by accident that I'd been…"

"What?"

"Going to watch you. On the surveillance cameras at the facility." He wets his lips and I can't subdue a flare of excitement at the sight. "Every day. Sometimes more than once. I abused my badge as badly as I abused my cock…and I couldn't help it. Being without you turned me hollow. I walked around starved for months, just waiting for your release. Counting the seconds."

Oh my God.

I should be screaming. Running.

Sprinting as far and fast as I can. For a very different reason than the first time I ran tonight. This man, Brody, my stepfather, has been stalking me. He coordinated our meeting, our living situation, everything. He planned on making me his before I ever knew who he was.

Watched me when I was unaware.

That is terrifying.

At least…it should be.

Why is there a coil of heat in my tummy? Pleasurable goose bumps on my arms?

Why am I relieved? It's as though I've been wrapped in a blanket fresh from the dryer.

There has to be something wrong with me.

"I will make her leave again." He comes toward me with measured steps, eyes steady and watchful and dark. "And you'll sleep in my bed tonight."

"I can't," I whisper, retreating. *Can I?*

A touch of madness flares in his expression. "You *will.*"

Wetness spreads between my legs, despite my mind telling me this is wrong. My body is disagreeing, insisting that being with Brody is right. That it's okay to feel relief and happiness that he's wanted me all along. Even obsessed over me. Stalked me. For once, something in my life was planned and not another mishap or kick in the rear from fate. This man is offering me a home—himself—and it's a home I want to live in. Desperately.

Gravity seems to stop me in my tracks, allowing my stepfather to reach me, hauling me up against his chest, pulling me onto my toes and groaning into the crook of my neck. "The way I want and need you isn't natural, I know that. It's fucked up. But it's real and it will never, ever go away. I'm permanent. I'll never move a fucking inch, London. Just give in to it."

My neck falls back as if a string has been cut. "I want to, but…"

He holds his head. "But what?"

"You're married to someone else."

"Ah, London." His hand slides up the back of my skirt to massage my backside. "I needed a way to get close. And I needed to be as close as possible. My obsession with you doesn't allow for anything less than the same house." His fingers bite hard into my flesh. "I want to devour you, do you fucking get it?"

More and more heat swamps me, a current carrying away my reservations. What feels right is obvious. It's this man. It's his devotion…and yes, even his obsession. It's calling forth my own and making it expand, whispering, *you will be obsessed with him, too. Maybe you already are.* "Yes. I get it."

His exhale of relief stirs my hair. "You will be my wife. Now that I don't have to hide this goddamn sickness, now that I can set it loose, there's no need to pretend anymore just to get close. I'll have a ring on your finger..." His teeth close around my earlobe and bite down. "And a baby in that little belly of yours so fast, your head will spin."

"Your wife..." I breathe, the permanence of that stealing my breath. Filling something inside me that has been empty my whole life. "Yes, I want that."

"You're going to get it. Wrap your legs around my waist, baby. Don't you know I'm gutted over seeing you cry?" He unzips and a second later, his shaft prods me between the thighs, hard and thick and ready. "Have to fuck, little girl. Have to orgasm you."

"Yes, Daddy," I whisper, clinging to him, wrapping around his big body like ivy. "Please."

His steel fills me in one thrust and I scream into his shoulders, my knees jerking where they rest on his hips. "London Allen, I'm in love with you," he says hoarsely against my ear. "I'll never spend a day apart from you for the rest of my life, so help me God."

Pleasure spears up inside of me and washes me clean, washes away every doubt in my mind, until there is nothing but a future with this man. And I can't wait to live it.

EPILOGUE

Brody

Five years later

I GRIP MY wife's hips and ride her pussy hard from the back, watching her eyes start to go blind in the mirror over the bathroom sink. Her ass cheeks shake with the force of my thrusts, her legs struggling to keep her upright under the onslaught of my lust.

Goddamn, she is so fucking hot, it pisses me off. And I don't bother to hide the irritation from my expression when we lock eyes. I let her know exactly what I think about her red high heels and leather skirt. At the sight of my annoyance, her painted lips curve up at both ends.

Baring my teeth at her, I wrap her long blonde hair around my fist and roughen my drives, making her moan loudly. "Do you actually have the nerve to smile at me after strutting out of the bedroom and making my cock stiff?" I draw her head back until her entire throat is exposed. "I think you're starting to enjoy your spankings too much, London."

I don't think, actually. I know.

Today is a huge day for London. She's helping cut the ribbon on the first roller coaster she helped design.

After graduating from engineering school early and interning with one of the best designers in the state, she's put her mark on the first of many projects. And it happens to be at the park where we made love for the very first time. Which might explain why she named the roller coaster Conquered and gave it a romantic theme, complete with mist and red lighting.

London entering the workforce and fulfilling her dreams has been incredible. Watching her grow in confidence only makes me love her more, which I didn't think was possible.

But her working around a lot of men—never mind that they're mostly of the nerdy variety—has led to a lot of in-office spankings for my wife. I like to show up when she least expects me and calmly close the door to her office. Then push her face down over her desk, ruck up her skirt and slap her gorgeous behind until she's wet enough to fuck.

Unfortunately, (or fortunately), London hasn't completely lost her rebellious streak and can't seem to stop dressing in a manner meant to tease. To incite me.

As she's done this morning.

I don't realize I'm grunting loudly in time with my thrusts until she glances back at me over her shoulder, her face flushed, eyes glassy. "Don't forget, the b-boys are downstairs with Betty."

Yes. Our sons.

Although it wouldn't be the first time they overheard me and their mother going at it. Nor would it be the first time our nanny overhears. She's walked in on us rutting like animals more times than I can count. Poor London can barely look the woman in the eye.

It can't be helped.

Over the last five years, my obsession for London has turned nearly unmanageable. She is on my mind every split second of the day. My desk drawers are now overflowing with items that belong to her. Scarves, photographs, and yes, panties, just so I can feel near her when I'm working. We've renewed our vows every year for the last four and I'm already considering making it a twice yearly event. Just to calm the beast inside me, reminding it that London is mine and she's not going anywhere. Obsession doesn't even begin to cover it.

Five years ago, when London ran from me and I gave chase, bringing her home in my arms, her mother was nowhere to be found. I think when she saw the fear and devastation in my eyes when London ran away, she knew I would allow no interference. That what I have with her daughter was bigger than anything she could understand—and it wouldn't be wise to disturb the waters. When I sent her the divorce papers the following week, they returned signed without a problem, and now London only receives birthday cards.

I asked her once if she was still sad about her lack of a relationship with the woman and she only shook her head. *There's no room for sadness when happiness is taking up all the space.* My heart still hammers in my chest when I think about London saying those words.

There's another throb hammering right now, too, concentrated between my legs. I'm squeezing in and out of her tight, wet pussy and she's doing that goddamn thing she does. Where she pulses her inner walls around my cock and looks me in the eye, her expression one of pure innocence in the mirror.

"Am I being a good girl, Daddy?"

I heave a groan, pounding into her all the harder, the slaps of our connecting flesh filling the bathroom. "You're always so good. Always so good for me."

She drops her voice to a whisper, as if we're sharing a secret. "Can you make me pregnant again?" She scoots her high heels wider and tilts her hips, so I can see where my cock disappears into her body. "I miss you coming all over my pregnant belly, Daddy. Please?"

My balls start to erupt, but I clamp down on my lust, clenching my teeth to stop from busting too early. She does it every time. Every single time, the fucking goddess.

Holding onto my last ounce of control, I reach around the front of her body, dipping my fingers between her legs and petting her swollen clit, listening to her sob brokenly at the slippery friction. And I know exactly what's going to push her over the edge. In the last five years, London hasn't merely embraced or accepted my violent preoccupation with her. She's become addicted to it. She craves the proof of my madness when it comes to her. So I press my mouth to her ear now and say quietly, "You're already pregnant, baby. I tracked you to the doctor a week ago. And they know better than to keep anything from me about my wife."

Her gasp is unmistakably excited, her affection reflecting in the mirror, along with her stark need. "I was going to surprise you tonight when we were celebrating."

"You should know by now that there are no surprises between us," I say, my middle finger moving in a blur on her clit until she screams. "I know everything about you. I love and worship every single part."

"I love and worship you, too," she gasps, deep in the throes, pushing me to a blistering peak. And later that night, when she cuts the ribbon on her very first roller coaster, I discreetly massage her stinging backside through her leather skirt, earning me a look of adoration, which I return, and will return for the rest of our lives.

THE END

CPSIA information can be obtained
at www.ICGtesting.com
Printed in the USA
BVHW051938231222
654915BV00012B/1407